La

MW01673124

Scraps and Sketches Gathered Together

Vol. 1

SALZWASSER VERLAG

Lascelles Wraxall

Scraps and Sketches Gathered Together

Vol. 1

Reprint of the original, first published in 1865.

1st Edition 2022 | ISBN: 978-3-75258-956-6

Verlag (Publisher): Salzwasser Verlag GmbH, Zeilweg 44, 60439 Frankfurt, Deutschland
Vertretungsberechtigt (Authorized to represent): E. Roepke, Zeilweg 44, 60439 Frankfurt, Deutschland
Druck (Print): Books on Demand GmbH, In de Tarpen 42, 22848 Norderstedt, Deutschland

SCRAPS AND SKETCHES

GATHERED TOGETHER.

BY

SIR LASCELLES WRAXALL, Bart.

IN TWO VOLUMES.

VOL. I.

LONDON

1865.

CONTENTS.—VOL. I.

GATHERED TOGETHER.

CHAPTER I.

A WEEK IN CONSTANTINOPLE.

After a very quick and agreeable passage from London, the good ship which bore me and my fortunes to the seat of war cast anchor at eight in the morning off Seraski Point, and, as you may suppose, the decks and paddle-boxes were soon crowded with spectators, anxious for the first glance of a city which will ever exercise a magic influence over our minds, despite the disillusionizing to which it has recently been subjected. It was late in the month of December when we arrived, and yet the weather was as mild and warm as a September day at home. The sun shone cheerily on the gilded minarets and cupolas of Stamboul, and the waters glistened with hundreds of gaily-painted kaiks, which really walked them like things of life. The prospect from the deck of our steamer was really magnificent: to the right was Scutari, rising upon the Asiatic hills in a dark setting of cypress-trees, indicating the celebrated Muhammedan cemeteries; below these, again, the enormous barracks; at the base, the charming Kadi-Koi, built on the classic soil where Chalcedon once stood. In the rear of this landscape we could distinguish the mountains of Bulgurlu and Kassi Dagh; while at their base lay slumbering the sea of Marmora and the Princes' Islands. In front of us frowned Seraglio Point, with its countless historical reminiscences; a little to the left, again, the steep ascent through Galata and Tophaneh indicated the way to Pera and the Frankish quarter. In short, the effect of my first aspect of Constantinople will never be erased from my memory.

It was only natural that we should feel a desire at once to subject all these wonders to a closer inspection; so, after donning our uniform and getting ourselves up to a very considerable extent, three of us hailed a kaik, and commenced our first experiences of Oriental life. It requires a very considerable amount of practice to enter these gondola-shaped boats; as they have no keel, the slightest oscillation would be apt to upset them, and hence the greatest caution is requisite, if the passenger feel no particular inclination to come to grief. However, we managed to make the traject from the ship to the Admiralty Wharf in safety, and a few moments saw us in Galata. But how fearful was the change produced by only a few minutes! At the first glance it seemed an utter impossibility even to move from the spot, so dense was the crowd, so gluey was the mud into which we were compelled to wade. The houses which, when seen from a distance, appeared to have been built by fairy hands, were in reality not worth one farthing more than those I had inspected at the miserable village of Dardanelles the previous day; the gaily-dressed and picturesque forms which the traveller sees wandering about the quays, and is disposed from a distance to regard as pachas and beys *pur sang*, are converted, on a closer approach, into ragged vagabonds —Turkish hammals, Greek scoundrels, and Maltese robbers. It was a pity that my fair dream was so soon dispersed, and I was more than ever disposed to admire the Englishman who—so the story runs—was told that he must not attempt to land in Stamboul if he desired to keep up the illusion; so he hired one of the small Greek peril-boats, sailed in it for a week along the Bosphorus, the Sea of Marmora, and the Golden Horn, and then returned home by the next mail steamer, without having once set foot on land.

But it was of no use giving way to such unpleasant thoughts. It is true that the quay on which I stood was a rotten edifice, into which I sank ankle deep; instead of the perfume of roses, a stench of fish, cucumbers, and garlic pervaded my nostrils; but for all that I was in for it, and the only plan was to go on. Our first halting-point was Missuri's hotel, the best in the place, and that in all conscience was bad enough; for a bottle of wretched Bass they had the impudence to charge two francs, for a mouthful of bread and cheese five more, and then the waiter was highly indignant because we declined to give anything *pour le service*. Of a verity, with such prices, Madame Missuri can very well afford to pay her own waiters. Strange to say, this house was always crammed with English officers, who quietly allowed themselves to be cheated, thinking it beneath their dignity to expostulate. The only thing note-worthy about Pera is the view to be enjoyed from the summit of the hill; but whether that be a fair compensation for the amount of actual misery undergone in obtaining it, I should not like to decide. For my own part, I went there once, and—never went again.

As for Galata, I dare not describe it to you: this entire suburb, from the Golden Horn as far as the Tower, is, with its filthy streets, its evil-smelling fish and vegetable stalls, its old clo'men, wool-carders, Christians, Jews, Greeks, Armenians, and German tailors, nothing better than one huge Circean sty; and it is a neck-breaking job to descend the street leading down from Pera after nightfall. In fact, I never could fully realize Muhammed's notion of not allowing his followers to drink wine or spirits until I had seen this city, for I am convinced that any drunken man, unless specially guarded by that Providence which is supposed to have charge of him, would inevitably break his neck before he reached his home. On both sides of the road are miserable huts, dignified by the name of houses, whose roofs extend so far that neither sun nor moon can penetrate, and these have been converted into shops for the special object of swindling strangers. There is, however, one green spot on my memory with reference to this street, namely the London Tavern, where you can procure a very decent glass of Bordeaux; and one clambering up from Galata requires a strengthening dose, owing to the heat, and I would advise him not to leave this house unvisited. In truth, there are so few public-houses in Constantinople which a man can visit who has any regard for his character, or any old-fashioned notions about morality, that I think this honourable exception deserves to be immortalized in my pages.

Let us suppose ourselves safely arrived in Pera. But how shall I attempt to describe a town which is renewed every eight or ten years, owing to the devastating fires that continually occur? The careless manner the Turks go about with fire and charcoal is quite characteristic of the nation. If a fire breaks out, in the Turk's fatalist view of matters, it is God's will, and nothing can be done. In such cases he generally carries off his wife and children from the haremlik, and leaves the house a prey to the flames. A short account of a fire at which I was present at Galata, will give a good idea of the way the Bono Johnnies manage things at home. We had just finished dinner, when our attention was attracted by the firing of cannon and the appearance of lanterns on the Galata Tower, a sure sign that there was a fire somewhere. We immediately pulled on land, and found ourselves speedily in the centre of a dense mob of firemen, çavasas, and soldiers, all shouting "Janjin var" at the top of their lungs, and attempting to stop the spread of the flames with the most primitive instruments that can be conceived. They consisted of an upright brass tube, resembling a field-gun, forming the cylinder of the pumping machine. Each of these machines is borne along by at least eight firemen, on two thick poles. All shouted "Janjin var," and sought to reach the place of the fire. But then came the question, Where was water to be procured? It had to be carried up with great difficulty in tubs and bags, perhaps even purchased from the water-carriers; and so, before they had succeeded in getting one squirt into working order, the fire had converted a street into a heap of ashes.

Formerly, the want of water was felt still worse, and it is even said that all sorts of scoundrels used to bring up squirts filled with oil, with which they threatened to sprinkle the neighbouring houses unless their owners consented to ransom themselves. The next morning after a fire has taken place curious gazers may be seen wandering about over an immense heap of smoking wood ashes. The Turks congregate, hundreds of "Mashallahs" and "Inshallahs" may be heard, and they puff away at their chibuks in rivalry with the cinders. The next morning, when the ashes have grown cold, you will notice on the spot a number of huts or tents being erected; the owner of the spot has taken possession of it again, and lives on in his tent till he can scrape up enough to build a new house. If he cannot do so, the spot remains empty; and so you may find at the present day whole streets desolate which were afflicted some ten or twelve years back by a fire. A curious preservation against fire may be noticed in Constantinople before the windows of the houses, namely, a pair of slippers and a bundle of onions; houses which are provided with these means of protection are generally found, however, to burn as fast as the rest.

Suppose now, my dear reader, that you accompany me to a Turkish bath;—but no, I should not like to practise such cruelty upon you; you had better stay at home, and let me describe it to you. The person desirous of bathing enters the hamam, and finds himself in a large hall, round the walls of which a gallery runs.

You then go up a flight of wooden stairs, where an hamamji take off the clothes of the visitor, then wraps him in several large blankets, and puts a pair of massive *sabots* on his feet, in which he descends the stairs. As a general rule, however, the shoes reach the bottom long before the wearer. From this hall the bather is led into another, out of which a considerable degree of heat pours forth to meet him. While the first chamber is lighted by large windows in the walls and cupola, the second apartment is found to be somewhat darker. The floor is formed of very fine marble, and a fountain is usually to be noticed in the centre; round the room are cushions, on which the visitor reclines for a few moments, to prepare himself for the bath. The Turks sit here in undisturbed, blessed rest, wrapped up in their blankets, and trying to acquire the proper state of mind for the impending performance. The visitor is allowed some ten minutes for the requisite transpiration, and all sorts of reflections about what he is about to undergo, and is then conducted by a servant into the sidjahlik, or hot room, where he finds a heat of about 130° Fahrenheit, and gasps for air like a fish pulled out of the water on to land. This apartment is also elegantly paved with marble, and the ground slopes towards the wall, so that the water may run off; the condensed steam keeps dropping down from the dome, where the only light penetrates through convex panes of glass. Round the bath-room are open cabinets, in which small marble benches are attached to the walls; above these are two brass taps, from which hot and cold water can be drawn, and there is usually a brass basin upon these benches.

The naked hamamji, generally a boy, who receives us here, intimates to you that you must lie down on a large plate of marble, about two feet high, in the centre of the room: for what purpose will be soon discovered. The stranger reclines on his back, the marble plate, like the whole floor, being heated from below, but not so much as to be unendurable. This second period of reflection lasts another five minutes. You perspire all you can; the dome, too, perspires above us, and huge drops fall on your face. On the marble plate there are usually five or six persons reclining, all motionless and perspiring with great assiduity. Then comes the hamamji, dressed only in a short apron, and the fun waxes fast and furious. He begins belabouring the bather with both hands; rubs, rolls, and kneads every limb; cracks all his joints, with the exception of his neck, strikes them with his flat hand till it sounds like the beating of a drum; and, as several other hamamjis are performing the same process simultaneously on other persons, the noise becomes slightly monotonous, to say the least of it. At last the bathman plants his knees on your chest, and gives you various other *coups de grâce*, making you feel as if your limbs were scattered about the bath-room. While this process was going on with me, and the hamamji had belaboured me in a most Vandalic manner, he ended by seizing my right arm, in which I had been nursing a pet rheumatism for several years. My blood boiled at such ill-treatment: following a very natural impulse, I liberated my arm, and was on the point of giving the hamamji a box on the ears, but reflected in time, and drew back my hand. The same circumstance must have frequently happened to him before with Franks, for he laughed, and bade me get up.

With a "Lord be praised!" I collected my limbs on the marble plate, and carried them, following the lad, into the side-room, where I seated myself near the water-taps. Here I had to decide what degree of warmth I would have my bath; the hamamji then produced the required temperature, by means of the two taps, poured the water over me, then put on a glove made of coarse, hard felt, with the effect of a currycomb, and began to rub me till he peeled the outer skin from my body. He then beat up some sweet-scented soap-suds in the bowl, poured them over me, and the bathing operations were concluded. I was finally wrapt up quite wet in new cloths, one of which the boy fastened round my head like a turban, and was led back again to the gallery, where I reclined on one of a row of mattresses; a chibuk was stuck in my mouth, coffee was brought me, and I gradually dried. This lasted an hour, during which I conversed, as well as I could, with a thorough-bred Turk lying next me, who asserted, with all possible earnestness, that such a bath was the most splendid and beneficial thing to be had under the sun. Other persons have already stated this on authority of the Turks, but as I have a special regard for my limbs, I cannot assent to the proposition.

One of the prettiest objects I saw in the streets of Para was the carriage in which the Turkish ladies make their excursions to the Sweet Waters of Europe and Asia. It consists of a long quadrangular frame, on which some six persons find room; round it runs a back about two feet high, generally painted a very bright red. At each corner of the carriage are poles of a spear-like form, supporting a snow-white canvas roof, as protection against the sun; along this run gold cords with large tassels. This carriage is drawn by two grey or perfectly white oxen, which are decked with very gay harness, and driven by a richly-attired cavass. When an araba of this sort is laden with half a dozen half-veiled and fantastically attired Oriental beauties, and you see them drive past, sitting cross-legged in the Turkish fashion, it is quite impossible to pass by with indifference or look in another direction. I for my part always ventured to have a thorough good look at the odalisks when they passed me, although I had been warned against rousing the fury of the people; and I never came to grief, though now and then a Turk would mutter a "Giaour!" between his teeth, and the way he spits it out is what the Americans would call a caution to any nervous man.

A great change, by the way, appears to have taken place with the Turkish women: formerly the yashmaks were so thick that no mortal eye could penetrate them, but at present even the veils have had to yield to the onward movement. Once on a time the veil covered the whole of the face, so that only the eyes were free, and the poor women did not even use a pocket-handkerchief, because they could not find the way to their noses; but now *nous avons changé tout cela:* the veils are so thin and gossamer-like in texture, that the features can be clearly seen through them, and, in addition, they only cover the forehead and the lower part of the face, while the eyes and nose are emancipated. A friend of mine, who has resided some time in Pera, tells me, too, that the Turkish ladies appear to have an especial fancy for the Franks and Giaours; and they cannot be blamed if they try to play their jealous husbands a trick, which is indeed the case now and then. They visit Pera in large parties, lounge about in their wide mantles and huge boots, under which they generally wear neat little slippers, and let the Franks gaze their fill of them, which evidently causes them great amusement. They look with great interest after any elegantly dressed European woman who may pass them: and what a difference exists between the wasp-like waists of the strangers and the clumsy cloak of the natives! Nor must we look at the feet of the Turkish lady, unless you wish utterly to destroy the advantageous effect which their interesting, even pretty faces may have produced: all the Turkish women waddle like ducks; all turn their feet in, probably a result of their way of sitting; and their walk is rendered still more clumsy by the immense yellow boots in which they wade through the mud. Generally, however, they are pretty—I saw very few who were ill-looking, at least. On the other hand, their faces are generally pale and sickly, which is rendered still more unearthly, almost spectral, by the yashmak. Their continual washing, and the use of all sorts of essences, render the skin flabby, and take away all its freshness; and the prison life in the harems is not adapted to give them a blooming complexion; but the shape of the nose, the mouth, and the sparkling eyes are generally very fine. An unpleasant effect is produced by the elder women, when they waddle along the street with a species of patriarchal dignity, bearing a chibuk and parasol under their arms.

We will now quit Pera and proceed to the adjoining Tophaneh, a not less interesting suburb. My first visit was naturally paid to the institution whence this quarter derives its name—the immense cannon foundry, situated at the confluence of the Bosphorus with the Sea of Marmora. This building is one of the handsomest of the sort I have ever seen, not merely for its splendid situation, but also for the cleanliness to be witnessed within it; such a rarity in Turkey, that any instance of it produces a marvellous effect. Any one who examines this foundry can quickly form an idea of the excellent condition of the Turkish artillery. In the large court-yard I saw a great number of guns parked: some of them were trophies of the earlier Turkish wars, and had been taken from the Christians; among others I noticed old French guns with the lilies, others bore the papal arms. I also noticed here four Russian guns, taken at Slatina from the advanced posts, and which the Turks pointed out with a very pardonable degree of pride.

In Tophaneh is the large and splendid mosque which the padishah is in the habit of visiting; here, too, are the head-quarters of the Tcherkess, who bring their pretty daughters for sale to Stamboul. These free sons of the Caucasus may be seen at any time in the streets and coffee-houses of Tophaneh, and always have a supply of their fair wares on hand. It has been calculated that, up to the present time, about five hundred Circassian and Georgian women were imported annually into Constantinople; but the trade has fallen away considerably lately, for the Turks appear to have given up their partiality for these daughters of the mountain, and describe the Circassian women as obstinate, extravagant, and sulky, the Georgians as stolid and awkward. A curious race of men these Circassians!—on one hand they defend their liberty to the last drop of blood, on the other they carry their own daughters to the slave-market! The friend to whom I have already alluded, and to whom I am indebted for a great deal of my information, described to me a visit he paid to a Circassian young lady, and it is so *piquant* that I venture to repeat it. He formed the acquaintance of a Circassian slave-dealer, and went with him to his quarters. They entered a small and comfortable apartment, in which he saw a girl, not more than thirteen at most, with light hair and most classical features. The poor little thing was playing carelessly with a water-melon, and regarded her visitor with kind glances, for the only desire of these poor girls is to be bought and make their fortunes. My friend, though not the most bashful of men, positively felt uncomfortable at the sight, and ashamed of the part he was playing through mere curiosity, so he rose and quitted the house. The Circassian followed him, and he heard the poor deceived girl utter some words of regret. As they would not let him go, he was forced to go to a coffee-house and ask the price demanded for the child. Six thousand piastres was the reply. He promised to consider the matter over, and so escaped; but he could not get rid of his uncomfortable feelings for some days after.

Like Galata, Tophaneh is built against the side of Pera Hill, and consists of dirty streets in which fever reigns with undisputed sway. The air is pestilential in both suburbs, but more especially in Galata, and it is excessively dangerous to pass through them at night, owing to the vicinity of the Maltese street, where a motley mass of ruffians is congregated ready to put any one out of the way for the miserable sum of sixty piastres. By great efforts the police have succeeded in preventing murders by daylight, but all their exertions are unavailing to prevent horrid scenes at night. Even in Pera, Englishmen have been recently attacked while going home to their quarters; and one night, when I was at the opera, a major of the German Legion was stabbed in four places, just after he had left the çoffee-house. But our countrymen run very foolish risks, more especially in the low drinking-houses near the bridge; many a man is hocussed and murdered for the sake of his clothing or money, and the Turk very quietly ejaculates his "Allah Kerim!" and goes on his way probably rejoicing that there is one infidel the less in the world.

One thing I forgot to mention to the credit of the Turks, namely, that although the city, and more especially Pera, swarms with beggars, you rarely find among these highwaymen any Muhammedans—they are generally Greeks and Armenians—although you find in Galata Tower-street, and on the stone steps leading to the Austrian Embassy, a quantity of old women lying down, who begin to lament directly they see a stranger, and even go so far as to seize him by the coat-tail. When the Turk begs, he generally does so in a droll and, consequently, successful manner, by calling you his kuzum, or lamb, and mentioning various pressing emergencies which compel him to become your suppliant. Generally, however, the Turk only takes to the trade when blind or a cripple. The real Turkish beggars take up their quarters on the Yeni Kuprï (new bridge), leading from Galata to Stamboul, over the Golden Horn, whither I now propose my reader shall accompany me. This bridge is one of the largest wooden bridges in the world, I should think, although I cannot say much for its architectural beauty. It is currently supposed that you pay to cross it, but I fancy it is optional. If you happen to have any change, you give two pacas; if not, you let it alone, and no one seems to bother himself on the score. The first object generally sought for on entering Stamboul is the bazaar, one of the largest buildings in the place, and well meriting the celebrity it has acquired. Even during the greatest heat you feel as if in an ice-cellar when within it, for not a single ray of blessed sunshine ever penetrates into this labyrinth of broad-arched corridors.

But before reaching the bazaar you are sure to have had your temper soured for days by the infamous interpreters, who stick to you like leeches, and can only be driven off by a hunting-whip. They are all rogues without exception, and if you employ one of them, you not only have to pay him twenty to thirty piastres for his service, but you find that your purchases cost you on an average one-third more than they should have done. "Capitaine," or "Signor Capitaine," greets the stranger's ear from every shop; one hands you a handsome tobacco-box, another a shawl, another the Lord knows what—you positively run the gauntlet. Your money is the article required; and since the presence of the Allies in the East, the English have behaved with such liberality that prices are nearly doubled for everything. This bazaar is immeasurable: in one street we find the tailors, then the shoemakers, then again the shawl, silk, and carpet dealers; a whole quarter is occupied by the goldsmiths' shops, the bazarlan, or bazaar for arms, &c. There is indubitably an immense amount of wealth collected in this covered market-place; but as a semi-obscurity always prevails in it, you can only see on returning to daylight what it is you have bought, and not unfrequently you have sold yourself in the bargain. On quitting the bazaar you generally feel inclined for a rest; so you go into the nearest Turkish coffee-house, drink your cup of coffee, and smoke your pipe. But those are luxuries I intend to describe presently, when I tell you about the Sweet Waters.

The Serai and the Aya Sofia possess even more attraction than the Bazaar, and away you clamber up the hill to the Seraglio, which may be reached from different sides. However, it was another illusion dispelled. The Serai, on closer inspection, consisted of a gloomy court-yard, surrounded by a high wall, in which all I had to admire was a magnificent palm-tree, occupying the whole of one corner. In addition, I saw the fountain near which the pachas used to be beheaded, and the iron hooks on which their heads were fixed; but that is nothing in a country like Turkey, where every inch of ground has some sanguinary reminiscence attached to it. From the court of the Serai I proceeded to the "Sublime Porte," which I had imagined a colossal gateway, but found it to be only a narrow one, to which a fictitious height is given by the contracted nature of the arch. Inside this door I saw on either side two glass-cases, in which were muskets with ornamented barrels, probably to pay honour to the padishah, for the guard carried the ordinary muskets. Two pretty marble pillars ornament the entrance; near them are two niches; above the arch numerous verses from the Koran are painted; while a row of wired, unglazed orifices above the Sublime Porte serve to disfigure its white-painted frontage. The prettiest object I saw was a small fountain, just in front of the gate, covered with numerous ornaments, gold and silver bas-reliefs, &c. All those Oriental ceremonies which formerly took place in the Seraglio are neglected; the building itself has lost its importance, for it is only inhabited by servants; the padishah himself now resides at his new palace on the Bosphorus.

Just opposite the Sublime Porte is the Aya Sofia, which, though not so elegant in form and construction as the Achmetji and the Suleymanyeh, still is rendered interesting by the numerous historical reminiscences attaching to it. Formerly no Christian dared to enter it; but at the present time any European officer or soldier is allowed to go in if he will go through the ceremony of putting slippers on over his boots. There is nothing, however, to be seen inside, save mats and carpets on the floor, as well as long strings suspended from the ceiling, to which ostrich eggs and flowers are attached, and the lengthy verses from the Koran inscribed on the wall.

The most memorable of all the public places in Stamboul is indubitably the Atmeidan or Hippodrome. Unfortunately, this square was sadly injured by the erection of the Achmet Mosque, and it is now limited to about one-third of its former space. To the north of this mosque, with its six graceful minarets, we find three monuments of antiquity, the only ones preserved in the whole of Stamboul out of the countless artistic treasures which once adorned the Rome of the East. Though of less importance, one of the most prominent objects in Stamboul is the "Burnt Pillar." This monument stands isolated, in the midst of Turkish vegetable stalls, cook-shops, and coffee-houses, which have collected so closely around this column that it appears to be growing out of one of these houses. At the first glance it might be taken for a huge smoke-blackened chimney, but it is supposed to have had a much higher mission, for folks say that it once supported a statue of Constantine. Its name it indubitably owes to the countless fires to which it has been exposed; it is beginning to look in a very tottering condition, and is surrounded by iron rings, which however afford it but scanty support, as they are perfectly rust-eaten.

One of the things to be seen in perfection in Stamboul is the out-door life of the Osmanli. They appear to perform every domestic duty in the streets, and all the artisans and mechanics work in the open air. This leads to a considerable amount of gossip, and were the work performed proportionate to the amount of chattering, the Turks would be the most industrious nation in the world. Indeed the preconceived notions of the Osmanli which we bring out with us are utterly knocked on the head after a close inspection of the Turks at home. They possess a very considerable amount of humour, and are fond of practical jokes, which they carry on utterly regardless of the annoyance they may cause. Thus, for instance, the other day in Kertch I saw some of the Contingent amusing themselves with an exquisite game, which consisted in their picking up a dead dog and throwing it at each other. But, hold! I have not yet finished with Constantinople; we have first to go to Scutari and the Sweet Waters, and then through the Bosphorus, so I am doubtful whether I can reach Kertch before next month.

It was at eight in the morning that I stood with three friends on the great bridge, and awaited the return of the Turkish steam-boat which was to carry us across to Scutari. A number of Turkish ladies, in the most variegated feridjis, or cloaks, were also waiting for the vapour, and had seated themselves with the greatest calmness on the rotten planks of the bridge while we were gazing down on the blue waters at our feet. At length the vessel arrived. Thanks to the Turkish carelessness in all matters relating to the public comfort, there is not even an opening in the railing of this bridge, from which all the local boats ply. The passengers arriving from Scutari—chiefly women—performed wondrous feats of balancing on the narrow plank laid from the vessel to the bridge, and crept under the balustrades, while we followed the same course, and had three things to guard against simultaneously—not to come into collision with the Turkish fair ones, hit our heads against the railing, or get our feet entrapped in the holes upon the bridge. Half an hour later we landed on the equally wretched wooden bridge at Scutari, and found on the quay a numerous party of horse-litters already assembled. Each of us hired a horse for the day at twenty piastres, and we then commenced our ride in the direction of the Kassi Dagh, the highest mountain on the Asiatic coast, whence a magnificent view may be enjoyed. I should recommend this ride in preference to that up the Bulgurlu, for though the distance to be travelled is greater, there is no comparison between the two views.

In the interior of Scutari there is nothing remarkable—the only objects to be visited are the barracks, hospital, and burial-ground, which we proposed to do on our return—and we continued our ride across the plateau to the Kassi Dagh. After passing the sacred fountain at the base of the hill, whence the water is carried for miles, we had half an hour's climbing over the rocks and through the bushes ere we reached the summit. Most magnificent was the panorama which here lay extended before us. To the left, Constantinople, with the Castle of the Seven Towers; to the right, the entrance to the Bosphorus; between the two, the Turkish city, Pera, Galata, and Tophaneh. To our extreme right we saw the mirrored surface of the Black Sea, at our feet the Sea of Marmora, about five hundred paces from us, washed by the sea, the Princes' Islands; to the left, on the Asiatic side, the snow-capped Olympus, veiled in light mist—an indescribably lovely tableau!

We soon found ourselves in Kadi-Koi, and hastened off, as evening was closing in apace, to visit the mighty burial-grounds of Scutari; an immense forest of gloomy cypresses, the twittering of millions of birds, and a thickly-strewn field of narrow Turkish gravestones. announced the kingdom of the dead. Here and there a couple of Turks were seated, with their chibuks and nargilehs, on the tombs; they had probably been there since the morning, so motionless did they appear. The

Turk is very fond,.by the way, of enjoying his kef in a churchyard, for gloomy death possesses no terrors for him. I attempted to climb up the steep road on horseback, and commenced picking my way through the countless gravestones, scarcely a foot apart. The road was fatiguing, and my exertions were fruitless: my horse was continually sinking in up to his fetlocks in the graves, or stumbling over upturned tombstones. I could find no monuments worthy of inspection—all the tombstones were equally insignificant — but I could not refrain from admiring the permanent brilliancy of the colours and gold fresco work with which the Easterns are so fond of ornamenting their graves.

On reaching Scutari we returned our horses, and had to hasten off, as it is difficult to procure a kaik after dark. Fortunately we succeeded in obtaining one, and after the usual amount of bullying the kaikji, who demanded about six times his proper fare, we reached our ship in time for a late dinner. I much regret that the length of our excursion prevented our having an opportunity to visit the hospital, and add my tribute of gratitude to Miss Nightingale for the devotion with which she has laboured to promote the comfort of our suffering soldiers. Others, however, among our passengers were more fortunate, and amply bore out the laudatory remarks which have already been published about this lady. She had succeeded in raising for herself a monument more enduring than brass, and the name of Florence Nightingale will be remembered when those of our heroes are forgotten.

Sunday, the last day of our stay in Constantinople, was devoted to an excursion to the Sweet Waters of

Europe, for which purpose half a dozen of us took the ship's boat, and set off for a long pull. For some very considerable distance we proceeded up the Golden Horn, underneath the two bridges, and passed the few Turkish men-of-war still in existence, which have been removed for protection as high as the water will allow. Those we saw were built on fine models, but suffered from the all-prevailing want of cleanliness. After a while the river narrowed perceptibly, and the mountains grew higher; but one great charm was wanting —namely, that the country was almost utterly devoid of vegetation or trees. Here and there a clump of gloomy cypresses revealed the presence of a Turkish graveyard; but, with this exception, the general aspect of the country was monotonous in the extreme. At length we arrived at the termination of our voyage, for we were stopped by a Turkish sentry, who intimated that we could go no further in that direction. It was impossible that we had arrived at the celebrated European Sweet Waters. All we saw was a half-decayed palace, situated on the banks of a muddy canal, and very much resembling Hornsey Wood House, near London. Our disgust was excessive, and to cure our spleen we started off for a long walk over the hills to gain some idea of the general aspect of the country.

The walk was pleasant enough, as far as it went, but would have been much more so had it not been that our olfactory nerves were being continually offended by dead oxen and sheep, off which countless lean and savage-looking dogs were making evidently a dainty meal. Here and there we came across a shepherd carrying a walking arsenal in his belt, and armed with a long spiked stick, forming a very formidable weapon. He would look savagely at us, mutter something, evidently not a blessing, between his clenched teeth, and retire slowly. After a while we grew tired of our ramble, and returned to our boat, when, after strengthening the inner man, we determined on making one supreme effort to discover the Sweet Waters. For this purpose we pulled to the other side of the river, and proceeded along a severely straight path, whence a view of a stagnant piece of water, about half a mile in length, could be obtained.

At the end of about half an hour's walking, in mud up to our knees, we at length reached a village, and discovered to our unmitigated disgust, that we had not been mistaken: we had visited the Sweet Waters, about which so many authors had joined in a conspiracy to humbug us. We turned into the only coffee-house the village possessed, and called for coffee and pipes. The operation of making the coffee took place before our eyes; the man took a little brass cup with a long handle, into which he put the coffee, very coarsely ground, sugar, and water. After a few minutes' boiling over the charcoal the beverage was ready, and handed to us in some porcelain cups, but I cannot say that I enjoyed it particularly. It may be habit, it is true, but I prefer keeping the coffee and the grouts separate; but here you had to eat them both with a spoon. Such a thing as drinking a cup of coffee must be unknown to the Turks. Nor did I have any much greater amount of success on trying the nargileh, or Turkish hubble-bubble, which requires the lungs of a horse before any smoke can be drawn from it. Now, as I particularly dislike making a toil of a pleasure, I was glad to exchange for the chibuk, which better responded to my English notions. The only thing I can honestly say in favour of the coffee-house was the excessive cheapness, for we only paid one piastre and a half for eight cups of coffee and pipes to match.

On our return to the ship, we were highly gratified to find that all the preparations were completed, and that we should positively sail on the next morning. Everybody was tired of Constantinople; tired of the dirt, the stench, the noise, the cheating—in a word, we were tired of barbarism, and longed once more to be among civilized beings. Nor were we disappointed in our expectations: the captain kept his word like a man, and the next morning found us steaming up the Bosphorus, and fully prepared to admire its beauties, for we knew that every rotation of the paddles carried us further and further from that sink of iniquity, the mere aspect of which is sufficient to prove the utter worthlessness of the cause for which so much of our best blood has been shed.

It is almost impossible to give any description of the Bosphorus: words are too weak to describe the beauties which are developed almost without interruption from Scutari as far as the entrance to the Black Sea. Fortunately, too, we should not have to land anywhere and dispel the illusion, so we sailed along in the brightest possible spirits, and were prepared to admire anything. The whole of the Bosphorus is so sown with cannon, that a mouse, one would think, could scarcely get through, and yet, at the commencement of the war, a Russian frigate ran the gauntlet, and escaped into the Black Sea. I was anxious to see Buyukderé, interesting to me as the spot where the Contingent had lain so long idly, and to the bitter discontent of the officers and men. But such good fortune was not granted me; a rattling shower of rain, such as can only be met with in Turkey, drove us below, and we were not released until our good ship was heaving merrily on the Black Sea.

CHAPTER II.

A WINTER IN KERTCH.

Nine times have I already taken up my pen to jot down my experiences of a winter in the Crimea, nine times has a numbing stiffness in my fingers compelled me to drop it again, and seek a welcome refuge by the side of my stove. No doubt many persons will imitate the example of Professor Koch, and write learned treatises on the climate of the Crimea, but as far as myself and winter are concerned, I can aptly describe it in one short sentence: "When it don't rain it freezes, when it don't freeze it rains." However, as we have now had two consecutive days of sunshine, and this 13th of April appears the turning-point of the year, I will venture to take up my narrative again, and proceed to describe in a rambling and desultory fashion our winter in Kertch.

On the 10th of December I was landed at Fort Paul in charge of our department, being responsible for their safe-conduct as far as Kertch. The change was anything but agreeable; it was nearly six, on a dark winter's night, ere we were all landed, and standing up to our knees in the loose washy mud, which represents the beach at Fort Paul. Add to this that several portmanteaux were dropped through the holes in the rickety wharf, occasioning a considerable amount of bad language from their owners, and it may be easily conceived that our situation was not the most pleasant in the world. But this was only the beginning of misfortunes: officers, men, and servants were huddled into one huge hut, and left there for the night, without food, water, or light. The last we were enabled to rectify by means of Clarke's candle-lamp—an invaluable companion on a campaign; but the other two appeared insurmountable difficulties.

At last, one of our officers took heart, and set out in search of water. He returned in about an hour, one mass of mud from head to foot, but bearing triumphantly a gutta-percha bottle, holding about a gallon of the precious fluid. Eagerly did we produce our panikins, but, alas! woeful was our disappointment. The water was half-warm and inexpressibly mawkish, and we found, on strict cross-examination, that it had been obtained from a condensing machine erected on the beach by her Majesty's steam-ship *Niger*. Supperless and quarrelsome we proceeded to rig up our camp-beds, and after many mistakes succeeded in rendering them sufficiently strong to lie down upon, and we gradually dropped off to sleep, with the pleasing consciousness that we should wake up in the morning with an astounding rheumatism; and such was the case.

Thus was spent our first night in the Crimea: the details may appear puerile, but still I fancy them valuable, as proving that a campaigning life is not all rosy-coloured; for my own part, I can only say that I entertained some very mutinous ideas, and would have gladly resigned all prospective glory to be once more seated in my own house. However, it was too late to repine, and I was compelled, *nolens volens*, to accept the situation. My bed, I found, was not so downy as to induce me to oversleep myself, and by six the next morning I had all the luggage packed, and off we started for Kertch, which we reached by ten, after wading five miles through the stiffest and most uncompromising clay I ever saw in my life.

The first view of Kertch is certainly very fine: there is a species of stern dignity in the rugged, treeless hills, at the foot of which the town stretches out in an amphitheatrical form, and a pleasant contrast is occasioned by the white houses, with their cheery green and red roofs. On a nearer approach, this feeling gave way to one of profound pity—the reader must pardon me, but it was my first introduction to the amenities of war. In the palmy days of Kertch, the Fort Paul road was bounded on one side for nearly a mile by magnificent storehouses and factories. All these were now utterly and hopelessly ruined. Huge fissures in the walls showed the ruthless passage of a shell, while the absence of doors, windows, and every particle of wood revealed that even a more cruel foe had been at work, in the shape of the barbarous Turk.

In truth, no words would be sufficiently strong to portray the desolation which reigned in Kertch on my first arrival. Everywhere might be traced the handiwork of an infidel and sanguinary band, who thought they were doing Allah good service by despoiling the Giaour; and blind to their own comfort, or that of their allies (Heaven save the mark!), their track was marked by wanton destruction, relentless ruffianism, and studied debauchery. Let it not be supposed that I am exaggerating. I could an' I would tell tales which would freeze my reader's very marrow, of the truth of which I cannot entertain a doubt, but they are not suited for perusal. The worst of it was that the French thought themselves in honour bound to follow in the footsteps of the Turks; and though not committing the same excesses, they entertained very indistinct notions of the laws of *meum* and *tuum*. Hence it was not surprising that the more respectable portion of the population should seek shelter in the interior, and leave their lares and penates to the tender mercies of Tartars and self-emancipated serfs, who sedulously completed the work of destruction by stealing and secreting everything which had by chance escaped the polite attention of the Turks.

On arriving at Kertch, I soon found the quarters allotted to the officers and men, and after a hard day's work retired to my own, which were excessively comfortable, and, strange to say, had nearly half the windows entire. By the sacrifice of a few copies of the *Times*, I succeeded in keeping at bay the wind, which was whistling more than sharply through the streets. After making myself as comfortable as I could, I proceeded to look for dinner, and found a good Samaritan in the shape of a restaurateur, who served you up what he called a dinner, for the sum of fifteen francs. With this the first day of my campaigning ended, and I need not further allude to myself, except in so far as my narrative compels me to speak in the first person singular.

Kertch, when belonging to the Russians, must have been a singularly clean and pleasant town. It possesses excellent fountains, and had abundance of sewerage, until the French took it into their wise heads to break it up, in pursuit of hidden treasure. The town itself is built in a quadrangular form, and the houses are generally large and stately. The streets are wide and airy —rather too much so in winter, but then it must be remembered that it is essentially a watering-place, and only fashionable in the summer months. This fact is proved by the large suites of rooms, innocent of stoves, to be found on the shady side of the Woronzoff-street, which formerly served for the dwellings of the Russian nobility, and afterwards, by sad mutation, for regiments of Turks. At one extremity of the High-street is the market-place, a circle surrounded by shops, and on one side a magnificent flight of steps led to the museum. The entrance-gate was guarded by a couple of griffins, and the same device may still be seen in a mutilated form on the barrier gate of the Arabat-road at the other extremity of the town. These steps are now, of course, nearly destroyed, but the Turks are not entirely to blame for this. The soft stone of which they are built is remarkably friable, and requires constant looking after, for the rain and frost cause it to give way almost at a touch. Still I would not have it supposed that the Turks had no share in the destruction, for I saw them myself one afternoon diligently engaged in upsetting one of the griffins, and bursting into uncontrollable shouts of delight when it fell down and smashed to pieces on the pavement. I need not say that, on our arrival, the museum contained not the slightest article possessing any intrinsic value: French artistic amateurs and Turkish iconoclasts had removed everything scarce, and only the *disjecta membra* of some pre-Roman or Genoese torsos showed that antiquities had once possessed at this spot a local habitation and a name.

On the extreme summit of the hill towering over Kertch, and on the spot called Mithridates's Chair, from a popular rumour that the great "Palmer" of the ancients here reviewed his fleets, is to be found a small temple, sacred to the memory of some Russian swell who deserved well of his country, and inscribed his name on the hearts of his loving compatriots in the usual Russian fashion, namely, by bullying the weaker vessels, and letting off the larger ones untouched. However this may be, his monument has been gutted, and the Turks have expressed their detestation of the Moscow Giaour in their usual practical fashion. These, I believe, are the only curiosities the town used to possess; there are, of course, the usual Greek churches filled with greasy pictures and still greasier papas, but these are elements to be found in any Russian town. And if I allude to the peculiar frousy smell pervading the houses of the townspeople, it is only as a proof that the Russians remain true to themselves even in this *ultima Thule* of their gigantic empire.

But now to allude to matters more nearly affecting the Turkish Contingent. We had hardly become comfortably settled in our quarters, when the alarm spread that our scanty cavalry had received a severe blow and heavy discouragement at the hands of the Cossacks. Unfortunately we could not prove that the jade Rumour lied on this occasion, for the news was confirmed that

Captain Sherwood and forty-six men had been killed by an overwhelming body of the enemy. They had advanced too far up the country—for what reason deponent sayeth not, although some Benjamin Backbite stated they were foraging for Christmas turkeys; but whatever the cause, they suddenly found themselves surrounded, and had no other alternative but to cut their way back. Poor Sherwood was killed at the first charge, but Captain M'Donald, the second in command, succeeded in forcing his way through, with the loss above detailed. How many Cossacks were sent to their last account it is impossible to say; but this much is certain, that had it not been for the strange fatuity which had hitherto attended every movement of the Contingent, and which very naturally accounts for the cavalry going into action without having their swords sharpened, the enemy's loss would have been severe. This affair cast a gloom over our Christmas festivities; and, worse than all, the presence of the Cossacks in our immediate neighbourhood put us all on the *qui vive*, and threw upon us a great additional amount of most unpleasant duty in fortifying the town.

We had just retired to bed at a rather early hour of New-Year's day, after seeing the old year out, not forgetting to drink the health of sweethearts and wives in merry England, when a breathless messenger arrived, stating that the walls—then only half completed—would be manned at half-past three o'clock, and preparations made to take up the siege guns without delay. This was not the most pleasant information in the world, but necessity knows no law, and we all had too great a regard for our carcases to neglect a warning so pregnant of meaning. At the time appointed we therefore set to work, and by twelve o'clock the next forenoon we had the satisfaction of knowing that the enemy, if he came, would meet with a warm reception. But, although he did not come, we neglected no precaution, I am proud to say; trenches were dug all around the town; walls were built, by the simple process of pulling down houses; every accessible point was defended by a gun, and we began to breathe freely again, and refresh our exhausted frames with ration rum. But the danger was not yet averted, the Ides of January were not yet passed, and on the 6th of that genial month was fought the tremendous engagement which will be known to our children's children under the name of the battle of the Moscov Yok.

Imagine the sensation which would be produced in a quiet country village, were a breathless messenger to enter the church on a Sunday morning just as service was commencing, and announce with face as pallid as that which drew Priam's curtains at the dead of night, that a rampant tiger had escaped from Wombwell's menagerie, and was quietly regaling on the parish bull just in front of the parson's bay-window. Such a feeling, I can assure you, I entertained when I saw a booted and spurred hussar enter *our* church at Kertch (generally supposed to have been the dancing-room of a boarding-school in the palmy days of the town), and whisper mysteriously to his commanding officer. How much was the feeling aggravated when the said commanding officer quitted the room, and the clergyman announced there would be no service that morning!

On reaching the street rumours fell thick and fast,

like leaves on Vallombrosa, but the favourite one was that Fort Paul and Yenikaleh were already taken, and that the Russ was within half a mile of Kertch. Endless were the gallopings of aide-de-camps about the streets; fearful was the discord of the fifes and drums among the Turks; direful was the commotion among the European officers; great was the glee of the Russian inhabitants at the thought that the Czar would have his own again. Unluckily fears, hopes, agitation, and forebodings were destined to be equally infructuous; no Russians made their appearance, and after four hours of anxious anticipation the troops marched down the hill again, to enjoy their pillaff, and boast of the mighty deeds they would have done if the Russians had only dared to attack the conquerors of the world. For my part, I can only say I am deucedly glad they did not.

Thus things went on through the month of January. Our leaders very wisely kept the troops on the *qui vive*, and ready to turn out at a moment's notice; and if it did nothing else, it gave them a healthy occupation, and opportunity to become acquainted with their European officers. The only apprehension I entertained was that the cry of "wolf" might be raised too often, but I am happy to say I was agreeably disappointed; at any hour of the day or night the Turks were prepared for a scrimmage, and I dare say if the Russians had come they would have fought bravely behind the stone walls which they had so admirably constructed. From all I have seen I should say that the Turks ought to make the finest masons in the world; their talent in building walls of surprising height and thickness is truly wonderful; and even if the said walls were only suited for an army of Brobdignagians to fire over, still the Lilliputian Turks had the advantage of being out of harm's way, and that feeling has a wonderful effect in arousing the pluck of even the most timid, whether Christian, Mohammedan, or Buddhist.

All this time, however, the Turks were getting into a very efficient state of discipline; at first, they had been difficult to manage, owing to their prejudices running counter to their interests, but at last the latter gained the day, and the victory was won—a harder matter, by the way, than the capture of the Malakhoff. Their native officers, annoyed at the subordinate position into which they were thrust, thwarted the European officers in every possible way. Add to this the prevalent ignorance of the language, and the foolish bullying of some European officers, who treated the Turks like a conquered nation, and there is very little doubt that we only owe our present existence to the marvellous foresight and cool calculation of our much-beloved commander, General Vivian. But to elucidate this matter I ought to give a short account of the formation of the Contingent.

When it first entered the wise head of Lord Stratford—a man who, whatever his faults of temper may be, has the most perfect appreciation of the Turkish character—that the Turkish army contained the elements of success, although thwarted by the incompetency of the pashas and native officers, he proposed that the Ottoman troops should be taken into English pay at the same rate as the Turkish, but with the advantage that they should be well clothed, well fed, regularly paid, and be officered by Europeans. The Sultan acquiesced, and with his peculiar Oriental slave notions, handed over various regiments, principally *mauvais sujets*, who were encamped at Biyuk Dereh, as the nucleus of the Contingent. Most of these men were Redifs, or militiamen, who had already served their time, and it is not surprising that the idea of being robbed of their liberty and being commanded by infidels induced them to desert. And this was the great mistake in the formation of the Contingent. Had they been removed immediately to some spot where they could not have deserted, much difficulty would have been avoided. However, they were at length taken to Kertch, and then the process of reducing them to a degree of discipline was heartily commenced.

And at this critical stage the conduct and consummate tact of General Vivian cannot be sufficiently praised. His life, and those of the few Europeans attached to the force, were at the mercy of a number of as unmitigated ruffians as were ever yet congregated together. It was impossible to say at what moment they might rebel and run amuck, thinking it no doubt a most meritorious action to extirpate as many of the infidels as they could. But General Vivian bided his time, and was well supported by his officers. Conciliation was his policy, and he succeeded, I believe, beyond his most daring anticipations. Within three months he converted a riotous body of Albanians, Arnaouts, and Pallikars into a highly-disciplined force, and this was effected without the slightest disturbance. The Turk, however bigoted, began to find out that, although three-and-fourpence per month was very small pay, still it was paid him regularly, without any portion adhering to the fingers of the pasha, and the clothes he received were far superior to anything he had seen in his beloved Stamboul.

Add to that, the European officers treated him as a fellow-creature: he had not to crawl before them and kotoo as if to a superior being; he had a right of appeal against injustice, and he gradually awoke to a perception that he was a MAN, enjoying the blessings and privileges of nature, and no longer the slave to accident and caprice. Here, then, was one great point gained, and at the same time the power of the native officers was sapped. They could no longer tyrannize over and plunder the troops with impunity, and although their hatred of the English was redoubled, still this was more than compensated by the interest and affection the lower ranks began to feel in us.

The difficulties the European officers had to contend with were not slight; their ignorance of the language, and being compelled to trust to dragomans, generally in league with the Turkish officers, were a great stumbling-block, but they managed to climb over it, owing to the peculiar position they held. This I had better attempt to explain as concisely as possible.

By the constitution originally given to the Turkish Contingent, each regiment consisted of eight companies, commanded by the usual Turkish officers, but actions being controlled by three European officers—the first in command, the second in command, and the adjutant. By this process the Bim-bashi, or Turkish commandant, was degraded to the fourth place instead of the first, and, indeed, became to all intents and purposes a nonentity, except as regarded the internal administration of the regiment, for he was converted into a species of intermediator between the European officers and the troops. This naturally enough galled the haughty Osmanli; but this was not the worst: in process of time supernumerary captains were attached to the regiments, all of them claiming and obtaining rank above the Turkish officers. In point of fact, the Bimbashi was converted into what in the Indian army is designated a Subahdar Major. The Turkish officers, as a natural consequence, detested us, and would gladly have induced a mutiny, I am inclined to believe; but they set to work too late. By the time they began to see the anomalous position they were called on to assume, the European officers, with few exceptions, had conciliated the Turks, who were willing to follow wherever they led. Had the Contingent, however, been a permanent institution, it was currently believed that the Turkish officers would have been gradually weeded, and others raised from the ranks to occupy their places. Had this been done, I have no hesitation in declaring that few nations would have had a finer body of men at their command than the Turkish Contingent.

But the moral effect produced by the presence of European officers was even more surprising than the physical. On first joining the Contingent, I heard of numerous murders and robberies recently committed; graves were desecrated, and women assassinated, after being exposed to the most shocking indignities. But, after a short space, all this ceased as if by magic. General Vivian, by an excellent system of firmness blended with kindness, showed the troops that he was determined to punish the guilty and reward the good.

In fact, it cannot be denied that the Turk, regarded as a soldier, is the very best raw material that can be procured. It would be difficult to find in any army soldiers so modest in their requirements as the Turkish, or any satisfied with so little, or, indeed, with nothing at all. With a lump of bread, some sugar, and cheese, in his pocket, this soldier will endure the greatest fatigue; he will follow without a murmur wherever his leader may take him, and when utterly exhausted he recruits his strength by singing one of the patriotic songs, which generally throw the Turks into a state of ecstatic delight.

It is curious to watch, as I have done, the utter contempt of death with which the Turkish soldier marches to meet the foe; he knows that his destiny has been fixed since the day of his birth; he knows that he *must* die whenever his time comes, and that a whole park of artillery would miss him, if his destiny so decrees it; finally, he knows that, if he fall in battle, he will go straightway to Paradise,—and won't he be better off there than in this world of cares? The same feeling, indeed, predominates with the Turks whenever the approach of death is felt. I have seen them dying here in the hospitals, and the calmness of their demeanour would shame many a Christian: let them once be persuaded that they are booked for another world, and the surgeon may lock up his medicaments again—no persuasion will induce the Turk to attempt to frustrate the designs of Providence.

Although the pay of the privates only amounts to twenty piastres a month, still the soldiers are so saving, and their wants so small, that it is amply sufficient for them. Many of them with whom I have spoken appear to prefer the old Turkish system of irregular payments to ours. In the first place, the Sultan's treasury served them as a species of savings bank, and relieved them of the necessity of carrying about their little capital in their waist-scarf. There is another light, too, in which the soldier regards the matter: if he happens to fall in battle, and does not happen to carry his money about with him, he is sure that it will not fall into the hands of the enemy after his death; and as the common Turk is generally very craving, or at least highly economical, he naturally prefers making a will in favour of his padishah than of the dogs of Moscov.

I have met Redifs belonging to the Contingent who have shown me savings to the amount of five or six hundred piastres, and regarded with inexpressible delight the beshliks, or bank-notes, which they carried about them. If we calculate that a soldier spends about a piastre a month on himself—and few do more, —after five years' service he can have saved at least five hundred piastres, or according to Turkish notions, is a well-to-do man, with taking into calculation the little backshish which he manages to draw out of English officers. One of their principal amusements during the winter, when the exchange was up at 147, was to stop us in the street with a "Sovran Johnny," displaying at the same time twenty shillings in silver, which they were prepared to exchange. We frequently humoured them, and no doubt they made a very profitable thing by it. In addition to his pay, the soldier receives an excellent ration of meat, bread, rice, and vegetables, and, in truth, has not the slightest cause for complaint.

When the Turks were first handed over to us by the padishah, nothing could have furnished a more striking proof of the state of his exchequer than their deplorable appearance. Even his crack regiments, that had fought so bravely at Silistria, were in rags, and armed with old flint muskets. But English money soon made an alteration in this: any quantity of new clothes have been issued; and had the war lasted, the whole of the Contingent would have been armed by this time with Minié rifles, obtained from Balaklava, when the new Enfield Pritchett rifle was issued to the English army. And I must say that the Turkish soldiers deserve good weapons: as a body they are the finest marksmen I ever saw, as their targets will abundantly testify, and their care of their muskets is beyond all praise. The sentries, when on duty, spend the greater portion of their time in polishing up their barrels with a piece of oiled rag, and rust is quite unknown among them.

Their great fault, however, is their unmilitary appearance, produced in the following way: no Turk was was ever yet known to throw away a rag as long as it held together, and consequently, when new clothes were issued, the Turks put them on over the old ones; which did not produce the most soldier-like effect in the world. Great were the exertions on the part of the English officers to rectify this, but I am afraid Turkish prejudices for dirt are irradicable. In truth, there never was a greater fallacy propagated than the one touching the cleanliness of the Turks. They may use plenty of water in summer, but I have not yet had an opportunity of seeing them at that season; during the winter I can only say they were fearfully suffering from hydrophobia. In fact, when we take into consideration that a Turk wears his shirt till it falls off his back, there can be little doubt as to the state in which he must be during the hot weather; and so, I dare say, from a motive of self-defence, he indulges in copious ablutions.

The Contingent affords any person of a speculative turn of mind ample opportunities to realize the alterations made by Sultan Mahmud in the organization of his army. The reform dates from the fall of the Janissaries: uniform, arms, and manœuvres (partly) were borrowed from the Europeans, and the government is still striving to perfect the process of transition; but the war allowed no leisure time to follow it up; and the hatred of the Giaour, summoned up and fostered by the Moscov, placed the Turkish soldier in a state of unpleasant opposition to his external appearance. The general spirit among the Nizam, is, in one word, bravery and blind obedience,—when not on duty a somewhat exaggerated cordiality between the privates and non-commissioned officers: the reason is, because the latter are very little above the others in education. Officers and privates sit in the same coffee-house, and if a mulazim happens to come in late, and cannot find a seat on the carpets, he may place himself very contentedly on the bare ground, for he is quite certain none of the men will move for him. And now for a word or two about the officers.

The education of the real Turkish officer may be regarded as an unknown quantity: the few to be met with displaying any intelligence, have been instructed in London, Paris, or Vienna, and these are certainly very polished and amiable men. Their scale of pay, especially among the non-commissioned officers, is very low: in the infantry a corporal has 30 piastres, a sergeant 50 piastres per month. A lieutenant gets his 180 piastres, clothes and rations; a captain 270 piastres and two rations. From this point a strange discrepancy commences, for a colonel receives 1800 piastres and 16 rations for man and horse, while the field-marshal receives 75,000 piastres per month, and rations worth at least 50,000 more. The principle of giving pecuniary compensation for surplus rations has been maintained in the Turkish Contingent, and hence arises the anomaly that the Bin-bashi is actually better paid than the English adjutant of the regiment.

One of the principal causes which has gained us the good-will of the Turkish soldiers, is the wonderful attention paid them by the English medical men. Any one at all acquainted with the utter ignorance of the Turkish Hakim-bashis, can easily imagine the delightful change the Turks must experience in being attended by highly-educated men. And indeed the medical officers have effected wonders: they have overcome prejudices which appear, at first starting, insurmountable; and though they had been severely tried by a very dangerous outbreak of scurvy, they were enabled (greatly assisted by the judicious arrangements of the purveyor to the forces) to check it, without any great loss of life.

Dr M'Pherson, the inspector-general of hospitals, has been indefatigable in bringing everything into good working order, and I am sure he feels amply satisfied with the result. Nor have the Europeans of the force been neglected: they had a fine hospital detached for their own use, and Staff-Surgeon Irvine and Dr Bogle have contrived to keep it remarkably free of patients. In fact, the healthy condition of the Turkish Contingent has been a matter of general remark at English head-quarters, and the correspondent of the *Times* spoke in high terms of commendation of the labours of our medical staff.

The amount of the Contingent at present quartered in Kertch, Yenikaleh, and Fort Paul, is about 16,000 men, composing 16 regiments of infantry, 6 batteries of artillery, and 1 battery of horse artillery. The latter is confessedly the crack arm of the Turkish army, and the men we possess do not belie their reputation. They perform their manœuvres most creditably, and I believe would fight bravely if an occasion presented itself. Indeed, there is no fault to find with the Turks as far as readiness to fight is concerned; and taking into consideration that they have been in front of the enemy the whole of the winter, in daily expectation of an attack, the general officer restricting the issue of Crimean medals to those persons who were present before the 9th of September appears to act with peculiar harshness towards them. I trust, though, that some gentleman of an inquiring turn of mind will yet bring this matter before the "House."

But, after all, Kertch was an abominably dull place during the winter months: one got tired after a while of inventing *shaves*, and when that occupation was gone there was nothing to be done. Salt pork, too, palled upon the senses, and fresh meat was not to be had, owing to the terror felt by the Tartars of the Russians. Hence the consumption of preserved meats was prodigious: still more prodigious that of brandy-and-water and Cavendish tobacco. From sheer want of something to do a man would invite his friends to a smoke, and the result would be a severe headache in the morning. One enterprising individual imported some soda water, for which he only charged 4s. 6d. a bottle; but that was soon disposed of, by the bottles bursting from the cold, leaving him a considerable loser by the transaction. But, by Heavens! the cold was intense; a piercing easterly wind would blow for weeks in succession, and the bay would be completely frozen over, so that it would have been an easy matter to walk across right to Taman. That, however, afforded some relief to our *ennui*, for at any rate we could go on board some ship for a change, instead of brooding round the stove. Books were at a premium, and newspapers priceless, for at times no mail would arrive for a month, owing to the ice, and we could procure no information, except the lies the Tartars chose to tell us.

About the middle of March some enterprising individuals got up races, which would have been all the pleasanter had the weather been warmer; however, they lasted three days, and afforded the topic of conversation for nine, so they were of some service in their way. The only other amusement I can specify during war-time was a ride to Yeni-kaleh, or Fort Paul, at the latter of which places a very good idea of camp-life could be obtained, as the troops were all hutted, and exercised many ingenious dodges in keeping out the cold. One of the best I saw was a wall of empty bottles, about nine feet in height, all of which the owner of the hut prided himself on having been emptied in his abode. The French quarters are interesting, from the fact of their having exercised their ingenuity in laying out gardens and terraces. I don't believe, for my part, that anything would grow on so barren a rock; but still the idea was good.

Yeni-kalch is a very peculiar little town of very dirty houses, built under an old Genoese fort. The streets are remarkable for being quite impassable during the winter months; being very steep, they are either too slippery for locomotion from the frost, or you stick up to your knees in mud, owing to a thaw: there appears to be no other alternative. I should say, of the three posts of the Contingent, it aspired to the superlative degree of dulness. One peculiar fact I may mention is, that there was not a single female in the town. Such an abyss of desolation, to use the words of the poet, may be imagined, but cannot be described; but we pass it over in mournful silence. It was in Yeni-kalch more especially that the scurvy housed, and the disease at one time attained such proportions that it was deemed advisable to remove the worst of the patients on board a transport, converted for the nonce into a hospital ship. Owing to the use of large quantities of rice, to which the Turks are especially addicted, the disease broke out without any preliminary warning almost, and it was not till the soldiers had their allowance of rice stopped that any head could be made against it. Now that the fine weather has arrived, we are quite clear of any diseases of an epidemic nature, and I trust will remain so, although the Russians in the town bid us beware of the Ides of May. I should think that Kertch would be a very unhealthy place in the height of summer; there are no trees to afford any shelter, and the dazzling white houses, combined with the dust, ought, by all the laws of physic, to have a tendency to promote ophthalmia; but I trust we shall be away from here before the summer sets in with its usual intensity.

The news of the armistice, it may be supposed, produced a very agreeable change among us, and many parties were speedily formed to make fierce attacks on hares which were said to swarm just beyond our outlying pickets. When the Contingent first came to Kertch a great number of ownerless greyhounds were picked up by the Turks, and now came into great requisition, quite at fancy prices. They are a very peculiar breed of dog, much larger and more powerful than the English greyhound, with long bristly hair. I fancy they are in some way related to the Persian dog of that breed. For once there was truth in a report arising in Kertch: there were oceans of hares, easily captured, and the consequence was that the Contingent was soon suffering from a surfeit of hare, roasted, jugged, or baked. At the same time large flocks of bustards were found, but they were very wary, and it was very rare to bring one down.

The other *feræ naturæ* of this part of the Crimea consist of wild duck, pigeons, hoopoos, and larks of fabulous proportions. The finest shot made during the armistice was by a medical man, who brought down two large eagles with one charge of No. 6. They were splendid birds, and possessed of extraordinary vitality, for though one of them had a penknife passed through his brain, he had sufficient strength an hour after to clutch me by his talons, and give me a very severe dig.

Another amusement we discovered was to go out among the Tartar villages, and try to fraternize with the inhabitants, by devouring their eggs and milk. The poor fellows are in a horrible fright at the thoughts of peace, for they fully anticipate having their throats cut by the Russians. There is probably some truth in this story, for we have shipped to Stamboul the whole of the Tartar militia we embodied; and it is very possible that the Cossacks may feel an inclination to revenge themselves on their next of kin.

These Tartars, though, are a wretched set; they are the biggest cowards on the face of the earth, and the fear they entertain of the Russians would be ludicrous, were it not, unfortunately, too well founded. They live in the extreme of poverty, and rarely know what the taste of meat is; the most striking proof of this is found in those who have been in our service during the winter, and are now so plump that they could not be recognized by their nearest friends. The only extravagance they appear to indulge in is dress; they wear large dressing-gowns, as it were, made of red and yellow striped silk, and evenly quilted, blue serge trousers, and kalpacks of Astrakan lambskin. They are very fond of riding at a break-neck pace, and how they stick on is a mystery; their saddle consisting of a hard leathern pillow, strapped on to a diabolical wooden framework, and looking like a patent method to dislocate your limbs. Their horses are not very bright specimens, being generally thin and badly groomed; in short, I was greatly disappointed with the Tartars, after all I had read of them; for I had expected to find a race of men only sullenly yielding allegiance to the Russians, while the bare truth was that they are so frightened that they dare not say their houses are their own. In person you find here and there some fine specimens, were it not for their Mongolian eyes and flat noses, while the absence of beards among the younger men gives them an appearance of effeminacy when compared with the Turkish soldiers.

The news of peace being proclaimed was a sad blow to the officers of the Contingent; for, apart from the loss of any opportunity of trying the mettle of our troops against the enemy, it is much to be apprehended that France and Russia may insist on our being disbanded. If so, many of the officers will be heavy losers; they have been to considerable expense in providing their outfit, and it is even a moot point whether we shall obtain any compensation. I have hopes, however, yet; the Turkish Contingent has cost so large a sum in formation that I do not think it would be advantageous to disband it, especially at a time when the peace of Europe is far from being ensured.

The great stumbling-block in Turkey has been the inefficiency of the native officers, and now, when there is an opportunity to improve the Turkish army to a wonderful extent, I hardly think it will be let slip. At any rate, whatever be the result of the next five months' deliberation, I am sure many persons in England sincerely regret that we were not sent direct to Kars, to the relief of General Williams and his gallant troops, but I am convinced no one can regret it more earnestly than we do. Besides, it should be taken into consideration that the Turkish Contingent is actually one of the cheapest armies that ever was embodied; the pay of the soldiers is very trifling, and although the English officers are suppôsed to be overpaid, it must always be borne in mind that we possess no prospective advantages like those enjoyed by the officers of the line. But a truce to politics.

April 17th.—We have just been honoured by a visit from a Russian general, who came in to look after his property—poor, misguided individual! he literally did not find two stones standing on each other on the ancient site of his domicile, but was shown them converted into the town wall of defence. The look of consternation with which he regarded the destruction is said to have been very great. What the Russians will do with the town when it is evacuated by the Allies is difficult to say, but I should advise, if they have any regard to their own interests, that they should desert it altogether, or else the stenches produced by the Turks will raise them up a foe in the shape of fever, more deadly than were the bayonets of the Allies at Inkerman.

I think I may say, without exaggeration, that there are not six houses in the town habitable by ladies: windows and doors were removed at an early date by the French chasseurs, who evinced a wonderful aptitude in appropriating everything that was not too hot or too heavy, and even the few sticks of furniture that had been saved were in most instances converted into firewood. Of course, when all the mischief possible had been done, stringent orders were issued to put a stop to the "looting;" and when our fellows left off, as in duty bound, the ruffianly Greeks and Maltese set to work on their own account. How well they succeeded may be seen from the fact, that during the whole of the winter pictures have been for sale, evidently taken from the Russian houses. Intrinsically they are of no great value,—the best I have seen was sold for forty-two guineas, being richly encased in silver-gilt, but they are interesting in consequence of their religious (?) character. A saint averages in the market about five shillings; a Bogoroditza about seven-and-six; while any allegorical picture, with a quantity of figures, will fetch from fifteen to twenty shillings. They are all of a very mediæval character, and would gladden the hearts of the pre-Raphaelite brethren, such impossible postures being only known to Byzantine artists. But these Greeks have found other occupations besides picture-dealing; they have recently taken to midnight assassination, and in one week murdered three unhappy wretches. All attempts to discover them have been in vain, and our only remedy is an increased amount of patrolling.

Since the proclamation of peace it is marvellous to notice the number of persons who have made their appearance in the streets. It is currently supposed they have been concealed in cellars during the winter, wisely objecting to expose themselves, after past experiences, to the tender mercies of the Turks. Shops, too, are being gradually opened, and, what is more, are well stocked, though where the articles come from is unknown. But the character of the Russians appears to be concealment.

By the word "shop," must not be supposed anything like what we see in civilized countries; they are generally gloomy holes, particularly dirty, and guarded by a female Cerberus, with her head bound in a white napkin, and herself muffled up in a long black cloak, which appears an heirloom, handed down through many generations. In fact, the only way to describe a Russian logically is a cloak-wearing being, for they never leave off those garments winter or summer, and are popularly supposed to sleep in them. But the horrible smell in their houses is past bearing; they are filthy in their habits, and do not possess even the commonest articles of civilization; and this rule is equally true both of great and small. In fact, there is not a pin to choose between Turk and Russian in the matter of dirt, except that when it is a wonderfully fine day the Turk may be seen washing his one shirt; but this I have never witnessed among the Russians.

The Turks, as may be imagined, are in high glee at peace, and the prospect of their returning to their beloved Stamboul. Their notions of the future of their country are, to say the least of them, curious. Yesterday I was talking with a Bim-bashi, and he kindly volunteered to tell me the arrangements the padishah had made. He stated that the Turks and English were going to combine to kick the French (whom he remarked parenthetically were "chok fenar") out of Stamboul: that after that the Turkish army was going to Inghilterra, and the English troops remain in Turkey, and that peace and fraternization would last between the two nations for ever. How it is the French have rendered themselves so odious to the Turks, I cannot say: but we have derived one advantage from the last war—if advantage it can be called—in making the Turks, as a body, love us, or our money. The same Bim-bashi told me another curious tale as current among his countrymen; namely, that in London there was a cave of fabulous proportions, brimming full of "liras," and guarded by an old woman of vinegar aspect; and that whenever our sultan wanted a few millions, he applied to the old lady, who accommodated him to any amount. I fancy I have read that this story was also heard in China; if so, it is curious to trace the tradition. It is utterly impossible, by the way, to convey to the Turks any idea of our being governed by a sovereign lady; if you try to explain it, they evidently mix her up with the aforesaid old woman.

I am afraid my readers will find this article very rambling and desultory, but it has one merit, that of being a faithful transcript of my experiences during a winter at Kertch. I have omitted much which is not of general interest, but I can say that, on the whole, I have been very comfortable in the enemy's country. Of course there was a good deal of grumbling at first, but it is surprising how soon one gets accustomed to minor privations. Thus I am perfectly contented to eat hare, although gooseberry-jam has to be substituted for currant-jelly; nor do I turn up my nose because I am forced to satisfy myself with a caper-sauce as a succedaneum for lobster with my turbot.

But I should be most ungrateful were I to close this chapter without referring to Commissary-General Adams and his staff, and thanking them for the exertions they made on our behalf. Not one single day have we been on short rations, and this was an astonishing feat, when it is borne in mind that for more than three months, off and on, there was no communication seawards, owing to the bay being frozen over. We have confessedly been better fed than the army at Balaklava even at the best period, and we have experienced none of those privations which are generally expected on the organization of a new force. So far, indeed, were precautions taken, that salt pork was never once served out to the Turks, and when we take into consideration that 16,000 or 17,000 men had to be rationed daily, it showed a wonderful amount of provision on the part of General Adams that all his arrangements were so well carried out.

Nor have we been over-troubled with red-tape, that usual curse of armies: it is true that a few instances have happened, but the dispensers of tape were so heartily laughed at, that they were only too glad to fall into the customs of the rest. An excellent *esprit de corps* has been maintained, and I may safely say that the Turkish Contingent, both under General Vivian and his successor, General Mitchell, has been rendered a most efficient force.

CHAPTER III.

FROM STAMBOUL TO PESTH.

Blessed is the man that invented sleep, says honest old Sancho Panza. Never was the truth of this more appreciated than after a weary trip by water and land across the European continent. Auph! I wearily stretch myself, and rise under the melancholy delusion that I have slept my sleep out; but all in vain. The future wanderer may lay it down as an axiom, uncontrovertible as any of old Euclid, of wearisome school and black-board mémory, that two nights' rest (Heaven save the mark!) in a railway carriage require ninety and six hours of consecutive feather-bed practice before the human frame is restored to its proper equilibrium. There is such a confounded angularity about a railway —such a tendency found among the cushions to establish a raw on the person of the sleep-desiring traveller —such a draughty predisposition on the part of the doors and windows, that rest, in the proper acceptation of the term, is impossible.

But even supposing that by dint of elaborate scheming and absolute disregard to comfort, the traveller succeed in snatching those forty winks in which our grandams indulged, he will surely be disturbed (supposing him to be bound across the Continent) by periodical visits from a gendarme, who can by no possibility be induced to believe that the traveller's passport is *en règle*, but that some deep design has been hatched to defraud his imperial royal master (or as the case may be) in some artistic manner, which only his (the aforesaid gendarme, I mean) remarkable talents can counteract. Then, again, the constant changes from motion to rest, entailed by the succession of stations, where the train must stop, if only that the conductor may drink his choppin of beer; the sudden inroad of frouzy, sleepy, bad-tobacco-puffing Germans, who make it a point to smoke themselves as they do their hams, by shutting out the external atmosphere; the shrill-sounding horn of the guard; and, worse than all, the palpitating motion of the carriage, when any acceleration of speed is attempted, and which makes one speculate on the advantages of the Railway Insurance Company,—a combination of all these renders it extremely difficult for the Continental traveller to snatch that fearful joy of sleep which his habits and education render a necessity of existence. After this preliminary outbreak of what the French would be disposed to call "English spleen," but what I term just complaining, I may as well proceed to tell my readers how it was that I underwent the above-described pleasing torture.

No very long time had elapsed since the post had borne away to England the account of the winter I had spent in Kertch, before the supposition, hitherto whispered in a doubtful accent, that the Turkish Contingent was on the eve of dissolution, became converted into a certainty. This was decidedly a most unpleasant fact, for no one cares to see his labour thrown away; and after working hard to convert the Turks into something bearing the appearance of an army, it was indubitably galling not to have an opportunity of seeing how the system worked in the field. Many officers deluded themselves for a time with the anticipation that the option would be given them of entering the Turkish service under English guarantee, and in this they were supported, strange to say, by the opinion of men high in command. In fact, this was the season for "shaves," wonderful in their audacity, and unparalleled in their success.

No information of an authentic nature could, of course, be obtained in Kertch as to the future fate of the Contingent, and all we knew was that the troops were being taken away as rapidly as possible, while the English regimental officers were kicking their heels about Kertch, and soothing their feelings with champagne. At length our eyes began to be opened; general orders were crowded with the names of officers whose services were dispensed with, and passages provided for them to Constantinople, when they would hear further. Eventually the lot fell on myself, and one morning about nine o'clock I received the pleasing information that I was to sail at twelve on the same day. Now, as I was troubled with various *impedimenta* —not the least being a wife—it may be assumed that the time was none of the longest; however, by various artful schemes known to campaigners, the most successful being to place the fragile articles at the bottom, the heavy goods at the top, and then dancing upon them with a severe aspect and indomitable energy, our trunks were strapped and at the wharf by the appointed time, and I said good-bye to Kertch, I sincerely trust for the first and last time.

In truth, I may consider myself fortunate in getting off so well, for many officers were driven from pillar to post in the most wonderful manner. Until you were safely on board ship you could not be certain of getting off, and even in some instance officers were removed into other vessels, after they had made themselves comfortable. In short, want of management was the rule, and not the exception; and the beautiful system of routine and red tape, I, as an Englishman, proudly assert was maintained in its pristine vigour, and even with some new offshoots, until the last moments of the Contingent.

Suppose us then safely on board the transport—let us call her the *Sparrowhawk*—built in Sunderland, and great in the coasting trade. The shady back slums of Wapping are probably the favourite haunts of her crew during their leisure hours; she possesses accommodation, somewhat scanty it is true, for captain and mate, though it is whispered that even their cabins are now and then laid under embargo, to be filled with wares, hard or soft. Of course she is the very vessel for a troop-ship; she can carry at a stretch 200 tons of merchandise in her hold; then why not a regiment? It is all nonsense saying there is no accommodation for officers; a paternal government has dispensed with their services, and they ought only to feel too happy to get to Constantinople at all. So in we all struggled, some 27 officers, into a cabin with accommodation for six; and it was only owing to the kindness of the captain, who gave up his own berth, that my wife was able to sleep at all.

There was certainly one other lady on board, but in

addition to having her cabin choked up with husband, grandfather, father, mother, four children, and a nurse, she was addicted to smoking cigarettes, which in a confined bunk is, to say the least, unpleasant to a lady still strongly addicted to English prejudices. I may as well remark that the lady with the family party belonged to the chief of the police in Kertch, who had received an amicable message from the Russians that he had better make himself scarce at once, or else they intended to hang him—what for, of course I can't say, but looking at the immense quantity of baggage, strongly suggestive in shape of pianofortes and bedsteads, I was led to presume that he, too, had been despoiling the Egyptian.

Our regiment of Turks behaved admirably on the passage down: it is true that their officers occupied the whole of the poop as dining apartment by day, and sleeping ditto by night; but that was nothing, for the English officors were too busily engaged at their one all-engrossing pursuit by day and night to require any fresh air. I don't know how the Queen's army got on before Sebastopol, but if the demon of play nestled there as comfortably as he did in Kertch, he must be quite a millionnaire by this time. As for the troops, they lay about the decks, indulging now and then in a hard biscuit and a draught of water, but always smoking or sleeping. Nor did they display the slightest vitality until they arrived in the neighbourhod of the Balta Liman palace, where the Sultan was then resident; but there, to the great horror of the captain of the vessel, who was carefully conning the ship through the Bosphorus, they began a diabolic charivari, with the united strength of their drums, fondly imagining it to be a salute. It was not till the captain threatened to carry them back to Biyukderéh, far from their beloved Stamboul, that they consented to hold their noise.

On our arrival in the Golden Horn, we had the first specimen of what the end of our twelve-million-costing Contingent was to be. Ships lay all around us crowded with Turks that had left Kertch many days before. The only anxiety appeared to be to get them away from the Crimea: what became of them after was not of the slightest consequence. Here and there a small tug-steamer might be seen dodging about with some two hundred troops aboard, and landing them appeared to be considered a capital day's work. As for any attempt to make the troops comfortable, that was too absurd: the war was over, and they were no longer required. What cared D.A.C.G.s, and such worthy gentry, for a parcel of Turks, whose occupation was gone, as far as England was concerned? It was not of the slightest consequence if they had only salt pork to eat—and knowing the decided preference Muhammedans entertain for such food, it was rather doing them a kindness than otherwise. Such is, indeed, the general way in which Englishmen render themselves beloved in the East: they are themselves so unprejudiced that they naturally strive to render all with whom they come in contact of the same mode of thinking as themselves. However, all things must have an end, and so eventually we got rid of our troops, and had time to look out for ourselves.

Of course we had to find lodgings of some sort, as

we could not sleep in the streets; and this was a matter of some difficulty, considering that Pera hotels have no expansive power, and were already uncomfortably crowded. However, after making the grand tour of the hotels, the L'Europe had compassion on us, and allowed us the divided possession of the landlord's own bed-room,—that is to say, it was already occupied by a vast quantity of quadrupeds, whose room is decidedly better than their company. The heat, too, was intense, and this, combined with bad food, such as can only be procured in Constantinople, very soon laid my wife on a bed of sickness. Considering, too, that we could have lived at the Clarendon at rather a cheaper rate than we were paying, it was decidedly advisable to look out for transport home.

As the Golden Horn was so crowded with ships that accidents were of daily occurrence, I was foolish enough to suppose that there would be no difficulty in obtaining passage to England; but I was still innocent of that peculiar institution known among us as the Transport Service. I found, for instance, after three days' diligent inquiry in various dark nooks in Galata, that although it was perfectly true transports of nearly 2000 tons were lying empty in the Horn, that was no reason English officers should obtain passage in them. They would probably be employed in taking home horses belonging to staff officers, and so on; but if I didn't mind waiting till the said horses were comfortably housed at home, why, perhaps,—and so on.

A very slight acquaintance with officials at times suffices to understand their meaning, so I politely bowed, and didn't trouble them again. As I did not suppose that the English government was going to establish a balloon correspondence for the service of Contingent officers, and as, moreover, my hotel bill was growing apace, I made frightful efforts, and after dodging the chief paymaster for two days, I at length had two minutes' conversation with that dread functionary. From him I received the information that I should be paid forty pounds for the passage of self and servant to England, and must do the best I could. Whenever my papers were signed I should receive the money I was entitled to, and there would be an end of my military services.

I trust I may be allowed to say a few words, even at the risk of being tedious, about the way we have been treated, as a warning in future wars for my readers aspiring to military fame *not* to go and do likewise. It is well known that the government was in sad want of officers when the Contingent was formed, because sufficient Indians could not be procured at a moment's notice. Promises costing nothing, we were fed with hopes, and many of us were fools enough to believe in them. We are forced to purchase an expensive outfit, and live seven months in a frightfully expensive place; for though, theoretically, rations may be very good fare, practically, the War department would not like to live on them for a day. We have no opportunity for saving money, consequently, and at the end of the period we are told our services are dispensed with; we receive two months' pay, and are got rid of like a set of scabby sheep.

Verily, England encourages her soldiers admirably: we go out of the kingdom, give up our various avocations, live in bodily fear of daily attack from the Russians, half starve ourselves, become morally and physically weakened, do our duty to the best of our ability, perform regimental functions which require great forethought, as we are mixed up with a set of demi-savages whom it is imperative to keep in good humour; bother our brains with learning a language which never can be of any use hereafter, save by accident; endure the horrors of a Constantinopolitan hotel; and for all this, and much more, we receive—two months' pay, and a polite bow from the chief paymaster, as her Majesty's representative. After this, we are left to our own resources, and, if at all of a cynical temper, can amuse ourselves by visiting Scutari, to look at the German Legion, who never saw a Russian, except as a prisoner.

But the mere pecuniary loss is not so hardly felt, although I know many officers who have had a sad deficit in their exchequer owing to their having joined the Contingent; there is one other point in which the English government has behaved most unwarrantably to us. By the conditions of the general order issued after the fall of Sebastopol, no officer was to receive a Crimean medal who had not entered the Crimea before the 8th of September, *unless engaged in presence of an enemy, or in an expeditionary force.* Could any one but the members of an English government pretend to assert that we had not fulfilled both conditions by our winter stay in Kertch? We were constantly in the presence of an enemy, constantly awaiting an attack. Cossacks prowled round us, and made prisoners of officers who ventured beyond the lines; our cavalry was engaged with a foe, and yet, forsooth, by some quibble, we are mulcted of our medal, which, by all principles of justice, we are entitled to.

But even supposing that the Crimean medal ought not to fall to our share, because the newspapers chose to run down a force they had never seen, and so bully a weak government into ignoring us, why should we be forbidden the acquisition of the Medjidié, which the Sultan would gladly give us, and we would gladly wear as a mark of distinction? *

One more point, and I will drop the subject. Why were we deliberately fed with falsehoods prior to leaving England? Why was it distinctly told us in Whitehall that the Contingent would be a permanent institution, and that whether the war continued or not we were sure of employment in the East? Why, as soon as peace is proclaimed, should we be dismissed as if under a cloud, and told we have no further claim on government?

Supposing, then, that ten days have elapsed, during which I have been running about to obtain the necessary signatures to my papers, for, although all the offices at Pera are within a radius of a quarter of a mile, it must not for a moment be supposed that business can be done at a railway pace in the East. Routine must be maintained at any risk: one office is only open between ten and twelve; another between two and three, and so on. You appear regularly each day: on the first, the officer you wish to see has gone to visit Lord Stratford, and won't be back that day; you put your name down as the hundred and nineteenth on the list, and hear that, if you call again in a week, your

* In 1863 we received the Sultan's Crimean medal.

business, consisting in obtaining one signature, may be attended to. Good; you wait a week, and then discover the gallant officer has actually devoted forty-two minutes during the week to his duties; he has been to Biyuk Chekmedje to cheapen a horse; he has attended the Baïram festival; the next day is Friday, and how could he miss the Sweet Waters? And so it goes on. Then, again, you nail your man; he is in his sanctum, and you swear a bitter oath you will not leave until you see him. *Victoria!* your turn has arrived; now all delays are over; but hold, a large brigadier, or such a one, makes his appearance, and you are shoved to the wall with a polite, "Call again to-morrow!" All the while—pray don't forget that fact—your hotel bill is running on faster than Jack with his seven-league boots, and you mentally resolve the problem: Given two months' pay, how long will that last against an hotel bill, which is as the xth power of your diurnal receipts?

But supposing all the signatures of the respected and respectable staff-officers have been obtained, and that Captain Smailes, of the smiling countenance and affable address, has, with his usual promptitude, handed you over the pounds sterling which dissolve your connexion with the British government, and that you have in return affixed your sign manual to a document disavowing any further claims on your part upon that benignant and paternal government, you are not to suppose you are yet at liberty to leave Constantinople. That dearly beloved Destuniano, of the European Hotel, still holds you firmly in his clutches, for you can't get away.

You hear a myth that the Messageries Impériales will bear you half-price to Marseilles, and in that way your £25 may be made to eke out; so off you hasten down that blessed institution, Galata Hill, at the imminent risk of ruining your nose by falling on it. You inquire about the truth of the story: "But certainly, yes!" says the civil clerk, "by the production of a certificate from General Storks, you can travel half fare." You bless the Emperor, and hurry to Scutari to obtain the all-important document; you rush back with it, rejoicing at the idea that you will leave Pera next Thursday afternoon. The clerk is still the cream of politeness; you produce your money, and have the satisfaction of hearing that if you will give yourself the pain of attending three months later, you may have the possibility of acquiring the refusal of a berth. But you naturally object; very few officers have hitherto left the Crimea, how then can the boats be so filled already? You appeal to the clerk's feelings as a Frenchman, a man, perhaps as a husband (at least, such was my excuse), and you hear that the French government certainly carries English officers at half-price, but infinitely prefers full-price passengers, who can always be procured in the shape of generals, staff-officers, and *commis-voyageurs*. He is of course *désolé* that he cannot arrange the affair, but, *que voulez-vous?* In despair, you repocket your money, leave the office, and do anything but bless the Emporor of the French.

In gloomy anticipation that for your sins you are compelled to remain during the term of your natural life a convict in Constantinople, you moon along the pleasant street of Galata, celebrated for its fragrant odours and agreeable society: you descend savagely into dark passages, on the extremest confines of which ship-brokers take up their residence, apparently from some predilection; you spend a day wandering about the Horn in a caïque; you tie your tongue in a knot trying to explain to the boatman what ship you want to visit. At last, just on the point of giving up the chase in despair, you suddenly find the vessel you are in search of, the tenth of a tier, jutting out into the Bosphorus; you ascend the side by an ingenious mechanism of hanging ropes and wooden steps; you feel as if your arms had been dragged out of the sockets, and you entertain doubts how you will ever get down again without tumbling into the water, or at least upsetting the caïque. But what matter?—you have found the object of your search! You go down a fearful companion-ladder, and are assailed by scents not emanating from Araby the Blest. In passing, you notice vaguely that the decks are crowded with lumps of coal, pleasantly suggestive of dirt. But what matter?—you must get away at any expense of annoyance and inconvenience. You enter the cabin, you find the captain, you deliver the card handed you by the broker—pray take a glass of rum—you obey, you light a cigar, for the odour is, if possible, rather stronger than what you are used to at Galata, and you unfold the purpose of your visit. The skipper is very sorry—you can have half a sofa or a berth under the table for thirty pounds—every other place is bespoken. You faintly whisper, "We are three, and one of them a lady," and somehow you find yourself on board your caïque again, gracefully bobbing up and down over the short, crisp waves of the Bosphorus, on your way to Top Khanéh Steps. You make up your mind that, although a transport is bad enough, a private merchant vessel is infinitely worse, and, in utter desolation of spirits, you recklessly order a bottle of champagne, and wake up next morning with a fearful headache, which you naturally attribute to sugar of lead.

At last, on an ever-blessed Wednesday, you see light! you hear there is still a way of release—there is a delightful institution called Austrian Lloyd's, which has a weekly communication with the Danube, *viâ* Varna, every Tuesday. You go in at once for the chance. What matter, be Galata Hill ever so steep—what care you for smells of bad drainage—what odds the clove of garlic, your usual detestation, which insidiously finds its way into your hollow tooth in your slice of mutton? You can look M. Destuniano, of dear memory, boldly in the face—you can afford to smile, though languidly, I confess, at the thought of your nocturnal visitors—you can forgive all, in the consciousness that you are in a fair way of attaining your liberty. The next morning you rise with the sun, and rush down to the office—of course it is not open yet—but you wait patiently; you distribute paras to the throng of Greek boys who congregate around you; you roll your cigarette in comfort, for are not your days numbered?—you are sure to leave Constantinople in five days. The doors are at length opened: you obtain your ticket; you are not the least anxious about the agio, even if you lose thirteen pence on each sovereign. You pay fifteen pounds for each ticket to Pesth; you hear mistily that you will be obliged to pay for your food as far as

Galatz, but thenceforward you will be free. What matter! take my *porte-monnaie,* take all I possess, only let me leave Pera before I die!

Your tickets once paid for, you feel a different man; you can afford to walk about the town; you can even make up your mind to go and see sights. You visit the Bezestan; the wife of your bosom invests capital in Brusa silks, which can be bought half-price in London; you find yourself laden with bundles composed of pearl-sewn slippers, yellow bathing papouches, attar of roses, and, perchance, if you have behaved yourself, a fez for yourself as an encouragement; you are cheated right and left, of course; but you pay willingly, for are you not to leave Pera next Tuesday? Then, again, you go by night to the artillery barracks at Top Khanéh; you submit yourself to the blows of the Khavasses, who lay about them furiously with their white wands; you take one of the culprits by the ear and whisper the magic words *Zubit Inglis,* and lo! they fall on their knees and howl, *Amaun, Bey Zadeh!* You forgive them, for you leave Pera in four days now; you mildly threaten the bastinado, but are pacified by the gates being thrown open, and you enter with all the pomp of a Briton, combined with the dignity of a pacha.

Then you hear that the Sultan is visiting the mosque; you take your place behind various French officers, who scowl at your uniform, and puff smoke in your face savagely from a *brûle-gueule,* regardless that a lady is with you; the said lady stands on tiptoe to see the sight, and of course can see nothing but the oil dripping from the tulip-shaped lamps on her dress.

Suddenly you observe a large pacha of your acquaintance, German by birth, Turk by habits and appearance; you shout in your joy and in his native dialect for his assistance; he takes no notice apparently, but soon returns with half a dozen Khavasses and a still bigger pacha: *Place pour une dame, messieurs!*"—the Frenchmen scowl still more ferociously, but give way. The lady obtains a chair and a body-guard of Turks, whom she regards curiously and pityingly as some unknown animals, whose brothers she has seen in the Zoological Gardens. You wait an hour, two hours, *que sais-je?* except that I am horribly thirsty, and the prayers appear fearfully long.

At length the padishah comes past; you recognize him by his pictures, but can that seedy-looking individual in the shady cloak and fez be the majestic Sultan, whose ancestors were the terror of the Christian world? But the Sultan has taken boat. "Long live the Sultan!" and so on. You next wander about the gardens and admire the Turkish tastes for illumination. You see trees formed of coloured lamps, exquisite in design, and looking like a fairy scene in the "Arabian Nights." You stand lost in amazement at the extravagant display of fireworks, of designs quite unknown in England, and you think how lucky the Sultan must be in being able to go into the English market to borrow millions, which he expends in smoke; you mentally calculate whether, if you were a reigning prince and could also borrow millions, you would not expend them in establishing schools and popular institutions; then, as a Briton, you consider yourself guilty of impertinence in daring to criticise any act of a reigning prince, and you cry, "God save the Sultan!" with as much fervour as any benighted Turk then present in the gardens.

But a sudden sinking warns you that you had better leave the gardens at once, if you wish to obtain any supper, for M. Destuniano, though a very dear man, is withal despotic, as it is only fit for a Pera hotel-keeper to be, and locks up his larder at ten o'clock. It is of no use knocking at that door, if you are only five minutes late; the verdict is, "Serve you right," and no compassion. You emerge through the iron gates, and find yourself in a dense throng of persons, whose appearance does not allow them access to the garden. You strive to force your way through the crowd, but in vain: no amount of objurgations or blows will help you on. A Turk bears the closest resemblance to a donkey of any European race I know. A pleasant variety is here and there occasioned by the passage of a carriage belonging to a great diplomatic card, and surrounded by mounted Khavasses; shrieks are heard at intervals, as people are knocked down and trampled under foot, but what does our diplomatist care—is he not the representative of a reigning prince, and, of course, can do no wrong?

At length, after waiting an hour or so, and having drunk up the establishment of a perambulating lemonader, you light your paper lantern, and make a bold attempt to force the crowd: you succeed in your design, but apparently your memory of locality has been squeezed out of you in the process, and you find yourself eventually, by the fitful light of your lamp, wandering about the *Petit Champ des Morts*. Of course your lamp goes out at the most interesting moment, and you go stumbling over tombs, and barking your shins against gravestones, until a watchman takes compassion on you. Such, or of such nature, are the evening amusements at Pera. Of course, I don't expect that you can be so verdant as to visit the Opera: nothing would induce me to believe that any one belonging to a nation flatteringly supposed to possess a more than average amount of common sense, could consciously endure three hours of such melody, under the pretext of amusing himself. Even a British ensign, the popular representation of folly *à tout prix*, would not be guilty of extravagance like that.

But I should do wrong were I here to omit mentioning the lamentable fate of the Contingent. It must be borne in mind that the English government had thoroughly clothed 15,000 men, and made the Turks a present of 13,000 stand of Minié arms, which had been obtained from Balaklava. Well, the batteries and regiments were handed over, and we indulged in the pleasing delusion that, at any rate, Turkey had been benefited by our temporary employment of the troops. How were we mistaken! Not three days after No. 3 Battery had been given over to the Turks, I was walking with Captain F——, the English commandant, up Pera-street. We met his Bimbashi, as woebegone as that interesting individual who drew Priam's curtains at the dead of night. On seeing us he positively burst into tears; and then told us the battery had received no rations since it had been handed over, that all their new clothes had been taken from them, and that they had been forced to dress in their old rags. Captain

F——, as an energetic Briton, naturally loving justice, proceeded straightway to the seraskier, but only obtained temporizing answers; and he might have spared his visit, for we found afterwards that the whole of the regiments had been treated in the same way, and the clothes and rifles sold to the great profit of the Turkish pachas. Such a practical satire on the outlay of 12 millions rarely comes to the knowledge of the English publicist, but I can vouch for it as a fact publicly known and spoken about in Pera.

At length the wished-for morrow makes a vigorous attempt to break through the hazy sky, but I am far from being absorbed in silent sorrow, for I know that I shall be released from purgatory by twelve o'clock precisely,—so the clerks told me on the twenty-fifth visit to make inquiries, and they cannot be mistaken. At an early hour I summon friend Destuniano: I demand his bill; I eat my last breakfast, all the while said bill is being prepared: I shudder at the thought how long that bill will be: I shudder still more as I turn over the pages and arrive at the sum total; I strive vaguely to knock off items, but I can see that my host has his soul in arms, and is eager for the fray. Discomfited, I try to escape by examining the mystery that renders me responsible for many pounds sterling, but the attempt is futile. Can *extuat* mean extras? I suppose so, and sigh as I suppose. I pass over sundry bottles of champagne, as they have the kindness to term it; but what can 2 *do d'al* mean? Did you ever drink *al*, beloved reader? I have journeyed over many lands, and many a clime I've seen, but up to the present I know not the spot where *al* ever was, or ever could be, an emblem, &c. With the sternness of a British paymaster, I demand an explanation. The mystic *al* is then converted into *bière de portaire.* This item I pass, for I own to the soft impeachment of being given to beer, no matter whether of Barclay, Allsop, or Bavaria. I should have to invoke the woodcutter's art, did I wish to lay before my readers the next item to which I made exception, but eventually I found it out to be three teas. Two *longe* I also pass, as representing bread and cheese, although I mildly repine at paying five shillings for the articles, without anything to wash them down. A *coniake,* too, I also made no objection to, although charged at two shillings, because I drank that interesting draught at a moment when I was apprehensive of cholera. The long and short is, I pay, and then wage desperate war with the waiters, who cannot be brought to agree to my ideas of what their service is worth. I can only remember that a bottle of beer always demanded seven peals at the bell-rope before I could obtain it, and any one who has experienced Constantinople in June, will agree with me in regarding that as a *casus belli.* But I pay, pay —what else can I do? and, besides, I leave Pera at 12 o'clock.

The Hammals are summoned: they perform sundry acrobatic feats with our luggage: they descend Top Khanéh Hill at a *pas de glissade,* for it has been raining all night, and the street is as slippery as glass. We reach the wharf: we dismiss the porters, after an awful amount of slang: we call a kaikji: we explain to him that we propose going on board the good ship *Bratwurst* as speedily as possible: we demand the fare; he answers, many piastres: we mildly object; he is steadfast: we begin to grow angry: we make allusions to his descent from a porcine race: finding this of no avail, we make further allusions to little dogs and his father's and mother's grave: we condemn himself to the mild tortures of Jehannum: in a word, we go through the whole *copia verborum* of Turkish slang, and end by giving him what he asks, for shall we not leave Pera at 12 o'clock precisely?

Still in the midst of my troubles, one star of hope gleamed brilliantly before me; on that same Top Khanéh wharf, in the midst of rain and vociferating boatmen, I had found one sweet item of consolation, for I had finally bidden adieu to that faithful but stupid servant, who had been the bane of my existence since leaving England. To him must I attribute the loss of unnumbered handkerchiefs and shirts, for was he not honest, and did he not credit other servants with the same divine characteristic? Through him, too, my dinner was always ruined, for he was too honest to forage, and a great deal too stupid to cook. Then his honesty induced him to lend money to other servants, which he never got back; not forgetting articles of my camp equipment, which went the same road, for his stupidity led him to lend them without my leave. Then, again, out of fear of the Turks, he would lay up a private armoury of weapons only dangerous to himself, and fancy the rats gambolling over his faithful but stupid countenance, to be fly-blow reminiscences of happy days in England. How often have I been locked out of my own quarters by that amiable youth, who began by being stupid and ended by growing deaf! But I shall reserve further allusion to this interesting subject until I write my analysis of army servants, which I intend to publish in the Philosophical Transactions.

After a certain amount of bobbing up and down the Bosphorus, imagine us—and by us I mean several fellow-officers and jolly fellows who made the same tour—climbing up the side ladder of the *Bratwurst.* We introduce ourselves to Captain Cassel, a Dalmatian by birth, an Everything-arian by education—a species of Jack-of-all-trades and master of none in philology, who speaks a polyglot of languages, but none of them in a manner to be comprehended of the Gentile. Our luggage is safely deposited in the hold, and we amuse ourselves with eating strawberries till 12 o'clock strikes, and yet the ship does not move. What can be the meaning of this? I rush frantically to the captain, and find that he cannot start till the mail comes on board. "When will that be?" I demand. "*No sabbe,*" is the reply, with an intense grin. We prowl about the deck—we indulge in bad language—but for all that the mail does not come; we pathetically entreat the captain to depart without the mail. "*Impossible,*" is the reply. At length four o'clock arrives, and with it the mail, just as I had begun to give up faith in everything; we slip from our buoy, cannon against various ships lying in our wake, at length find a clear track, and go down to dinner with an intense sign of satisfaction, for are we not leaving Constantinople at last?

Is there an old saying somewhat to the effect that you must not commence ejaculating or shouting *Evviva!* until you have left the forest safely in your rear? Such was our case; we ate our dinner—rather worse, by-the-way, than at the Europe—and began to feel the vessel grow lively. The ladies disappeared one after the other, and, just as we left the Bosphorus, two persons were still seated at table. A heaving, stretching, tearing of bolts from their sockets, told us the Black Sea was striving to render itself worthy of its old name *αξενος*; and, after a desperate struggle with the elements, we found ourselves compelled to put back and take shelter in the Bay of Biyukderéh. The next day we met with the same fate: the sea was still rough, and there was a strong head-wind, and as the Austrian Lloyd only allow their steamers forty-eight hours' coal, it was not advisable to be left to our sails alone in the centre of the Black Sea.

At last, however, all was propitious, and we really left the Bosphorus for good. As the weather, moreover, was most favourable and serene, we had an opportunity of seeing our other passengers, of whom we had hitherto only obtained fitful glances as they rolled in agony about their cabins. Of course, there was no lack of princes and princesses, for those individuals swarm all over the Principalities; they certainly did not come up to our preconceived notion of those exalted characters, for they looked rather seedier than those Italian Principi who eke out a miserable existence in England by giving music lessons: they indulged largely in caviare, pickles, and pudding, and performed gymnastic exercises with their knives and forks which could never have been intended by the original inventor of those useful household articles.

Their luggage, too, appeared somewhat scanty, but that was amply compensated by the gorgeous apparel of the ladies, who displayed every hue of the rainbow in silks and velvet. Jewellery also formed a heavy item of expenditure, but I did not notice that any great attention was paid to the design as long as the article was heavy, no matter how clumsy it might be. I know a nation, I fancy, far more civilized, in which the same principle holds good. I try to enter into conversation with these fair dames, but am balked at once; they inquire whether I am going to Bucharest, and on my replying in the negative, they regard me as an outer barbarian. They describe to me the pleasure of that town in glowing colours; it evidently ranks in their idea next, and only next, to Paris. As for London, I am told (in bad French) that it is well adapted for the Rosbifs, but no good can come out of Nazareth. I turn the conversation to politics, the late war, and so on. I speak of portions of the globe which they have evidently never heard of; all they know of geography is comprised in Paris, Petersburg, Bucharest, and Constantinople. They speak many languages, but all equally incorrectly; they appear to my unaccustomed eyes somewhat forward in manner. I regard them as a rare and interesting branch of the human family, which I am bound to *approfondir.*

In the midst of my researches I stumble across a Hungarian, who is eminently acquainted with Moldo-Wallachia, and from him I learn many new and remarkable particulars. I find, for instance, that the man with the very dirty face and no whiskers, whom I took for the manager of a perambulating theatre, is a very great Moldavian Boyar. I am sure he is a patriot, and has sworn to debar himself from the use of water till his fatherland is freed from the yoke of Mahound. I learn again that these princesses are contented, at home, to live in houses where we should object to put a favourite dog; that their principal amusement is running in debt wherever they can procure credit; that their education is limited to a study of the French fashions as published monthly; and as for their morality, the less said about it the better.

As for the vaunted Bucharest, it is a thoroughbred Turkish town, with an external varnish of Gallicism; when dust does not blind you, mud suffocates you, and *vice versâ*. There is certainly an hotel, popularly supposed to be maintained on European principles, but unfortunately these have been grafted on Turkish ideas, and the only difference the traveller perceives is in the exaggerated proportions of the bill, which would drive Biffin into a state of frantic rebellion.

As we have not yet crossed the Austrian frontier, I venture to allude to politics. I find that the Moldo Wallachians have astounding ideas of their importance, and aspire to the establishment of an independent kingdom—a regular Utopia, where no taxes will be paid, but each will do right in his own sight. I am not quite certain whether the first law of the constitution will not be that each Boyar will have his debts paid for him, and be at liberty to commence afresh. At any rate, he will maintain unlimited power over his serfs, buy them, sell them, flog them, murder them, according to his good pleasure; and, probably, after a few years of self-government, sell his country to Russia. He will then become a respectable member of society, and spend his days and his pension in strong drinks and gambling.

For my own part, I don't see what better end could be devised for the Modo-Wallachian Boyar.

During the time that I have been collecting these data, we have been bowling along merrily towards Varna, which interesting spot we reach at four in the morning. It takes us till ten to coal, for no one puts himself out of the way in the least, even supposing we are thirty-six hours behindhand, and stand a great risk of missing the boat at Galatz. In the interval we go on shore, and telegraph to the agent *viâ* Bucharest, stating that many British officers have been detained by the weather, and the ship must be kept from starting until we make our august appearance. Of course the Austrians, through their love for the English, will do anything to oblige officers who have been fighting against Russia. At any rate, Hope tells the flattering tale, and we believe it; hence we start again with renewed spirits, partly attributable to the stock of porter we have laid in at Varna. By the next morning we arrive off the Sulina mouth, and receive a striking impression of the beautiful results of protection, by the sight of the countless wrecks that block up the passage. We spend an hour, profitably we trust, in speculating on the benefits which would accrue to Europe by Russian ascendancy; we realize the blessings of the continental blockade system, which would be so speedily introduced, and wonder what would then be the price of the bottlo of English porter with which we are now moistening our matutinal clay. We enter the bocca, and turn our eyes to the right bank, and gaze over the boundless expanse of marsh and plain which will so soon be handed over to the Turks; we think of the period when those grey-coated statues, who line the bank at distances of two hundred and fifty yards, and form a living telegraph, will disappear, probably for ever, and the Danube once again become the silent highway of nations.

How much of that corn, now stored up in the countless *entrepôts* of Bulgaria and Wallachia, will soon find its way to England, and bring down the price of bread to what bakers will call starvation prices, but which, this winter, will save many a hollow-eyed wife a march through rain and slush to her only friend in the time of need—the pawn-broker? Come, war is not so bad after all; and when I think that the next time I go up or down the Danube, I shall have my choice of various competing steam companies, and save several pounds through honest rivalry, I fancy that I, too, in my humble way, have done my share towards promoting the comfort of my fellow-man.

On Sunday night we arrive at Galatz, and find that we are in time for the steamer. We go through an interesting process at the office of having our luggage weighed, and pay an exorbitant sum for its carriage to Pesth. I, as the only German scholar, have a fearful wordy combat with the ragged youths who have carried our luggage, twenty yards from one steamer to the other: I offer a rational amount, while they demand an exorbitant one: the dispute suddenly takes a favourable turn, by the violent outrush of a uniformed clerk with a rope's end, who starts the ragamuffins from the yard, and leaves me in peace.

The Danubian steamers are certainly very magnificent vessels: the saloon is brilliant with gold and painting; the food is excellent, and appears even better than it really is to a traveller recently arrived from the East; but why on earth should the sleeping-room be in the hold? Why should 50 berths be squeezed into a space hardly large enough for 24? And why should there be only one washing-basin and towel for so many? Water, too, one would imagine easily to be obtained from the river on which you are floating, then why should the cistern be always empty? It is strange that, though so many thousand travellers yearly traverse Germany from one extremity to the other, there is still the same lack of that virtue which is currently supposed to rank next to godliness.

At Galatz we received a vast accession of company; many more princesses, all most magnificently dressed, and a number of Russians who had arrived with the corresponding boat from Odessa. The presence of the latter had a very quieting effect on the Moldo-Wallachians, who left off laughing in a very loud key. I heard from my Hungarian friend that this Danubian trip was their one great event of the year; they can earn enough ready money to pay their expenses up and down the river for a week, during which time they throw off their fine clothes, and then return home in perfect happiness to their pig-sties. Among the Russians I found one very interesting acquaintance in the secretary to Prince Gortschakoff; he was a captain in the navy, but his ship having been sunk at the commencement of the siege, he had occupied a military post. Speaking English most fluently, it had devolved on him to examine the deserters, and make *résumés* of the contents of the English papers. I found from him that many more deserted from our army than from the French, and that these were principally Irish. The work in the trenches, joined to want of food, drove them to desperation. Of all our troops, the Russians appear to entertain the best opinion of our riflemen, who bothered them sadly, and were such excellent shots that it was highly dangerous to draw near an embrasure. It appears that Sebastopol could have been repeatedly taken during the last spring, for many times there was not 24 hours' ammunition in the fort—but where fresh supplies were obtained from he declined to tell.

Now here was a simple captain, who was better acquainted with our institutions, civil and military, than probably nine-tenths of our staff-officers. Not a book of importance was published in England of which he did not receive a copy, and he was as well up as any government hack in the House. I should like to know why information of the same nature about Russia and the European nations could not also form a part of our military education? Why we so obstinately persist in rendering the finest raw material in the world so unavailable, as was the case in the last war? Are officers' commissions such sacred objects that we dare not entrust them to any one but the members of a favoured clique, and know-nothingism must always be the first recommendation to a military appointment? It is all very well saying we live and learn, but I am sadly afraid we don't go the right way to work to profit by our learning.

There is nothing worth seeing on the Danube till you reach the Iron Gates and New Orsova. I must say the Austrian Douaniers do their spiriting gently; all they appear to be anxious about being Turkish tobacco. Before leaving Stamboul we had purchased an okka, or three pounds of Turkish tobacco for our use on the voyage; by the time we reached Orsova it had shrunk to one half. This remainder I had to declare, and was requested to pay nine shillings duty on it. I explained that we were not going to smuggle it, and that it would be used up by the time we reached Pesth; but all of no avail. I then stated very particularly that I would not pay a halfpenny duty, but that they might confiscate it. That they could not do, but I was requested to throw it overboard. Casually inquiring whether none was allowed for my personal use, I heard I might keep two ounces; on pursuing my inquiries, I found each passenger might keep the same quantity; I, therefore, very quietly divided my tobacco into 14 lots and requested the passengers to help themselves. They entered into the joke, and the tobacco was saved, much to the disgust of the Douanier, who walked away in the midst of a general shout.

The whole scenery of the Danube is comprised in about four hours' steam after leaving Orsova, and is certainly very fine, but whether it can compensate for a week spent in the company of Moldo-Wallachian princesses, I leave my readers to decide for themselves. For my part, I was excessively glad to reach Pesth, where there is more opening of trunks, and have a quiet night's rest.

CHAPTER IV.

A DAY IN CAIRO.

One of the pleasantest reminiscences of my Eastern tour is the first day I spent in Cairo. As the train had been delayed for several hours at Alexandria for the passengers of the Indian mail, I reached the capital of Egypt after sunset. A travelling companion, resident in Cairo, quickly led me through the throng of porters, waiters, donkey-boys, camels, and omnibuses, congregated at the station door beneath the light of a hundred torches and hand-lanterns, to a carriage, which bore us through the darkness along several broad streets, and across the Esbekieh-square to the Hotel des Pyramides. The quickness of the drive and the darkness had allowed me to see no more of Cairo than a few camels' necks, some black-striped leaves and palm-tops that peered over the garden walls, and where a lantern or torch moved along, a white turban; and the supper-table at the hotel and the arrangement of the bed-room made me miss my native land but little.

The morning, however, produced other and almost magical impressions. Even in the silence of night I fancied I could hear distant singing to a solemn tune in the streets; and, indeed, the Praise of Allah is chanted from the minarets of the principal mosques throughout the night. When I awoke, words smote distinctly on my ear through the open window; it was the Adan, or summons of the Muezzin to morning prayer. I walked to the window, and witnessed a scene that harmonized with the sound. Beneath me, on a small triangular space, partly overshadowed by a thickly-leaved acacia, stood a khavass before a cloth spread on the ground, on the point of performing the genuflexions prescribed by Islam. A little further on a shepherd, surrounded by his flock, was lying with his head in the dust. Above the roof of the house behind the tree rose some lofty palms, whose crowns, moved by the wind, bowed also in the direction of Mecca. Further back rose three graceful minarets, lit up by the yellow shimmer of dawn. The cry that had aroused me came from the gallery of the nearest of them. On the others the Muezzins, with their white turbans and light blue caftains, were still standing, and singing down into the silent lanes and gardens their "Allah akbar!"

While I was mentally recording the main features of this picture, the yellow dawn was followed by the red, and lastly by the sun. The city was awake, and louder and louder grew the murmur of traffic in the streets below me. With the buzzing of the Semitic guttural tones, the donkeys, now beginning to collect before the houses, blended their ear-piercing braying; the market-folk flocked in and praised their wares with lengthened shouts; workmen walked towards the building-places with a melancholy song; a shrill female voice contended—and, as it seemed, victoriously—with a dozen masculine voices; goats bleated their complaints at being milked so roughly; buffaloes bellowed; camels grunted the bass to the concert, in which gradually joined the water-carriers with the tinkle of their brass cups, the street changers with the regular rattle of their copper piastres, the coachmen with their whips, and the runners who here bound before every vehicle with their incessant "Guarda, guarda, ya chowadja!"

A bell summoned the guests to breakfast, and I was again in Europe. The Oriental divans against the walls, the carved-work on the back windows, and a few tarbushes did not harmonize, but the company at table was as European as any to be found between Hamburg and Venice. The situation of the hotel, immediately at the entrance of the main street of the Frankish quarter, which is the liveliest in the whole city, enabled me to carry out my plan of letting Cairo defile before me ere I entered the streets. The large bay-window of the dining-room was admirably adapted for the purpose, for I could stand here for hours and watch the heaving current below. On one side of the square, close to my window, was a cluster of donkey-boys with their animals—the cabs and strangers' guides of the Egyptian capital. While the donkeys were provided with red-cushioned saddles, and hung with tassels and brass ornaments, shaved all over, and in some instances gaily painted, the boys looked like walking rag-bags. Not one had shoes; few had more clothing than the blue cotton shirt of the lower classes, over which one or two had drawn an old military jacket or European coat, minus sleeves and collar. Though constantly quarrelling and fighting, on the approach of a foreigner they began swarming like a disturbed beehive. They flocked round him, praised their donkeys in broken English, French, and Italian, and, to show their value, leaped into the saddle and performed wild caracoles, until the stranger either yielded or forced his way through by the help of a stout stick.

On the other side of the square, under the great acacia which overshadows the office of the Transit Company, a no less interesting group—a study for Murillo—had assembled. Near a chibouque-maker, who carried on his trade in the open air, crouched Fellah women with trays of bread, which they offered to the passers-by with shrill yells. Close to them lay a half-shaved head in the lap of a turbaned barber, who, holding the lock of Paradise in his left hand, the gleaming razor in the other, was busily engaged in producing the customary baldness, while behind him a girl's active fingers were performing an operation in the hair of a dirty brother, which needed a similar position, but no razor. Between these stationary groups in the foreground moved a mass of men and women, of pedestrians and riders on donkeys, horses, and camels, of white, yellow, dark brown, and black faces, of white, red, and green turbans, of uniform and striped cloaks, sulphur yellow and linnet-green caftains, of embroidered jackets, wide trousers, laced gaiters, tasselled hoods, veils, monks' gowns, ragged beggars, naked children, and state coaches, cane baskets, and sacks. It is evident that I am in the capital of a riding nation; nearly a fourth of those who throng past are in the saddle. Camels take the place of wains, donkeys of trucks. The rolling of wheels is hardly heard, for the few coaches visible drive over unpaved ground.

Countrywomen tripped past in dark blue chemises, with their head, shoulders, and back covered with a hood of the same colour, and their fellow-faces sometimes hidden behind a narrow yashmak, but more frequently unveiled. One carried on her head a big-bellied two-handled jar, while a naked child sat on the shoulder of another, in the posture of a horseman. Among the unveiled women I noticed several whose chin and even cheeks were tattooed with blue dots. All wore broad silver bracelets, and the majority finger-rings of the same metal, with coloured stones. The nails on the hands and feet, as well as the palms, were dyed a brick red with henna, and several had the back of the hand tattooed. The elder women were, without exception, hideously ugly, and the young, too, had little attraction in their features, save the fiery almond-shaped eyes; but the figure of the majority, which fashion does not forbid them displaying, was irreproachable.

Through the dark-robed band of women marched a troop of soldiers in white cotton jackets, over which were the white cross-belts, white knee-breeches, white stockings, gay girdles round their waist, flint-lock muskets on their shoulders, and a red tarbush with a blue silken tassel on their shorn heads. They were all young fellows, with yellow faces and jet-black eyes, beardless, apparently weak, and badly set up. Near them a line of donkeys tried to force their way through, laden with dripping goatskin water-vessels, and which must inevitably upset a fat grey-bearded mollah who was trotting towards them, holding his rosary in his left hand, the reins of his mule in the other, and evidently lost in thought on some abstruse doctrinal subject. Behind the donkeys cavasses were leading a drunken soldier to the flogging-bench in the *saptie*, or guardhouse, where he would probably receive the hadd, or eighty blows, prescribed by Muhammed for the cure of drunkards. Light blue fluttering cotton shirts, a yellow burnouse much embroidered and trimmed, a coal-black Abyssinian with snow-white turban and robe, a band of Amants in red and blue faced jackets, with a broad leathern belt round the loins, out of which a very magazine of murderous instruments, consisting of long-necked yataghans, crooked daggers, and silver-mounted pistols peeped, and a swarm of children, each with a dirty nose, and at least a couple of dozen flies on its eyelids, followed as spectators.

Ever and ever the life-current of the great city brings fresh pictures past the window. Greek dandies appear to lounge about the Esbekieh. The tall red cap sits impudently and self-assertingly over their right ear, and they have an inimitable knack of making the fustanelle fold gracefully round the knee. Copts follow in black caftains and dark blue head-clothes, with the tin box of pens thrust like a pistol through the girdle, and paper in their hand, for they are the secretaries of the street population. Another wave brings up sherifs, whom the green turban indicates as descendants of the prophet, and who are in Cairo at present largely represented, as about this time the small annuity is paid them which reverence for the sacred blood flowing in their veins procured for them. Then another wave brings before me a medley of Persians, with black lambswool caps, dervishes, who in their shaggy dilk, and with their fearfully matted beards, more resemble wild beasts than human beings; long-bearded, bare-footed monks in brown robes and black standing collar coats, in which smooth-shaven English missionaries wander about. Among these ride or walk other persons in European garb, with a rhinoceros whip in their hands, and their heads bound up in the kuffish, a striped yellow and red cloth, terminating in long lace. With them came Englishmen, whose helmets tell us they are bound for India, and English ladies, everywhere distinguishable by their blue and green veils.

A harem rides out to enjoy the air. The donkeys of the great ladies are covered with carpets, and all the dames, without exception, have their eyes and forehead covered by a white veil, and are attired in the chabarah—a black silk mantle—which the wind puffs out like a balloon. Under these may be seen parrot green, pink, and yellow tunics and trousers, clocked stockings and pointed shoes. By the side of each lady walks a valet, to hold her in the saddle, which she bestrides after the fashion of a man. The ladies get out of the way of a running footman, who, with multitudinous cries, warns them of the barouche behind them, in which the Armenian or Greek bishop is taking a drive. At the spot where the barber recently sat a half-naked Nubian, with his hair growing like a mane down his back, is offering for sale broad straight swords, such as the Barabras wear near the Nile cataracts. Close to him a Bedouin, from Sinai, is selling sausages, made of dates and almonds, sown up in gazelle hide. Proudly rides past him another son of the desert, armed with a long lance, whose plain brown burnouse and lean horse form a marked contrast to the splendid Turkish bey following at his heels on a well-fed steed, and whose cloth jacket is so covered with gold lace that the foundation cannot be seen.

A little on one side a white and a red turban are saluting each other. They join their right hands, then raise them to their lips and forehead, and then lay them on the breast, while mutually exclaiming, "Peace be with you;" or, "I wish you much good fortune." A little further on death forces its way through the living crowd, in the shape of a funeral procession. First come six poorly-clad men, in two rows, incessantly repeating the Muhammedan Confession of Faith. Then follow the relatives of the deceased, his friends, and several dervishes, with the red flags of their order. Behind the latter walk several boys, one of whom bears, on a reading-desk of palm-wood, a copy of the Koran, covered with an embroidered cloth. They sing in a shrill voice a hymn of thanksgiving to God:

"Praised be the perfection of Him who created everything that has shape, and subjugated His servants through death. They will all lie in the graves. Praised be the perfection of the Lord in the east, the perfection of the Lord in the west, the perfection of Him who lit the two candles, the sun and the moon. His perfection, how merciful He is! His perfection, how great He is!"

Then comes the dead man on the bier, head first, with his hands laid on his bosom, covered with gay shawls, and carried by four friends. Next follow a band of veiled women, with dishevelled hair, weeping, and uttering loud lamentations. Some have bedaubed their head, brow, and bosom with mud and dust. They are hired mourners, who from time to time utter a shrill, inarticulate yell, to which they wave their handkerchiefs, while the real mourners of the family evidence their grief by outcries such as "Oh my consolation! oh my father! oh my lion!"

The passers-by turn their faces to the procession and murmur, "God is very great!" The body is first carried to the Morgue, where a sort of funeral service, consisting of chapters of the Koran and prayers for the deceased, is held, after which the khialib summons the congregation to give their testimony about the dead man, which is done with the formula "He was one of the righteous." Prayers are again recited, and the procession then sets out for the cemetery, where the body is deposited in the ground without further ceremony. The procession has passed, and round the corner press the head of a camel followed by others. The caravan draws near, and the ugly though so useful animals pass one after the other, with their snake-like necks, their pendulous lips, and their warty and abraded bodies. Some carry large mill-stones in cocoa fibre nets; others are loaded with mountains of grass and clover; others, again, with chests and sacks. Their rough growl is audible for a long time after they have passed, above the exclamations of the street salesmen who have now congregated in front of the hotel.

"The lupins of Nubali are sweeter than almonds!" a blue caftain, with a sack on his back, announces. Soon after is heard the cry of a water-carrier, "May God requite it to me!" accompanied by the clatter of cups. Almost at the same moment I heard the cries, "May God grant that I easily get rid of them, oh lemons!" and "Fragrance of paradise," with which the dealer in henna-blossoms tries to induce the passers-by to purchase. "Oh arouser of compassion, oh Lord!" a beggar grunts, and a member of the same guild, possessed of greater self-respect, shouts almost simultaneously, "I am the guest of God and of the Prophet!"

Then appears the sherbet-seller, who carries on his head a round copper tray, on which cans of cooling date-juice stand. Then comes a man, also carrying on his head a heavy basket of pipe bowls, which he declares to be of Sycet manufacture. Then appears sundry dellals, or street brokers, who for a certain per-centage dispose by public auction of any goods a private person may wish to get rid of. Near the Nubian, who is now chaffering with two Englishmen for a sword, which in the German factory, whence it indubitably came, cost a dollar, but will here, I presume, be sold for a couple of sovereigns, as made at Habesch, a ragged fellow is squatting, whose shapeless feet show that he is tortured by elephantiasis. Close to the cripple a brown woman, of the race of the Ghawaggi, is performing, to the sound of a drum and small brass castanets she strikes above her head, those sensual dances which the monuments of Thebes tell us date from the time of the Pharaohs. On her head she wears a tarbush, adorned with gold coins; her eyelids are stained of a dark colour, and wide yellow and red striped trousers are visible under the fluttering blue chemise, which only half covers her bosom. The performer on the drum is her husband, and procurer. Mehemet Ali banished these wretches to Upper Egypt, but they have since crept back, and the passers-by exclaim, "Allah Keriar! God is kind and merciful! and the present pacha's government is also merciful."

Very surprising is the number of blind and one-eye

persons who pass, and I am almost inclined to believe the assertion that of the five hundred thousand eyes in Cairo, at least one hundred thousand cannot see the sun. At any rate, among the party of blue and brown caftains, now passing the pater-pipe from mouth to mouth beneath the acacia, five eyes out of twelve are closed; and since I began my observation, I have noticed many begging Belisarii, who, led by little girls, groped their way through the crowd.

I had been looking into the street for several hours without feeling the slightest weariness. Suddenly I heard at a distance Arab music, the clang of cymbals and the sound of flutes and drums. It was a marriage procession, passing from the Esbekieh to the interior of the city. Such a procession is formed to conduct the bride to the bath. It usually takes place at twelve o'clock before that day on which the bridegroom receives the bride's veil, and as Sunday evening is selected by preference for that ceremony, usually on a Saturday. The procession I am about to describe was got up by rich people, and, as frequently takes place, the circumcision of a boy had been combined with it.

The procession opened with two mountebanks, busy with long sticks in knocking the three-cornered hats off each other's heads, and followed by a third on stilts. Then came a barber, with a small box, containing the instruments for the circumcision, and which was of the shape of a semi-cylinder, ornamented in front with pieces of glass and brass bells. Behind the barber walked four bare-footed musicians, in blue shirts and white turbans, and after them the boy on a horse, held on by two footmen. He was a short, stout, ill-tempered lad, with a female tarbush on his head, covered with gold coins. The bridle and saddle-cloth were also richly decorated with gold, silk, and precious stones. He held to his mouth an embroidered handkerchief, probably to guard himself from the evil eye, which alarms all respectable mothers in Egypt as it does in Italy and Greece. As a further protection the boy wore a triangular neck-amulet, wrapped in paper. After the little horseman came other musicians, one with a dervish flute, whose sound can be best compared with the squeak of a new-born child, and a second with a drum, like ours in shape, but not producing so deep a tone.

After these came the bridal procession proper. First stalked two footmen, carrying in silver salvers the bride's bathing appliances. After them came a third, swinging a censer; and a fourth, who scattered rose-water over the passer-by from a porcelain can. Then came twelve white-veiled maidens, to judge from their stature, very youthful; and then the red-and-yellow striped canopy, under which the bride generally walks. This canopy, of silk, only open in front, and about the size of a small marquee, was borne on poles by four men. The bride generally wears a small coronet of gilt pasteboard, but I did not see it, for her whole form, from head to ankles, was wrapped in a bright red shawl. Probably to prevent her for from falling, the young lady was supported by two elder women. Behind the canopy walked several female relatives, who from time to time burst forth into a piercing, tremulous yell of joy, not unlike a horse's neighing, and which quite drowned the sound of the instruments. Four musicians, with drums and tambourines, closed the procession, which reached the bath, in a side street no great distance from the hotel.

Towards evening my friend invited me to take a stroll with him on the Esbekieh. This square, formerly a lake for one half the year and a swamp for the other half, was drained by Mehemet Ali, and converted into a very pleasant promenade. Walks of splendid leafy acacias, between whose trunks the white walls of lofty acalio houses, several large hotels and palaces, and two or three minarets are visible, run round plantations of tamarisks, sycamores, and mimosas. On one side Greeks have erected various arbours and booths, before which the swells smoke chibouks or nargilahs, and drink coffee, or a glass *or* so of rakih when the police are not looking on. Further a-field the lower classes amuse themselves with swinging, or a mountebank, with a learned donkey or ape, collects a circle of blue caftains and yellow faces to admire his tricks.

When we came forth and seated ourselves in front of a coffee-stall, that orange-coloured light which leaves the foliage its hue streamed over the bushes. Soon after it was changed into a pale pink, in which the lower part of the trees turned quite black. At length this last gleam was extinguished, and the feather crown of the palm-tree, which is said to have been planted by Napoleon himself in the garden of the French Consulate, also became quite black. The intoxicating aroma of the mimosa flowers floated in the tepid air, while the mild Schiraz tobacco exhaled its fragrance around us. On the road, a few white and red paper lanterns seemed like glow-worms; lights were visible from the windows, and the stars of Orient shone down on us from the light-blue sky.

All had become silent around us, and I gradually fell into a reverie, from which the shrill whistle of the locomotive and the noise of the carriages and horses dashing into town from the station, scarcely aroused me.

When all became quiet again, the magic of the warm, odorous night regained its full might over me. The stars turned pale, and the moon rose between Napoleon's palm-tree and a minaret. High in the trees above us a nightingale began singing, and I felt no surprise, for I had long before forgotten that it was in January. Bulbul continued her song, and, when she ceased, a companion began in the next tree the same song of love and roses in the same melodious voice.

Such were my first impressions of Cairo. I regret to say that, ere long, all the romance was knocked out of me, but I shall never forget the first day I spent in the capital of Egypt.

CHAPTER V.

REMINISCENCES OF BADEN.

It was our lot to reside for many years at the Queen of Watering-places, and during the course of that time we witnessed much, both curious and instructive. We lived in the midst of the storm-boding events of 1848, and the awful desolation of the ensuing year, after the thunder-cloud had burst. We saw princes tottering on their thrones, and even then breaking their plighted word; and a nation so intoxicated by the first fumes of liberty, that it slept away in inglorious inactivity the fair season in which to become great and free. But beside all this, much has attracted our attention which casual tourists would be apt to neglect; and this we now humbly venture to submit to our readers, our purpose being to amuse those who have not been to Baden, while at the same time we trust we shall not fatigue those who have already visited "les Eaux" and "la Foret Noire;" and, as the Limonadier of the Quartier Latin remarked to his "pratique," when expressing their astonishment at the alarming development of hair on his upper lip, drunk "la bonne Bière de Mars" at the fountain head, which Major H., of the Baden Artillery, so aptly rendered by a "verre de Brasse."

This hero, who was more conversant with the word of command than the French language, once had occasion to pay a visit to Strasburg. In great doubts as to his own capacity to express his wants, he was still so overcome by his natural thirst and the heat of the weather, that a "choppin" of beer was alsolutely necessary before he could go further. Imagine his joy at seeing the magic word "Bierbrauerei," painted in large letters on a board beneath the word "Brasserie." By a mental operation, as Aldrich, in his Logic, hath it, he soon discovered that "Brasserie" and "Bierbrauerei" must mean the same thing: and by a further process of ratiocination, concluded that "Brasse" must be the French for "Bier." So he boldly walked in, and summoned the waiter with the authoritative command, "Garçon, un verre de Brasse."

Baden-Baden is, in sooth, a pleasant place, which none can leave without regret; some at their losses to Mons. Benazet, others at being compelled to bid adieu to the delightful scenery. A philosopher might here study, with advantage to himself, the mutability of fortune: he may see a "Milord" arrive with a dashing equipage, and observe him, within a week, modestly retiring from the stage of his late splendour, leaving behind him horses, carriage, and all!

But of all the gay scenes, none surpasses the Promenade in front of the Conversations Saal, where, on a fine afternoon, the company sit beneath the orange-trees, sipping coffee and listening to the band. To this circumscribed sphere every nation of the civilized world sends its representatives. Here may be seen Americans glowing with all the hues of Parisian fashion, and, like Christmas turkeys "hung in chains," as retiring and modest as they usually are. What more striking proof can be furnished, than by a conversation which the writer had the fortune to hear between two of these gentlemen and the proprietress of the Reading-room. They were engaged in paying their subscription, and in the course of the conversation one of them asked:

"And what countrymen do you suppose us to be?"

"Englishmen, of course," the lady replied.

"I thought so," was the next remark, accompanied by a bland smile of pity at her ignorance. "Let me inform you, my good lady, that when you hear English spoken with remarkable purity, you may lay it down, as an established rule, that the speaker is an American, not an Englishman."

Poles, who are always disappointed in the arrival of their remittances, which have been unaccountably delayed, and who, in consequence, are ever ready to borrow from the person to whom they impart their anxieties any sum from a franc upwards, to be repaid on the arrival of the said remittances, but as they never do come, the liquidation of the debt is deferred to the Greek Calends, Chevaliers d'Industrie, and of the Legion d'Honneur, who yet have no honour but that typified by the red ribbon attached to their button-holes—Alsacians of a cunning and astute appearance, who realize Æsop's fable of the bat, which was neither bird nor beast, by being neither French nor German, and speaking a "Kauderwelsch," which bears no resemblance to either language: and, indeed, where but at Strasburg would it be possible to hear such an apostrophe as the following? which we carefully recorded in our note-book on the market-place of that city:

"He da! Bourgeois! Voulez-vous des navets? 'sind nit hölzig, 'sind nit pelzig (*i. e.*, they are neither woody nor woolly). Prenez où prenez pas—wenn Sie aber nit nehmen, so kimmt Mnsieu le Caporal und giebt mir un sou davantage."

Then there are Russians, bearded like the pard, who, by avowing liberal principles, induce their countrymen to give expression to their complaints, and then, on returning to their hotel, transmit to the paternal government of St Petersburg a full account of all that has been said, with the additional "haut goût" of their own inventive talent. Now and then, too, may be seen a swarthy and scowling "Sclave," wrapped in his dingy Bunda, and carrying a bundle of mousetraps, which he offers for sale while cursing the Suabes to whom he offers them. Swarms of artists flock hither from Germany, from Dusseldorf to Munich, and line the passages and stairs of the hotel where any exalted personage takes up his abode with their own productions, in the hope of covering the expense of a "Bad reise" by the sale of a picture. Next we have a heap of Puseyite parsons, who glow with a mild fervour when speaking of the splendours of a Catholic church, and praise the wondrous effect of a brass band that plays in the Cathedral of Cologne at high mass, while they mildly repine at the crass obstinacy of their parishioners, who cannot be persuaded to regard the matter in the same æsthetic way as themselves. Then the peasants who flock in on Sundays, the women in red petticoats and black bodices; the men in blue cotton coats, flat three-cornered hats, red waistcoats, and high well-greased boots, who expend their "hoarded

Batzen" in cheap jewellery, and gaze with wondrous looks on the tightly-laced Parisian mam'selles. And here let us not neglect to record an anecdote relative to one of these peasants, who, on the railroad being opened from Baden to Oos, had a great desire to travel by it, and so went to inquire the price by the Steh-wagen. On being told six kreutzer, with the love of bargaining so peculiar to this race of beings, he offered four, which was of course refused, and he walked away. He had not gone far before the whistle was sounded on the train starting, and thinking it was a signal to him that his offer was accepted, he turned round and said:

"Ihr mögt peifen—i kimm nimmi zurück"—"You may whistle, but I shan't come back."

Besides all these, there are our own exports and specimens in the great foreign exhibition; but these deserve a separate paragraph.

Make way there for the great Captain Bobadil. Who does not know him, that has visited those towns on the Continent where Englishmen most do congregate? Admire the pendant moustache and huge beard, which render him so like one of Salvator Rosa's brigands modernized. The gentleman he is walking with is Mr Theophilus Muff, as we learn by the "Fremden Buch" of the hotel where he is stopping; B.A., or, as he has written it, "Bachelier ès Arts," of Teakettle Hall, "Gebürtig aus," Sappington, "Wohnhaft in," Oxford, and on the road to Rome—not the only B.A., be it said parenthetically, who is bound the same journey. We also happen to know, fortunately for our readers, that Theophilus Muff, in the opinion of his friends, wrote the best prize poem for the Newdigate, but by some unaccountable mistake the palm of merit was awarded to another. He lately passed his examination in a manner so creditable to himself and his tutors, that it has gained him immortality in the columns of the *Sappington Independent*, the paper which bore such an undaunted front in the great Gorham case, and whose letters, signed "No Humbug," are confidently said to have materially influenced the Privy Council in their late decision. The paragraph to which we allude commenced thus:

"It affords us great satisfaction to be enabled to inform our readers that the worthy head-master of our excellent grammar school, Dr Ferule, has gained fresh laurels for his brow by the unexampled success of our talented townsman, Mr Theophilus Muff," and so on.

Muff, of course, learned French when at school, but it appears to him that there must have been a great change in the pronunciation since he benefited by the instruction of Monsieur Tabatière; but, as he justly remarks, "With a people so fond of changes in the government, it would be surprising were no alteration in the language to take place." See how well satisfied he is at walking up and down the Promenade side by side with the distinguished Captain Bobadil, who, with that condescension which is the characteristic mark of a truly great man, addressed him during the morning in the reading-room. With what reverential awe he listens when the captain, in his off-hand manner, speaks of the intimate terms on which he stands with kings and their ministers! Let us, too, listen for an instant.

"You came through Brussels, I presume, sir? It is a very nice town. I lived there for some time, to be near my friend Leopold; but, 'egad, sir, I was obliged to leave, the place became so low, and the society at the Royal Balls was infernally mixed. I warned Leo of it, when he asked my advice about accepting the throne; but wilful men will have their own way. He used often to send me a boar's head when hunting at Laeken, with a hint that he would drop in at six to dinner—and, 'egad, sir, I never begrudged a couple of hundred francs to do honour to the royal guest and his present."

Were we to tell Muff that Bobadil has only a lieutenant's half-pay to support himself, his wife, and six children, would he believe the malicious tale? We unhesitatingly answer, "No."

But, see! a sudden gloom has overspread the captain's countenance. Now he is speaking of the brutal conduct of the government towards him. "The first lord was jealous, sir, of my humble abilities—you understand me?"—and so on. The rest is lost in his ample beard.

Bobadil, however, once had his revenge in rather a comical way. One of England's most distinguished statesmen visited a much-frequented Bad for the benefit of his health, where the captain was for a time residing, and, in accordance with the custom of the place, went to the reading-rooms each morning alone. Here he fell into Bobadil's clutches, who was frightfully enraged at not meeting with that attention which he considered he merited; in point of fact, Lord —— paid no regard to him or his complaints. On this account Bobadil vowed vengeance, and he had it. Lord —— read the papers for a fortnight, and never thought of the daily twelve kreutzer he ought to have paid. The old Jew who kept the rooms fell into a frightful state of alarm, as he did not know his visitor's rank, and asked his old friend the captain whether he knew the gentleman. "What, hasn't he paid you?" asked the captain; and on hearing it was so, he added, with fiendish joy, "Then he never will—he never pays anybody; but as the first loss is the best, I would recommend you to ask him for the money the next time he comes." The Jew followed his advice; in expressive, though not very choice French, he informed Lord —— he expected to be paid at once; and if not, he should summon the police to his aid. Of course a most ludicrous scene ensued when the Jew learned the nobleman's name; and thus Bobadil repaid his insulting silence.

The next specimen is the Honourable Captain Fitzpavin, without exception the best *cicerone* a philanthropist like the revered Howard could have, for he is intimately acquainted with the interior of every gaol on the Continent, and is equally great at selling a horse or a friend. He must have obtained some money somewhere, for, see how eagerly he rushes up the steps which lead to the Conversations Saal. He'll now play till it is all gone, and then he will exert his wits in devising some fresh scheme to replenish his pockets. It is strange that a man so clever in gaining money should be so deficient in the requisite talent to keep it; but, "ainsi va le monde."

You are looking at that portly gentleman with the sleek smile and sparkling eye; surely you recognize him? It is the Reverend John Doubleface, who edified us so greatly at Xhausen by the refreshing sermon he preached. If you happen to be in the Kursaal next Sunday evening, you will see him, when he thinks nobody is looking, with his eyes fixed on the ceiling, and pushing a Kronenthaler on to the zero rouge.

But these pictures may be multiplied *ad infinitum.* Let us turn to more grateful subjects. The Lichtenthaler Allée is a pleasant scene on a bright summer afternoon, filled as it is with carriages, from the King of Würtemberg's coroneted and well-equipped calèche down to the banker's wife from Carlsruhe, who parades her Iris-rivalling splendour in a humble drosh, while her husband is essaying his infallible martingale at the green table. And then, again, at the end of the season, Monsieur Benazet, with a count as his huntsman *en chef,* gallantly provides stags from the grand ducal park, and gives luncheons worthy of Apicius to those who have confided their money to his coffers, or else brings boar pigs from France to be speared by the chivalrous nobility of Europe. How pleasant, too, the balls in the "Salle des Fleurs"—heretofore so free from the taint of exclusiveness which the travelling English have lately introduced—the air redolent with the sweet-smelling orange-trees, and the thousand-and-one perfumes to which odoriferous Paris gives birth; or the Trinkhalle, with its frescoes, which allure the gazer to visit the fairy scenes which Götzenberger has so well depicted; or else the Restauration Saal, with its dainty *table d'hôte,* where such conversations as the following may be heard between stout Englishmen and waiters:

"Garçon, un biftek."

"Oui, monsieur; avec blaisir."

"No, no; avec des pommes de terre."

One of the pleasantest amusements we know is to sit in front of Mellerio or Buffa's shops, at the little round tables, and play at chess or dominos; nor is any lack of opponents to be feared, for there is an *habitué* of Baden, who is such a *fanatico* that he constantly walks about with a chessboard beneath his arm.

And if none of these scenes satisfy our craving, we can take an agreeable walk to the Alt Schloss, and breakfast beneath the umbrageous oaks, whence, by-the-by, the writer had the fortune to see the great Lola expedited by two fierce gendarmes, and convoyed to the railroad station, in 1846, on account of certain eccentricities of behaviour she had displayed on the preceding evening in the Kursaal. She, however, escaped on this occasion better than she did in 1848, when passing through Baden from Switzerland, for then the students shamefully ill-used her at the station in Heidelberg, and compelled her to fly further. In spite of Lola's almost sovereign authority in Munich, the pot-valiant Münchener gave vent to many sly jokes about her, the *Fliegenden Blätter* taking the lead, and cleverly managing to evade the censorial shears. One caricature had a great run, representing the king as Io, and Lola as the vengeful *οἰστρὸς*, in the shape of a huge Spanish fly. The following lines excited considerable attention, for the author had the audacity to affix them to the door of the Countess Landsfeldt's mansion:

Un jour Lola,
Bel oiseau, s'envola
Vers un pays chéri de Loyola:
Elle trouva là
Un roi poète—et puis—le cajola,
Et de caresses l'accabla

Du roi la tête se troubla—
Il affubla Lola
Dans un beau falbala—
Des titres, des bijoux, en veux-tu—les voilà.

Le ministère s'assembla
Et voulut chasser Lola—
Mais c'est lui qu'on exila,
La cour bêla.

Le bourgeois beugla,
On siffla Lola,
On persiffla le roi—hola!

Malgrè cela,
Lola est toujours là,
Et puis voilà—
Vive le roi, Lola et Loyola!

Spite of all her faults, Lola did some good in her unquiet way, and the king was perfectly right when he wittily said, "Had her name not been Lola, but Loyola Montes, she would still have been in Munich." A plain proof in what awe her power was held, is furnished by the well-avouched fact that not only the so-called Austrian party at court offered her £20,000 to go away quietly, but that the ecclesiastical and temporal nobility, who formerly managed state affairs in Bavaria, had, on several occasions, shown themselves well disposed to form a coalition with, and gain an ally in her. Even the ministers who had been appointed through her influence would have gladly conceded her a certain share in the government, had she not wished to become more than the other royal mistresses, Mesdames Lizius, Dahn, &c., had been—that is, mediators between the king and ministers. These ladies had been satified with receiving advice and hints from ministers in weighty state affairs, and with cleverly conversing with the king about them, discovering his views and wishes, and then imparting them to the ministers. But Lola would not be servant to any one—she wished all to become her slaves. She hated the ecclesiastics—she detested the nobility—not through any democratic feelings, but because the laws of society prevalent in Germany did not suit her; for even in Munich they set certain bounds on her passions and her avarice, which despised every effort at concealment, and she deemed even common prudence a restraint on her liberty.

Still, though Baden is so delightful a place in summer, yet we must confess we prefer it in winter. At that season the amusements are ever varying, and a sociability exists which it is not possible to maintain during the summer months. We have balls given by the "Leseverein" and the "Bürger-Gesellschaft;" the haute volée also play their part, by holding, fortnightly, reunions at the Zähringer Hof. The pedestrian may find ample entertainment by a walk to Lichtenthal, where Graf is ever ready to welcome him with a warm room and cold beer, and a hissing caldron on the top of the stove, filled with "Knoblauch, meth, or Blutwürsten," while his Jung Bier preserves its well-merited reputation, and is even better than the "Lager Bier" he dispenses in summer; these being the names given to the winter and summer brewage, as during the former season beer is being constantly brewed, but in the latter they are obliged to brew it all at once, and lay it up in a "Felsen Keller," whence it derives its name of "Lager Bier." At the Fremersberg, too, he will always find a welcome and a shelter, go when he may; or he may extend his walk to Ebersteinburg, Sinzheim, or Steinbach. One great amusement, to which we can hardly grant the name of sporting, is the "Meissen fang," or capture of titmice, which occupies a large proportion of the population at large during the months of November and December. The orthodox method of proceeding is by carefully searching for a place in the surrounding woods, generally near the Yburgh, where the birds usually feed, and there a hut is formed of pine boughs, large enough to conceal two persons. An aperture is left in the front, through which a piece of wood is extended, with springes of horse-hair hanging on either side. A tame titmouse is fastened on the other end of the stick, and by his twittering he induces his unfortunate relatives to enter, when they are soon despatched by having their necks twisted. We have known two persons catch as many as 1500 birds in the course of an afternoon. They are esteemed a delicacy, and are eaten like larks in England. If snow intervene, still there is no cessation to our amusement, for then the sleighs come into use, and fly with hundreds of tinkling bells through the streets. The chief inconvenience of winter is the "Glatteis," formed by rain falling on the congealed earth, and making one entire sheet of ice; and as the streets are all paved with small round stones, tumbles in abundance may then be predicted. At such times it is a common occurrence to see a party of citizens, on leaving their tavern, deliberately pull off their boots, and walk home with stockinged feet, which is the only safe method of locomotion. The Carnival is also kept up to a certain extent, and a "Narren-Verein" hold its sittings during the month of February.

As regards legitimate sporting, shooting may be

had in abundance, extending for miles round the town, as, since the revolution of 1848, the crown lands, heretofore so strictly preserved by the grand duke, have been given up to the corporation, and they have let them to a party of citizens, from whom permission to shoot may be purchased for about eight florins annually. Roebuck, hares, partridges, woodcock, and snipe, may be met with, the two former in considerable abundance, though the chevreuil have been sadly thinned by the peasants, who, on the abolition of the game-laws, went out *en masse*, with every description of firearm—muskets, pistols, and the long rifles with which their fathers had so mercilessly received the French, when they tried to force their way through the Acherner Thal. It may be imagined what devastation was done, when the writer states that upwards of 200 head of roebuck were sold in one day on the market-place of Strasburg for half-a-crown apiece. Another sad blow and heavy discouragement for sportsmen was the so-termed revolution of 1849. On the Prince of Prussia passing through Baden-Baden, martial law was proclaimed, and all guns, &c., ordered to be given up, and deposited in the Town Hall, under pain of death. This was, of course, directly complied with, and all went on quietly till six o'clock in the evening, when the Prussians marched to Oos, where they encamped for the night. At about eight, however, the Nassau and Mecklenburg contingent marched in, and in a very short time broke into the Town Hall, and carried off nearly 200 fowling-pieces, all of considerable value, and among them eight belonging to a Prussian Graf. Maugre all our exertions, we never saw any of them again, though we heard of them all up the country to Constanz, and found they had been sold to Jews from Strasburg, who doubtlessly made a rich harvest by them. All the satisfaction we obtained was, that we should send in our claims to the respective governments, and when matters became quiet again, they would be examined into. One trick, however, these godless soldiers practised at Lichtenthal is too rich to pass unnoticed. They persuaded a poor simple gardener of the convent to purchase a gun of them, inducing him to do so by the low price they asked. He was foolish enough to buy it for about a pound, but had scarce arrived home when a picquet seized him for having arms in his possession, in contravention to martial law, when he was imprisoned for three weeks, and sentenced to five-and-twenty blows with the haselnuss stock, while the informer, the very fellow who sold him the gun, received a reward for his keen scent after hidden weapons.

It appears to us that the whole affair of 1849 has been greatly misunderstood in England. It has been termed a revolution, though, in point of fact, nothing of the sort took place. A public meeting was convened at Offenburg on the 6th of May, at which a petition to the grand duke was drawn up, strenuously urging the necessity of the constitution being called into life—a step considered requisite, as the grand duke had been playing fast and loose for a considerable time. On the following Tuesday some drunken life-guardsmen, who had been conducting prisoners to the Penitentiary at Bruchsal, on returning to Carlsruhe, gave three cheers for Hecker. In consequence of this, the duke expressed his opinion that it was impossible to live in such a state of things, and therefore quietly departed. The chamber was taken unawares by this unexpected defection, and, as the government was at a stand-still, eventually established a dictatorship under Brentano.

It was, in truth, curious to see the different manifestations of joy and sorrow on the countenances of the bourgeois of Carlsruhe when this event took place—those notable heroes who, in the stormy times of 1848, after being enrolled in the Burgerwehr and armed, patrolled the streets without any weapons of attack or defence, for fear the workmen of the "Kesslerche Fabrik" might fall on them and deprive them of their weapons. But now their ardour was excessive in all the Bier and Wirth Stuben, and all vowed they were ready to fight, and, if need must, die for the republic, though, when called upon to furnish their quota to the expenses of the war, all set more value on their money than their lives. Oh, these bourgeois! whose salient points Glasbrenner has so excellently described in his "Hauptkennzeichen eines Philisters."

The Philistine is either noble or a government employé, or else hath a business which provideth him with a respectable livelihood. He also hath several children, whose clever sayings it delighteth him to repeat.

The Philistine formerly felt an agreeable sensation on hearing the word "Liberty," and would even read forbidden books, or was pleased in his heart when despotism was cursed and reviled. But when the light of freedom dawned, things were not sufficiently quiet for him, and he now heartily wisheth himself once more beneath the protecting wings of absolutism's police, though he dareth not give expression to such sentiments, "for fear of being laughed at."

He also attacheth to the words "Popular Representation" the idea of murder and rapine; and if he heareth of a public meeting, he diggeth a hole in the ground and hideth his money, though he hath no objection to the windows of his richer neighbour being broken now and then.

The Philistine also termeth each person "a Foreigner" who was not born in his own town.

Whenever he readeth a satire, he always feeleth himself the subject of it, and he therefore abuseth violently or giveth vent to his spleen in the daily journals of his town.

Under the term "Freedom of the Press," he understandeth that each must hold the same opinion as himself.

From pure anxiety and fear of excesses, he continually causeth disturbance and unpleasantness.

These were the men who, in contradistinction to Napoleon's Garde Imperiale, were ready to reply, "La Garde se rend mais ne meurt pas"—pot-bellied citizens, who would march to the exercising-ground on wet days with an umbrella in one hand and a musket in the other; for even if they were about to lay down life for their country, that was no reason they should suffer from a cold, like the man left for execution who complained that his sheets were damp. Others walking to parade in uniform, while the maid-servant carried musket, sabre, and cartridge-box after them, for they had no wish to appear in the streets as common soldiers, although they were compelled to exercise;—men, who were all anxious to be elected officers, and so caused a wit to propose that they should proceed to elect a private. All this was of daily occurrence in Carlsruhe. But when the time for real action arrived, a sad change came over the spirit of their dreams, and few, very few, were to be found among them ready to march to the frontier; so, to prevent such an awful catastrophe, they commenced caballing against Brentano, and doing their utmost to evade the collectors of the voluntary loan. At length they succeeded in carrying a measure that only the young men of the 1st "Aufgebot" should be marched to the seat of war, while they remained behind and pledged themselves to fight *pro aris et focis.*

But, in sober sadness, the whole affair was a melancholy mistake. Brentano, to whom we are inclined to attribute the purest motives, was in a serious state of ill-health, and was driven by his colleagues to proclaim a Republic. From that moment the fate of the country was sealed. Besides, too, their leaders were enough to ruin any cause, however righteous; such men as the two Mieroslawskis, who make a trade of rebellion, and care for nought but plunder and good cheer, continually intoxicated, and only mindful of their own safety. The odium thrown on the whole cause by the shamelessness of the military leaders checked the growth of the young Republic, and caused the ever-careful Suabes to ponder ere they raised the standard of insurrection. And still, in spite of all this, they fought bravely. It was great to see the youth of the whole land foremost in the van at Ladenburg, Mannheim, and Muggensturm, and, though conscious of the impossibility of success, through a mistaken sense of duty standing firmly to their ground. How many mothers had to mourn for sons laid low by the Prussian tirailleurs with their murderous "Nadel-Gewehre;" how many had to weep for their children's blighted hopes; and how many families have been condemned to the bitterness of poverty to afford their relatives a sustenance in a foreign land! God knows! the country has suffered enough, and years must elapse ere Baden become again the happy and prosperous Garden of Germany it formerly was.

CHAPTER VI.

A DAY AT THE BARRICADES.

Fortunately for themselves, few Englishmen are in a capacity to join with me in saying that they have also spent a day at the barricades; the inhabitants of this happy island are still blessedly ignorant of even the first principles of their erection, and none of our generals have been yet compelled to exchange the sword for the pen, and explain the proper method of scaling them. The only barricades we ever see are those raised in our thoroughfares when repairs are going on, to the profit of our cabmen; and the only weapons with which they are assailed are winged, but not death-dealing, consisting, as they do, of a volley of objurgations on the heads of the leaders of the destructive and constructive band.

Our political excitement ends in a very different fashion from that which was formerly *en vogue* on the Continent; when a thing grievously annoys us, and cannot by possibility be endured any longer, we even join together in a peaceful conspiracy, and abolish it by the employment of moral force—a more powerful weapon than all the warlike equipments to be found in Woolwich Arsenal. For all that, though, our cousins-german must not be utterly blamed for their appeal to the sword: they never were in a position to understand the real blessings of liberty, and persons under such circumstances are only too prone to be seduced by the meretricious blandishments of that painted lady, Democracy.

For my own part, I was led to comprehend the delights of revolution by a very peculiar process: at the first outbreak of hostilities I may safely avouch that there was not a more peaceful *Civis Britannicus* in the whole territory of Baden than myself; but I presume the enjoyment of revolution is something like that of opium—the first taste is inexpressibly nauseous, but, by degrees, it becomes a necessity to existence. At least, it was so in my case; when the news arrived across the frontier that Louis Philippe had scented the danger and betaken himself to England, under the vulgar name of Mr Smith, I felt rather more than curious to know what would be the result of the movement in the ducal residence of Carlsruhe. Thither I went, and had the distinguished honour of forming one of the body-guard hurriedly raised to protect the grand duke from any hostile attack. Fortunately for myself, the only opportunity I found of exhibiting my prowess was in wielding my knife and fork, and drinking several bottles of the celebrated white wine from Eberstein, which, though heretofore exclusively kept for the grand ducal table, was, by the levelling process going on, considered not a whit too good for his gallant defenders.

As the political excitement waxed fiercer, in equal ratio did mine, and I gradually found myself shouting vehemently for Hecker and other worthies, who have since left their country for their country's good, although up to that time their names were almost unknown to me, and it was a matter of perfect indifference whether the National Guard were formed or not. But here I must correct myself; for, after it came into existence, the unlucky drums used to beat the *reveille* every morning at four o'clock, and I, consequently, lost a considerable portion of my natural rest.

The first great popular meeting that was held took place at Offenburg, and an ominous sign of the times was rendered by Hecker's reply to the request that he would accept office as minister of justice, "Ich kann kein Fürsten Diener seyn;" words which, although placed by Schiller in the mouth of the Marquis Posa, had a terrible significance here, as they left the people to choose between a grand duke who was indifferent to them, and a man like Hecker, who was born to be the darling of a mob.

The popular ferment increased instead of becoming diminished; armed meetings grew into fashion through the whole length of the land, from Heidelberg to Basle, and, to my sorrow I must confess, I went regularly to all of them. Hecker and his friends retired to Switzerland after the breaking up of the Vor Parliament, and all threatened a very lively episode in the history of Baden.

Towards the close of the month of May, the political refugees, wearied of the monotony of peace, thought it high time to have their innings, and word was soon brought that they were moving on the Rhine, as some said, with half a dozen red-trousered French regiments at their back. The excitement was of course intense, and a popular armed meeting was immediately convened at Freyburg, to see (in the words of the programme) what encouragement should be given to the progress of the Republic. But, before telling you what they said and did there, I may as well give a short description of this most interesting town.

Freyburg is situated in an exquisite valley in the Black Forest, at no great distance from the Swiss frontier and the Rhine. It contains a population of about 10,000 souls, and enjoys the usual gentle dulness of collegiate towns. It is the seat of the Catholic University of Baden, and would scarcely ever be visited by strangers were it not for the very splendid cathedral it boasts. It is, in fact, the finest specimen of Gothic architecture in a complete state to be found in Germany, or, I might almost say, in Europe. At least I cannot, at the moment, recollect any other great church completed in accordance with the original design, except, perhaps the Madeleine in Paris, or our own St Paul's. The cathedral of Cologne may be grander in conception, but it is not yet finished, and never will be, unless they progress considerably faster than they are doing at present. "Besides this, Freyburg cathedral is remarkable from being the result of the united energies of the people, for they completed it, after kings and princes had given up the task in despair. Houses and lands were mortgaged to raise the money; and where a man had neither, he voluntarily gave his days and labour to complete the noble work: the result was one of the most beautiful buildings it is possible to imagine."

The presence of the cathedral in Freyburg has had considerable influence on the fortunes of the town; the inhabitants are perfectly well acquainted with the current value of English sovereigns, and do not evince the slightest objection to receive any quantity their distinguished visitors may feel inclined to exchange for Dutch clocks and straw hats, the staple articles of barter drawn from the Black Forest. From these data it might be inferred, naturally, that the population of the town would be disinclined towards revolution, or rebellion, if you like to call it so; and so they would have been, if the season had commenced. As it was, they felt dull after a severe winter—their blood had been put in active circulation by the various *émeutes* all around them—strangers had not yet begun to appear, that is, those who were worth shearing, and the consequence was, the good people of Freyburg thought that they would have their fun as well, though it might be death to others: nor were the means and appliances wanting.

At the close of May, then, the long-talked-of armed popular meeting took place, and thousands flocked to Freyburg, myself among them. My knowledge of such assemblies was becoming rather extensive, and I soon saw that there was some mischief in the wind, through the number of strange faces I perceived, and which could only belong to Poles, those carrion crows of revolution. It was a most peculiar fact that, during the whole progress of the outbreaks in Vienna, Berlin, Frankfort, &c., Poles were immediately found in the front ranks as soon as the first gun was fired in anger. Whence they came nobody appeared to know, or how they disappeared; as soon as hostilities ceased they modestly retired, without waiting to receive the meed of valour at the hands of a grateful mob, or anticipating it by carrying away with them a few dozen silver spoons, and such unconsidered trifles, as a reminiscence.

As for the rest of the assembly, they were the old

familiar faces; the detachment of blouse, or scythe men, as they were indiscriminately termed, I had seen before, but as my readers may not have enjoyed that peculiar good fortune, I may as well devote a few lines to them. They were a corps of picked men, of herculean forms, dressed in blue linen blouses and grey-felt somberos, adorned with red feathers, and carried a most extraordinary weapon, formed of a combination of scythe and reaping hook, fastened to the end of a pole about five feet long. This curious instrument was a reminiscence of the last Polish war, and was intended to be employed in repulsing cavalry attacks: the reaping-hook serving to catch the rider by the neck and drag him from the saddle, when the scythe effectually settled him. I believe, however, its value was never properly established, at least by a fair trial, for when it came to cavalry attacks the rebels used to remember the adage of "running away" in order to "live to fight another day," and very speedily took themselves out of harm's way.

The remainder of the mob collected on the market-place of Freyburg consisted of Turner, or members of the gymnastic societies, dressed in their white linen jackets and trousers, and armed with muskets the grand duke had been good enough to give them, at considerable expense to the country, and a vast number of long-booted, red-waistcoated peasants, whose armament was, to use the mildest term for it, extraordinary. An antiquarian would have gloated over the guns and pistols, swords and daggers, there brought to light, with intense satisfaction. There were the long rifles with which their forefathers had repulsed the

French in 1794, now quite disabled by rust, and weapons of such quaint and peculiar form that it would not have required any great stretch of imagination to suppose that they had been employed in the terrible peasant war of 1525. Add to these a quantity of fat citizens from the towns of the Underland, some dragging huge sabres rattling at their heels, others tripped up by their straight court swords, and the reader may form a tolerably correct idea of the components of a German armed meeting in those days.

As heterogeneous, however, as the assembly was, it was just the same with their opinions. The majority of the peasants were only animated with one wish, that of eking their revenge upon the Jews, who certainly deserved punishment if all behaved in the same way as one of whose villany I was once witness. I had been out shooting, and in the afternoon turned into a village inn to have some refreshment. The only inmates of the room where I sat were an old peasant and two children of Israel, money-lenders or corn dealers, for in Germany they generally unite both professions. The peasant wanted to borrow the sum of 40 florins, or about three pounds ten, on mortgage of his farm, to which the Jews consented, but the main difficulty appeared to be that they had not so much money with them, their united capital only amounting to 26 florins. They, however, drew up a bill, handed over the 26 florins to the peasant, inserted the amount in the document, and all appeared to be going on correctly. One of the Jews, however, suddenly recollected that he had some money to receive in the village, and promised the peasant that, if he succeeded, he would let him have the other 14 florins. He went out for a time, and returned with the money, which he handed over to the peasant, and duly inserted in the document. I had forgotten all about the affair, when, some three months afterwards, the old peasant came to call upon me in a state of terrible tribulation, and begged in the name of all the saints that I would help him. It appeared that the Jews had begun an action against him for 2614 florins, which they swore they had lent him, and which was borne out by the bill he had signed. They had put down the first 26 florins they had given him, and added the other 14 close by their side afterwards, so that it read 2614, and had it not been for my active interference, and after an infinity of trouble, caused by the Jews' perjury (for they would not give in until the chief rabbi of Carlsruhe was summoned to take their oath by some dreadful process peculiar to themselves), the poor old peasant would indubitably have been sold out. Nor was this an isolated case; but as it occurred in my own presence, I can vouch for the fact. Indeed, in Alsace many of the Jews were terribly maltreated about this time, and even the great Israelite, Baron von Rothschild, according to popular rumour, was glad to remove his treasures to the strong fortress of Mayence, not deeming them sufficiently secure in Frankfort. By the way, I wonder what his mamma, Madame Rothschild, if she be still living, thinks about the complication with Russia. It is said that, at the time when a war was apprehended between France and Germany, several years ago, one of her *commères* ran in to tell the old lady the terrible news; she was, however, speedily consoled by the reply: "Pah, pah! my son won't permit it—he won't lend them any money." Surely Mr Cobden must have derived his notions of finance from this worthy dame, when present at the Peace Congress at Frankfort. After this long digression, let me return to the good town of Freyburg.

The balcony of the first floor windows in the Hotel zum Ritter was selected as the oratorical tribune, and it was soon densely crowded with students, newspaper editors, and other dissatisfied heroes, who wished to make a little noise in the world. The usual turbulent speeches were held, the flags were waved from below, guns and pistols were continually fired, regardless of danger and expense, and I breathed somewhat more freely, for I fancied things would end in the accustomed manner. In this, however, I was lamentably mistaken, for a horseman came suddenly riding in who brought the news that Hecker and Sturvé had, that afternoon, passed the Rhine at Lörrach, and were hurrying with forced marches to Freyburg, fully determined to do or die. It was surprising how this intelligence inflamed the hearers. Hecker's name was idolized by the people, and the feeling had been maintained by many artful rumours. One, for instance, I remember, was universally circulated and believed, that he was the second son of the Grand Duchess Stephanie of Baden, and carried off, when born, by the White Lady from the palace of Carlsruhe. This was an adaptation of the Caspar Hauser legend, which had never been satisfactorily cleared up, but was so fully credited that reputable persons pointed out to me the actual murderer of the boy, who was a gentleman held in high repute, and personally received at the grand ducal court. But this is ever a misfortune contingent on absolutism, that the most *outré* stories obtain credence through the exertions of the police to suppress them. For my own part, I succeeded in procuring the secret history of Caspar Hauser, and studied it carefully, and I have no doubt that the suspicions cast on the Grand Duke Leopold could have been easily dissipated at the time; he, however, dared public opinion, and has gone to the grave with the unenviable reputation of having been implicated in an assassination. Be this as it may, the original story had been so successful, that it was thought advisable to spread reports that Hecker was the younger brother of Caspar Hauser, and removed by the same process; and it was not at all a bad scheme, for it reconciled many, who would have shrunk from rebellion, to an armed interference in favour of the legitimate heir.

As I said before, the arrival of the messenger caused the greatest excitement in Freyburg, and the armed meeting formed the groundwork for a very successful attempt at rebellion. A student of the name of Von Langsdorff proposed that the town should be held on behalf of the "Apostles of Liberty," and the regular troops kept in check until Hecker and his merry men threw their weight into the scale. This proposition was unanimously agreed to, and a "rider" was appended in the shape that no one be allowed to quit the town, but all be tarred with the same brush. I now thought it time to beat my retreat gracefully, but on wending my way to the gate that led to the railway station, I found it already held by a party of the scythe men, who would not allow me to pass. My attempts at the other gates were equally unsuccessful, and I found the rather unpleasant conviction forced upon me that I must stay in Freyburg and be witness to a real contest, my only experience in that line having been hitherto confined to theatrical combats of two—up to—a dozen.

The night was passed in various preparations for the anticipated fight, for two regiments of infantry and a field-battery lay within twenty miles of the town. The plates were pulled up for some distance on the railway, the omnibuses and various carriages confiscated and formed into barricades in certainly a very practical manner by filling them with paving-stones, but the great achievement consisted in carrying too four-pounders to the top of the Schwaben Thor. The citizens of Freyburg had amused themselves in happier times by playing at soldiers, as is the case in every German town, and their scarlet-fever broke out in the form of an artillery corps. The grand duke had very kindly made them a present of four little field-pieces, which they had been accustomed to limber and unlimber, load and fire, at every possible opportunity. These guns, when not in active service, were kept in the Town Hall, together with the fire-engines, and thence the rebels carried them off in triumph, after intimidating the porter by holding a pistol at his head. I may as well state that it was unloaded, and the official was perfectly well aware of it; but then it is just as well to go through the proper form, and I believe the worthy janitor received afterwards the Zähringer order of the twenty-ninth class for his heroic conduct. After this affecting scene, two of the cannon were planted in the centre of a barricade at the Schweizer Thor, and the other two dragged by sheer strength to the top of the Schwaben Thor, where they were loaded with old iron, nails, and stones, in readiness for the morrow.

I retired for the night to the Zähringer Hof, where I found quarters at the very top of the house, whence I could enjoy a view over a broad expanse of country. The town remained in a state of great confusion during the whole of the night, as the insurgents ransacked every house from top to bottom for arms, and even stripped part of the lead from the roof of the cathedral to melt into bullets. I obtained an hour or two of broken sleep, and as soon as day dawned, I posted myself at the window, to see if anything fresh had turned up. The first thing I noticed was a body of about 600 men, as it seemed to me at a rough calculation, collected in a narrow valley, about three miles from the town, but strange to say in a remarkable state of inaction. I soon found, however, on looking to the other side, what it was that held them in check. Two regiments of Hessians, and a field-battery of six guns, were drawn up close to the railway station, and evidently meant mischief. I had not much time, though, to watch them, for the door of my bed-room was suddenly burst open, and a party of armed men rushed in, who, with many fierce oaths, insisted on my coming down and helping to remove the barricade at the Schwaben Thor, so that their friends might come in. With much repining at my folly at running my head into such unnecessary danger, I went down-stairs, and betook myself under a guard to the gate, where I found several more involuntary revolutionists assembled. The policy of the insurgents was, however, far from being despicable: the barricade was the most exposed place in the whole town, being only four feet high, and covered by the enemy's guns; only those, therefore, were to be employed in its temporary removal by whose fall the ranks of the fighting men would suffer no loss. At it we went, then, and very rapidly cleared away the paving-stones, carts; &c., of which the barricade was formed, being much hastened by the dropping fire of one of the Hessian regiments, who seemed to make us their especial target. Fortunately, though, they, in all probability, aimed at us, and this accident saved our lives, for regulation muskets are notorious for not carrying straight. Be this as it may, the barricade was very speedily removed, and all the neighbouring houses lined with tirailleurs to repulse the soldiers if they attempted a storm. It was all of no avail; the insurgents in the valley either would not, or dared not, face the enemy's fire, and they could not be induced to make a bold rush, and enter the town. In fact, we were again driven to rebuild the barricade; and I may as well mention here, that, although we carried it away three consecutive times, the heroes without had too much regard for their skins, and gradually retired farther and farther up the valley.

This, of course, inspired the soldiers with fresh courage, and they soon commenced a tremendous cannonade upon the barricade at the Schwaben Thor. Myself and a few others mounted the cathedral tower, whence we had an uninterrupted view of the whole engagement. The soldiers soon gave up the use of their artillery through fear of injuring the cathedral, and prepared for a storm. They were twice repulsed with considerable loss by the insurgents, who were materially aided by the two little cannon on the top of the gate, which were served with very great precision.

At length the barricade was captured, and the soldiers rushed in; the fellows on the gate, with a courage worthy of a better cause, would not desert their guns, but were cut down to a man. This, I must candidly state, I was not an eye-witness of; for being tolerably well acquainted with the amiable disposition of soldiers after an engagement, and their proneness to shoot people first and inquire into their guilt afterwards, I had gradually found my way to the top of the castle hill, whence I hurried off, with several other co-revolutionists, into the recesses of the Black Forest.

I was not at all deceived in my anticipations as to the conduct of the soldiery, for I afterwards learned that they had killed everybody they found in the street, without any compunction. They merely requested them to hold out their hands, and the least trace of dirt upon them was a proof of complicity in the rebellion. The victim was then planted against a doorway, and either impaled on a bayonet or else shot. An old English gentleman, so the story ran, who was very far from feeling charitably disposed to the insurgents, opened his shutters to cheer the soldiers, but, in doing so, had two of his fingers shot off.

After we had succeeded in placing some six good miles of ground between ourselves and the soldiers, we held a consultation as to our future progress. We were six in number, and if it be true that "poverty makes us acquainted with strange bed-fellows," I am sure it may be said with equal justice of revolution. The party consisted of two students, two handwerksbursche—a tailor and a shoemaker, the editor of a Mannheim newspaper, and myself. Our united property amounted to seventeen florins, and the only persons laden with luggage were the journeymen, whose knapsacks were arranged on little trucks for the purpose of easy locomotion. We lit our pipes, had a pull at the "Schnaps budel," and talked about our future prospects. The world was certainly before us, but not where to choose: behind us were the Badenese troops—before us Switzerland, where we well knew it would be no use for us to go in the present state of our finances. After a long deliberation, it was agreed that we should separate and shift for ourselves; so, after fairly dividing our money, the students went off for the Rhine, in order to take refuge at Strasburg; the journeymen determined on going to Switzerland; and the editor and myself decided on trusting to our good fortune to return home safely. We had not much to fear as long as we kept out of the way of the soldiers; our passports were *en règle,* and our only apprehension was that we might starve on the road. As it was, we remained nearly six weeks in the Black Forest, where we were most hospitably treated by the peasants, and lived on the fat of the land, for my comrade was a famous singer, and that was enough to secure him a hearty welcome among the unsophisticated sons of the mountains. At length we were reluctantly compelled to quit this happy spot, for detachments of soldiers were sent into the Black Forest to rout out the refugees, and we trudged off to the Lake of Constance, stopping at Schaffhausen by the way to "do the falls" as long as our finances would permit us, which was no great length of time, for we indulged rather too extensively in wine, after having been subjected during nearly six weeks to the annoyance of drinking potato-brandy —the most horrible decoction that can be conceived. How we eventually got to Stuttgardt has ever been a mystery to me, for we positively walked upwards of one hundred miles without a penny. We did get there, however, and our troubles were at an end; we procured money and clothes, and set off leisurely on our homeward route to Heidelberg. By the time I got back to Baden-Baden, though, I had had quite enough of revolutions for some time at least, and I consequently soon packed up my portmanteau and returned to England, where I had no fear of being forced to build barricades, or become a firing mark for soldiers.

CHAPTER VII.

A WALK TO WILDBAD.

Doubtlessly many of my readers were struck, on perusing the tales brought by English newspapers of the almost daily outbreaks in the German Annus Mirabilis, 1848, at seeing the Turner assúme a notorious pre-eminence as the instigators and promoters of rebellion. This was more especially the case with the Turner of Hanau and the Oberland, on account of their proximity to Frankfort; and as I am not aware that any detailed account of them has been submitted to the English reading public, and as, besides, they were my companions on my present tour, a few remarks may not be out of place.

The Turner, then, are ostensibly a number of young men who meet for the purpose of developing their bodily strength by gymnastic exercises; but, in reality, as one of their first laws states, the Turner Bund is constituted for the physical and moral improvement of the members. Each separate Turnverein is under the jurisdiction of a Kreis Verein, and these again under that of the Haupt or General Verein, which held its periodical meetings at Hanau—a town, by the way, which has always been looked upon suspiciously by the government ever since the meeting of students in 1832, at the Hambacher Schloss. Vater Jahn was for a long time president of the united Turnverein of Germany, till his senile vanity led him to apprehend danger at the hands of his sons. He therefore uttered his recantation, or, as he termed it, his *Schwanen Rede,* in the St Paul's Kirche, at Frankfort, though his opponents were inclined to regard his swans as geese. He was the first originator of the Turner Bund, probably from some fond reminiscences of the Prussian Tergend Bund, to which he had belonged in his young days; and was ever a conspicuous object, from the immense white beard he wore flaunting in the breeze, and the linen jacket he never exchanged for warmer clothing in the severest weather. Under his presidency, the Bund consisted of 150,000 members, and would have formed a dangerous body, had they at all interfered in politics. This fortunately was not the case, and their youthful effervescence found a vent in singing patriotic songs, directed against the French, especially Becker's Lied, "Sie sollen Ihn nicht haben, den freien Deutschen Rhein," written in 1842, when M. Thiers made some tentatives to regain the Rhenish shore as the natural boundary of France. However, in 1848 the revolutionary caldron boiled over. Jahn was weighed in the balance, and found wanting, and a more energetic man chosen to occupy his place. Many new laws were made, and a deliberative council summoned to Hanau, to which all the Turnverein were invited to send representatives. About 800 responded to the call. After a *séance* of two days, during which many violent speeches were uttered, the Empire was carried against the Republic by a majority of six. But this was in the time of the "Einheits Schwindelei," and the King of Prussia's hollow toasts; and the executive council plainly showed afterwards which way their wishes tended. Among the laws relative to the government of the Turnverein, one was passed by which each member was bound to pay one kreutzer weekly to the Haupt Cassa in Hanau, making an annual sum of 130,000 florins, or rather more than £10,000. This fact throws a strong light on the frequent outbreaks at Frankfort, Mayence, and elsewhere, for we now see whence money was derived to set them in motion, and men collected for such purposes. In addition to this, subsidies were voted to Hecker and Struvé on their irruption into Baden, and after they were repelled the exiles in Strasburg were supported from the same source.

All the members wear the same uniform—a linen jacket, loose trousers of the same material, and a cap bearing a silver cross formed of four F.'s, the initials of the words "frisch, fromm, frey, froh," the motto of the society, set in a wreath of oak leaves. The head covering, however, differs in nearly every town, many wearing Schlapphüte of grey, black, or white felt.

The Turnlocale is a large room in an inn, where the members assemble, filled with pictures, caricatures of every description, while the red flags of the different companies hang round the walls. Beer and tobacco, without which nothing can be done in Germany, help to wile the hours away while the business of the society is being discussed, and new members enrolled. In the summer months, on *fête* days, Turnfahrten are held; and during holidays, such as Easter and Whitsuntide, more extended expeditions into the country are made, at one of which, to Wildbad, it was my fortune, as the French say, to assist.

At four in the morning of Whit-Monday, we assembled, in number about eighty, before the railway station, to proceed in that manner to Carlsruhe, as there was nothing worth visiting *en route* to that city. The band was among the number, and as they were public-spirited enough to encumber themselves with their brazen instruments, we presented a very martial appearance while marching through the more sequestered villages. My readers must be pleased to bear in mind that this was the very season of disturbances, when each man spoke of wars and rumours of wars, and the peasants had hardly got over the fright to which they had been subjected in the preceding February, when hourly expecting the French to pass the Rhine.

We arrived at Durlach after an hour's sharp walking through a magnificent avenue of lime-trees, which extends the whole way from Carlsruhe. Durlach is a fine old-fashioned town, once the residence of the Markgraves of Baden Durlach, the elder branch of the present reigning family. A round tower, currently stated to have been built by the Romans, overlooks the town, to which a melancholy celebrity is attached, in consequence of a lady of high rank throwing herself and her two children from the summit of it, in consequence of some family jealousy. Thence our road led us to Wilferdingen, where it was arranged our first night's quarters should be established. As it was impossible to obtain beds for such a numerous party as ours, the landlord was necessitated to strew a quantity of trusses of hay in a barn, to which the majority retired, after discussing a hearty supper of potato-soup.

At three the next morning, the *reveille* was sounded; and after a refreshing turn at the pump, we set out for Pforzheim, a large manufacturing town, filled with jewellers and tobacco merchants, who, by the way, favoured the Exhibition with specimens of their industry. The church, which we visited, is a very handsome Gothic edifice, containing some remarkable monuments; among them one of marble, raised by the present grand duke, to his father, Carl Friedrich; and another, erected by public subscription, in memory of the 600 Pforzheimer who fell in the Thirty Years' War, at Wimpfen, while fighting for their religion and their country against Tilly. As it was no part of our plan to expend money in luxurious living, we remained no long time in Pforzheim, but set out for a small village called Tiefenbronn, where we actually took the inn by storm. Linen jackets might be seen in every part of the house, from "garret to basement," or looking from "window and casement." The landlord was so utterly dumb-foundered (the only word which will fully convey my meaning), that he let us do much as we pleased, and I really fancy would have suffered us to depart without payment, had such been our intention. He put me much in mind of Willet, senior, after the rioters had visited him; for he faintly remarked, he believed there was a trifle to settle.

Our next march brought us to Maulbronn, in Wirtemberg, through an extraordinary quantity of apple and pear trees, which lined both sides of the road, and the fruit of which we appropriated, thinking it but right to despoil the Suabes. I imagine the Chancellor of the Exchequer must have an annual sum voted in his budget for the proper maintenance of the frontier, for we passed at least 200 sign-posts in a distance of about ten miles, painted with the Wirtembergeois colours, and bearing the royal arms. Every now and then we were reminded of our being in a Catholic neighbourhood, by seeing gigantic crucifixes, carved in wood, and bearing all the insignia of our Saviour's passion—for instance, nails, dice-boxes, swords, &c. At Lautenbronn, by German measurement about a pipe and a half from Maulbronn, we passed a very beautiful Gothic chapel, now, unfortunately, converted into a cow-shed—the high altar and crucifix carved in stone still remain entire. At Maulbronn there are fortunately two inns, and we therefore contrived to procure beds for the whole party, though at only one of them could anything eatable or potable be procured, for at the other they had positively nothing in the house but an execution. Our arrival excited no small alarm among the Beamten of the town, and the Burgermeister had some thoughts of calling on the Rathsdeiner to arrest us all, but his fears were assuaged when he found that we were only on pleasure intent. This most servile servant of his most transparent Majesty doffed his dignity, and even accepted our invitation to crack a bottle. Maulbronn was, in the good old times, perhaps the most splendid of all the monastic buildings in the south of Germany; ample traces of this are furnished in the beautiful though ruined building, and in the care with which the surrounding country is laid out in terraces, for the proper cultivation of the vine. It has been secularized, and converted into a Protestant government school. The Burgermeister, on the next morning, was kind enough to act as our cicerone. He first led us into the chapel, which bore evident proofs of its pristine splendour, in the beautifully carved sedilia; but the painted windows have been removed by the abovementioned "transparency," to decorate a pet church of his own at Cannstadt, near Stuttgardt. That which struck us with the most surprise, was to see the marks of monastic feet deeply worked in the oaken floor, where the monks had literally shuffled off their mortal coil—this was a convincing proof of their piety and their weight. The seats themselves were a perfect specimen of ingenious torture; they were so contrived that the sitter would require all his wits to keep his balance, and if happening to fall asleep, he would inevitably come down with a squelch on the ground, no doubt to the great amusement of his brethren. The worthy Burgermeister next led us to the refectory, now converted into a barn, where he directed our admiring glances to a large pillar with an orifice in the centre, through which, he asserted with the utmost seriousness, a stream of red wine used to pour while the monks of old where dining. But now no signs bore evidence of the jovial race they were, and the loud "Ha, ha!" which shook the old oak wall, had been long hushed. Thence we proceeded to the cloisters, which are somewhat larger than those of St Mary Magdalene at Oxford, but the carved-work is much more elaborately executed. The predominant figure is that of the Maulcsel or Mule, which gives its name to the town, and is represented in every possible ludicrous position. In the centre is the large fountain, or Bronn, in a better state of preservation than any other part of the building—probably because monks are usually afflicted with hydrophobia, and holiness and dirt generally go together.

At about eleven o'clock we took leave of our friendly guide, and started for Neuenbronn, which place we reached about nightfall, after a lóng walk through some very romantic scenery. As there was a little difficulty about procuring sufficient food for so large a party, the landlord placed his nets at our disposal, and after pulling off our shoes and stockings, we had a glorious haul of trout in the river, which is strictly preserved for the use of amateur fishermen.

The next morning we set out for Wildbad, along a most exquisite road, which wound round the base of a huge mountain, till we arrived at a village called Cawl, where we made mid-day. And here occurred the most extraordinary incident of our whole journey. Will my readers credit it, that, in this sequestered Wirtembergeois village, I saw the wires and posts which usually indicate the presence of the electric telegraph on our railways? I instinctively felt that I had made a grand discovery, which would serve to enrol my name on the pages of history by the side of those of Cook, Humboldt, and Layard. The present claimants of gratitude and renown for the invention of the electric telegraph were evidently base impostors—had shamelessly taken advantage of the science of a Suabe, who was born to blush unseen, and robbed him of all the credit due to him. In my generous indignation, I determined his merits and name should no longer be hid under a bushel, and, therefore, began inquiring of the landlord where this wondervoller kopf resided. To my dreadful abashment, I found I had been a little too precipitate in drawing my conclusion, and that my fancied telegraph was merely a method of communication with the village constable—probably invented by some lazy Burgermeister. The wire, commencing in the dread functionary's bed-room, was attached to a bell in the Rathdiener's house; and when the night was cold, or the Burgermeister tired, he could summon his assistant to his aid whenever a pothouse dispute required his presence. As too, in this instance, they lived at different ends of the village, this only served to render the affair still more conspicuous.

We arrived at Wildbad about two o'clock, fired with the expectation of seeing some really glorious scenery—as the name led us to infer; but this, too, was a mistake. There was nothing at all wild about the place, and the landscape was of an every-day sort of character. Besides, however picturesque the place might naturally be, the presence of the great overgrown hotels would be sufficient to destroy the effect. The Badhaus is a very handsome edifice, built at the expense of the government, containing four public and some 20 private baths. The water is excessively hot, and beneficial in scrofulous and rheumatic complaints, ample proof of which we had while walking through the streets. Barring our own party, I really believe we did not see half-a-dozen people in the proper possession of their health; at every corner we stumbled over Bath chairs, in which the valetudinarians were being dragged to or from the Kursaal. To the credit of the government, there is an excellent hospital open to all, without distinction of country or sect, where a trifling sum is demanded for board and lodging, and this only in the case of a patient being in a condition to pay it.

Wildbad must have suffered an extraordinary change since the time when, as old Uhland sings to us, the Count Eberhard der Greiner was surprised here by his arch-enemies, the Counts Wolf von Wunnenstein and Ebersteinburg, while trying to get rid of his gout. He escaped on the back of a faithful shepherd, who hid him in one of the surrounding forests. Our poet-laureate was never weary of repeating the ballad, and pointed to the neighbouring mountains, in the vain hope of discovering the forest-clad retreat he reached in safety.

It is seldom that the popular voice errs in assigning a nickname to its oppressors, and none was ever more merited than that given to Count Eberhard of Wirtemberg—*der Greiner*, or "The Quarrelsome." His whole life was spent in a series of disputes with the citizens of the few imperial towns within his principality, and in checking the progress of civil liberty. Encouraged by the unexpected result of the battle of Sempach, and the decided repulse it gave to the aspirations of the house of Hapsburg, the cities of Ulm and Augsburg placed themselves at the head of the Suabian Confederation, and demanded the same privileges conceded to their brethren in Upper Germany, or, as it is now called, Switzerland. The Greiner was, of course, furiously incensed at such audacity, and summoned all his vassals together to punish the rebels. The hostile armies met on the 14th of May, 1377, beneath the walls of Reütlingen, and the Count suffered an ignominious defeat.

Still Eberhard, like many other great men, did not know when he was beaten, and though his son Ulrich was severely wounded in the battle, and narrowly escaped captivity, did not for a moment relax in his efforts to subjugate the rebels. By the aid of money and promises, he induced the knightly order of St George to help him, and the war was carried on with great animosity for several years. At length the Confederation, in 1388, seeing the injury done to trade by the continuance of hostilities, determined on risking a decisive battle. This took place at Dossingen, in Wirtemberg. The Greiner, who was aided by the Markgrave of Baden, the Bishop of Wurzburg, the Count von Ottingen, and several other nobles, was enabled to bring into the field a force of more than 7000 men. But not caring to trust entirely to the army, he also had recourse to treachery, and bribed the Count von Henneberg, the leader of the Nuremberg contingent, with 1000 florins, to quit the field at the critical moment. Count Ulrich commenced the attack, burning to wipe away the disgrace attaching to him from the defeat at Reütlingen; his repeated assaults failed, however, to break the enemy's line, and he and several other nobles fell in the engagement. At this moment, when victory seemed to hover over the townsmen, Count Henneberg commenced his retreat. Another circumstance especially favoured Eberhard, and materially influenced the fate of the battle. His old enemy, the Raging Wolf of Wunnenstein, was so conscious of the danger which would accrue to himself if the townsmen asserted their liberty, that he proffered his services to aid in subjecting them; and although Eberhard haughtily declined his assistance, still he appeared on the battle-field, with his robber hordes, almost at the same moment when Count Ulrich fell, and Henneberg's treachery was being carried out. The consternation of the townsmen at the sudden defection of the Nuremberg contingent, was naturally enhanced by the appearance of fresh combatants in the hostile army. Still the concurrence of so many unfortunate accidents did not shake the courage of their heroic leader, Conrad Besserer. The Suabes willingly responded to the summons of their brave compatriot, and remembered the glorious prerogative assured them by imperial edict, of ever being first in attack and last in retreat. With Conrad Besserer, however, the banner of the United Cities sunk to the ground, and when the signal of liberty vanished, the remnants of the allied army commenced their retreat. Such was the deplorable result of the battle of Dossingen, the most important of all those chronicled in the pages of Germany's history. Had the townsmen conquered, no princely coalition would have been sufficiently strong to prevent the liberty and unity of Germany. The mainspring of both, the imperial dignity, would have been re-established in its pristine vigour, and we should not have been witnesses of the lamentable mistakes and failures of the year 1848.

But *revenons à nos moutons.* We soon made our arrangements for leaving such a melancholy place as Wildbad, for all we had to do was to find a guide to lead us over the mountains into the Murgthal; and this we fortunately effected by falling in with an old peasant who lived in Baden, and had come across to visit some relations. The only disagreeable thing was that peculiar effluvia emanating from two immense bags of *sauerkraut* and pickled beans, which had been graciously presented to him by his friends; but this we rectified by keeping as far as possible from him. The road he led us was up an excessively steep mountain, immediately in the rear of the Bad, which gave our legs plenty of exercise. On reaching level ground, the first thing that struck us was a large square tower, or blockhouse, about 30 feet high; and this we found, on inquiring from the guide, had been erected, in communication with several others we afterwards passed, in the war of 1792, as a line of defence against the French. They had been of some service in their day, but were now in a decayed condition, and only served as a refuge for the charcoal-burners. These fellows, by the way, must have a merry time of it in summer, and many a fine roebuck is set to roast before their fires. It is rather strange we never hear of young adventurous spirits taking to this line of life. Perhaps, however, it is not sufficiently romantic, though, at any rate, it would be safer than the robber line, which, thanks to Schiller, so many untamed youths selected.

After a few hours' walking we arrived at Kaltenbronn, a *Jagd Haus* belonging to the grand duke, and chiefly maintained for the purpose of shooting the *Auerhahn*, or bustard. It is a very strongly-built house; and it is, indeed, requisite it should be so, for the gamekeeper assured us that it was no uncommon occurrence for himself and family to be snowed up for weeks together. After refreshing ourselves with beer and wine, we descended into the Murgthal, where we stopped for the night at Forbach.

We were induced to stop here longer than we had originally intended, by the intimation that the *Schwellung* was about to take place, a sight well worth being present at. The next morning a party of us accompanied the Revier Forster along the banks of the Murg to Schwarzenbach, in Wirtemberg, from which place we climbed up a hill, and at length arrived at the sluice-gates. About half a mile of water had been dammed up, covered with timber of every description. Two large wooden gates, somewhat resembling our English lock-gates, confined it at one extremity, about 20 feet above the bed of the stream; so that, on their being opened, the wood and water would gain sufficient impetus to find their way down the mountain into the Murg. As the Revier Forster told us we had better witness the progress of the water from below, we went down the other side of the hill looking towards Forbach, and took up our position on the other side of the stream, beneath some fir-trees, waiting patiently till 11 o'clock, when the gates would be opened. We could see before us about 400 yards up the stream, which, immediately in front of us, rushed beneath a solid stone bridge with a fall of about 15 feet. We heard the pent-up waters long before we could see them, as they bore their crashing burden towards us, till suddenly the first log made its appearance round a projecting rock. In its wake came every description of timber—pine, elm, oak, ash, &c.—all leaping frantically one above the other, and of all dimensions, from the stately tree, which would hereafter find its way to Holland, down to the humble *Brennholz*, about to seek an ignominious fate in a *bourgeois* kitchen. This waterfall of wood lasted about three-quarters of an hour, and we were informed that upwards of 60,000 *Klafter* had been floated down. The *Klafter* is something like what the Americans call a cord of wood—a solid cube of six feet in length by six in breadth. These *Schwellungen* take place twice in the year, and are usually witnessed by a considerable number of persons. It is, in truth, one of the most picturesque of the various methods by which timber is transferred from its native forest to a home on the watery deep.

On our return to Forbach, we started homewards along the Valley of the Murg, the great attraction to visitors at Baden-Baden, on account of the magnificent view to be enjoyed, especially from Schloss Eberstein. The scenery the whole way from Forbach to Obersroth is exquisitely beautiful, the brawling stream making its way through a succession of orchards, prairie, and masses of rocks, while villages in abundance give a charming relief to the picture. Weissenbach is the chief place in the valley before arriving at Gernsbach, and is rendered conspicuous in the view from Eberstein, on account of the Gothic church lately erected there. The path from Obersroth winds through the vineyards which produce that famous wine called Ebersteiner Blut. It may be procured at the *château*—that is to say, the red sort, as the white is exclusively kept for the grand-ducal table. The writer was once fortunately witness of a glorious night illumination which took place here under the auspices of the people of Gernsbach, as a token of gratitude to the grand duke for the establishment of a bailiwick in that town. A procession of 250 persons, each bearing a lighted torch, ascended the path from Obersroth; the bridges of Gernsbach and Weissenbach were brilliantly illuminated; floats bearing huge bonfires descended the stream, while blazing beacons were suddenly kindled on the surrounding hills. The effect was superb in the extreme, and, to enhance the general satisfaction, the grand duke was graciously pleased to express his thanks from the balcony: to which a worthy citizen replied, "Brauch' nit zu danken, Majestät!"

From Eberstein we proceeded along the new road to Baden, formed by the grand duke at a vast expense, and which put his engineering staff on their mettle. On arriving at Lichtenthal, we found a number of tables prepared for us on the *pelouse* before the Gräfshe Bierbranerey, where we sate till a late hour, refreshing ourselves with beer, and telling of the wonders we had seen in foreign parts.

The following extract from the "Stuttgardter Beobachter," done quite literally into English by that eminent hand, the writer, as the old newspaper advertisements would say, served to recall our trip to our memory, when it had almost been forgotten in the weightier political events of the season:

"Information being received at the Royal Police Bureau, that a party of rebels (probably belonging to the band of the God-forgotten Hecker) had crossed our frontier, and sought to enkindle in our peace-loving peasantry a desire for innovation and outbreak against our beloved monarch, the heroic Sergeant Mangelbacher was detached to hold them in check. However, on arriving at the place indicated, it was discovered that the so-called patriots had retired, evidently disconcerted by the fidelity and obedience to the law which our worthy compatriots ever display in the hour of need."

CHAPTER VIII.

A CHAPTER ON GAMBLING.

Very little doubt can be entertained that gambling is rapidly falling from its pristine eminence in the fashionable world: we seldom or never hear of thousands being now lost at a sitting; and those of the present generation can scarcely credit all that is said or written of the doings of their forefathers, or that whole estates were set on the hazard of a game of piquet, as a certain Irish writer veraciously informs us. Railway coupons have usurped the place of the cue and the dice-box, and the greedy passion finds an outlet in Capel Court. We do not for a moment mean to assert that gambling is dying away—the countless betting-lists in town and country furnish a melancholy proof of the widely-extended contagion—but still we do say that its very universality has brought it out of fashion, and that it is not regarded with that indulgence it formerly claimed, but is rather looked upon as the "dernier ressort" of the hard-up man about town.

Such being the case, it may cause our readers some surprise, on referring to the heading of this paper, to find it termed a chapter on gambling. Let them not expect any piquant details of English folly, or a peep behind the scenes of Club life. We have no wish to lay bare the secrets of our own land; and, indeed, too much has already been written on the subject; be it our task to give an account of the doings in foreign countries, and for this purpose we must ask them to accompany us across the Channel.

After the villanous dens in the Palais Royal were rooted out, the proprietors, who found the business much too profitable to be tamely resigned, turned their gaze beyond the Rhine, where a fair field for their exertions in the pursuit of a livelihood presented itself. After many weary negociations with the several governments, a company of banquiers, with M. Chabert at their head, simultaneously opened their establishments at Baden-Baden, Wiesbaden, and Ems. It was a very hard contest between the Regents and the Frenchmen before the terms were finally settled, and they had to expend much money and many promises in getting a footing. But they evidently succeeded, and a few years saw their efforts richly rewarded. As they had a monopoly, they could do pretty much as they pleased, and made very stringent and profitable regulations relative to the "aprés" and other methods of gaining a pull. On the retirement of M. Chabert with an immense fortune, the company was dissolved, and M. Benazet became ostensibly sole proprietor of the rooms at Baden-Baden. The terms to which he had to subscribe were sufficient to frighten any one less enterprising than the general of an army of croupiers: he was compelled to expend 150,000 florins in decorating the rooms and embellishing the walks round the town; and an annual sum of 50,000 florins was further more demanded, for permission to keep the establishment open for six months in the year. The company, which leased Wisbaden and Ems, was treated much in the same manner, but still they progressed most successfully, till they were frightened from their propriety by Monsieur le Blanc. This gentleman, after struggling against immense opposition on the part of the Frankfort merchants, who were naturally alarmed at the danger to which their "commis" and cash-boxes were exposed by the proximity of a gambling-table, obtained a concession from the Elector of Hessen to establish a bank at Homburg-an-der-Höhe, which he speedily promulgated to the world, with the additional attraction of being open all the year round, and only a "trente et un aprés" for the players to contend against. Some time after, Wilhelmsbad was opened as a rival to Homburg, with no "aprés" at all, and the above mentioned, with the addition of Aix-la-Chapelle and Cöthen, form the principal establishments where "strangers are taken in and done for" through Germany.

The games universally played are "rouge et noir" and "roulette," the former also denominated "trente et quarante," though both titles insufficiently explain the tendency of the game, especially as "noir" never has any part or parcel in the affair, all being regulated by "rouge" winning or losing. The appointments are simple in the extreme: a long table, covered with green cloth, divided into alternate squares marked with red and black "carreaux," and two divisions for betting on or against the "couleur," three packs of cards, half a dozen croupiers armed with rakes, and a quantity of rouleaus and smaller coin constituting the whole *matériel.* A croupier commences the pleasing game by dealing a quantity of cards till he arrives at any number above thirty (court-cards counting as ten), when he begins a second row, the first representing "noir," the other "rouge." The "couleur" is determined by the first card turned up. The two great pulls in favour of the bank are, first, the "aprés"—that is, when the two rows amount to the same number, and the croupier calls out "Et trente trois," or any other number "aprés,"—the stakes are impounded, and can only be released by paying half the money down, or else by the same colour winning; and secondly—the chief thing—*the bank never loses its temper.* As a martingale, or continual doubling of the stakes after losing, would infallibly cause a player to win in the end, there is a law in force that no stake can exceed three hundred louis-d'or without the permission of the banque: a permission it very rarely grants, except in extreme cases, as, for instance, at Homburg, when the Belgians so nearly broke the bank; but then it was "conquer or die." The lowest amount allowed to be staked is a two-florin piece. The expression, "V'la banque!" which we so frequently hear quoted, has its origin from this game. After a player has passed, that is, won, on the same colour two or three times consecutively, the croupier, to prevent any possible dispute, asks whether he wishes to risk the whole of the money down; if he intends to do so he employs the above cabalistic formula.

Roulette is a very much more complicated affair; for this, a table is required with a basin in the centre, containing a spiral tube with an orifice at the top, through which the ball passes, and falls into one of the thirty-eight holes in the basin, which are respectively marked with figures, and alternately painted red and black. There are four projecting pieces of iron, one of which the croupier twirls, crying, "Faites votre jeu, messieurs;" when he says, "Le jeu est fait, rien n'va plus," no more money can be put down. In the middle of the table are the numbers, from one to thirty-six, going regularly downwards, in three rows, while at the head of them are the two "zeros"—rouge single and noir double. On either side of the numbers are three divisions; on one hand, marked "rouge, impair et passe," on the other, "noir, pair et manque." Besides these, there are three compartments at the end of the columns, for the purpose of backing the numbers contained in the column; and three others on each side of the numbers, in which to bet on the first, second, or third series of twelve. The odds are regulated in the following fashion. If a player back a single number, he receives thirty-five times the amount of his stake, in the event of its coming up; if he back three at once, he only gets eleven times; if six, only five times the amount. For either of the other compartments he receives, if he gain, the simple amount of his stake, with the exception of the divisions at the end of the columns, and the series of twelve, when he receives double if he win, as the odds are two to one against him. The banque has a most iniquitous advantage in the two zeros, which are calculated to recur once in nineteen times: if the single rouge turn up, they sack all the money, except that placed on the red; if double zero, they take all.

The amount of the stakes at roulette is limited to two hundred louis-d'or on a colour, and six on a single number; the lowest stake allowed is a florin. Though it may be supposed that a run at "trente et quarante" would be a much more likely occurrence than a roulette—and, indeed, we can remember at the former game the "noir" passing two-and-twenty times, though no one had the courage to take advantage of such an extraordinary circumstance—yet it is a very frequent thing at roulette for the ball to have a predilection for a certain series of numbers—probably through the croupier twisting the machine with the same force each time—and on such occasions a good deal of money may be won by a careful observer. One young Englishman, who was perfectly ignorant of the game, we saw at Wisbaden place a five-franc piece on the last series of twelve, and he left his money down six times, winning double the amount of his stake every turn. He then discovered the money was his, by the croupier asking him if he wished to stand on the whole sum; but he never gave the banque another chance, for he picked it up, and quickly went off with it.

Every player at roulette seems to have a different system: some powder the numbers with florins or five-franc pieces, in the hope of one coming up out of them; others speculate merely on the rouge or noir. One Spaniard at Ems, we remember, made a very comfortable living at it by a method of playing he had invented. He placed three louis-d'or on the manque, which contains all the numbers to eighteen, and two louis on the last series of twelve; that is, from twenty-four to thirty-six. Thus he had only six numbers and two zeros against him. If manque gained, he won three louis and lost two; if a number in the last twelve came up, he won four and lost three; but a continuation of zeros would have ruined his calculation. Some, again, back the run, others play against it; a very favourite scheme, and one generally successful, being to bet against a colour after it has passed three times: but then, again, there is no law on the subject, and a man may lose heavily in spite of the utmost caution. In short, the best plan by far would be, if play one must, to stick to "rouge et noir," which bears some semblance of fairness.

The *habitués* of the rooms are well known to the croupiers. At Baden-Baden we had for many years the old ex-Elector of Hesse, who made his money by selling his soldiers to England at so much a head, like cattle, during the American war, and who was easily to be recognized by the gold-headed and coroneted rake he always had in his hand. He was, indeed, a most profitable customer to Monsieur Benazet. But, alas! the superior attractions of Homburg led him away, and we never saw him again in Baden: the revolution of 1848 frightened, or angered, him to death. Wiesbaden boasts of a banker from Amsterdam, who usually plays on credit—that is to say, he pockets his winnings, but, if he loses, borrows money of the banquier, squaring his account, which is generally a heavy one, at the end of the week; and an English baronet, who always brings a lozenge box with him, which, when he has filled, he retires with; and this he frequently contrives to accomplish, for he possesses his own luck, and that of some one else in the bargain. Ems is the principal resort of Russians, who play fearfully high, and a good deal of private gambling is done there on the quiet; while

Aix-la-Chapelle appears only destined as a trap for incautious travellers, many of whom, in consequence, never see the Rhine, and return to England with very misty ideas about Germany.

Aix-la-Chapelle will never be erased from our memory, on account of a most ludicrous scene which happened on our first visit to Germany. Being unacquainted with German at the time, and our French being of the sort which Chaucer calls "French of Bow," we had selected one of our party, who boasted of his knowledge of most foreign tongues, and installed him as "Dolmetcher." His first experiment was in ordering supper, which he proceeded to do in something he was pleased to call German.

"Plait-il, M'nsieu?" said the waiter.

The order was repeated.

"Would you have the kindness to spik Angleesh?" remarked the garçon.

Though this raised some doubts in our minds as to our friend's capacity, yet one of our party, feeling indisposed, invoked his intercession for the sake of procuring some Seidlitz powders. However, in his indignation, he refused to have anything to do with it. In this dilemma, the sick man called in the English-conversing waiter to his aid, who readily offered to help him, and soon returned with a bottle of Seidlitz *water*, which he persuaded our unwary friend to make trial of. Now this water happens to be the strongest of all the mineral springs in Germany, and the consequence was, the poor young man became very shortly alarmingly unwell. In his anxiety, he fancied himself poisoned, and summoned the waiter once more. On his reappearance, he compelled him to finish the whole of the bottle, which contained nearly a quart, to prove it was not of a dangerous nature; but, in point of fact, he proved it to be so by nearly killing the wretched garçon.

The company to be seen round the table consists usually of Russians and French, both male and female, with a sprinkling of Germans, who escape from their own police in order to satisfy their itching for play. Thus, for instance, we have Nassau and Darmstadt people at Baden-Baden, while the Badese and Suabes rush to Homburg and Wiesbaden. There is a very salutary law in every land where gambling is permitted, that no inhabitant of that land be allowed to play at the public table, and if any one is caught red-handed, he is usually imprisoned, and his winnings, if any, confiscated. We can call to mind a laughable instance of this at Wisbaden. Two old peasants, who had probably come for a day's pleasure and to see the sights, managed to find their way into the Kursaal, and stood all entranced before the roulette-table. One of them, imagining it a right royal way of making money, and much better fun than ploughing, lugged out his leathern purse and began by staking a modest florin on the rouge. In the course of about half an hour he had contrived to win a very decent sum, and was walking away in great glee, when a gendarme, who had been watching him all the while, quietly collared him, and dragged him off to the Polizei, where, as we afterwards learned, he was incarcerated for three weeks, and his "addlings" employed for the good of the state.

It may naturally be supposed that the presence of so much circulating medium in one place, and the *prestige* attaching to the banquier's coffers, which are currently supposed to contain a sum

> "More precious far
> Than that accumulated store of wealth
> And orient gems, which, for a day of need,
> The sultan hides in his ancestral tombs,"

would induce many depredators to make an attempt on them, but we generally find that cunning is much more in favour than any open attack. Thus, for instance, Monsieur le Blanc, who, we may add, has been more assailed than any other banquier, was nearly made the victim of a stratagem, which might have entailed serious results. A fellow contrived to get into the "Conversations Haus" by night, and blocked up all the low numbers in the roulette machine in such a manner that the ball, on falling in, must inevitably leap out again. On the next day he and his accomplices played and netted a large sum by backing the high numbers. They carried on the game for two or three days, but were fortunately overheard by a detective while quarrelling about the division of their plunder, in the gardens behind the establishment. They were arrested, and the money recovered. A very dangerous design was also formed against him by one of his croupiers, who, being discontented with his lot, determined to make his fortune at one *coup*: and the plan he contrived was this. He procured a pack of pre-arranged cards, which he concealed in his hat, and when it came to his turn to deal he intended to drop the bank cards into his *chapeau* and cleverly substitute the others; but this artfully-concocted scheme was disconcerted by one of his confederates considering he might make a better and safer thing of it by telling Le Blanc beforehand. His most imminent peril, and the occasion when his very existence as a banquier was at stake, was the affair with the Belgian company, of which Thackeray has given us such a detailed account in his "Kickleburys up the Rhine."

The "proprietaires," besides, suffer considerable losses by the dishonesty of the croupiers; for, although there is a person expressly employed to watch them, who sits in a high-backed chair behind the dealer, yet they are such practised escamoteurs, that they will secrete a piece of gold without his seeing it. One fellow was detected at Baden-Baden, who had carried on a system of plunder for a long time with security. He used to slip a louis-d'or into his snuff-box whenever it came to his turn to preside over the money department; he was found out by another *employé* asking him casually for a pinch of snuff, and seeing the money gleam in the gas-light. These croupiers are the most extraordinary race of men it is possible to conceive. They seem to unite the stoicism of the American Indian to the politeness of the Frenchman of the *ancien régime*. They are never seen to smile, and wear the same impassive countenance whether the banque is gaining or losing. In fact, what do they care as long as their salary is regularly paid? They seem to fear neither God nor man: for when a shock of the earthquake was felt at Wiesbaden in 1847, though all the company fled in terror, they remained grimly at their posts, preferring to go down to their patron saints with their rouleaux, as an evidence of their fidelity to their employer. Perhaps, though, they regarded the earthquake as a preconcerted scheme to rob the banque, the only danger they are apprehensive of. You may beat them, and yet they smite not again; for when a young Englishman, of high repute and bearing an honourable name, vented his rage at losing by breaking a rake at Baden-Baden over the croupier's head, he merely turned round and beckoned to the attendant gendarme to remove him and the pieces, and then went on with his parrot-like "rouge gagne—couleur perd."

The most amusing thing to any philosophical frequenter of the rooms, is to see the sudden gyrations of fortune's wheel. One gentleman at Baden-Baden, a Russian, was so elated after an unparalleled run of good fortune, that he went out and ordered a glorious feed for himself and friends at the restauration; but during the interval, while dinner was preparing, he thought he would go back and win a little more. His good fortune, however, had deserted him, and he lost not only all his winnings, but every florin he was possessed of, so he was compelled to countermand the dinner. On the arrival of his remittances, determined not to be baulked of his repast this time by want of funds, he paid for a spread for twelve beforehand; but his luck was very bad, and he actually went back to the restaurateur, and, after some negociation, sold him the dinner back at half-price. The money he received was, of course, very speedily lost. Another, a student of Heidelberg, won at a sitting 970 florins, but disdaining to retire without a round thousand, he tempted fortune too long, and lost it all back, as well as his own money. The most absurd thing was, that not having any friends in Baden, he was driven to return "per pedes" to his university, a distance of more than 100 miles. It is a very rare occurrence for the banque to be broken, though the newspapers state that such a thing happened three times at Baden-Baden during the present season, —a statement which we are inclined to place in the same category with the wonderful showers of frogs and gigantic cabbages which happen so opportunely to fill any vacant corner. When, however, it really takes place, the rooms are only closed for an hour or two, and the play soon commences again.

The most painful incident is, the frequency of suicides during the season, any account of which Monsieur Benazet, for obvious reasons, prevents reaching the public. When anything of the sort occurs, the place most commonly selected for the tragedy is a summer-house a little way out of the town, on the road to the Alt Scholl, whence the poor victim can take a last lingering look on the scene of his ruin. One young man, in our time, attempted to blow out his brains at the roulette-table, but was fortunately prevented, and a fortnight's detention in the House of Correction very much cooled his ardour for making a "dem'd disgusting body" of himself. Indeed, it has ever been a passion with your Frenchmen to cause a scene when dying: they would not give a "thank you" to cut their throats in private.

On the 31st of October, the day on which the rooms close for the season, an immense quantity of players throng to the Kursaal; for though they have withstood temptation for so long a time, they cannot possibly suffer the season to go past without making one trial. On the 1st of November, those birds of ill-omen, the croupiers, set out to hybernate in Paris, and the rooms are closed, not to be re-opened till the 1st of May.

It has long been a question most difficult of decision whether, leaving morality entirely out of sight, the watering-places of Germany are benefited or injured by the continuance of gambling. We are inclined to the latter opinion, for, though it may be said that it brings a deal of money into circulation, yet your true gambler is a most unsocial and inhospitable fellow, and one of the worst visitors an hotel-keeper can have. Besides encouraging, as they do, all the riffraff of Europe to pay periodical visits to Germany, they thereby prevent many respectable persons from settling in that country; for any wife or mother who has the interests of her family at heart, would fly from a place where gambling is allowed, as from a pest-house. At the same time, a very lax tone prevails in these towns, and every finer feeling is blunted—in many cases irreparably—by constant association with hard-hearted, callous, and unscrupulous gamblers. That this was a view taken by the more enlightened of the Germans, is proved by the fact that the parliament of Frankfort decided on the abolition of all gambling-houses by a considerable majority, but unfortunately there was no time to carry such a salutary measure into effect. Had it been otherwise, the Regents in all probability would, through very shame, have hesitated in giving their assent to the re-establishment of such a crying evil.

CHAPTER IX.

A PLEASANT NIGHT OF IT!

What a very happy period of my life that was when I was supposed to be studying Roman law at the feet of the great Professor Mittermaier, at Heidelberg. Little did my fond parents reck the way in which I spent my nights, or the mad scenes in which I, a respectable British citizen, was a sharer among the feather-brained Burschen. I had only recently quitted Oxford, after four years of college experience and forgetfulness of what I had learned at school, and the contrast a German university presented was most striking. Still I took to the new mode of life very kindly, and by the time I was enabled to express my wants and wishes in fearfully broken German, I was perfectly happy, for life is so pleasant at twenty!

Perhaps, though, I enjoyed my vacations even more than I did my terms, for I was my own master, and could wander whither I pleased. I had a Foreign-office passport in my pocket, and a respectable amount of florins, and with knapsack on back I trudged through the whole of the Black Forest, learning German (of a sort, it is true) rapidly on the road, and meeting with various queer adventures. One of the queerest, however, that befell me was in the Vosges, and I may as well narrate it here, as another instance of those strange things which travellers sometimes see. I had ever a predilection for Alsace, for in that happy land the quart bottle holds not merely a quart, which is a rarity, but just three pints, which is a marvel. Nor is the quality of the wine depreciated by the quantity: on the contrary, Chablis is not a patch (to use a chaste Americanism) upon the white wines that grow on the sunny slopes of the Vosges. "If you doubt what I say, take a bumper and try;" which you can easily do, reader, on your next visit to Strasburg, by calling in at the Rebstock, and asking for a *litre* of white wine with the ochre seal. However, as I knew that I was going into the country where the delectable wine grew, I did not dally at Strasburg, but strode manfully away towards the Vosges, full of glorious anticipations, and carefully studying the patois by conversing with every peasant I fell in with. There is a very simple plan, however, to make yourself comprehended in Alsace: always use a French word and a German word alternately; it is wonderful what success you meet with. An infallible rule to make yourself liked is by lugging in the name of Napoléon le Grand on every possible occasion, and if you are sufficiently cosmopolitan, you may tacitly assent to the fact that he won the battle of Waterloo. Thank Heavens, there are very few Englishmen who would be disposed to grant that fact! However, I throw out the hint as useful to the members of the Peace Society, who seem so fond of evincing their pacific tendencies by depreciating the value of our army, to the augmented glory of foreign powers.

There is only one defect connected with Alsace: when it rains there, there is no mistake about it. I really believe the Vosges are superior even to Plymouth in the annual rainfall. I was fated to discover this interesting meteorological fact at the expense of a thorough wetting. I had dined at a little village inn on the inevitable cold veal and pickled plums, when I set out on my jaunt to my night's quarters, seventeen miles off. The clouds were beginning to collect ominously in the west. I buttoned my blouse round me and trudged manfully onwards along a road which had not been traversed by a respectable conveyance within the memory of man. It was full of ruts, hard enough at first, but which the persistent rain, which had commenced by this time to fall, converted into so many pitfalls, into which I was continually slipping. To add to my troubles, night set in with that rapidity peculiar to Southern Germany, and there was no sign of the village at which I intended to spend the night. Not a creature did I meet: nobody was foolish enough to venture out in such weather, save pleasure travellers like myself, and on I went, making about half a mile an hour, and growing very savage: whether the result of the wetting, or of indigestion, I really cannot say. My brandy-flask had long been emptied: there was no chance of filling it, and I was wearied—so wearied that I could have lain down to sleep in a dry ditch, had there been one handy; but against that the elements had carefully guarded. There was no hope for it: I must trudge onwards.

Suddenly, through the rain, I fancied I could see a light glimmering a short distance from the road. I stopped, and looked steadily; it was no Will-o'-the-wisp, and by a sudden impulse I bounded over the low hedge, and went stumbling over a ploughed field towards the house, as I now felt certain it was. Up to the present I had regarded the peasants' cabins with considerable aversion, and *pour cause:* they were the dirtiest places imaginable, and I had no desire to sleep in them so long as an *auberge* could be found. But now I would have gladly paid a handsome sum for the use of a dog-kennel, so long as it sheltered me from the pitiless rain, and held out the prospect of a glass of brandy to warm my inner man, which stood so much in need of that refreshment.

I soon approached the cabin, which stood beneath the shade of some gloomy trees, and the light, which probably came from the fire, burned so dimly, that I hesitated for a moment; all appeared so unutterably wretched about the house, that I had a nervous timidity about approaching it. I am not constitutionally fearful; on the contrary, I am usually too prone to run into foolhardiness; but now, whether it was the soaking or the veal, I felt horribly nervous. A moment, however, sufficed to recover me, and I walked across the yard, and knocked boldly at the door. All remained perfectly quiet in the house, except that I fancied I could hear the growling of a huge dog, like distant thunder; then I knocked again somewhat more loudly, and a dog began barking violently. At the same time, however, I had the satisfaction of hearing footsteps approach the door.

"Who is without?" a voice was heard saying, in execrable Jewish-German; "is it you, Benjamin?"

"'Tis a stranger," I shouted, fearing any hesitation might render my friend inside suspicious; "I want shelter for the night, and I will pay you handsomely for it."

"Are you alone?" the voice asked again. "Quiet, Nero! down, dog! what do you mean by growling when I did not order you to watch him?"

"All alone, but as wet as if I had been dipped in the river."

"You'd be clever to keep yourself dry this day," he said, as he pulled back the bolts, and opened the door slowly and cautiously. "Come in—the dog won't hurt you when I'm with you. What weather! Come to the fire, and dry yourself."

He walked in front of me to the fire, stirred up the smouldering wood, and threw a few sticks upon it. All this while I could notice he was taking quick, sharp glances at me; then he went up to my knapsack, which I had laid on a chair, appeared to feel its weight for a moment, and brought it up to the fire to dry as well as myself.

"And you're hungry, too, I suppose? out for pleasure, eh? Young blood! young blood!" and he grinned in a manner to me quite diabolical. He then went to the table, spread a very dirty table-cloth, on which he placed a loaf of black bread, stuck a knife into it, and then produced a large green glass jar, containing the much-desired fluid. After filling an iron saucepan with hot water, and putting it on the wood, he quitted the room for awhile. During his absence I surveyed the room in which I was seated, and the very sight of it made me uncomfortable. It was quite destitute of furniture, contrary to the usual fashion of the peasantry, and I shuddered involuntarily. But, nonsense, it could only be the cold and the moisture the fire was drawing out of my clothes, and yet, for all that, I began to wish I had trudged on through the rain. And then, that immense dog that lay close to the fireplace, and kept its small, suspicious eyes fixed on me! And the walls were shining with grease and soot, and the small cupboards fixed against them, and shelves—But, Heavens, I could hardly suppress a cry of surprise when my eye fell on an old mummy-like woman, who rose from the dark corner where she had probably been sleeping, and walked towards me and the fire. She was a model of ugliness and disgust, this old woman, with her tangled masses of grey hair hanging over her forehead and temples, her sunken cheeks, hollow eyes, and wrinkled neck, as she stood there shivering with cold, and stretched out her thin bony hands to the fire. I fell back a step to give the old creature room, but on my first attempt to quit the chimney-place the dog growled, and, as I turned towards him, his eyes sparkled so vividly that I thought it advisable to stay where I was, and not anger him unnecessarily. The woman now turned her face to me, and after gazing fixedly at me for a moment, whispered a few hurried words in a language of which I did not understand a syllable.

"What a pity," I thought to myself, "I did not go in for the Pusey and Ellerton Scholarship when at Oxford, so that I might have understood a little Hebrew." I then looked carefully at the old woman, trying to find out from her gestures what she really meant. Again she began her whispering, turning her head timidly towards the door, and pointing at the same time to the table.

"I can't understand you!" I said, in the usual patois, hoping she would understand me, at any rate.

"Hush!" the crone said, quickly and fearfully, holding up her finger in warning; at this moment the door opened, and the Jew, on seeing the old woman by my side, went up angrily to her, and spoke harshly in the same unknown tongue. The woman crept timidly away, wrapped herself more closely in her old cloak, and lay down again in her corner. The Jew then said, pleasantly enough, to me,

"Don't bother about the old gal; she is quiet and harmless, but not quite right here," he said, pointing to his forehead. "When we're alone, I let her do much as she likes, but when strangers visit me, which is seldom enough, she must keep in her corner. But here," he added, in a louder voice, "is something for you to eat—bread and Münster cheese I lately brought from Strasbourg, and a famous glass of brandy which will do you more good, I fancy, than all the rest; the water will be hot by this time. Ah, I see it's boiling, and I'll mix you a glass of punch in the meanwhile. So, now, go to the table and begin."

I was really almost starving, and yet I could not swallow anything. That confounded dog had his eyes still fixed so dangerously upon me.

"The dog won't hurt you," said the Jew, calmly; "he is only not accustomed to strangers."

"But if I'd stirred while you were out of the room he would have sprung at me," I said, rather angrily.

"It's an old dog," the man continued, with a smile, "and hasn't a tooth left in his head, but he often pretends to be savage. The time is long past since he bit any one, and you can go up and pat him, and he won't say a word."

However, I did not feel the slightest inclination to try the experiment; I therefore proceeded to the table and cut a hunch of bread and cheese, while the old Jew stooped down to the fire, and after shaking something out of a paper into the glass, poured the water upon it.

"There!" he said, as he came to the table, "now put in as much brandy as you like, but the stiffer the better, for it will keep you from catching cold."

"What have you put in the glass, my friend?" I asked, as I held the glass to the fire.

"Sugar and water; the sugar is good, and takes off the strength of the brandy."

"I'm not fond of sugar," I replied, suspiciously; "and, if you've no objection, I'll mix it for myself."

"Not like sugar! why it's the best part of it," said the Jew; "only taste it, and you'll soon see how good it is."

However, I persisted in throwing the mixture away, and, after carefully washing the glass out, I filled it afresh with water, and poured in some brandy.

"More, my friend—more," the Jew advised me; "that's not half enough, and won't draw the cold out of your limbs. Why, my old woman will drink stronger punch if I give it to her."

"Thanks, thanks!" I said, as I turned away the bottle, from which the Jew persisted in pouring more into my glass. "I'm not accustomed to strong drinks, and shall have a headache to-morrow morning."

"Oh! to-morrow! I'll guarantee you against that," the old man laughed to himself; "the brandy is capital, and no one has a headache from it."

I really felt such a shiver come over me at these words (though, of course, I ascribed it to my wet clothes), and the brandy really tasted so good, that I took up the glass and emptied it at a draught. By Jupiter! how it burned!

"And now you had better lie down," the Jew said, after removing the brandy and the other things from the table; "it is late in the night, and, after your sleeping draught, you will sleep sound in spite of your hard bed. The best place for you will be here by the fire. Before we go to bed I'll put on some fresh wood, and by the time that is burnt out you'll be warm enough. The nights are beginning to grow fresh."

I was glad enough to lie down, so I took up my knapsack, which had dried a little by this time, to serve as a pillow, and the old man brought me a blanket and a sheepskin, regretting that he had nothing better to offer me, but all his beds were occupied. "But I'll bring you something to keep your feet warm," he added, "that's the chief thing, and by the morning you'll be all right again." With these words he took a canvas sack, which appeared to me to be ominously stained, from the chimney-nook, and then bringing it to my feet (for I had lain down by this time), requested me to put them in it.

"In the sack?" I said, in amazement—"why?"

"Oh! you'll see how warm that will keep your feet."

"No, I'd rather lay it over them; that will answer the same purpose."

"Not half so good, I tell you," the old man continued, and tried to draw the sack over my feet, but I strenuously resisted. There was something so dangerous, in my opinion, in knowing my feet were in a sack, which I could not easily remove in the dark, if I were obliged to spring up in a hurry. If——? Besides, the old fellow's pressing made me feel uncommon uncomfortable (I may tell you so in strict confidence). What on earth reason could he have for insisting on my putting my feet in the sack? However, when the Jew found that I was obstinate, he laid the sack over my feet, and went back to the fire instead of retiring to bed as I had expected, and sat cross-legged, staring fixedly into the flame. Well, I shut my eyes and tried to go to sleep, but somehow I could not manage it; the fire burned low, and I could see the old fellow still sitting there, but I *felt* that his eyes were fixed upon me, and that he was watching my every movement, every breath. Why? I lay thus for half an hour, and the strangest feelings came over me. Then I had a curious taste in my mouth—the brandy, of course, but why was it so metallic? And my head began to go round, and my eyelids grew heavy as lead. At last, I could stand it no longer, and determined to jump up, but I was unable to do so; my limbs refused me their service, a veil seemed to be let down over my eyes, and I felt that a deep, irresistible sleep was overpowering me.

How long I lay in this sort of half dreaming condition I do not know, although I struggled against this unnatural state with all the strength of my mind, and I should finally have yielded to it, had not a slight sound just at the right moment come to my aid in resisting it. The Jew, who was still seated at the fire, moved—gently and noiselessly, it is true; still he got up, and now stood with his face turned towards me. I tried to close my eyes, and dispel the odious vision which my fancy seemed to summon up, but at that moment I felt the light, crawling steps of the old man on the floor, felt that he was drawing nearer and nearer, and when I half opened my eyes, cautiously enough lest the scowling fellow might see I was awake, I saw him standing a few paces from me, with his body half bent to listen, and watching my every breath. What was he about?—what did he want? Should I jump up and meet him, in case he attempted to attack me?—but then the dog, which was still lying in the room? And, again, was the Jew really going to attack me, or might it not be anxiety whether I slept comfortably? I determined to wait and judge for myself, even at the risk of exposing myself to his attack, for I was young and strong, and if the old man designed evil he should meet with a resistance he little anticipated. So, in order to leave the old man at leisure to carry out his designs, whatever they might be, I began breathing loudly and regularly, while watching him carefully through my half-closed eyelids.

The Jew remained for a while observing me, as if to make sure that my sleep was real; but then, as if every doubt were removed, he crept quietly back to the chimney, threw some brushwood on the glimmering charcoal, which began to glisten and crackle, and went to the opposite end of the room, where the crockery was kept. Anxiously I watched him; but I must confess that my blood appeared to stagnate, and an icy feeling ran down my back, when I saw him take up a long gleaming knife, and while trying its edge with his thumb, seem to measure the distance between himself and his victim.

As I have told you before, I believe I am anything but a coward: I have stood behind a four-foot barricade, and looked into the gaping muzzles of the cannon as they poured a shower of bullets on our slight defences, but I am bound to say that the present was the most uncomfortable moment in my life. The calculating villany of the old scoundrel, and the simplicity with which I had entered the snare, seemed to render escape almost impossible. Still I made up my mind to sell my life as dearly as possible. Fortunately I had in my pocket a Spanish spring-back stiletto, generally employed in the peaceful duties of cutting bread and cheese—German and French knives being made, like Peter Pindar's razors, to sell, and not to cut—and I cautiously moved my hand to my breast-pocket, and noiselessly drew it out. When I once held it in my hand, my confidence returned to me. I opened it very quietly, and then, laying my left arm across my breast, to parry the first blow, which would probably be aimed there, I held my knife firmly clutched in my hand, and awaited the attack with ground teeth, but no failing determination. My heart, though, *would* beat so loudly and violently, that I feared the Jew must hear it; but when I saw him approaching, with the knife cautiously held behind his back—when I felt his foot against my own—when he bent over me, and felt along the wall with his left hand, to find a spot on which to rest it and give his blow more certainty, my fears entirely disappeared. It is a well-known fact that danger really exists only so long as it threatens us, and is robbed of more than half its terrors when it breaks over us with undiminished force. This was just my case. I had felt terrified, and could hardly struggle against the feeling, so long as the danger was drawing nearer and nearer to me, but every thought save that of self-defence disappeared when I knew that the knife was directed against my heart. So soon as he struck at me, I determined to parry the blow by means of the left arm, and the blanket lying over it would afford me great protection; but then I would start up and bury my knife in the villain's ribs, before he could recover from his surprise or summon the dog. I should soon be able to overcome the weak old man, and as for the brute, once on my legs, I dare say I could keep him from doing me an injury.

Such was my line of thought, and I was quite prepared to carry it into effect. But why did the Jew hesitate so long? He had advanced his left foot a little, his arm was still supported against the wall, yet he did not raise his other arm to strike the blow. Was he afraid? I bit my teeth more closely together, and almost longed for the decisive moment to come, so excited did I feel—anything, sooner than endure this horrible suspense. Suddenly, the Jew drew back; he did not strike at me—his left arm quitted the wall, and he held in it—I hardly knew whether I was awake or dreaming

—the same loaf from which I had previously been eating. He walked with it to the fire, cut off a hunch with the fearful long knife, laid the remainder on the chimney-board, and, after poking up the wood fire till it threw a brilliant light over the room, he began quietly eating, without troubling himself any further about my presence.

I drew a deep breath—it was as if a large stone had been rolled off my chest—and I lay for a long while in a sort of dreamy condition, hardly able to realize this state of perfect security following closely on the danger which I had fancied so shortly before had menaced me. I really began to feel ashamed of the cruel injustice I had done—though only in thought—to a man who had so hospitably entertained me; and I almost felt inclined to jump up and tell him of my foolish suspicions. But no, that would not do—he would laugh at me; still I felt I must do something, if only to reconcile my own conscience. I, therefore, shut up my knife as quietly as possible, returned it to my pocket, and then, pretending to wake from a deep sleep, I threw off the blanket, took the sack, and put my feet quietly into it.

"Aha!" chuckled my host, who, on hearing my movement, turned his head quietly towards me, "one's feet generally get cold of nights, if they have been wet during the day; but the sack will keep them warm enough."

"I think so, too. I fancy it will be better so," I replied; then fell back on my somewhat hard pillow, drew the blanket up to my chin, and in a few seconds had fallen into a deep and sweet sleep. When I woke the next morning I found that the sun was high in the heavens, and on the table a comfortable breakfast had been laid. A pretty little girl was tidying the room, and her presence really rendered it quite cheerful.

"So, sir," she said, good-humouredly, "you are awake at last. Uncle did not like to disturb you. I am sorry, though, you had no better bed than this, but I only came home last night from Strasbourg on a visit, and we had all gone to bed for the night."

The old Jew now came in and gave me a hearty welcome. I hardly had the heart to look him in the face. I was then forced to sit down to the breakfast-table, at which the old man's son, a fine young fellow of twenty-four, joined us. Hearing from him that he was going back with his light cart to Strasbourg that morning, I willingly accepted his offer of accompanying him. I had had quite enough of adventures for this bout, and, besides, sundry rheumatic twinges told me that I ought not to venture away so far from civilization, lest I might be laid on my back in a rustic village, and my mourning relatives never learn where they should set up a cenotaph to my memory.

When the light cart came up to the door, I inquired what I had to pay; but the old Jew could not be induced to accept a farthing for the accommodation. Bed and breakfast, he said, had both been poor enough; and I shook his hand heartily upon leaving him. And, upon my honour, in the bright sunshine, he wasn't half such a bad-looking old fellow. There was something quite patriarchal about him.

Now, I dare say, you'll all laugh very heartily at my story, and fancy I must have been a great cur to let myself be frightened by an old man; but really, even now in writing it, I have had an uncomfortable feeling crawl over me at the reminiscence. It's a good many years since it happened, and there's not much prospect of my having any more adventures of that or a similar nature; and, between ourselves—in strict confidence, mind—I prefer making "a pleasant night of it," with Smith, and Jones, and Thompson, after a very different fashion.

CHAPTER X.

SCORING THE KING.

WHO of my readers has not visited Mayence the Golden? Where is the man with soul so dead who cannot to himself have said that he has drunk Rüdesheimer at the fountain-head? And, of truth, Mayence deserves its name of Golden were it only for the sparkling wine which is pressed out in the vicinity beneath the clumsy boots of the peasants. Golden Mayence! What vinous visions float across my brain, as I revel over my modest pint of porter, of thy stores of liquid amber, in which I have heretofore imbibed more than my fill, and could proudly smile at all notions of matutinal headache.

It is not generally known to the cursory traveller that, if he would visit Mayence aright, he must visit it after passing through the hot-water ordeal of Wiesbaden. If ever a man sincerely wishes himself at the antipodes, it must be when the cruel fates force him to a compulsory stay in that capital of Nassau during the summer months. I have read, in an interesting work called, I believe, "Sandford and Merton," that bears are taught to dance by making them hop on plates of iron gradually warmed beneath their feet. Wiesbaden should be the head-quarters of this trade, for the streets are positively boiling hot with the water running away beneath the pavement. You try every possible experiment against the disturber of your rest; you wear heavy boots and lame yourself; then you try thin ones and blister your feet; then you swear savagely that you will confine yourself to your room, and are eaten alive by mosquitoes; in despair you rush to the Kursaal, and are devoured by croupiers; in short, do what you will at Wiesbaden, you are a victim to miseries of every genus.

But, given that you are the most stolid of Britons, and insist, on the Mark Tapley principle, upon being jolly under whatever circumstances may turn up, I defy you to be unhipped after a week's stay at Wiesbaden. That eternal *Platte* stares you in the face, with its whitewashed tawdry front, whenever you take your walks abroad. Before long it becomes your moral nightmare; it enters into frightful combinations in your dreams; you swallow it with your first spoonful of soup, and it reappears with your last glass of Liebfrauenmilch. Go where you will, that whitewashed sepulchre haunts you; and at last, in despair, you determine to beard the lion in his den. Of course it is the hottest of summer days when you set about your terrible resolve; you pant up the hill past the weeping oak (which looks wonderfully as if some nest-robbing boys had broken down the branches); you pass the duchess's mausoleum, all blazing with (mock) jewels and gold; you fraternize with sundry stags, who playfully display their affection by butting at you, and forcing you to take shelter behind the nearest tree; for though you know what horse-play may be, you are dubious as to the results of stagging—unless you were a railroad director in 1846. At length you reach the summit of the hill and the Platte. You need not expect any refreshment after your walk, for hospitality is not the forte of German princes, but you pass through a suite of rooms in which the furniture is made of staghorn, and you scale the roof of the house to enjoy a magnificent view, over the tops of the trees, of nothing. Mournfully you wander homewards; you ponder as you go on the nothingness of human wishes, and the strong affinity between the German princes and the Platte; very distinguished objects both, when seen at a distance, but on nearer approach proved to be lacquered shams, the poorest windbags, which deserve an annihilating prick from the point of the Carlylean Gillott. But, heavenly powers! I am talking the most arrant treason, forgetting to tell you the while all about scoring the king.

You must know, then, that in the year 18—, I won't tell you when, for I am arriving at that period of life when my age is becoming a mystery to my dearest friends, I was sent by my anxious governor to study German, after wearing out my brains at Latin and Greek. I, Brown, proceeded to Wiesbaden, because it contained a large proportion of English, and I could there display my Britannic airs without running any risk of being kicked. While residing there, I formed the acquaintance of Jones and Robinson, which soon ripened into an intimacy. After enjoying the delights of Wiesbaden, such as it has to offer, and losing a whole year's allowance at the table (which the govenor repaid honourably, under the impression that the money had gone in German tutors, and several artful presents I had procured on account, and sent home as specimens of native manufacture), I began to find Wiesbaden more than slow. At the end of the week it became positively unendurable, for swarms of Frankfurt Hebrews came over to spend the "Shabbes." Hence the triumvirate established it as a rule to evacuate Wiesbaden on a Friday morning, and not return till Tuesday, unless a refreshing shower of rain had washed away the Semitic taint during the night of Sunday. Ah me! youth is impertinent! Since that happy period I have been only too glad to dine with a Hebrew, especially if I had a little bill which I wanted him to discount.

Our principal refuge from the Jewish invasions was Mayence, because in those days the *Anlagen* on a Friday afternoon presented the fairest assemblage of women, and the finest music to be found anywhere on the Continent. I've journeyed over many lands, and many a clime I've seen, but never yet have I found such a combination of beauty and intellect as that presented by the public gardens of Mayence any Friday afternoon prior to the revolution. As for the women, *cela va sans dire* that any Chiswick meeting would display a finer growth of feminine roses and tulips than ever yet was seen in Germany; but on the other hand, the band was sublime. Imagine one hundred and sixteen Austrian musicians, every one fit to perform the onerous duties of *maître de chapelle,* playing the finest opera music in the open air! There is a fine classical German song called "Strauss in Olympus," which pays due honour to the German taste for music, but I fancy that orchestra at Mayence surpassed anything the *dii majores* could have executed. The mere fact of the revolution of 1848 having broken up that magnificent band was enough to convert me into the most ultra aristrocrat.

To the observer, these Mayence gardens afforded much instruction and amusement. Here you might see Lord Polyanthus in his own hair (for had he not paid for it at Trufitt's), ogling the fat and rather greasy German Frauleins, and fancying he had made an impression on their susceptible hearts, when all the while they were merely smiling at the thought of the *sauermilch,* which would form their vespertinal repast. There, too, might be noticed the Vicomte de la Cruchecassée scowling on the Prussian officers, and fancying himself engaged on the plains of Germany, and defeating the *Pru-chiens* and *les autres chiens.* Or, again, the Count of Zobelwitz, a distinguished Pole, with a fatal facility for English, would accost you, and after giving a general and particular account of the wrongs of Poland, would end by asking a donation of five francs on behalf of his oppressed brethren. You gave it, feeling all the time that you were being swindled; but then how could you, as a Briton, refuse so slight a mark of esteem to the red ribbon of the Legion of Honour, or the green distinguishing mark of the St Vladimir. When you had got rid of your Pole you could afford to smile at the tightly-laced, swaggering Austrian officers, as they lounged along, striking their sabres against every chair and table, and evidently fancying that the world was too narrow for a *roturier* to come between the wind and their nobility. Then, again, you would become lost in admiration of some Mr John Bull, out from home for the first time, and whose cup of coffee was evidently embittered by the thought whether Thomas had met the bill which was due that morning. Bless the English! no nation in the world can so perfectly carry its home with it; I verily believe that my commercial countrymen are truly unhappy when they go abroad; and yet they behave like the Spartan, who suffered the fox to gnaw his entrails sooner than betray his secret. I am only afraid that the *primum mobile* in both cases may be the fear of detection.

I have already mentioned the Vicomte de la Cruchecassée in this veritable history, and as he is the great individual of my story I will safely lodge him at once within the comfortable walls of the Katzenellenbogen Hôtel, where we always put up. On the eventful night of my domestic drama, we had dined—that is to say, the English reason had been sapped by sundry extra bottles of wine we had drunk. Hence we condescended to talk with the vicomte, and soon found him a most agreeable companion. Nor were we averse, such was our thirst for liquor, to initiate him into the mysteries of the "odd man out" for sundry bottles of champagne. After various interludes of fortune, and the emptying of some dozen of bottles, it was found that the vicomte was let in for the whole. In our British generosity, we could not stand this; and feeling morally convinced that no Frenchman's purse could survive the payment of fifteen or sixteen bottles of champagne, we proposed to pass it off as a joke; but to this our Frenchman would not consent. He insisted on paying the amount, and some additional compliments to ourselves, for our affability of manners and extreme courtesy, so different from the usual caste of

"Angleish," as he affectionately termed us. Of course we would not stand this, and, by some extraordinary fluke, it was proposed that we should play a quiet game of écarté, to give the Frenchman his revenge.

Now, the last words my respected governor addressed to me on the pier at Blackwall were, "Whatever follies you commit, never play écarté with a stranger—above all, with a Frenchman—or else you will come home not merely fleeced, but without your skin." Now the governor's advice had been bought dearly, I knew, so I set a proper value upon it, and declined the party. Jones and Robinson, rather more intoxicated than myself, if that were possible, sat down to play *poule* with the stranger, while I looked on. For a time the stakes were moderate enough, limited to five francs, and no one was a loser. At length my friends, tired of the monotony, proposed an augmentation, to which the vicomte assented. They played on with varying success until the stakes grew alarming, reaching five louis generally, and at the same time luck veered round to the Frenchman. Jones and Robinson, let them play all they knew, could not win a single pool. The matter was becoming serious, for they had already borrowed twenty pounds of myself, and yet their luck did not appear to turn. The stakes were increased, and at length Robinson retired from the table utterly rooked, while Jones continued his game. During this time, I must not forget to mention all of us had been drinking heavily, although the want of excitement had kept me more sober than the rest. On the contrary, I began to grow misanthropical and philosophical at the same time, and during my reverie

I kept my eyes unconsciously fixed on the Frenchman. The game was four to three, and the vicomte's deal. There, I thought, is a true emblem of hope. Jones fancies he will gain a vole, the Frenchman hopes he will turn up a king and end the game; and, by Jove! so he did, but from the bottom of the pack instead of the top. I could scarcely believe my eyes; and I only fancy the extra amount of wine the Frenchman had imbibed rendered him so clumsy that he was detected. At any rate, I did not dare speak, but I watched every movement closely. The next game was much the same, except that the Frenchman, confident in the drunkenness of his adversary, turned up the king twice. At length, in the third game, I had opportunity for interfering. They stood at four all, and the Frenchman deliberately drew the king from the bottom of the pack. Flesh and blood of an Englishman could stand no more of this, and I rushed forward to seize the vicomte's hand, exclaiming:

"Jones, my boy, the Frenchman's cheating you like mad!"

"Is he, by Heavens! I trust to you! Here's at him!"

With these words he seized an empty champagne bottle by the neck (he had sense enough left to choose an empty one) and hurled it at the Frenchman's head. Owing to his drunkenness, he missed his shot, but followed it up by a heavy right-hander, which floored his man, to use a classical expression, as flat as a tesselated pavement. Up sprang the Frenchman: with one glance he measured the athletic proportions of his opponent, and rushed from the room with a hideous howl. Foreseeing that there would be a tremendous row, as the quickest mode of attracting attention I flung a bottle, in my turn, through the window of the comptoir, and in rushed an agitated mob of waiters, porters, and lacqueys. In two words I explained matters, and implored them to rush for the nearest guard. The room was scarcely cleared when our Frenchman returned with a pistol in either hand. He flung one across the table to Jones.

At the same moment, he raised his own pistol to fire. But I had watched all his movements, and, at the decisive moment, I put one leg behind him, and delivered a heavy facer. Down he went, the pistol going off at the same time, and making a dismal hole in our host's favourite mirror, where it remains to the present day, for the admiration of British youth. The Frenchman being thus disarmed, I determined to render him perfectly innocuous; so I dropped on his stomach heavily with my knees, when the guard came in, and we were all marched off ignominiously.

Fortunately for us, these events happened before a Crimean war had destroyed our prestige on the Continent, so we were let off by the confiscation of our passports, and our promise to appear whenever called upon. The vicomte was not so fortunate: he possessed no passport, and this led to some unpleasant inquiries, not at all in his favour. He was proved to be an arch rogue, whom the police had been inquiring after all through the Continent, and would have been severely punished, had it not been for the fear of compromising ourselves. He was mercifully let off by extradition over the French frontier, and I believe he has since expiated his numerous offences at the Bagne.

But this proved the turning-point in my German career: I was so frightened by the events I had risked, that I formally cut the acquaintance of Jones and Robinson, and proceeded to Frankfort, and thence to Heidelberg, where I studied the law. Unhappily for me, at that period the Badois University was the stronghold of the wildest Englishmen. But, for all that, I managed to learn something at my German university, which had not been the case at Oxford; and my experience at Mayence stood me in good stead when I finally migrated to Baden-Baden. There I was utterly stoical to every invitation to play écarté; I had had a sufficient lesson in the art of scoring the king; and if I ever went astray from the rule I had laid down, by giving a turn to the table or playing a hand at piquet, it was merely for amusement, or, at the most, to gain a cup of coffee.

I have already so amply dilated on the joys of Baden that I dare not venture here on saying another word on the subject; but I may be allowed to give my readers a word of advice: the game of écarté is as dangerous there with strangers as I found it at Mayence. It is true that the rooms close at eleven; but many Englishmen, who have not found sufficient excitement, are very prone to visit surreptitious places in the faubourg Lichtenthal, where high play is carried on through the night. All I can tell them is, not to allow themselves to be deluded by great names: as much swindling is effected in Baden by a lord as by a *nouveau-né* Smith; and I would recommend none of my readers to trust to old family as a criterion of fair play. That accursed thirst for gold pervades all classes; and it can make very little difference whether you are robbed by a Smith or a De la Cruchecassée, for the result is always the same—you have to draw on your circular banker; and I sincerely hope you return home a wiser and a better man.

But it is absurd to try to argue with gamblers innate. I address my remarks solely to those young men who go abroad under the impression that they will learn German at a cheap rate, and, with their strong common sense, elude the traps so sedulously laid for them. You are lamentably mistaken. You may be the most knowing dogs in England, the delight of the casino, and the darling of the café chantant, but you have not yet passed your apprenticeship on the Continent. You are delivered like lambs to the slaughter; and the less you are robbed of, the more fortunate you may esteem yourselves.

To you, then, youthful Oxonians and Cantabs, I address these solemn words of warning. If you trust yourselves unfledged among Continental crows, be careful of your society: if you must play, resort to the public gambling-tables; but, above all, be extra careful never to engage in the hazardous game of écarté, unless you feel yourself equally conversant with your adversary in Scoring the King.

CHAPTER XI.

A DAY IN THE DESERT.

I WILL ask my kind readers for a brief season to leave far behind them the continent of Europe, with its hills and vales, forests and meadows, its rivers and streams, towns and villages. We will hurry across the heaving sea which separates sunny Italy from the black mountains of Albania, and hold a south-eastern course to the African continent. Even Alexandria, with its world-famous Cleopatra's Needle, and its Pompey's Pillar, with its catacombs and graves, and the new town, offering so much that is strange to the astonished traveller in its motley mixture of Eastern and Western life, is left behind, and we will finally halt between the 31st and 32nd degrees of latitude on an Egyptian dahabiyah, near the Arabic village of Terraneh. But we shall require some rest after such a long *trajet*, and we will therefore enjoy it with truly Eastern *far niente*, on the deck of the vessel during an Egyptian February night in 1854.

In the bows of the dahabiyah the silence of night is suddenly interrupted by the melody of a national song, in which a young Arab sailor is imparting his woes to his only friend, the night. He produces simple sounds from the darabuke, the earthen drum of Eastern singers, and finally concludes his chant in the usual fashion of all Arab love-songs:

> *Ja lèle! ja lèle! ja chabibti, ja lèle!*
> Oh night! oh night! my own, my lovely night!

Suddenly the dark forms of his sleeping comrades on deck are seen moving, for the magic power of the words *ja lêle* reaches the heart of an Arab even in sleep. The repeated ejaculation "Allah!" "Allah!" and deep-drawn sighs, the usual symbols of applause among the Orientals, reward the amatory singer, who hangs the darabuke on a pin in the mast, wraps himself up in his camel-hair cloak, and lays himself down to enjoy a refreshing sleep by the side of his comrades.

Just in front of the vessel four swarthy old fellows are cowering, cross-legged, among the reeds on shore. A white turban covers the smoothly-shaven head, and the thick, broad-striped abaje protects the lean, sunburnt body from the unusual freshness of the February breeze. A half-burnt fire of durra branches throws a flickering glare upon them. Only rarely do they remove the Arab's inseparable companion, the glowing chibouk, from their mouth, to carry on a short conversation about the gins, or evil spirits, that sit at the cross-roads and mock the good Moslem; or about the Franks, who have come so great a distance to pay them a visit; or about other strange things which fill the head of the smoking Arab with utter confusion, while not forgetting to praise the singer and his ballad. Four lances, adorned at the top with a short tuft of black ostrich feathers, are fixed in the ground near the old men, and prove their owners to be the guardians of the vessel.

Gradually the Great Bear draws near the verge of

the nocturnal horizon, and shows that the midnight hour is already past. The sound of men and animals moving rapidly is heard from the neighbouring village. It draws nearer; a shot is fired, and flashing torches of wood illumine a grotesque congregation with their blood-red glare. The hand-shakings continually exchanged between the new arrivals and our four watchmen, and a repeated "*Salam alëik ja achûje, taibîn?*" ("Peace be with thee, O my brother! Art thou well?") calm our apprehensions as to the designs of the strangers, which are anything but hostile. They have come to escort us as expected friends on a tour through the Libyan Desert to the valley of the Natron Lakes, for the road is unsafe, and predatory Bedouins carry on their plundering trade on the caravan route, especially before midnight.

The occupiers of the vessel are aroused, and the huge stable lantern, in whose flame hundreds of large and small buzzing musquitoes terminate their brief existence, throws a dull light over the deck of the dahabiyah. Three Europeans leave the vessel, armed with guns and pistols to the teeth, and join the motley group, where they are reverentially greeted by the Fellahin and the Sons of the Desert. The latter, a Bedouin tribe, which lives in peace and amity with the inhabitants of the village of Terraneh, have solemnly pledged themselves to provide for our safety; and the old Schech of the caravan route, who also escorts us, has offered his life as a guarantee for ours. They are tall, handsome fellows, of a swarthy complexion, beardless, with small twinkling eyes, caused by the blinding rays of the sun, all young men, and full of the highest spirits. A simple white cotton robe covers their hardened bodies as an under-garment; a broad cloak, slung round the head and neck, protects them from wind and cold. They are armed with flint firelocks above six feet in length, and carry powder and ball in a leathern pouch, while others bear in addition long lances, like those already described. The animals they have provided for our excursion consist of the three most useful representatives of the animal world which modern Egypt can produce —of four long-pacing camels, a good-tempered, much-enduring horse, and ten donkeys. The camels are dragged down to the ground by means of the neck-rope; they are then laden with instruments, portfolios, provisions for three days, and, above all, with water-skins. With ear-piercing yells, their thick tongues protruding from their dripping mouths, the ships of the desert receive their burden in a kneeling posture. The European swings himself into the cushioned Turkish saddle of the only horse which Terraneh can offer, thrusting his feet into the comfortable crescent stirrups, and seizing the rope which serves as bridle to the noble animal. The remainder of our party and a portion of the Bedouins try with a clever leap to reach the back of the little swift-footed donkeys, whose proverbial laziness is belied in Egypt. But we are worse off than if we had to perform our travels on foot through the desert. A rough, tremendously broad cushion occupies the place of the saddle. The donkey goes wherever it pleases, unless the Frank is acquainted with the extraordinary method of guiding it, which is also applied to the camel. A little bent stick, with which the animal is struck either on the right or left of the neck, is the bridle which directs it. A more careful study of our donkeys, for which our desert ride affords us ample time and leisure, leads us to the remarkable observation that they may be divided into three categories—the long-eared, the short-eared, and the intermediate. This strange definition will be readily comprehended, if we add the remark, that whenever an Egyptian catches a strange donkey *in flagrante delicto* grazing on his pasturage, he cuts off the upper part of the ear; in case of repetition, performs the same operation on the other ear; and, on the third occasion, kills the sinner. I was allotted a grey donkey, with both ears lopped, which its owner recommended to me with a remark I did not understand at first, "*Hua charámi kebir, lakin maschi taïb.*" ("He's a great scoundrel, but he is a good one to go.")

The procession is gradually arranged. The camels in front, we Franks in the centre, surrounded by the armed Sons of the Desert, march in the darkness from the bank of the river up an acclivity towards the desert. It is about four in the morning, the air seems terribly cold, a penetrating mist thoroughly drenches the cloaks in which we had, shivering, wrapped ourselves. Suddenly, an obstacle checks the course of the silently-moving caravan. A broad canal, cut to carry the waters of the Nile to the higher land at the period of the inundation, appears an insurmountable difficulty. There is no bridge, so nothing is left us but to wade through it. We clamber with difficulty on the tall backs of the camels, or mount upon the Arabs; the Bedouins cleverly wrap their garment like a turban round their heads, and with noisy shouts men and animals enter the cold element. Upon the other side of the canal we find that the luxuriant display of organic life has deserted us, and with solemn reflections we cross the desolate border of an immense tract utterly devoid of vegetation, and thrice the size of the Mediterranean.

Gradually the night, with its sea of stars, disappears; but for a long while a dense mist prevents the desired prospect of the desert, and we are only able to distinguish that the rarely-trodden road beneath our feet is composed of pebbles, from which at rare intervals a scrubby bush, more prickly than leaves, laboriously forces its way into daylight, to have its brief existence cut shorter by a long-haired camel or hungry donkey. Suddenly a pale strip of light on the eastern horizon lightens up the dark earth, and long, bright, grey shadows precede the caravan. But these soon disappear in turn, and a dazzlingly bright orb rises above the white strips of mist, surrounded by coruscating beams, like the head of a saint with a brilliant *gloriole*. It is the sun, which has gained the victory over night. For the first time we salute it in the desert, and for the first time it displays to us the picture of the desert in all its horror. Not a tree to cheer the anxiously-seeking eye with even a slight mark of vegetative life, not a verdant spot inviting us to rest and refresh ourselves, but, as far as the eye can reach over the dead scene, only desolate fields of boulders and pebbles, which seem to us like the surface of a petrified ocean. The desert plateau, itself from 100 to 200 feet above the level of the sea, frequently rises in elevations of 200 to 300 feet, then sinks into deep ravines, through which timid herds of active black-eyed gazelles bound away, or a band of black snorting buffaloes rushes, with their tails high in the air.

Our idea, that the desert was a plain covered foot-deep with a layer of soft sand, is soon found to be erroneous, for it is in fact a mountainous country, with a hard stony soil, on which the shifting sand only collects in parts protected from the action of the wind. Furrows of a foot in breadth, 10 or 12 of them side by side, and not unlike the tramways of a railroad, run along in a winding direction, and traverse the desert diagonally from one point on the horizon to another. These are the sole marks of a road, the sole consolatory witnesses of humanity in these deserts. Here and there we come upon a pile of stones, or the bleached bones of fallen camels, which serve as sign-posts to the Bedouin; at times the eagle-traps (*nisbe e' nisr*), artificially arranged piles of stones, with the carcase of a donkey in the centre, serve to measure distances, which he is wont to calculate by *mulaquas*, as the boatman on the Nile does his by *birkes*.

The mid-day sun is at its zenith. Its burning beams pierce through the white cloths that shield the brow, and its dazzling glare at length utterly wearies the smarting eye. At the same time, transparent mists rise from the ground, and play around us in immense circles. They are the children of the sunbeams, which rise from the heated ground, and float restlessly above the surface, rising and sinking irregularly. Utter prostration at length seizes on the wearied body, arms and legs are affected with a spasmodic trembling movement, and the parched tongue pants for water. But the caravan does not halt yet, and the "*lissa schueisse*" ("a little further only") of the Bedouins no longer satisfies the impatient inquirer. But see! at some distance in front of us, close to the horizon, what a glorious scene presents itself to our delighted eyes! A lovely lake with its blue waters is extended before us, shady trees grow on its banks, on which human forms are moving back and forwards. With renewed strength and fresh courage we begin to hasten towards the sea; but the child of the desert knows it better than we do, and remarks, with a smile: "No, Lord, that is no lake, but only Satan's waters—*moïje Scheïtân.*" One of the frequent mirages in the desert has bitterly deceived us.

Our young Arabs hardly share at all in our fatigue, for they step out heartily over the burning soil, and sing separately, or in chorus, verses from the Koran, or love and war-songs. The last consist of a short triumphal pæan, generally ending with the verse, "The tents of the foe are destroyed!" At the same time they execute their war-dance, in which they twirl their long guns round their head like their reeds, and with a shout of joy fire a salvo into the air. Above all, we most admire the merriment of a Bedouin about seventeen or eighteen years of age (for in the true Arab fashion he is ignorant of his own age), the son of our caravan Schech, who puts no bounds to his love-songs, which he causes the desert to re-echo with in a loud, harmonious voice. He is about to visit his second wife, who is staying with her father in the Natron Valley, while he has left the other behind in Terraneh.

About one o'clock we halt in a ravine. After a hurried, frugal meal, we start afresh, and, after going up and down hill till four in the afternoon, we at last mount a steep acclivity, after a march of about fifty miles. There, in a long, narrow valley, whose opposite wall rises almost perpendicularly, we see six lakes, with dark blue glistening water, before us, surrounded by a dense belt of reed and grasses, and in this hollow, some distance apart, four long buildings resembling fortresses, which seem to invite us to seek repose within their walls. What a cheerful, smiling scene, in comparison to the melancholy desert! And yet the vegetation even here is so uniform, so scanty! Herds of buffaloes traverse the valley; and a motley mass of voiceless birds—chief of all, the long-legged flamingoes, with their gaudy plumage—congregate on the shores of the lakes to quench their thirst with brackish water.

We descend slowly to the plain, and soon after a dense forest of reeds (carix cyperus) impedes the progress of our stumbling animals. The ground creaks beneath their feet, for it is covered with a thick coating of salt, which bears a great resemblance to hoar-frost. This salt, which effloresces from the ground by capillary attraction for miles around the lakes, is the Natron, which has given a name to the whole district. We approach the largest of the Natron Lakes. Several Arabs, who live here in this boundless desert as watchmen, receive us with a well-intentioned fantasia—as they term it—of gun-shots, and greet our Bedouin companions with real Arabic flowers of eloquence. There is an unending questioning and answering, a repetition which makes our heads giddy. "O my brother," one asks the other, "how are thy father and thy mother, thy son, and thy horse, thy ass, and thy goat." And if they are on very friendly terms, the long query is terminated with the otherwise improper remark, "And how is the mystery of the people of thy house?" which is a somewhat extraordinary paraphrase of the simple "How's your wife?" But we survive this scene with true Arab patience, and are quartered in an old boarded salt-room, without a door, in which reed mats are stretched out upon the sandy soil. We have hence a view of the lakes, whose shores are covered with a number of large and strangely-formed logs of petrified wood.

We pass a restless night in our Natron room. The camels, ruminating with a loud noise, and with their knees fastened together, donkeys and horses, with their fore-feet hobbled, lie in company with the smoking Bedouins before our room. But in what condition does the next morn find us? Stung and bitten by fleas and buzzing musquitoes, and two other members of the insect family, which the Bible quotes among the plagues of Egypt, and which, at the present day, French wit in the land of the Pharaohs designates "light and heavy cavalry," we can hardly discover a square inch of surface on our bodies unattacked.

The beauty of the morning soon dispels any melancholy reminiscences of the past night of horror. We talk with the watchman about the nature of the Natron Lakes, whose fall and rise is in inverse ratio to the inundations of the Nile, noticing at the same time that their stagnant and salt water is dyed of a blood-red hue when near, probably by infusoria, but at some distance off appears dark blue, and when set in motion by the wind produces crimson waves. And, in conclusion, we visit the ruins of a small Roman fort at no great distance from the lakes.

At three in the afternoon the caravan starts afresh,

to visit the largest of the four ancient Coptic monasteries, which is situated about 15 miles further on. A leave-taking, rich in words, accompanied by the tinkling reward of Backshish, that magic word which buzzes in the traveller's ear for years after his return home, separates us for a lifetime from the Natron-guarding Arabs. We surmount a rather steep acclivity, and see from the broad crest of the hill three monasteries before us, bathed in the yellow light of the setting sun, in the centre the one which is the object of our expedition. They appear to us so near that we can clearly distinguish the different parts of the buildings, and even the tops of the palms, which rise from the garden above the lofty walls. While we fancy we shall reach the monastery in half an hour, we are compelled to ride three good hours at a sharp trot ere we stand beneath its walls. The evening bell, which summons the pious brethren to prayer, sends its clear clang across to us. How strangely we are affected by the familiar sound in the desert. A thousand sweet reminiscences of the distant home and the beloved family rise before the dreaming mind, and deceive the longing heart, in the same way as the mirage does the pilgrim in the desert.

For the last time the sun casts its beams athwart the melancholy desert, then it disappears, and with it the last degree of its precious blessing—heat. A cold, almost freezing north wind blows across the desert, and compels us to wrap ourselves in thick shawls. The loud *harr, harr!* of the Bedouins drives the animals on at a quicker rate, and at last the monastery wall, with its turret-like entrance, is close before us. Three Bedouins, at their head the cautious old Schech, with their guns cocked, hurry forward to reconnoitre whether any predatory Arabs may not be lying in ambush. Their caution is, fortunately, unnecessary, and so they soon pull lustily at the long cord which hangs down from an orifice in the tower, and sets the strangers' bell in motion. We must wait a long while ere an answer is given us, and have, consequently, time afforded us to examine the locality more closely. A strong, insurmountable wall forms a large quadrangle round the building, rising to a height of about 60 feet. The Coptic cross is let into the wall above the gateway. The small, low door, through which it is only possible to pass in a stooping posture, is almost entirely blocked up by two huge masses of rock, and, in addition, guarded by a door thickly mounted with iron. The tops of fruit-bearing palms rise above the top of the wall.

In the mean while voices become audible in the interior of the gateway, and an animated discussion is carried on with the Bedouins, who thrust a letter of recommendation for the Europeans under the door. After a long discussion, the bolts are finally withdrawn, the door creaks on its rusty hinges, and a dozen human forms march out like denizens of the tomb. Their appearance has something gloomy and awe-inspiring, which is augmented by the melancholy *entourage* and the twilight. A black or blue turban, the distinction of Coptic Christians in Egypt, is closely wrapped round the pale, sickly face of each individual that emerges from the darkness of the gateway. A long dark robe surrounds their wasted bodies. Evidently pleased, they seize our hands with many polite speeches, press them to their lips, and almost put us to shame by their fraternal conduct. They make incessant excuses for not having opened the door immediately, but they fancied we were Bedouins, come to take the monastery by stratagem. At length they invite us to pass through the narrow gateway, while the animals and a portion of the Bedouins are compelled to camp without: we traverse a narrow passage, and at last reach an open hall, in which other monks, with their yellow wax tapers in their hand, politely receive us. They hold their hands before their eyes, which are swollen with illness, in order to defend them from the yellow glare. Each new arrival approaches us reverently to kiss our hands and cause us fresh embarrassment. In the mean while a room is being got ready for the Frankish guests. We are conducted across two court-yards—the last being ornamented with a garden, in which tall palms rise up from the centre of low bushes, a real oasis in this desert scene—to the uppermost of two terraces, up a flight of stone steps, in such dilapidated condition that we are obliged to employ extreme caution in scaling them. Our room is rather spacious, and pervaded with that disgusting odour which betrays the vicinity of a Copt. It is divided into two parts by a small wooden lattice, and covered with old mats and carpets. It contains two low windows, looking out on the court, a strongly-grated hole affording a prospect of the desert, and, in addition, somewhere about ten orifices, through which the draught whistles its pleasant tune. All the monks collect in and before our apartment, and the proper introductions now commence. Two very aged blind

Patres stand at the head of the community. With real Arab loquacity they tell us that the monastery is about 1500 years old—just about 33 centuries younger than many of the mortuary chapels at Gizeh—and is named after the Syrian virgin, because in earlier time Syrians inhabited it in common with Egyptians. "We pray thrice a day to God," thus they conclude, with a certain amount of self-laudation, "in the morning before sunrise, at mid-day, and in the evening. We fast on Tuesdays and Fridays; and, as we eat no meat on those days, we consider you fortunate in coming to-day (Saturday) instead of yesterday. In addition, we fast for 40 days at Easter and Christmas.

After expressing a wish to be present next morning at early mass, we are invited to supper. With our legs crossed under us we crouch in a fatiguing position with the fathers of the monastery round a circular board, which stands on a supporter hardly a foot in height, and forms with it a moveable table. Soup, with sweet potatoes, and cold veal, form the bill of fare; and there are about thirty small loaves, made of maize. The water, which we drink out of earthenware vessels, called *qullen*, tastes salt and bad, and would furnish a naturalist a famous opportunity for the study of the varieties of infusoria. The monks obtain it from a deep well within the monastery. The food is rapidly devoured without the aid of spoons, forks, or knives; and though we strangers cannot in consequence manage the soup with any degree of success, the old Coptic fathers are practised hands. With reverent gestures they draw back the long sleeve of their robe, and dip the bread, together with the half of their right hand, into the wooden bowl, and then carefully lick their fingers. We notice with surprise that these Christian monks neither commence nor terminate the meal with a prayer, and we already begin to form well-founded doubts as to their piety. After the termination of supper we descend with all the monks into the court-yard, where a violent wind is blowing among the branches of the palm-trees, at a temperature of 16 deg. Reaumur. The yellow tapers, which are frequently blown out, cast a sickly glare over the cells of the monks, but it is sufficiently strong for us to discover a horrifying want of cleanliness in them. In the church, which is divided into two parts by a carved screen, into the naye (hêkal) for laymen, and the choir for the priest, we are shown with almost childish glee the wretchedly-painted pictures of saints, and the mummies of two holy Copts, who once lived in the monastery. Ostrich eggs are suspended by long cords from the roof of the church. Upon a reading-desk lies a rather old Coptic-Arabic book of Gospels. Each page of the vellum is disfigured with spots of grease and dried yellow wax, and is just as dirty as the desk on which it lies, as the church, and the whole body of Copts inhabiting the monastery. The curious Franks are then led further to a quadrangular basin, filled with dirty, brackish water from the deep well, into which the monks go once annually in memory of Christ's baptism by St John. A second chapel, in which during the fast the service is performed in a kneeling posture, is broadcast with a coarse variety of corn. Most peculiar is the effect made on us by a long arched room, with traces of coarse old painting. A long table is in the centre, a hundred small loaves lie upon it, and a stone bench runs down either side of it. But who and where are the guests, who will take their places at this long table in the heart of the desert? The monks explain to us that it is always in readiness for the wandering Bedouins, who are driven by hunger to pull the strangers' bell, and by the monks for a hospitable reception.

Only with visible repugnance, and after long entreaty, are we conducted to the last spot in the whole monastery most deserving inspection. We slowly climb on to the terrace of a small building; a board is then laid across it from the projecting threshold of a small door which we see slightly above us. The brother who conducts us warns us to cross the tottering bridge with caution. The heavy bolts are drawn back, and we enter a confined space, from which another door equally well guarded leads to a separate room. The dignitaries of the monastery follow at our heels, and closely watch our every movement. This is the library, which they guard with Argus' eyes. We fancy we shall find a collection of books well arranged, rich in all MSS.; but what a chaotic disorder reigns in this apartment! Some forty large volumes, mostly containing Arabic and Coptic documents, lie confusedly on a bench: torn-out pages of parchment or cotton paper cover the filthy ground, the covers are nearly all rotting, and worms have disfigured the leaves by making deep holes. Some of these MSS. are probably four or five centuries old, but we cannot induce the monks to part with them, either by money or persuasion. "Lord!" says the prior of the monastery, "these books were written by brethren who have rested in the lap of earth for ages.

At the end of each document, they have solemnly bound us not to part in any fashion with any of these blessed heirlooms, on peril of our salvation." Of course we can make but slight objections to this; and with a glance of compassion at the old, uncomprehended Coptic books, we lament their unworthy fate of being so carefully treasured through ignorance. After being obliged to admire a species of chapel in the rear of the library, with several badly-painted pictures of Miriam (Mary) and St Makarios, as well as a carved screen, behind which are the glass communion vessels with their proper coverings, we wander back to our cells in considerable dissatisfaction, and stretch our wearied limbs on the mats, to enjoy the sweet gift of sleep in the Desert Monastery of the Syrian Virgin.

We dream of the old Copts, whose miserable representations our hosts of to-day were; we look back on old times, and see about a hundred monasteries in the valley of the Natron Lakes, from which the Emperor Valens once drove no fewer than five thousand monks into the Byzantine army; we look further back upon the infancy of Christianity, when Egypt was the refuge of the first Christians; we dream of St Anthony—of the hermits and penitents—of the pious Pacomius, who, in the middle of the fourth century, built the first monastery on the fertile Nile Island of Tabium; suddenly the walls of our chamber rattle, and the earth trembles; a fearful crash breaks over our heads, and wakes us from our short sleep. Under the combined influences of alarm and surprise we rub our eyes. Forked flashes of lightning illumine the white lime walls of our cell, the boisterous wind howls through the numerous openings, and the rain pours in torrents aganst the building. To judge by the short intervals between the lightning and thunder, a tremendous storm is raging somewhere in our immediate vicinity. Wrapped in our cloaks, we go out into the elements upon the open terrace, and from the parapet are witnesses of the magnificent spectacle, so rare in Egypt. Flash on flash lights up the boundless desert, which seems converted into a glowing sea of fire. The black clouds come in collision with a fearful crash, while the hymn of the trembling monks rises up to us from the lighted church, like the faint groans of dying men, between the pauses of the rolling thunder.

After an hour the storm passes away, which commenced about two o'clock, the streams of rain cease, and the desert is once more shrouded in night. We spend the remainder of it in restless sleep. The tormenting occupants of the Natron chamber, of blessed memory, appear to have the head-quarters in the monastery, and full of vain fury, and tortured by the pain, one sleeper imparts his sufferings to the other. Silent resignation alone can support the usual phlegma in such a truly Egyptian state of things. Woe to that man in the land of the Pharaohs who cannot resignedly endure such a trial of his patience!

At five in the morning the bell rings in three intervals, for early mass. We quit this terrestrial Hades, and go down to the church, in which the monks are already assembled. The sanctity of the day enhances our feelings of reverence, and with a silent prayer we cross the threshold of the Coptic temple, which is dimly lighted with ampullæ, and powerfully scented with incense. But what is the appearance of the church itself? The little community appears to be a congregation of idlers, who strive to render their standing position more supportable by leaning one arm on tall crutches, and support their backs against a wall, or crouch in a corner. We also receive similar crutches, on which we support ourselves like cripples, following the evil example, and not wishing to attract attention. The officiating clergy wear white robes, or, speaking more correctly, robes which had been once white, and which they have bound round their heads and necks after the fashion of the Bedouin cloaks. Red Coptic crosses are sewn on the chest and sleeves. The priest reading mass is continually in motion, bending back and forwards, smoking the saints, then the pictures or the Book. The Gospel is first read in Coptic, not a word of which a Copt now understands, and then chanted in Arabic. The monks repeat it after him, at the same time correcting the priest who is reading the Holy Word, until growing impatient he repels the nearest critic with the coarse words, "*Oskut hansir!*" ("Silence, pig!") Full of astonishment, we hear this strange exclamation in a Christian church, and when we look round to discover any one sharing our well-founded displeasure among the congregation, we notice that some of the monks have rested their heads on the crutch, continuing their sweet morning sleep, as is evidenced by their snoring; others are chattering and laughing, or yawning in a most unseemly fashion, and stretching their limbs. It seems as if all this formed a part of the Coptic ceremonial. After this so-called mass had lasted an hour, the priest distributed small loaves of blessed unleavened bread. We also receive one, and eat it, after the fashion of the others, in the church.

We thank God when we again reach the open court, where the Bedouins are already awaiting us. After giving the monks a present of money, which appears to afford them more pleasure than the visit of Europeans, they wish us a successful journey with their usual loquacity, and all lay the right hand incessantly on their chest, mouth, and forehead, as a sign of leave-taking. The same narrow passage leads us out into the desert, which looks remarkably fresh under the blue vault of heaven. The sun has already risen, the animals are impatiently scratching up the wet earth; we mount, and the return journey to Terraneh commences. After a visit to the monastery, the desert seems to us to have become a pleasant place; timidly and cautiously we pass the second monastery, and then strike out in an easterly direction. A twelve hours' march, during which we only rested once, brings us to our destination. The animals have been unable to quench their thirst for three days, and we ourselves are so fatigued as almost to sink from the saddle. The road seems never ending; one *malaqua* follows the other, and yet the sun is already setting on the verge of the desert. The camel stretches out its long neck, the horse whinnies merrily, and the donkeys, pointing their ears, redouble their pace. The Bedouins discharge their guns with a chorus of triumph, and all indicates that we shall soon be restored to the luxuriant abundance of vegetation.

Before the sun has thrown its last parting beam on

the earth, the fertile Nile Valley, with its light delicate verdure, lies stretched out at our feet. The boat is at the same spot, but the whole landscape, so simple in its components, seems to us to have become tenfold richer, tenfold more beautiful and pleasant. With a hearty *El hamderlillah!* (Glory and praise to Allah!) our expecting friends on board greet us, for we have gone through the first excursion into the Libyan Desert without meeting with any dangerous adventure.

CHAPTER XII.

A DAY'S HUNTING AT BADEN-BADEN.

READER, did you ever have the good fortune to be present at a boar-hunt—a real, legitimate boar-hunt? Do not lay the flattering unction to your soul that you have done so because you witnessed the so-called sport of catching greasy-tailed pigs among the old English games at the Jardin d'Hiver at Paris, but answer candidly, laying your hand upon your heart, have you ever seen how a boar should die, surrounded by a score or more of dauntless youths, "their souls all fire, and their swords all flame," as some one has said, or rather sung, before me? If not, have patience with me for a few pages, and I will tell you all I saw at an "Eber Jagd" which came off at Baden-Baden.

M. Benazet, chief proprietor of the gambling-rooms, I must, as a preliminary measure, inform you, considers it his best policy to do his utmost in furnishing amusement to those who honour his tables with a visit; and wisely deeming there may, peradventure, be something monotonous in continually losing money or pricking off the run of the *couleur* on a card, strives to provide them some relaxation in the pleasures of the chase. These manly sports do not, however, commence till September; because in high summer, as the German phrase runs, there is no lack of quieter amusements more congenial to the state of the thermometer, and partly, *pour encourager les autres,* the later flock of migratory birds, whom he thus induces to prolong their stay, and to whom he seeks to offer some compensation for the buried glories they were too late to share in.

As long as I can remember, I have ever felt a strange inclination to be present at a boar-hunt. Surely it could not be reminiscences of Meleager and the fierce Hyrcanian boar. But no; these and other heroes of antiquity could only summon up recollections of many a dire flogging they had cost me. But still the fact remains the same; the name itself possesses something very exciting for me. It reminds me of legendary lore—of scenes of danger and strife, baying of hounds, trumpet-sounds, glittering dresses, and all the gorgeous panoply with which the great Magician of the North has invested the creatures and creations of his fancy. At length my long-nursed wishes were to meet with realization.

M. Benazet had expended all the *Edel Hirsche* he had been furnished with from the grand ducal park at Carlsruhe, and, like a clever manager, who reserves his chief attraction for the season when the public taste begins to pall, suddenly came out with a flaring *affiche* that a boar would be started on the ensuing Monday; the meet, a forest, about two leagues—or, according to German admeasurement, three pipes and a half—from Baden-Baden, and at no great distance from the willow-covered banks of Father Rhine.

A party was soon formed at the *table d'hôte* of the hotel where I was accustomed to dine; horses ordered to be sent on, and a calêche to be held in readiness for us on the Monday morning.

The eventful day soon came, and at a very early hour the loud and joyous fanfares of the Jäger horns sounded the *réveille* through the quiet streets of the town. I sprung out of bed, and began dressing in frantic haste. I pulled on a pair of "canonenstiefel," or jack-boots, I had borrowed from a friend of mine, a student at Heidelberg, girded on my hirschfänger, and seized my boar-spear, which rested gracefully in a corner of my room: these two articles, I must remark, were my own property, and expressly ordered for the occasion, as I was determined to "do or die," and flesh my maiden lance in the carcase of poor piggy.

All my preparations being made, I sallied out to join my "compagnons de voyage" at breakfast. I found them also all armed and eager for the fray. They were three in number—an Englishman, a Frenchman, and an Italian. Let me describe their appearance minutely. The first was attired in immaculate tops and leathers, and a well-stained coat, which had once been red, but was now purple. Having almost lost all recollection of our national (hunting) costume, I took him for one of the grand duke's footmen on furlough—an opinion in which I was not singular, for later in the day a party of God-forgotten students saluted him with the rattling Commers Lied, "Was bringt der postillon?" The Frenchman was dressed in a green velvet hunting-frock, and wore a many-tasselled, much-befringed *gibecière*, large enough to contain the boar we were about to hunt. On his head was a black velvet jockey-cap; on his shoulder a double-barrelled carbine. The Italian resembled nothing, except a mild edition of "Fra Diavolo," wearing, as he did, a tall conical felt hat, and a belt graced by a couple of pistols. With these companions I ascended the creaking steps of the Droschki, humming, as I did so, the time-honoured "refrain," "Arise the burden of my so—ng, This day a stag (it was a boar we intended to kill, but then I was in no way particular) must die—this day," &c.

On starting, the morning was beautiful and fresh, and we merrily rattled along the road to Oos, through orchards of apple and pear trees, the Alt Schloss frowning down upon us in all its ruined majesty. But all this soon changed; one of those detestable mists, the curse of Baden, covered the valley, and rendered us cold, uncomfortable, and prone to quarrel. Cigars did their part in keeping us warm; and soon after, arriving at a "public," we made fierce onslaught on the potato-brandy, dignified with the name of "Kirschwasser," which, while warming the inward man, seemed to exert a sympathetic influence on the outward, for from this moment I heard no more complaints of damp.

In a short time afterwards we arrived at the *rendezvous de chasse*, the village of Sandweier, when we were enabled to watch the other noble sportsmen discontentedly spurring on through the rain, as we stood very contentedly smoking our cigars at the window of the village inn.

In a short time the place began to get very animated. The stragglers came in by twos and threes, some on horseback, some on foot, while carriages of every description followed each other in rapid succession, filled with elegantly dressed ladies, whom no weather, however bad, would have deterred from being present at the throw off. Every door in the village was thronged with peasants and their families, all wearing that peculiarly stolid look, the concentrated essence of *Sauerkraut*, which is characteristic of every uneducated German. The scene soon became very lively, especially as the sun broke through the mist, lighting up the medley of horses, hounds, jäger, and servants, or glancing from the spear-heads and *cors de chasse*, though it could not pierce through the dense cloud of tobacco smoke which, like a halo, surrounded the whole group.

The pack was the most lamentable part of the whole affair; Jorrocks, that M.F.H. of facetious memory, would have shed tears had he seen it; it was composed of foxhounds, harriers, lurchers, turnspits, even the "cur of low degree" was not absent, all making a horrible noise and yelping fearfully whenever M. le Comte de S——, Benazet's huntsman *en chef*, rode in amongst them and liberally laid about him with his double thong. The whip-smacking and trumpet-blowing seemed to have no end.

We were soon marshalled in proper order, holding our boar-spears erect, like Paladins of yore, and set out for the forest glade, where the boars were cabined and confined. They were penned up in hutches, about six in number, with trap-doors to turn them out at. The huntsman then arranged the meet in proper order, beaters in front, horsemen in the second rank, and the carriages in the rear. About half an hour was consumed in making these preparations, and I had ample leisure to notice and admire the picturesqueness of the whole group. I think it is old Beckford who, in his history of hunting, expresses a wish that an artist sportsman had been present on a certain occasion to paint the glories of a successful death; we were, in one way, more fortunate than the veteran, for before starting I noticed an artist very busy with his sketch-book, and was, indeed, at a later date reminded of the fact by his honouring me with an invitation to subscribe for a proof.

However, let me get on with my history. About five or six couple of the most stanch-looking hounds, in whom Count S—— seemed to place implicit confidence, were brought to the rear of the hutches, just near enough to get sight of the "varmint." The dogs made a great row, and certainly seemed to justify the confidence that was placed in them. How they did so, the sequel will show.

The beaters were drawn up in a dense semicircle, so that the boar could only have one way of escape when turned out upon a flinty world. All waited in eager expectation for the decisive moment.

The jäger horns sounded cheerily. "Lässt gehen!" shouted Count S——, a cry which was taken up by a thousand throats, and in every possible variety of translation.

Out the boar stalked, and amused himself by a long and pertinacious stare at the scene which met his astonished vision. He was an animal of very respectable size, and in the possession of a considerable amount of sharp and well-whetted tusk. At length he seemed to have decided on his proper course of action. Shaking his head very significantly, he came along at a quick, shuffling trot towards the beaters, as if intending to force his way through them. But we were not to be balked of our pleasure by any such display of valour; and as soon as he arrived within assailable distance, they attacked him with their long staves. At first he was inclined to show fight; but not relishing, and probably not expecting, such a reception, he gave a few angry growls, and then turning tail, started for the wood in front of us. Five minutes' grace was generously conceded him, and then the dogs were laid on the scent, apparently as dreadfully eager to be at him as was the Earl of Chatham, who, with his sword drawn, was waiting for Sir Richard Strachan, or *vice versâ*, I hardly remember which, to be at the French.

An extraordinary scene now commenced. Every horseman seemed to consider it his bounden duty to be foremost in the fray, and, in consequence, two or three of the most valuable dogs were ridden over and spoiled for the day. The result may easily be imagined. Many ardent sportsmen, disgusted by the jostling and noise, turned angrily back, and gave up all hope of participating in the chase; while many, only too glad of the excuse, hurried back to take up their posts each by the side of *la belle dame* in the light of whose eyes he delighted to sun himself.

Those who were left, and would not be daunted by a slight annoyance, pressed on after the boar, who was very calmly pursuing his course along a glade in the forest. Finding the hounds close at his heels, he fiercely turned at bay, and then the valorous pack—ran in and finished him, the reader may imagine. German dogs are too well bred to be guilty of such rudeness; so they stood at a respectful distance and barked at him. After awhile, the boar, getting tired of this amusement, or probably warned by the sound of coming horses, forced his way through a thicket, and disappeared from sight. My French friend had already taken aim at him with his double-barrel, to the certain disgust of the red-coated Englishman, who bitterly complained of the crime of shooting "Mr Reynolds" in face of the pack. The poor gentleman had by this time become almost as enthusiastic and insane as if following the hounds in his own native land. Fortunately there were no bullfinches for him to break his neck over. After two hours' hard work, chasing our bristly friend from thicket to thicket—which, by the way, caused awful havoc among the gaily-checked trousers of *la jeune France*—we drove the boar from his last entrenchment, and had a capital run after him through corn and potato-fields to the village of Iffezheim, when he took refuge in a pigsty, among his porcine relatives. A second time we set the dogs upon him, but they fairly showed the white feather, and the old adage was fully verified, "their bark was worse than their bite."

We were not sorry for the *intermezzo*, as our horses—not at the most favourable season brothers or sisters of the wind—had been completely pounded by the last burst. We could have killed the boar as he stood defying us, and, indeed, the Frenchman begged most earnestly to have a shot at him; but the sun was still high in the heavens, so we lighted our cigars, and passed the *kirschwasser* from hand to hand very cosily.

At length the Count gave the signal to start him afresh, and one of the *piqueurs* gave him a persuader with his hunting-spear. After a fierce grunt of dissatisfaction, the animal made up his mind to leave his present comfortable quarters, and started off towards the Rhine, apparently with the intention of taking to water. The best mounted, therefore, hurried along to cut him off, in which they succeeded, and he sulkily bent his way once more to the forest. Only a few of us managed to keep up with him at all; as for the dogs, they had long been left behind. Had he managed to reach the wood again, he would certainly have escaped us, and adieu then to all the fun of the *curée*. It was, therefore, time to end the farce; with levelled spears we pushed on after him, and soon brought him to bay. A sporting publican of the town was the first to dismount, and, drawing his *couteau de chasse*, he advanced boldly to deal the *coup de grâce*. But, alas! that hand generally so sure when about to tap a cask of beer, failed its master when about to tap the blood of the boar, and, his foot slipping, he fairly lay at the mercy of the now infuriated animal. Fortunately for him, the broadest part of his person was exposed to the assault of the boar, and the latter, making a furious rush, dug his tusks rather deeply into him, before any of us had time to prevent it. A shrill yell ensued, accompanied by the last savage growl of the boar, whom young L—— coolly transfixed at the moment when he was drawing back for a second edition. I also had the pleasure of having a drive at him, and thus tarnished the hitherto unsullied spotlessness of my spear.

Four *piqueurs* now dismounted, and forming a *brancard* of their spears, laid poor piggy, once the hero of the day, upon it, and we marched off at a quick pace to receive the meed of valour at the hands of the expectant ladies. When we arrived at the *rendezvous de chasse*, there was no time for anything of the sort, as every one seemed only awaiting our advent to make a still fiercer onslaught than on the boar, on the comestibles M. Benazet had so bountifully provided for them. A striking change had taken place during our absence. A tent had been raised, in which we could see casseroles stewing, and hear frying-pans hissing; fires were blazing in every direction, soup boiling, fowls roasting on spits, coffee exhaling its fragrant aroma. Tables, too, had been spread *fronde super viridi*, covered with drapery, white as the driven snow, and all the paraphernalia of the Kursaal Restaurant's *table d'hôte*. We willingly resigned all claim to soft speeches, and fully coincided with a stout German, who exclaimed, with a greasy smile of pleasure, "*Das lass' ich mir gefallen.*"

The silleri soon began to mantle in the glasses, and endue the ladies' sparkling eyes with still greater brilliancy. Each hunter bold began speaking of the perils he had undergone, except the publican, who seemed somewhat disconcerted, and writhed uneasily on his seat whenever any allusion was made to his misadventure. As the Vicar of Wakefield would say, "if there was not much wit, there was plenty of laughing," especially at our end of the table, for we had bribed a Kellner to make us a potent brewage of "croc." In short, all seemed delighted with the pic-nic, and ready to join in the chorus—"A Life in the Woods for me."

After everything eatable and drinkable, except the

water, had been demolished, the chasseurs attached to Benazet's wilde Jagd, came in for their share of the day's amusement. A mark was set upon a tall pine-tree, and money-prizes offered for the successful competitors. It was quite a realization of the opening scene of "Der Freyschütz." The *piqueurs* were, on the whole, excellent marksmen; and, O ye Gods! how the trumpets brayed, and what shouts were raised by beer-bemused peasants at each successful shot! Many amateurs also tried their hand, among them my French friend, who thus had an opportunity of discharging his gun—a cause of heartfelt joy to me, for I had been in fear, if not in danger, during the whole of the day. Extempore matches were also got up; in fine, no one seemed to think the sports of the day would ever come to a conclusion, and we were all surprised by the approach of nightfall, and the preparations for the *curée*, the last scene of this exciting drama.

The Count now ordered torches to be lighted, and the dogs brought up, who had arrived at the rendezvous, straggling in one after the other, weary and way-sore. A circle was then formed round the dead boar, and the mystic rites of the *curée* commenced. The count doffed his coat, tucked up his shirt-sleeves, and commenced cutting up the boar with all the grace of a professional butcher—the *cor de chasse* sounding the *mort* during the whole scene. Ultimately, the hounds were fed, much better, in my opinion, than they had deserved after the day's exhibition.

We were then marshalled in the same order as upon our arrival, the *piqueurs* carrying the *reliquiæ* of the boar before us to Sandweier. After this we started home for Baden, impressed with an exalted opinion of Monsieur Benazet's generosity; and I can safely avouch that he must have made a handsome profit by the day, after all expenses were paid. Each felt bound in honour to give the table a turn; for my own part—but it is unnecessary "infandum renovare dolorem."

All I can say in conclusion is, that I trust my readers will feel more pleasure than I do at these reminiscences of a "Day's Hunting at Baden."

CHAPTER XIII.

IMPERIAL PARIS.

WHEN future historians sit down calmly to discuss the merits and demerits of the Second Empire, it is quite certain that they must be unanimous in their praise of the improvements to which Napoleon III. has subjected the capital of his empire. It was the boast of Augustus that he found Rome of brick and left it of marble. The flatterers of our George the Fourth said the same thing about the conversion of Swallow-street into the Quadrant; but all such improvements pale into insignificance when compared with the alterations which the Emperor has produced in Paris. Not alone that Paris has been adorned with magnificent buildings, but the streets have undergone a thorough renovation, and it is possible now to walk in comfort through the penetralia of the *Cité*. To the Emperor the great credit is due that he has not sought merely to aggrandize his reign by the erection of stately buildings, which will form an epoch in French history, but at the same time he has ever kept in view the wants and wishes of the inhabitants.

Our first acquaintance with Lutetia Parisiorum dates from the Revolution of July, and on our last visit it seemed to us as if the city we remembered had disappeared from the face of the earth to make room for some gorgeous creation of John Martin. In those days Paris was essentially black, crooked, and uncomfortable, and the painters of the Romantic school had opportunities in abundance to represent mediæval Paris. At that time the city possessed its hills and its valleys; the bridges were admirable counterparts of the Montagnes Russes; and, on the slightest suspicion of frost, the horses found it impossible to ascend the acclivities of the Pont Neuf and the Pont de la Tournelle, while the Boulevards and quays were in a deplorable condition, fully justifying the remark that Paris was the inferno of horses. A smart shower rendered Paris inaccessible for the pedestrian; water-pipes had not then been invented, and the rain poured down from the roofs through the gaping mouths of the stone spouts, and gave the passer-by a shower-bath. In a few minutes the gutters were converted into rivulets, for the present system of sewerage was a thing unknown; streets became lakes, and the tradesmen hurriedly closed their shops to keep the water out. When the rain had ceased, the doors were again opened, and the apprentices began removing the water by means of large sponges. The wayfarers emerged from the gateways in which they had taken shelter, and crept cautiously along the slippery trottoir. Then came some clever speculator to earn a few sous by laying a plank across the road, on which only a tight-rope dancer could keep his balance—but we seem to be only repeating in halting prose what Boileau wrote in mellifluous verse about the discomforts of Paris, and yet we are describing matters from nature. It is not our fault if Paris in 1834 too often resembled the Paris of 1693.

These things struck us at once while pursuing our researches in new Paris—the absence of the gutter running through the centre of the causeway, the disappearance of the trottoirs, and the abolition of reverbères, of revolutionary notoriety. In the time we first saw Paris, the paving-stones formed a hollow along the centre of the street, which, though not an actual gutter, retained the moisture even through the summer, for the sun found it impossible to force its way between the bulging houses and lick up the water. Even the broader and more convenient streets in the middle of the city were always either wet or covered with a black layer of mud, less offensive when it rained than when the sun had imparted to it a degree of consistency. However active you might be, you could not for any length of time continue your peregrinations through the streets of Paris; for while you were soon fatigued by incessantly slipping off the greasy trottoirs, the stench emanating from the filth which was being continually stirred up by passing carriages made one sick at the stomach. In winter, again, the pedestrian ran considerable danger of being injured by the carriages, for, owing to the greasiness and high pitch of the streets, the wheels persisted in making eccentric revolutions, which inevitably brought them on to the trottoir.

It must be borne in mind that we are not writing of barbarous times, but of a recently passed lustre, of a blessed time of peace, of elegant manners and civilization: but the pedestrian was not taken into account. The small space left him by the vehicles he could only attain in the sweat of his brow. Now, broad footpaths are his property, which no coupé or cabriolet dare invade. He can now walk firmly with clean boots, even if it have been raining furiously for hours. So soon as the storm ceases the population of idlers and flâneurs reappear and lounge along the asphalt pavement; while, though their noses may be unpleasantly affected by the gutters running along the pavement, at any rate their stomachs are no longer upset. But the greatest change has taken place in the night of Paris. Formerly, it is true, the streets were not quite unilluminated, but the reverbères could hardly be regarded as lighting, although they produced a remarkable change, and lengthened the daily traffic of the city by six hours. In the reign of Louis XIV. commercial Paris closed its doors at nine in summer and five in winter; but the introduction of the reverbères effected an alteration, more especially as, with the Revolution, they were lighted every evening. Under the Monarchy, the lighting of Paris being farmed out, the good citizens had often to wade home through a sea of mud in the dark, or hire a boy at the corner of the street to light them to their houses. Paris of to-day and Paris of yesterday are as different as light from darkness. The light destroys those places and schemes which depend on darkness for success, and shun any illumination. Light kills like the Delian Apollo destroyed with his golden arrows the dragon Python, the father of the Gorgon and the Hydra. When Boileau writes that the most dangerous and desolate forest was a secure place as compared with Paris, it was no witty exaggeration. In any rich city, where the night is longer than the day, there is an endless succession of crimes, and murderers and robbers find certain shelter. Even at the close of the seventeenth century there were in Paris twelve publicly privileged robbers' dens, known by the name of "Cours de Miracles," of which Victor Hugo gives us such an admirable description. Unfortunately, our prosaic age cannot tolerate the romance of robber-life, and the Courts of Miracles have been put down by the strong arm of the law. Still, so long as Paris exists with its startling contrast between unbounded riches and the extremest poverty, it must be a prey to the dangerous classes that war against society. So late as 1836, these rogues regarded the night as their exclusive property. With the twilight, the veriest scum of Paris congregated on the Place de la Concorde. No honest man ventured among them, except under the most pressing necessity, and he might esteem himself fortunate if he escaped with only the loss of his watch and purse. After dusk no one ventured to walk along the Boulevard des Filles du Calvaire, or the Boulevard of the Bastille. Paris ended with the extreme verge of the Marais. On the other side was the town wall, with a prospect across the Rue Basse of wood-yards, fields, and nursery-gardens. Further along the Boulevards you came to the remains of Beaumarchais's splendid house and gardens, a half-finished basin in which stood the column of July, and a plaster model of an elephant, designed for a fountain, but never completed, and which eventually became a colony of rats. Round about these a spacious open quadrangle indicated the spot where the Bastille had formerly stood. Not a trace was to be seen of the once terrible building; the moat, a pestiferous swamp, with a green covering of festering weeds and some blocks of stone which peered out from the dank vegetation, were the only visible proofs of the existence of the Bastille. The long walk along the Boulevards ended as it began: in desolation and uncompleted monuments. At one end the elephant fountain, at the other the Madeleine church; on all sides there was something to complete or remove. The Seine had to be freed from the old houses which obstructed passage; the quays must be levelled to form a long, straight route from the Pont d'Jéna to the Pont d'Austerlitz, from the granaries to the garrison bakery; the river must be hemmed in between lofty insurmountable walls, the public buildings restored from the unclean and tottering condition in which they vegetated; the wretched shops and stalls removed from the immediate vicinity of the palace. But there was much more to be done besides all this: the Louvre to be restored, Paris rebuilt in accordance with a regular plan, the old *Cité* reformated, as Medea renovated Œson; gardens must be laid out, trees planted, lungs for the city arranged, the miracles of art and science introduced to every-day notice; and hundreds of other equally important matters. Well, reader, everything that seemed impossible has been proved not merely possible, but carried into effect—and that, too, with a rapidity that you can hardly believe it has all happened within your lifetime. New Paris in so far differs from old Rome, that it has been built in a day.

During the last half-century the population of Paris has more than doubled, and the measure of its prosperity increased proportionately with even greater rapidity. It was necessary that new houses should be built and suitable sites selected. The north-west side was preferred; and hence Paris has not grown equally in every direction. As in other great cities, the population of Paris has collected in districts, so that similar trades are assembled in the same part. Thus, the great manufactories may be found in the Faubourg St Antoine; the smaller factories, such as the bronze foundries and smithies in the Marais; the dealers in imported articles are found in the district between the Hôtel de Ville and the Canal St Martin; in the vicinity of the Rue Hauteville, the commission and export agents have collected; further on, near the Place des Victoires, we find the dépôts of woollen goods; while across the water, in the Quartier Latin, the tanpits and dyers' establishments occupy the banks of the Bièvre, and the printers, bookbinders, &c., are congregated around the schools and university. Hence it is seen that each part of the city possesses its elements of prosperity; but they are too unequally divided, and too much isolated. The great object, then, is to approximate them, and the greatest want hitherto felt in Paris has been of broad bridges and chaussées, which would accelerate the communication between the various suburbs. The towns of Flanders were at least three centuries in advance of the capital of France in this respect. The first trace of design in Paris will be found in the reign of Louis XIII., who had the Marais laid out after a regular plan, with a large *place* after the pattern of the Netherlands. The Place Vendôme and the Invalides, the chief monuments of the lengthy reign of Louis

XIV., are sufficient to show what that monarch might have made of Paris, had he not devoted his attention almost exclusively to Versailles. From that time Paris was left to its fate, and although a few streets were opened, and the most crying defects repaired, still the centre of Paris has always proved the stumbling-block which prevented any material improvement. This was the narrowest, darkest, and dirtiest part of the town, a chaotic mass of filthy houses, and narrow winding streets, into which the sun never penetrated: in this confined sphere lived some fifty thousand people, and the number was indefinitely increased during business hours. As was natural, this was always the unhealthiest part of Paris; the tables of mortality show that while the average deaths in the more open parts of Paris were one in fifty, in the centre one in thirty died. Here, too, epidemic diseases raged most severely. In 1832 and 1848, the cholera was fearful in the centre of the city, and in the confined region round the Hôtel de Ville the mortality was five times as great as in the open, healthy neighbourhood of the Chaussée d'Antin. Everything tended to prove that, if broad streets were made through the centre of the *Cité*, this quarter would not only become more convenient and ornamental, but at the same time the inhabitants would be healthier and have increased facilities of trade communication with the faubourgs. In this sense the present government has perfectly comprehended its mission, and immortalizes itself by commencing its improvements in that portion of the *Cité* where the want was most pressingly felt.

It would be unjust to assert that since the First

Empire no French government has made attempts to remodel or improve Paris. During the Restoration but little was done, and private buildings as much surpassed the public edifices as the reverse had been the case under Napoleon I., but the dynasty of July did much to improve the city. The formation of the Rue Rambuteau, running parallel with the river, and forming a better communication between the Place Royale and the Halles, was the greatest and most useful of the undertakings made by that government. The partial removal of the buildings round the Hôtel de Ville, the formation of the Rue Lobau, Rue du Pont Louis-Philippe, and of another street running from the rear of the Hôtel de Ville to the gate of the church of St Gervais, also in some measure ventilated the centre of the city. Still, the Citizen King, in this as in too many other matters, allowed himself to be directed by accidental circumstances rather than a given plan. A wise and powerful ruler, faithful in peaceful times to the principles of the founder of his dynasty, was destined to reconstruct Paris. Napoleon III. was the restorer of public peace and security in France, and with these trade and commerce emerged from their torpor. So soon as the community felt itself saved from the horrors of internecine war, the confidence it displayed in the new system was extraordinary. The numerous joint-stock enterprises, the enormous state loans, suddenly produced an incredible mass of easily convertible capital, and the spirit of speculation became so powerful among the Parisians that even the war could not damp it. Entire quarters disappeared and rose again by magic; and it would be incredible, if it could not be proved by documents, that during five years of the present régime four times as much was effected for the improvement of Paris than during the thirty-one years of the Restoration and the July dynasty. The sums expended in the improvements of Paris from 1816 to 1830 amounted to 10,250,000 fr., and from 1831 to 1847 to 24,500,000 fr.; while between 1851 and 1855 the enormous sum of 157,651,000 fr. was expended for the same purpose. Even more admirable than this is the design accompanying these magnificent works, for every day the spirit becomes more visible which has actuated Napoleon III. in all his undertakings. He has proved to his people not only that he ever studies their welfare, but that he possesses the head with which to find the means.

Paris is not a commercial and manufacturing city, which, like London, can be independent. The enormous population it contains lives almost entirely on the luxury and expenditure of rich Frenchmen and foreigners, who spend their revenues there, and consequently furnish employment for all hands. The rich foreigners, however, were driven from France by the Revolution, the rich people of France were afraid of attracting attention by any profuse outlay, and consequently the trade of Paris, being entirely dependent on them, was utterly stagnant. Every government, then, whatever name or form it might have, if it desired stability, was forced to find employment for the poorer classes, and set money in circulation; not merely because the workman must eat, but because an idle man is a dangerous man in any state, above all, in one that is insecure. After the *coup d'état* Louis Napoleon, consequently, sought to consolidate his power and make a powerful impression on public opinion, and he chose the improvements of Paris as the best and most effectual means. According to an old French proverb, "all goes well when *le bâtiment* goes on;" and by this is understood a quantity of special trades, which furnish employment for at least 50,000 workmen, or about one-fourth of the industrial population of Paris. In consequence of this new impetus the amount of money employed in private building soon grew from twenty-eight to two hundred and fifty millions, and the quantity of work for the labourers increased in an equal ratio.

If, however, the primary cause of the Parisian improvements may be of a political character, there is a second cause of much more important and beneficial aspect. A portion of Paris was immoderately populous and industrial, another almost lifeless and dull. Every one thronged round the Palais Royal, the Louvre, and the Halles. This was an admirable situation for the retail trade, from its vicinity to the Boulevards. Houses were expensive here, but any one who possessed one considered his fortune as made. On the other hand, the once rich Quartier du Marais, the handsome Faubourg St Germain, and the West-end had so sunk in public repute that they appeared like a city of the dead. The farther one went from the centre the broader and longer the streets became, but trade was stagnant. The more distant Quartiers had no intercommunication, and lay round Paris like villages. In Chaillot and the Roule, behind the Chaussée d'Antin, and the Faubourgs Montmartre, Poissonnière, St Denis,

St Martin, &c., on the right bank, as well as in the district between the Gobelins and the Invalides, resided many thousands who belonged only topographically and politically to Paris, but seemed to have no connexion with the city, which they only visited on business or on holidays. All these districts were once villages, which gradually joined themselves to the colossus, and were finally included by a common wall, during Calonne's ministry in 1784. In these village-like districts everything was quiet and rustic. Here you might see, within the banlieue, fields of wheat, spacious orchards, large nursery-gardens, dépôts of wood and stone, and those factories which required large space, which could be obtained here at a cheaper rate. In short, while one part of the city was overcrowded, another was almost deserted. So soon, then, as the number of houses in the populous quarter was diminished, the inhabitants were compelled to emigrate to the desolate portions of Paris. Such has been the object for which the present government of France has been striving, and it has met with perfect success.

The new Louvre was designed as the nucleus of new Paris. The completion of this palace has so long been regarded as impracticable, as the creation of the brain, that it is difficult to believe in the realization, even when it is visible to us as a gigantic fact. The Parisians had for so long a period known the court of the Louvre as a cloaca, where at night four wooden posts stretched out their arms to the passengers, diffusing a sickly light, and the Carousel-square, as a fair-ground, full of booths and stalls, that they had at last persuaded themselves that the dirty streets, gallows-like lamp-posts, and neck-breaking holes, formed an indispensable adjunct of the royal palace. And, in fact, is it not a dream? Five years have scarce elapsed, and the whole disgraceful heap of pigsties, stalls, pot-houses, and tapis francs has disappeared. The holes are filled up, the ground levelled and covered with magnificent buildings, and, strange to say, the eye accustoms itself so entirely and rapidly to the change, that the memory can hardly summon up the old aspect of the place; we seem to forget utterly the but recent buildings that covered it. At length we vacantly look round for the Rue du Doyenné, a species of Invalid quarter; the Hôtel de Nantes, a large house standing alone in the centre of the Place, where it looked like a pyramid, and served as a house of call for all the omnibuses of the city and the banlieue; the Rue St Thomas du Louvre, the most respectable and cleanest in the quarter, and which ran to the Château d'Eau: gone too is that labyrinth of dirty and scandalous streets that formed a chain of villany between the Louvre and the Palais Royal, in which no honest citoyenne dare appear by day or night, lest she might be subjected to insult. It is difficult *now* for us to comprehend how such a swarm of scoundrels could find shelter on a spot which is only just large enough for the new Louvre buildings. All this and much else existed five years ago—a miserable sight for the philanthropist; now it is almost an obliterated reminiscence, attaching itself to the archæologic memories of the Bastille and the Carillon on the Pont Neuf. The boarded stalls of the Carousel are as much a Parisian tradition as the old wooden gallery in the Palais Royal, once known as the "Camp of the Tatars."

The Parisians have certainly witnessed eternal repairs and improvements on the Louvre and the Tuileries, but they progressed so slowly that they might have gone on building for ever, for before one part was finished another had fallen into a dilapidated state. Now the Parisians see with amazement that the two palaces are connected, and the new Louvre built and decorated with magical rapidity, before they had time to form an idea of its extent, arrangement, and plan. The huge block of buildings now covering the Place de Carousel is of very recent date, the foundation-stone having been laid in July, 1852. Since that date the wing on the north side of the Tuileries, begun by Napoleon I., and extending from the Pavillon de Rohan to the Rue de Marengo, has been completed, thus forming the connexion between the Louvre and the Tuileries. At the same time two other wings have been added, running parallel from the old Louvre to the Place du Carousel, and forming a large square, which has received the name of the Place Napoléon III. Round the new wings, along the Place du Carousel and the Place Napoléon III., run covered walks, with terraces, in which an army of statues of celebrated men stand in rank and file, like soldiers in the battlements of a fortress. Doubts may exist as to the æsthetic value of the new edifices, and we are not disposed to agree with the French critics when they say that it is "le plus beau monument d'architecture moderne qu'il y ait dans l'univers;" but they certainly possess two incontestable grounds for attracting our attention and justifying our amazement—the magnitude of the design, and the wondrous rapidity of execution.

The same merit may be justly claimed by the new Rue de Rivoli. This magnificent street, running parallel with the quays and Boulevards, now extends to the Fontaine de Birague, opposite the church St Paul St Louis. From the Place de la Concorde, where it commences, it runs along an endless succession of stately art monuments, such as the Tuileries, the Palais Royal, the Louvre, St Germain l'Auxerrois, the Tower of St Jacques la Boucherie, the Town House, and the Column of July. The portion of this street extending from the Rue de Rohan to the Rue Culture Sainte Catherine furnishes the fairest evidence of the humanity that suggested this great artery. More than thirty pestilential streets and alleys have been removed, and a whole quarter cleared and ventilated. The Tower of St Jacques has been restored in its pristine pomp and surrounded by a handsome garden, and the Town House has been thoroughly cleared from obstructions; in the rear is the colossal barrack called Caserne Napoléon, a perfect fortress, connected with the Town House by a subterranean passage; and in front, a magnificent new street, christened Avenue de Victoria, in honour of our Queen's visit to Paris. Another great artery is that known by the name of the Boulevard de Sébastopol, running from the Strasbourg Railway station in the Faubourg Poissonnière to the Place du Châtelet. These streets have cost an enormous sum in payments to leaseholders and running up the new buildings; thus, the new Rue de Rivoli, which swallowed up more than five hundred old houses, cost

81,563,000 fr. But, in spite of this, the Emperor has been indefatigable, and it is an extraordinary fact that the restorations have been carried on in every quarter of Paris almost simultaneously. On the island of the *Cité* important works have been undertaken: a broad street has been laid down from the Parvis Nôtre Dame, running to the Council House, over the Pont d'Arcole, which has been converted from a suspension-bridge for foot passengers only into a handsome stone bridge with a broad highway. Great improvements have also been effected in and around the Palais de Justice; the block of houses between the Sainte Chapelle and the Quai des Orfèvres has already been pulled down, and the quay widened up to the Rue de la Barillerie. On the left bank of the Seine equally surprising alterations have been effected. The Faubourg St Antoine naturally afforded no great opportunity for demolishing; still the architects have found it necessary to pull down some houses in order to form new routes of communication. In the Quartier Latin enormous alterations are projected, which must drive the students to despair. Four wide streets are to be formed, crossing each other at right angles, and intersecting the entire Quartier. The two streets running from east to west, parallel with the Seine, are the Rue des Ecoles and the Boulevard St Germain; the two running from north to south are the Rue St Jacques, a continuation of the Rue St Martin on the right bank, and the Boulevard de Sébastopol, which is intended to run as far as the Barrière d'Enfer in the Faubourg St Jacques, and intersect entire Paris for a distance of nearly three miles. These streets are to be completed in five years, at a cost of

37,650,000 fr.; and thus a stop will be put to the complaints that have been prevalent as to the left bank being neglected.

One of the principal results produced by the wholesale demolition of houses in the centre of Paris has been that the faubourgs have greatly increased in population. The Faubourg St Antoine has been thus enriched by upwards of thirteen hundred new houses, or more than sufficient for a population of forty thousand. A similar phenomenon is now visible in the Faubourgs St Germain and St Marcel, and the buildings will grow up with magical celerity so soon as the Boulevard de Sébastopol has become an established fact. In the first and second arrondissements a multitude of new houses have also sprung into existence, and the Tivoli garden has entirely disappeared. This garden lay at no great distance from the northern boulevards, in a quarter between the Faubourgs Montmartre and St Honoré, opposite the Pavillon du Hanôvre on the Boulevard des Italiens, and extended thence to the Barrière de Clichy. Even though it might appear a paltry spot when compared with Horace's Tibur Supernum, the Roman Tivoli, whence it derived its name, it contained within its ample space every requisite for pleasure gardens; but the greedy eye of speculation surveyed it, and Tivoli was doomed. The ruthless axe was laid to the root of the chestnut-trees and silver poplars, the grass-plats were cut up, the visitors were expelled, and some dozen streets soon occupied the fairy spot. For awhile the gardens might still be traced, however; the first purchasers of "eligible building spots" considered it a point of honour to leave a clump of trees or a bosquet near their houses; and in some places entire alleys and gardens might be traced. But the quartier soon began to be regarded as fashionable, and the demand for building sites rapidly destroyed all the trees. On the Place Vintimille, in the Rue de Douai, Rue de Calais, &c., the trees have all been cut down, and the quartier now resembles any other, except that the houses are eagerly caught up, and frequently entered upon before the building is finished.

The park of Monceaux, near the Barrière de Courcelles, which reverted to the state by the Orleans succession, will soon endure the fate of its pristine neighbour Tivoli, which it far surpasses in convenience and space. The speculating builders have already invaded it, for it is known that two main roads, the Boulevard de l'Impératrice and the Boulevard Malesherbes, are to run through it. Even the Champs Elysées, which so reluctantly allowed admission to bricks, appear fated. An Anglo-French company has been established, under the title of the "Company of the Champs Elysées," and holds out most flattering offers to shareholders, great and small. It has already purchased a piece of land of more than one hundred thousand metres, and, we believe, has commenced operations. Every available spot between the banlieue and the wall of circumvallation is by this time built upon, and even beyond them the Parisians are now setting up their lares. There seems, in truth, no end to the extension of the city, for the entire population, down to the poorest labourer, is affected by a desire for living out of town.

The botanist, who not long ago was enabled to herbalize near the Barrière de l'Etoile, on now seeing the Bois de Boulogne converted into a Parisian promenade, may perhaps be justified in giving way to a gentle sigh; but while he is compelled to go farther afield to follow in the footsteps of Jussieu, the inhabitants of Passy, Boulogne, and Auteuil sing a pæan of praise at the conversion of their scrubby wood into a magnificent park. An ordonnance of the 8th July, 1852, gave the property of this wood to the city of Paris, on condition that it expended two millions of francs upon it in four years. This condition has been more than fulfilled: in three years the city laid out three millions and a half in converting the sandy plain into a garden. If we take into account the four million francs expended in forming the Avenue de l'Impératrice, with the two millions spent in building the new hippodrome of Longchamp, as well as all the improvements projected, we must allow that the city of Paris has spared no expense in producing a pleasure-garden such as the Parisians could desire. Under the management of Monsieur Varé, the old scene of duels and suicides has been converted into the Paradise of Imperial Paris: it already displays trees and bushes of every variety, hedges and labyrinthine flower-beds, shady walks and elysian alleys, rocks and grottoes, a hill with a gentle slope and pleasant view of the surrounding scenery, silvery ponds and foaming cascades, green islands with flower-gardens, châlets, and harbours; boats and swans upon the water, stags and deer upon the meadows, singing and chirruping birds in the trees and bushes—the whole produced, as it were, by a magician's wand. There are also numerous respectable hotels, where refreshments of every description may be obtained, a magnificent room for concerts and balls, and a hippodrome, where thousands of persons may drive and ride without impediment. The Bois has justly become the favourite resort of the Parisians, and we may say it assumes the character of a botanic garden, as almost every variety of tree has its habitat here, having been brought from all parts of the world to satisfy the luxurious desires of the Parisian populace.

Since the gardens of Paris have been destroyed for building purposes, it was found advisable to take especial care of the few oases left. Hence a commission has been appointed for this purpose with a very efficient staff. The city of Paris now holds possession of eight enclosed grounds, forming promenades or squares; on one side the Bois du Boulogne with its annexes, the plain of Longchamp and the Avenue de l'Impératrice, on the other the Place Royale, the Place de l'Archevêché, and the squares round the tower of St Jacques, in front of the church of St Clotilde, at the Temple, and at the ruins of the old Roman palace of the Thermæ. In addition to these, the city possesses more than fifty-seven thousand trees, planted in the Champs Elysées, the quincunxes of the Trocadero, the inner and outer boulevards, the quays, and a few open spaces; the whole of the plantations occupy a space of more than two hundred acres; the oldest, on the Champs Elysées, dating from 1617. The outer boulevards are adorned in some parts with double rows of lofty trees, dating from 1760; but the inner boulevards lost nearly all their trees in the revolutions of 1830 and 1848; those left are too stunted, and the newly-planted trees too young, to offer any shade. As a general rule, the trees planted in the streets of Paris have proved a failure, in spite of the care devoted to them; they die off rapidly, and the gamins do their part in accelerating their death. The authorities have recently planted large nurseries in the Bois de Boulogne, where they experimentalize on the best varieties of trees, and arrangements have been even made with the gas companies, which will in future prevent the trees being poisoned by the exhalations from the pipes. If these prophylastic measures are in any way successful, we may live in hope of seeing trees planted in our own streets—somewhere before the advent of the Millennium.

It would lead us too far, were we to stop and discuss the result of all these changes in the aspect of Paris. For a time rumours were prevalent of discontent at the great increase of rents, but these appear to have subsided, and the population of Paris to have "accepted the situation" with resignation. There appears to be more truth in the statement that, in these new buildings, internal comfort has been too often sacrificed to external effect. Among the numerous jeremiads we have heard, the principal refer to the instability of the houses and the thinness of the walls. Another inconvenience is the immoderate height of the windows, which open after the Italian fashion from top to bottom, and are fastened by a heavy iron bar, which a puff of wind is sure to blow open. Then, again, we are told that the chimneys are of extravagant dimensions, occupying more than half the side of the room, and costing a small fortune in firing. But the true Parisian cares little for these things; so long as the exterior of his house is handsomely decorated with stucco, gilding, and statues, he is perfectly satisfied, and these things are lavishly expended in Imperial Paris. At the same time, Paris has been newly furnished to correspond with the new style of building, and thus an immense sum of money has been brought into circulation; and if such amusements keep the peeple quiet and contented, who are we that we should gainsay the wisdom of the Imperial policy?

In so slight a sketch as ours it would be impossible to give more than an outline of the improvements in Paris which the Emperor has effected; but what we have said will suffice to prove how admirably he has provided for the physical comfort and well-being of the lower classes. By a stroke of his pen he has effected a marvellous change, such as we have so long desired at home, which has been debated and discussed under a hundred different aspects among us without producing the slightest satisfactory results. It is true that eminent philanthropists have subscribed to build model lodging-houses, but we doubt whether St Giles has lost one denizen by their erection; and though schemes have been ventilated for lodging our artisans out of town and enabling them to come to their labour each morning by train, we do not find any prospect of its fruition. And yet it is a question which will have to be grappled with sternly before long: the safety of our population demands that such lurking-places of disease must be eradicated, and the legislature is alone capable of strenuously interfering. The pleasing fiction that "every man's house is his castle" has, like so many other fictions, been overturned by the Board of Health, and it would require but a step to carry out in London all that the emperor has so successfully achieved in Paris. At any rate, we are forced to admit that they "manage such things better in France" on the *sic volo sic jubeo* principle than we can effect by the united efforts of our Board of Health and Sanitary Commissioners.

CHAPTER XIV.

ALPINE GRASS FARMS.

Those monarchs of mountains which we know under the name of the Alps are most prosaically called "hills" by the denizen of the district, for to him they are hills, and nothing more. While red-booked tourists gaze with admiration on the giants, and can glibly run off the name of each soaring pinnacle, it is rare for the peasant to possess any such knowledge, unless he has a desire to earn an honest penny by his visitors. The wondrous sheen of the ice-crowned crests, the majestic appearance of the Alps, and the dread secrets of their glaciers and caves, are matters of perfect indifference to the Swiss Peter Bell. His only regret is that the naked rock bears no vegetation: he would give for an acre of fertile soil square acres of glacier, and good fodder is dearer to him than the most enthralling landscape. By the term "Alps" he only comprehends the mountains in so far as they supply his cattle with pasturage; the "Alp" of the Swiss and the "Alm" of the Tyrolese is, therefore, only a grass farm. Those portions of the Alps on which nourishing fodder grows are called "matten," and they do not generally extend beyond seven thousand feet above the sea level. In the Grisons, however, some meadows are found at a height of ten thousand feet, and stand amid the eternal snows like the exquisite "gardens" seen on the glaciers, where sunny flowers exhale their perfume among the frowning ice. The Alps are divided by the Swiss peasant into lower, central, and upper; the first is nearest to the habitations, and is frequented by all the domestic animals, including horses, which at times, however, accompany the kine to their true habitat, the central Alp; while the uppermost is left principally to the sheep and goats, the cattle only ascending to it during the hottest months.

The ingenuous reader has probably formed a very incorrect idea of the vegetation of the Alps, and fancies that only the sweetest and most odorous plants, like thyme and marjoram, grow on them, affording magnificent pasturage. Here and there, I grant, there are rich meadows, but they are exceptional, and in most cases the Alpine rocks are covered with scarce an inch of humus, on which a very scanty vegetation grows. Much of the grass is also unfit for pasturage, owing to the incessant wet; and many noxious plants grow there, which the cattle, however, have the sagacity to avoid. On the highest stages of the mountain the best sorts of fodder grass are generally found, the most highly esteemed among them being the Alpine clover (Trifolium Alpinum), the Alpine plantain (Leontodon aureum), the tragacanth (Astragalus cicer and aristatus), the fescue grass (Festuca montana), the milfoil (Achillea millifolium), the succory (Hieracium pilosella), yellow clover (Medicago lupulina), snail clover (Medicago minima), accompanied by spring grass, quaking grass, timothy grass, salsify, spikenard, &c. The most favourite growth with the neatherds is, however, the

Alpine bear's-wort (Meum mutellina), with its graceful leaves and bright red sweet-smelling blossoms. The bear digs up its roots, and the marmot eagerly collects it for its winter stock of provender. The "nardus stricta," which is looked down upon in the plains, is also considered very excellent fodder, as it makes the milk rich; sheep are very fond of it also, and it forms the staple nourishment of the Bergamasque flocks. The nearer we arrive to the snow line, the more the vegetation changes; dwarf trees, among which the mountain pine occupies the chief place, grow more and more stunted; large surfaces are covered with the bright green leaves and pinky blossoms of the Alpine rose, among which flower the ranunculus, and red, blue, and yellow gentian, whose roots are eagerly sought by the digger, for the purpose of preparing a tonic spirit; then Alpine blue-bells, mountain asters, columbine, saxifrage, anemones, and a thousand other pretty children of Flora, which, however, gradually disappear as the Alp ascends. Their place is taken by moss, and last of all by lichens, which, as the last relic of vegetation, cover the highest peaks. Still, the summer tourist, in the midst of the snow, may come across a very garden of fair flowers in some sheltered nook.

The vegetation of the swampy Alpine meadows is similar to that in the plains: oat grass (Melica nutans) and cotton grass (Eriophorum angustifolium) are found in the lower stages, intermingled with Alpine sorrel (Rumex Alpinus) and guinea wheat (Holcus lanatus). Very curious here is the appearance of many poisonous plants, among which the foxglove is most striking. Untouched by cattle, even by the nibbling goat, it grows in thick patches, and to a great height, in the damp meadows, even as far as the snow line; it is found, too, very frequently round the milking huts, and is no slight ornament to the otherwise monotonous landscape. This is, however, the only value it possesses, except that, when dried, it can be employed for burning. Near it grows the white hellebore (Veratum album), often in incredible luxuriance, equally avoided by cattle, and only welcome to the root digger. Mezereon, madworts, &c., are frequently found on the Alps, but no instance has been known of cattle injuring themselves by browsing on them. The most valuable growth of all is the true timothy grass (Phleum appinum), a very soft, juicy, and productive fodder, which frequently grows to a length of two feet, and hangs picturesquely over the rocks.

The summer trip of the cattle to the Alp usually lasts four or five months, though in rainy seasons it only extends to two. The ascent, as the departure of the cattle is called, generally takes place at the end of May or beginning of June, and is a scene of jollity to the whole village possessing the Alp. In front of the procession gravely marches the leading cow, wearing a red leathorn collar, to which a bell often a foot in diameter is suspended; next comes the patriarchal bull, also wearing a bell; then follow the others carrying small bells, which now-a-days produce a species of Dutch concert, though formerly some attempt at harmony was made. The prettiest cows are generally decorated with flowers and streamers, and the milking-stools are fastened between their horns. As the procession passes those châlets where the kine are kept at home, a melancholy lowing greets it, for the cattle all know the season of liberty for which they long. As the summer advances the cows ascend higher up the Alps, and many a squabble takes place about straying cattle. In the olden times the farmers would defend the frontiers of their pasturage staff in hand, but now they content themselves with impounding the errant kine.

The cattle are generally waited on and looked after by a neatherd (the Senn) in Switzerland, by a milk-maid (Sennerin) in Bavaria and the Tyrol. As a general rule, however, men are considered preferable, for it has been found by experience that cheese, when made by women, is not so good, as the necessity of turning the millstone-like cheeses daily during the operation of salting, demands a considerable expenditure of strength. Curiously enough, though, in Switzerland the gravest charge brought against the milk-maids is a want of cleanliness. The hut in which the neatherd lives is usually built of coarsely sawn fir stumps, the interstices being filled up with moss; a chimney is a rarity, and the door serves the purpose of a window. When wood is difficult to obtain, the hut is built of unmortared stones, also covered with moss or earth, and generally stands in a pool of dirty water, where the cattle collect at night, and which is produced by the neatherd emptying the rinsings of his milkpans before his door. The furniture principally consists of a cheese caldron, and the neccessary articles for making that produce; now and then you may see a rickety chair, but the herd generally contents himself with his milking-stool. I need hardly say that the bed is distinguished by its absence, for the uncivilized fellow prefers sleeping on the hay he has cut for his cattle in the event of bad weather setting in.

The treatment of the cattle is generally kind, and if you can abstract the prevalent dirt, it is a pleasant sight to see them collect round the herd when he has put on his "licking-pouch." This is a large leathern bag in which he keeps salt, sometimes mixed with grasses, which the kine lick out of his hand; at times, however, he spreads it over the back of the cattle, so that they may lick one another. Another agreeable sight is the air of freedom the cattle gradually assume; they play about and indulge in all sorts of tricks, not unfrequently combining to attempt an assault on the unsuspecting visitor. At times they are careless, and commit suicide by falling off the rocks: thus, in 1845, two cows that were settling a private dispute fell over a precipice near the Staub-bach, and were literally dashed to pieces. It could not have been worse had they met with an English railway accident. In less dangerous instances the neatherd is compelled to help them out of their difficulty by means of ropes; this is more frequently the case, however, with the curious goats, whose boldness impels them to take the most daring leaps, but they suddenly lose all their courage when they find that they cannot get back from their dizzy perch. Man, who imitates the chamois, and surpasses it in daring—else he would not kill it—is consequently obliged to go to the help of the better organized animal, and generally succeeds in rescuing it. The goat does not possess the courage of the chamois, which, when driven into a corner, will leap down a sheer fall of a thousand feet, for it prefers to die of hunger when not rescued from its awkward situation.

The danger to which Alpine cattle are exposed from predaceous animals has now greatly decreased. In Styria or Carnia a bear may still carry off a calf or a goat, but such a foray is the signal for immediate pursuit on the part of the neck-venturing hunters, and Bruin rarely carries his fur back to his lair. Still less frequently does the lynx emerge from its Alpine den, although it is a bloodthirsty and crafty foe of the sheep and goats; but the wolves at times prowl about and commit ravages among the flocks, the great preservation against them being found in the long shaggy Italian dog, which attacks them most furiously. The lambs and kids fall more frequently a prey to the Lämmer-geier, which either pounces down upon them, or drives them off a rock into an abyss with its huge wings. In times of starvation several of these birds will combine to attack a larger animal, but only succeed in overpowering an inexperienced creature, as the old hands remain perfectly passive, and wear out the patience of their assailants.

As the main object of Alpine grass-farming is the production of cheese, I may be permitted to dwell a little longer on the process. In Switzerland various sorts of cheese are made, which, however, may be classified in two categories for my purpose, namely, Gruyère and herb, or green, cheese. The former is subdivided, according to quality, into extra rich, rich, half rich, and lean cheese. The first is rarely made, the last is consumed entirely on the Alp, while the two other sorts are introduced into trade. Their preparation only varies in the richness of the milk employed, and may be shortly described as follows: In the morning, so soon as the neatherd has milked the cows, he proceeds into the dairy, where the previous evening's milk is standing in pans, and the cream has already settled. If rich cheese is to be made, this is mixed, unskimmed, with the morning's milk; if it is to be extra rich, only the cream from it is employed; for half-rich cheese the cream is taken off the evening milk, and the morning milk is added to the residuum; while for thin cheese only the skimmed evening milk is employed. The whole is placed in a caldron, and warmed over a slow fire to between 25 deg. and 30 deg. Réaumur; but the richer the milk is the warmer it must be made. When the required temperature is attained the caldron is removed from the fire, the runnet put in, and the milk left to stand for a quarter of an hour. After the curd has set, the next process is to express the whey, which is effected by cutting the former into small pieces with a wooden instrument called a sword: the smaller the pieces are the better the cheese will become, as the whey can be more thoroughly removed. When all this has been done the caldron is again placed over the fire, and the mass is heated to 40 deg. Réaumur: this is done not only to separate the whey from the curd, but also to render the latter more cohesive. When the mass has attained this heat the neatherd removes the caldron from the fire, and swings it round rapidly until the curd has formed a globular and compact mass, floating in the whey, along with which it is then placed in a flat milk-pan. After the greater portion of the whey has been clumsily squeezed out, the cheese is placed in the form, where it lies for an hour with a heavy stone upon it, which squeezes more and more whey out; at the expiration of that time it is placed in the cheese press, where it remains some four-and-twenty hours. When there is no longer any fear of its losing its shape, the next process is salting, which takes place in the cheese-cellar; the rind is washed with a strong solution of brine, which is rubbed in with a clean rag, and fine salt strewn over the surface. In twenty-four hours the salt is brushed away, and the cheese turned to undergo the operation on the lower side: with large cheeses this has to be done daily for four months. The richer and larger the cheese is the longer it must lie—in some cases for a whole year—during which it has to be constantly turned. But this task does not devolve on the neatherd, for he either sells his cheeses when the salting is completed, or they are carried down into the valley to be stored. It is calculated that to make one pound of cheese twelve pounds of rich milk, fifteen of half-rich milk, or twenty of skim-milk, are required; and the cheese also loses from twenty to twenty-five per cent. of its weight while stored. The green cheese is made of the whey that remains over with an admixture of herbs, and I may also mention here, that considerable quantities of goat's cheese are made on the Alps for home consumption.

For keeping the milk, flat wooden pans called "mulden" are in universal use, but the finest specimens may be seen in Switzerland. They are washed immediately after use in the whey, and a deposit gradually forms on the bottom of the pans, called "milk-stone," or a combination of saccharine matter with a few inorganic salts. As this prevents the acid contained in the milk from penetrating into the wood, no consideration would induce the Swiss farmer to remove it.

The neatherd rarely makes butter, save when specially ordered; but, if firewood be abundant, he produces a large quantity of sugar of milk by evaporating the whey, and this commands a ready sale. In his leisure hours he may make baskets, wooden spoons, and clothes-pegs—at times, too, he will be observed knitting stockings, like the German peasant. No more monotonous life can be conceived than that of the Swiss Senn: he has said good-bye to all the comforts of existence, and has only what is absolutely necessary around him. His clothes are as simple and durable as possible; he usually wears a round leathern cap, which presently becomes quite greasy from leaning against the kine while milking, and short leathern trousers, footless stockings, and wooden shoes, complete his costume, though he is glad to kick the latter off. He does not trouble himself much about washing, or changing his linen, and his food mainly consists of dairy produce. He drinks cream instead of coffee, and whey as a substitute for water; fat cheese represents meat, and he eats goat's cheese in lieu of bread; or if he desire a dainty dish for a change, he will beat up cream into a species of syllabub. Even if he had meat and bread daily, he is much too lazy to cook, or entertains a prejudice against them, for he considers that the true neatherd ought only to live on the produce of his own hands. Recently, coffee has found its way into some of the huts, and nowhere in the world is cream so extravagantly drunk with it as there; plain milk is never used. But the tobacco-pipe is the Senn's great consolation, and the milkmaids even are partial to it. "Tübackle" represents to these hermits all the other enjoyments of civilization. The neatherds, as a general rule, are a contemplative and indolent race of beings: they do their work, but nothing beyond. If they have to carry wood, for instance, they do not load on their shoulders one log more than is absolutely required for boiling the caldron. The herd who repairs his cabin, or cleans anything further than his milk vessels, is regarded as a phenomenon. On the higher Alps, the Senn sees but few human beings throughout the summer; at times, his sweetheart, or wife, or a friend may visit him; the owners of the cattle may come up once or twice to look after them; or a neighbouring mountaineer run across to smoke a pipe with him, that is all. He has, however, no craving for society, the place of which his cattle amply supply. If he be young and jolly, he may give a colleague on an adjoining Alp a shrill yell, but you never hear from his lips those bepraised Alpine Lieder, which have been fashionable ever since Rossini composed the Ranz des Vaches for "William Tell."

Owing to their mode of life, the herdsmen are generally powerful and healthy men, whose astonishing strength has become proverbial in Switzerland. They are mostly short, with a very large bust, and an extraordinary development of shoulders, the consequence of playing with hundred-weights of cheese daily, but their lower works are not so satisfactory, and the majority of them have bandy legs, which they ascribe to the milking-stool. The once widely celebrated hospitality of the Sennhuts is now-a-days only to be met with in those which are rarely visited, and the ordinary herdsman generally expects hotel prices from mountain tourists for what he sets before them. If their liberality does not come up to his expectations of the right thing, he is apt to give them anything but a blessing on their journey.

When the Alpine meadows are close to the villages, the kine are driven up to them in the morning and home again at night: it is in many districts considered better, however, to leave them out all night, and the boys and girls go up at daybreak to milk them. The goats, in such cases, always return home at night, and it is a pretty sight to see them descending the mountain-slopes under the guidance of the goat-boy. Rich peasants also keep goats, employing their milk for the daily consumption of the family, while that of the cows is reserved exclusively for cheese-making. In many villages what is called a "cheese club" is formed, to which a party of peasants send their milk in common, keeping a man specially to make cheeses: in the larger villages, indeed, two or three such clubs exist, which carry on a profitable business. And this reminds me that Jeremiah Gotthelf has given a charming description of such a club in one of his village tales, which only deserve to be better known in this country to be preferred to Auerbach's peasant stories.

I may allude, in passing, to the Sheep Alps on the southern slopes of Savoy, the Tyrol, and Lombardy. The mountains there are so extensive, and the population so sparse, that the parishes and landowners generally let a large portion of their Alp to foreign speculators, principally Italians from the province of Bergamo, though the collective name of "Bergamini" is not absolutely indicative of their fatherland. As a general rule, only the plateaux from six thousand to nine thousand feet above the level of the sea are let in Switzerland, and those chiefly in the Grisons, Tessin, and Vaudois. A speculator, generically known as the "pastore," hires a certain district, on to which he turns his sheep, rarely exceeding three hundred in number, under the sole charge of a man and a boy. Milking sheep is a far more difficult task than with cows, and demands practice and patience. The milk is usually mixed with that of cows: a portion of it, made into sweet cheese, produces the celebrated Stracchin, known as a dainty all over the world, while the other milk is curdled, and made into a cheese not known in trade. The Bergamasque sheep are shorn in autumn all on the same day, for which the sheep of an Alpine district are drawn to one spot. Each sheep produces, on the average, seven pounds of wool, sold at the rate of £4 a hundredweight. Of the system pursued in the Italian Alps, I borrow the following interesting account from Stefano Jacini:

"From the time when the snow begins to melt until autumn the solitude of the mountains is populated by wandering cattle-owners. Cut off from human society, they observe a purely patriarchal mode of life, and have no settled residence, putting up wherever they may be a species of hut, in which they make cheese. If the snow expel them from the Alp, they put their traps on the bât-horse, and drive their flocks before them into the plain, where they wander about till they find pasturage. Among this nomadic race the actual shepherds must not be confounded with the Malghesi, or cowkeepers: the former pass a wretched life of poverty, owing to their ignorance. When they come down into the plains they are a thorn in the flesh of the farmers, who follow them up as thieves, because their flocks on the long road down to the plain are not merely satisfied with the grass growing by the wayside or on the banks of torrents, but take tithe of the winter fields, and commit such damage in them that they are not permitted to pass through many parishes. The cowkeepers, as a rule, are much better off than might be supposed from their boorish attire and mode of life. The value of their herds is often considerable, and there are cowkeepers possessing a fortune of 100,000 lire, which does not prevent them, however, from milking their own kine. In autumn they come down from the Alp, and bargain with the farmers in the plain to keep their herds for them during the winter. Sheep-breeding is falling off greatly in Lombardy: banished almost entirely from the more southern mountains, it is now confined to the upper part of the Val Canonica and the Valtelline, where wretched flocks of sheep browse close to the eternal snow, as the shepherds are unable to pay a high rent. But even in these districts the number of the sheep is diminishing, and the breed deteriorating, from year to year; thus, the parish of Ponte di Legno, which only a short time back drove six thousand sheep on to the Alp, has scarce half that number now. All attempts made to promote sheep-breeding at the beginning of this century, when the price of wool and meat was so high, failed. Though the Alps may support sheep during the summer, the best pasturage is reserved for cattle, and sheep are no longer tolerated in the plains, where they injure the growth of useful plants."

I may mention, in a parenthesis, that in the mountain ranges of Norway and Sweden the Alpine grass farms find a colourable imitation. There, also, the cattle, sheep, and goats spend the summer on the mountains; and the manufacture of cheese is the great staple, though large quantities of butter are also made. The northern herdsmen, or Seter, are, moreover, expected to collect a sufficient quantity of fodder for the winter, though that rarely happens, and the cattle are compelled to put up with dried fish and other supplementary stock.

The return from the Swiss Alps usually takes place in September, the goats and sheep remaining on the mountain as the rear-guard, and being gradually driven down by the snow. The descent is similar to the ascent, with the exception that it is not so merry, for the men and girls are so attached to a vagabond life, in spite of its privations, that the winter appears to them as bad as imprisonment. During that period of the year they are indolent and obstinate, steal hay and corn whenever they can, and become a nuisance to everybody, not excepting themselves. Unfortunately, the manufacture of cheese in winter is exceptional; very foolishly so, I fancy, for there is no reason why it should not go on, were proper attention paid to the forage.

I have only a few words left to say about the cheese trade in the Alps. It is well known to be not merely a lucrative, but a large branch of commerce, for Gruyère cheeses may be found all over the habitable world. Of course the producer derives the smallest profit from it, and the "cheese gentlemen," or wholesale dealers, take advantage of all the chances of demand. As a rule, a cheese-market is held in some central point of the Alpine districts, where buyers and sellers congregate; only those cheeses are offered for sale which will bear transport, and the sellers are bound to deliver the cheeses, free from charge, at the buyer's place of business. As I have stated, only the rich and half-rich cheeses are represented in trade; for instance, the Emmenthaler belongs to the former class, the Parmesan to the latter. When extra rich cheese is made, it is solely for home festivities; it is perfectly hard, yellow, and bears a close resemblance to frozen butter. If exquisite cheese is wanted for marriage feasts and similar occasions of rejoicings, it is wrapped in linen cloths, and sprinkled with wine daily.

A good cow will produce twelve hundred pounds of milk during the summer, and its value may be estimated at three pounds ten shillings. Deducting the wages of the man, salt, firing, the price of utensils, &c., each cow produces about a net profit of a pound for the summer. No wonder, then, that many Swiss economists set their faces against this system as unfitted for the age we live in, for not only is the manure of the entire summer lost, but the kine deteriorate alarmingly, through the in and in breeding. No German farmer thinks of buying an Alpine cow now-a-days, though formerly they commanded the market. The Swiss government has, however, taken the initiative, and I may venture to say that, what with increased attention to arboriculture on the Alps, and the gradual introduction of improved means of cultivation, Alpine grass farms will ere long become a thing of the past.

CHAPTER XV.

WANTED A WIFE!

If the reader of this true story wishes to be informed who I am, I can tell him in a very few words. I'm a poor devil without money, position, or prospects, and yet, I may be allowed to say without flattering myself, I am highly deserving of all three. As long as I was young, I was a spoiled child of fortune—that is to say, through the indulgence of my excellent father, a doctor in large practice, I gratified every wish of my heart. Oh, those happy university days!—though they were not spent in the lecture-room. I was always considered a lighthearted, lightheaded lad, and, as long as I was so, fortune granted me her sweetest smiles. But she is a woman, like all whose name is weakness and frailty. Now that I am a man, and would gladly put away childish things, I am the very lowest on her wheel. My father is dead, and left me nothing. Eight-and-twenty years of age, I am not able to calculate with certainty on my next day's dinner. I have eaten my terms, it is true; but the road to practice is a thorny one at the best. And then there are certain leeches belonging to an earlier period, impertinent, dunning scoundrels, whom I cannot possibly make believe that *ex nihilo nihil fit*.

It is equally true that I have an aunt living at

Cheltenham, who is said to be fabulously rich. She is a widow, and childless, and I have some faint recollection of her, when she came to pay us a visit, as a stately, though somewhat capricious and haughty, dame. Unfortunately, we have had a quarrel, an eternal quarrel. It came about thus. About five years ago I took a walking tour through Wales. I was then at the acme of my youthful happiness. Healthy, cheerful, full of brilliant anticipations, I regarded the world in the rosiest colours. I was in a glorious temper, and yet, at the same time, I felt a foreboding that something exquisitely pleasant was about to happen to me. Up to the present I had never been really in love: such feelings had only been transitory. In these hours of my solitary tour, surrounded by the beauties of nature, my heart expanded and gave way to its best feelings, earnestly longing for that which I still wanted to render me perfectly happy. How could I imagine that the object of my wishes was so close at hand?

While climbing a steep mountain path beneath the leafy shade of some majestic oaks, I became an involuntary witness of a most charming scene. Before me, in a grass-covered glade, whence a splendid panorama of the vale below could be enjoyed, I perceived a happy party of ladies and gentlemen, and the sight had really something fairy-like about it from the contrast it presented to the silent, solitary woods around me. I stopped as if spell-bound, bowed, spoke—I know not what—and in a very short time I was enjoying their merry frolics heart and soul. There were several elder and younger ladies present; among the latter a young girl of some sixteen years of age, who resembled a budding rose among less noble and precious flowers. But no, I will not describe her: it would be impossible for cold, dead words to do justice to her countless charms.

I requested and received permission to join the party for the rest of the day. Oh! what a day it was! I rarely quitted Lucy's side—that was the dear girl's name. We chatted, jested, and laughed together as if we had been acquainted for years, and the rest of the party were too liberal to see anything improper or dangerous in our harmless frolics. How quickly the hours passed away, and ah! how soon was evening there, and with it the hour of separation. The ladies of the party, fatigued with their day's amusement, returned to their inn, but my hopes of drinking deeper from the cup of bliss the next morning were most terribly frustrated. An accident had happened to me. While walking along the side of the hill, Lucy suddenly exclaimed, "Oh! what a lovely flower that is below there!" I ran down with lightning speed; but, unfortunately, my foot slipped, and I rolled a considerable distance down the hill. I quickly regained my feet, and Lucy's cry of terror at the moment of my fall, as well as her pallid face and gentle, grateful smile when I handed her the flower, were an abundant recompense for the fright and the slight pain in my foot which I at first felt. In truth, there appeared to be nothing the matter; but on walking further the pain grew more violent—at last even insupportable—so that with difficulty I reached the inn. All the remedies employed were of no avail, and during the night my foot swelled so, that any chance of continuing my journey was lost, and I could not even leave my bed. I have never seen Lucy since: before daybreak the party quitted the house.

Who can describe the misery of my situation? The bodily pain of which I was a martyr appeared a mere trifle; but the feelings I now experienced for the first time in my life agonized me. Not a word of love had been breathed between us, and yet my whole manner on that eventful day had revealed it. Did Lucy return my love? Should I ever see her again? How should I live without her smile to cheer me? These and a hundred other questions, with a multitude of extraordinary schemes and plans, which only the madness of a loving heart at the age of three-and-twenty can invent, tortured me during the eight days of my confinement. Alas! my hopes were very slight! Lucy had passed away like a dream that leaves no trace behind. I knew not whence she came or whither she had gone, her name, nor her abode. She was in a similar state of ignorance about myself. I had intended to reveal this to her the next day.

Just at this time, when I was full of my love-dreams, a letter came from my aunt at Cheltenham, with the strangest proposition in the world. The worthy lady wished to marry me. She had an adopted daughter, whom she had brought up since the death of her parents, a pearl, a jewel, the ornament of her sex; her dearest wish was to see this her favourite happy, and she had at the same time thought of me, whose fortune was equally dear to her, if I showed myself deserving of it, that is, if I studied industriously, and had prospects of success at the bar. We could some day form a happy couple, for she would assuredly treat the good child as her beloved and real daughter. The last words were underlined, and struck my father most of all. "Accept," he said; "she's a bird of Paradise!" "I won't!" I replied with heart and mouth; and, in truth, treated the affair with my usual levity. How could I, whose sole thought Lucy was at that time, think without repugnance and horror on an alliance with this orphan—this adopted daughter?

My over-kind aunt received from my father an apologetic letter of refusal; from myself one that was rather merry and humorous (I will say that much for it). The latter excited her utmost fury against me, and very justly too. Since that time no communication has taken place between herself and us, and from a friend of mine at Cheltenham, who is also an acquaintance of my aunt, I know that the vials of her wrath against me are still full. Perhaps, too, my foolish larks, with which she is sure to have become acquainted, have done their share in the matter. If, then, I could so far master my pride as to seek favour in her eyes, I should have reason to fear an uncourteous and abrupt refusal from her, to which danger and humiliation I will not expose myself. I must e'en think of something else.

A shipwrecked man, as I am just at present, catches at a straw. I think no more of marrying Lucy. All my attempts to find her again have been fruitless. Still I cannot forget her. She is enshrined in the innermost recess of my heart, like a beloved and revered talisman, and surrounded by the fairest flowers of memory. To speak the truth, it is a matter of perfect indifference to me if and whom I marry. But I cannot be equally indifferent to the storms and breakers which have cast my ship of life ashore, and now tear away one plank after the other. A wife might be the hawser to bear me safely on shore. I will try it. Daily I read in the papers matrimonial advertisements, in which bashful youths or honourable widowers desire a companion for life in this "no longer unusual manner," either through "a lack of female society," or else "great pressure of business." They are all excellent fellows, true phœnixes of men, generally young, well educated, sound in mind and limb, possessing a competency, &c. It is only surprising that they are so modest in their demands. Of course it is but natural that the lady wanted should be young, pretty, amiable, and domestic, and that is the least that can be asked. More serious certainly is the inevitable mention of "a fortune in her own hands of from one to three thousand pounds, which can be secured on herself, if desired." But it will always be worth notice, with what amiable, I may say bashful, reserve this harsh point, which in this naughty material world cannot be omitted, is placed at the very end of the advertisement, and under what flowers of eloquence it is usually concealed. This "no longer unusual method" I will try, or rather, I have already done so.

I have diligently studied this branch of literature, and believe I am perfectly conversant with it. The chief thing is to be as careful and select in what one says, as in that which is left unmentioned. A wide and free field must be left for feminine anticipation and curiosity, so that they may be irresistibly attracted like the bird by the fowler's call. I think I have succeeded in producing something super-excellent. My advertisement lies finished and sealed up before me, and will immediately wing its way to the office of the *Morning Post.* I hope and wish the best success; for only this very morning I had a pleasant visit from an old friend, far too closely *lié* with me, who inquired in a sympathizing manner after the state of my health, and examined my poor furniture with strangely-longing glances.

A very unpleasant thing has happened at first starting in my search for a wife, which has quite spoiled all my anticipations. I had several letters to write on that day; two of them, the one to my friend already mentioned at Cheltenham, the other to the newspaper, lay sealed before me, both exactly similar in shape and size. At the moment when I was going to address them I was interrupted by a visitor, and when left alone an hour later, I most unfortunately mistook the letters. Thus my advertisement went to my Cheltenham friend, while the other reached the *Post.* Both were of course sent back to me. My friend, an honest, worthy fellow, poured forth a deluge of good-humoured satire upon me, but concluded thus: "Try it! you do not seem to me condemned your whole life long to bear the ill-humour and caprice of Dame Fortune. Perhaps you may be successful, and then you will be all right for life."

If I must speak the truth, I had an indescribable feeling of shame on reading this letter. So long as the secret was my own, the affair appeared to me pleasant and attractive; but now, when a second eye had peered into it, it seemed to me absurd and out of taste. I had the greatest inclination to throw my masterpiece into the fire, and bid adieu to my scheme for ever. But a glance at the penniless condition of my purse, at the desert of my future life, on which I could see no green or freshening spot, overcame my feelings of repugnance and drove me to act. I fancied myself a gambler who stakes his last sovereign on a card, to have either everything or nothing: the present stake was my own charming person, and so gloomy and miserable were my feelings at the moment, that, contrary to my usual practice, I had a very mean opinion of the value of the stake. I carried the advertisement myself to the office, and had the extraordinary gratification of seeing it the next day snugly ensconced between two other advertisements, one offering a reward for a dog, while the other promised the highet price for cast-off apparel.

For a whole week I daily visited the post-office to which I had directed my letters, and constantly my bashful inquiry was responded to by the postmaster's reply of "Nothing!" With each negative my hope sank a degree nearer zero, and it was just verging on the freezing point, when, on the ninth day, it rose ten degrees through a sudden change in the temperature. At last there was a letter with my initials: a gracefully folded *billet doux*—the seal, a dove with a branch of olive. My hand, trembling with excitement, treated the note rather roughly, and before quitting the post-office I read the following:

"SIR,—I have read your advertisement in the

Morning Post, and, assuming the honesty of its purpose, am not indisposed to enter into correspondence with you. Come to-morrow morning at ten to Edward's Hotel, where I shall expect you in No. 3. But one stipulation is absolutely necessary, namely, that I may appear at our first interview masked. I have most urgent reasons for this, which you will yourself approve of eventually."

No signature, no further explanation! I was in an extraordinary state of excitement, which became almost insupportable during the day and night intervening ere the eventful moment arrived. I read the note at least a hundred times. The handwriting was elegant and ladylike: the scent of the paper, the emblem on the seal, seemed to promise happiness. But the stipulation, so absolutely necessary? Why masked? A nervous shudder and cold fit came over me. If she was young and beautiful, why then wear a mask? In my rather extensive practice I knew no instance in which young and pretty women had the courage to conceal the sunshine of their countenance behind an envious cloud. And if old and ugly——? I was certainly disposed to make some concessions on these two chief points. If she was rich, very rich—that is, if there was a cool thousand, say, to represent each year of her life, then it certainly appeared reasonable to close one's eye to a few years more or less, as well as to any lines in the face and form which deviated in a slight measure from the line of beauty. But that could only go to a certain limit. Thirty years I would put up with, no more. While thinking of this I still felt the before-mentioned shudder. I have assuredly the highest respect for the fair sex when they pass a certain age, and no one can be more willing to recognize the merits and dignity of a matron; but the thought of such a one as my wife, to have the June of my life frostbitten by such a January—no, that is past a joke.

But all my thinking, fancying, and planning over the letter were of no further service than to make the hours slip away more rapidly. No one can be angry with me for saying that on this morning I paid more than usual attention to my toilette. My glass told me many flattering things when I turned a last inquiring glance upon it. The light indescribable traces which the stormy season of youth had left upon my face disappeared entirely beneath my practised hand, and I could with some degree of confidence meet a lady who, as I now felt assured, had not assumed a mask lest she might annihilate a poor mortal by the divine brilliancy of her beauty. A few moments after ten I stood before the mysterious door, on the other side of which I should be either unmeasurably happy, or make myself unspeakably ridiculous.

A gentle "Come in," in harmony with my gentle tap, opened the door to me. I entered a richly and elegantly furnished room, indubitably one of the best in the hotel. That was a good sign. From the window a female form advanced to meet me. I could only distinguish her height, nothing more. Her face was hidden by a velvet mask, her head covered by a veil; from her shoulders downwards fell a wide silk dress, which completely concealed her shape. It was absolutely impossible for my generally sharp eye in such matters to form the slightest idea as to age and figure.

In addition, there was no time for observation: the moment for speaking had arrived. But what to say? In my whole life I never felt in such a state of embarrassment. My insinuating manner, generally so successful with the fair sex, utterly deserted me. I knew nothing better to do than to lead the lady to a sofa, with a grace which would have done honour to a dancing-master, and then placing myself on a chair before her, I at last stuttered, rather absurdly, I must allow:

"I received your kind note, which procured me this happy interview."

"What have you to say to me?" was whispered gently and timidly from beneath the mask. But though the voice was so subdued, my sharp and practised ear immediately perceived that it wanted the freshness of youth.

"Madam, I am in such circumstances, and have reached that time of life when it is not desirable to live alone."

"You, therefore, want a companion. But you must confess you have chosen an unusual method for finding one."

"Not so very unusual," I replied, with the consciousness of returning courage. "In all the public papers there are repeated notices like the one which procured me the happiness of this meeting. And if report may be believed, those are generally the happiest marriages which are formed without any previous acquaintance and through a pleasant accident."

"Still, sir, there must be some special reason why a person should trust to accident in such an important step as marriage. May I be permitted to ask what induced you to look for a wife in this way, however usual it may be?"

No question could be more unpleasant or unexpected. In my advertisement I had artistically veiled this point in a mystical obscurity, and it will be remembered how much I based my hopes on this clever silence, which I trusted would excite female curiosity. And now an importunate hand tried roughly to raise this veil. What should I say?—the truth? But with what face could I confess that only the most terrible embarrassments had forced me to take this step? Would not all the charming illusions, beneath which I desired to conceal my reasons, be dissipated immediately by the coarsest, most vulgar prose? I must consequently try to escape by some side-path. "May I reply by asking," I said, "what induced you to grant me this interview?"

"We will speak of that presently," she answered very calmly. "We must naturally become acquainted with each other, and by all the rules of society it is your place to begin our confidences. I cannot conceal from you that it seems to me almost inexplicable why *you* seek a wife through the papers."

"Why do you think so?"

"Are you astonished at it? Why, such a young, and may I be allowed to add, elegant man." I bowed with a pleasant smile.

"In addition, your manners can only have been acquired in the most select circles. I am quite certain that it was not 'the paucity of your lady acquaintances' which caused you to take this step."

Had the matter not been so confoundedly serious, I must have laughed at these words. Good Heavens! it had been constantly my misfortune that I had known too many of the sex.

"No, no!" I exclaimed, assuming a jocular tone, "I cannot complain in that respect. But do you consider it so strange that a man may know many ladies, and yet not find one of them with whom he would venture to spend his whole life?"

"Perhaps you have never meant it or tried seriously. Or, as I would most be inclined to fancy, you have not the time for it. You are a much occupied, active man. Your hours are precious; you do not wish to waste them in long searching and selecting. Am I right?"

I would have given much at this moment to see the lady's face. I could not in any way judge from her calm, regular tone, whether she was making a fool of me or speaking seriously. But however it might be, satire or seriousness, both were equally unpleasant to me. I found myself exposed to the purgatory of an examination to which my "great go" had been child's play.

"I like," she continued, as I did not immediately reply, "men of activity. Hence I shall be excessively pleased, and my respect for you be increased, if I hear from you that you have an honourable, even if slender, mode of life. At any rate, you owe it to me to tell me this, ere we can proceed to the chief point of our interview."

What evil demon was hidden behind this mask? She attacked the most susceptible spots with a calmness which was too natural to be studied and too pointed to be quite purposeless. I felt like a new patient at a hydropathic establishment over whom a bucket of water is every moment poured. Still I plucked up a heart, and answered, boldly,

"I have studied the law."

"Have you any official appointment?"

"No; I am still a barrister without much practice." For all in the world I could not have uttered the word "briefless." But she released me from my anxiety, and said, with an incomparable naïveness:

"Then, in fact, you are a briefless barrister. That is certainly bad; but still such a person may become lord chancellor, if he possesses talents, industry, and a little money," she added, with an almost satirical inflection of her voice.

The last word was the most reasonable she had yet uttered. My almost frozen hopes were slightly revived, and I listened with a deep breath of satisfaction to the following words:

"Come, sir," she said, good-humouredly, "let us be candid to each other. Why are we attempting mutual deception? I think I see it all clearly. You are looking for a wife who has money."

"Not that alone," I cried quickly, and felt that all the blood in my body flew to my cheeks.

"Still, that's the main point. Confess it would not have occurred to you to select 'this no longer uncommon' method, unless you were seeking a handsome fortune; and at the same time—as the two cannot be separated—a wife."

"Oh, you are severe—very severe."

"Only true," she replied, calmly. "And now, sir,

we have reached the point where we can begin our bargaining. I possess fortune. Come, now, what price do you set on yourself? But no, that would be really an impertinent question. How much do you fancy you require to make you comfortable for life?"

I cannot deny that the rather sarcastic tone which I fancied I caught in these words, horribly annoyed me. The blood poured to my heart, and, rising from my chair and feeling for my hat, I said, very seriously:

"It would be perhaps better, madam, for us to break off our negotiation. All that you have said up to the present appears to me strange, and does not please me. I am by no means certain whether you are jesting with me or speaking seriously. Were the former the case, you have quite mistaken me. This step of mine, I confess, was induced by a harsh necessity, but, nevertheless, was honourably and seriously meant. If that is not recognized, I shall not say another word, but take my leave."

"No! stop, I beg you," she replied quickly, and gently pulled me down again on my chair. "We have not yet come to the main point. You mentioned a harsh necessity. It is certainly hard for a young man like yourself, young, ambitious, and full of hope, to sigh beneath the yoke of depressing cares and embarrassment. I possess, as I said, the magic staff by which to dispel them at once. What do you say to thirty thousand pounds?"

Thirty thousand pounds! I started, as if a cannon had been fired close to my ear, at hearing this immense fortune stated. I probably cut a very absurd face, for the lady continued:

"Pray do not doubt the truth of my words. I am ready to give you, presently, every possible proof of my circumstances. You will perhaps convince yourself that I have spoken somewhat under the truth."

"But, gracious Heavens!" I cried, "thirty thousand pounds are a fortune which would bring as many men to your feet. Why seek a husband in this manner, when you could have a free choice among the best and most distinguished?"

"You had your reasons—cannot I also have mine?" she whispered, very gently and bashfully.

Ah! I guessed her reasons only too correctly! What a monster must she be, when even thirty thousand pounds were not able to endow her with youth and beauty! But though I felt in a complete whirl, I forced myself to say with pretended calmness: "I fancy I can guess your reasons, madam. May I express my sentiments?"

"Speak, sir. It is of no avail making any mystery of what must be at the next moment revealed."

"You desired," I continued, "to be masked at our first interview. Perhaps you distrust your beauty!"

"My beauty? Oh, sir, do not force me to a painful confession. I am not handsome." She uttered this with a sigh which expressed more than did her words.

"No one can be judge in his own cause. There is a beauty which is not found in the features, but in the mind, and which impresses the signet of its divine origin and nobility on the least beautiful countenance. Why will you not leave the verdict to me, by removing this envious mask from your features?"

"No, no; I cannot," was her reply, in a most decided tone. "You will not see my face till all is decided between us, either yes or no. What you said about beauty could be true—if I was young."

"Not young, then?" I asked, in an almost doleful tone, for the sake of saying something.

"No, sir; the days of my youth appear to me like a dream."

"In this instance, too, persons' views are very different," I replied, eagerly. "What you call 'not young' is, perhaps, only a decided, matured, and staid age, when solid and valuable qualities are a rich compensation for the transitory and always doubtful charms of youth." It can be seen from this answer what deep root the £30,000 had taken in my mind, and how I was determined to defend them *à outrance*.

"What do you call a ripe and matured age?" she asked, so gently that I could scarcely distinguish it.

I hesitated for a moment ere I answered—"I have known most amiable ladies, who had reached the middle period of life, between thirty and forty."

A loud "Ah!" of pain reached my ear, and I cannot deny that this "Ah!" gave me a shivering fit.

"I will not deceive you," the lady whispered, in a tone of unspeakable embarrassment and shame; "double the thirty, and then you have my age."

Had a flash of lightning separated us, I could not have been more startled. "What—sixty?" I cried as I started up.

"Yes, sir, sixty summers have I already seen; and when I tell you that I am a widow, you will know enough to decide either for or against me."

"Yes, I know enough," I said, bitterly, "to see

that my foolish step has caused us a most painful scene. It will be best to come to a speedy decision. I am afraid, madam, that the inequality of our years will form an impassable barrier between us. As we fortunately are unacquainted with our mutual means and circumstances, we can part, and forget all that is past."

"Not so, sir," she said, earnestly and firmly. "I am by no means disposed to let you off so easily. You have induced me to take this foolish step, which must compromise me both in your eyes and my own. I have a right to demand that you should decide in this affair, which is mine as well, not with passionate haste, but after calm reflection. I will give you till to-morrow at this time, when I shall expect your final decision."

"And if it is in the negative?"

"Then I shall be content. You will come, then? I ask your promise, that you will come."

"On my honour," I said, as I rushed away.

No, it would be impossible to form an idea of my feelings and temper when I found myself once again in the open air. I could have laughed, and, at the same time, vexed myself to death. Why should I deny that the £30,000 had exercised a potent charm upon me? That exceeded my highest aims and boldest expectations. All my cares and troubles would be at once removed, and my most high-soaring wishes and plans fulfilled. But on the other side, the charming widow of sixty! I mentally pictured myself marching by the side of the dear, hobbling old woman, saw the glances of my friends and acquaintances directed sarcastically upon me; heard their jests and jibes, which wounded me like poisoned darts. Impossible! impossible! But to do myself justice, something better than vanity was stirring within me. I found it utterly incompatible with my notions of honour to make such a bargain. And what else would it be than a disgraceful bargain, if I gave up myself, my youth, to an old widow, for dirty pelf, with the certainty that we should both be wretched? In truth, it cost me no great struggle to remain true to my previous determination, and firm as a rock, I proceeded at the appointed hour to the hotel. I found the lady in the same room, and masked as she had been the day before.

"Madam," I said reverentially to her, "I have in the first place to offer my most humble apologies for placing you in such a cruel position through my inconsiderate conduct. I know not what induced you to enter into negotiation with me in consequence of my advertisement. But whatever was the cause, I beg you earnestly to give up every thought of a union between us. We could not be happy. My conscience and my honour forbid me offering you my hand, or accepting yours. The inequality in our ages is too considerable, and your fortune too large, for any one else to imagine that any but the dirtiest motives impelled me to such a step. And so let us part."

"Is that your last firm determination?" was asked in a low, scarcely perceptible, voice.

"My irrevocable decision," I replied, firmly.

"Well, then, there is no danger in my taking off my mask."

With these words, uttered rapidly and merrily, the lady tore off her mask.

Good Heavens! what did I see! a youthful countenance! and a second glance caused me to exclaim, "Lucy, Lucy!"

It was my fair unknown: more beautiful and blooming than ever my imagination pictured her. I was about to rush towards her.

"Keep back, sir!" she cried, in her clear silvery voice and with sparkling eyes; "you have rejected my hand."

"Not you, Lucy, not you! No, I have not been guilty of such treason to youth, beauty, and love."

At this moment a door opened, and another voice was heard:

"Good gracious! what is the matter?"

I looked round. A fresh surprise, fresh astonishment—my aunt stood *in propriâ personâ* before me. I was as motionless as if I saw a ghost before me.

"Eh, eh!" she said, scolding good-humouredly, "it's you, nephew? What have you to do with my daughter?"

The scales fell from my eyes.

"Oh! now all is clear!" I shouted. "You—you were the good kind widow who led me yesterday to hope I should possess your hand?"

"Yes, you young rascal, you rejected me point-blank. Get out of my sight."

"No, aunt, here is a magnet which irresistibly attracts me. Then Lucy, my Lucy, is your adopted daughter?"

"Your Lucy! you are mad, my boy. You rejected her five years ago."

"Oh, why do you remind me of it? Who could imagine that the Lucy of the Welsh mountains and the Cheltenham orphan were one and the same person? If I answered then impertinently and negatively, was it not through my excessive love for her? You should not reproach, but rather praise me for it."

"And reward you in the bargain with this angel's hand? that's what you mean, you young rascal?"

"I dare to hope it, dearest aunt," I replied, in the most caressing tone I could assume. "Oh, surely, when you answered my advertisement it was with the purpose of bringing us together."

"Well, you cannot be so mad as to fancy I did so on my own account."

"But, my dear aunt, it was a dangerous experiment. What a fearful trial you exposed me to; only think of thirty thousand pounds! If I could have blinded myself and taken your richly gilded hand?"

"Then you would have had neither myself nor Lucy, but a very serious lecture, which would have put an end to all your wishes of getting a wife in that way."

"You see, then, that I am not so bad as you fancied."

"I do not think so, or else we should, most assuredly, not have come. Thank your friend Watson, in Cheltenham, who has long been your most zealous advocate. Through him I know that you have been guilty of levity, but never of deliberate crime, and that you had made up your mind to settle down and be respectable. Through him, too, I learned your precious matrimonial project."

"Oh! how glad I am at the mistake in the letters, which at first caused me so much shame and annoyance."

"Certainly; it was the happiest mistake you ever made in your life. By your friend's persuasion this plan was formed and carried out."

"But, dearest Lucy"—and I turned affectionately towards her—"did you know that you would meet your chance friend of Wales here?"

"Yes I knew it," she said, in charming confusion, and blushing to the very roots of her hair.

"But how was that possible? I do not remember telling you my name."

"Your friend helped you here, too," my aunt explained. "He told us of your adventure, without the least idea that Lucy was so intimately connected with it. As she displayed the greatest emotion during the story, I inquired further, and she revealed to me that she must be the young lady who left such a deep impression on your heart."

"Then you must know, too," I said, fervently, "that I was rendered most wretched by losing her; that I never forgot her, have ever loved her—yes, loved her to this hour. Lucy, dare I hope the same from you?"

I needed not to wait for an answer. Her beaming eye, her face suffused with blushes, said more than a thousand words would have done. What she might have replied was lost in the first kiss which I ventured to imprint on her pouting lips.

CHAPTER XVI.*

A NIGHT IN CALIFORNIA.

In the furthest east of the Californian gold-mines—that is, as far as the daring miners had, in that day, penetrated towards the east and found gold, and at the spot where the waters of the southern streams, the Macalome and the Calaveres, divide—a little mountain torrent rushes through the centre of the romantic scenery beneath the leafy covering of gigantic trees, and a little further below, though always precipitous and foaming, dashes down into the southern arm of the Macalome, which follows its noisy course at a great depth beneath it.

This little creek, or "Gulch," the Californian name which such streams have gradually acquired, though the word "Gulch" really means the ravine through which the stream rushes, had been named by its first discoverers, Germans, "Mosquito Gulch;" for, in the wildly overgrown thicket that filled the lower part of the gulch, and mainly consisting of a species of wild cherry and hazel trees, a very respectable number of these charming little creatures took up their abode during the summer, and spurred the workmen to fresh

* This chapter is an adaptation from the German of Frederick Gustäcker. I give it room here, as it conveys a capital idea of Californian life in the early time.

activity whenever they rested for a little while in the cool shade of the really gigantic cedars and pines, and wished to let their shovels and pikes "grow cold," as they called it. The mosquitoes make capital overseers.

But, speaking parenthetically, they were not so bad after all; the fact was, that the people who christened the clear merry stream thus, and so gave it a bad name, had not seen any places where the mosquitoes really swarmed; they had not visited the banks of the Mississippi, for instance.

About half-way down the mountain stream, at about the same distance from its source and its mouth, and on the slope of the hill, which was bounded on three sides by deep ravines—in the north by the Macalome itself, while from the hill a glorious view could be enjoyed of its fir-clad banks, and from the depths below, its hollow roar, as it leaped over masses of rocks and trunks of trees, reached the ear of the spectator; on the east by a little, dry ravine, and on the west by the deeply-cut Mosquito Gulch—down to which a precipitous path of about 200 yards in length led—stood a small camp, as it is called in miners' parlance, consisting of four tents, three white and one blue, nestled together closely and comfortably under tall pines and dwarf oaks, while at night a tremendous fire crackled in the centre.

These four tents were inhabited by just so many companies (as the two, three, four, or more, who work together, are called), and they were, with the exception of a single American, all Germans, the greater part of whom had come with the Bremen ships *Talisman* and *Reform*, but some from Australia and other parts of the globe, and had met togethor here, in true Californian fashion, on the retired, but exquisitely situated, mountain slopes.

At about a hundred yards distance stood another tent, in which a company of English and Irish miners lived; and still further back a Pole and a German, who had both come from Texas, camped under the open sky; for the rainy season had not yet set in, and the nights were generally bright.

If you have an inclination, reader, and nothing better to do, we will spend the present evening—it is Sunday—among them; we shall find a hearty lot of fellows, good company, and most assuredly a kind welcome.

It is about four in the afternoon, and the camp remarkably still: what can have become of all the men who usually make it so animated?

Yes, friend, we live here at a distance of about five English miles from the nearest store, and so at least one of each company, but usually several, goes on a Sunday on horse, mule, or donkey-back—for these three modes of transport exist here together—to "Charles' store," a place well known in the whole neighbourhood, to buy the necessary provisions in the shape of flour, potatoes, meat, sugar, onions, &c., for the next week, and frequently return in a remarkable state of beer on this particular evening. These usually very jolly fellows seldom come back before dusk, and it's often 10 or 11; and if the donkeys were not more sensible——but I am getting on too fast.

In fact, till now, only a single figure had been moving about the tents, a man in a cleanly, but old and repeatedly patched, red woollen shirt, and grey linen trousers, with dark brown curly hair, small but sparkling eyes, and broad hands well used to work—we might almost call them fists. He worked with another, of the name of Panning. Panning had been coachman in Germany to a Count So-and-so, and had come to California to make his fortune. Albert had driven a team of oxen over the Sierra Nevada for Uncle Sam—he was fond of talking about this journey; afterwards, I believe, he had "left of his own accord," as deserters usually called it, or had been dismissed; in short, he was here on Mosquito Gulch, and "made good out." Dear reader, you will have to accustom yourself to many mining expressions, and must not begin shaking your head over them already.

Albert was busily engaged in carrying his mattresses and blankets, which had been lying in the sun during the day, back into the tent, and in taking down the articles of clothing he had washed in the morning, from a line expressly fastened between two young oaks, and was now carrying in wood for the evening. He had been sewing and repairing the whole day, and was, in the bargain, a very industrious man and excellent workman.

Panning and Albert possessed a white mule as joint-stock property. In the blue tent some one was also stirring; its solitary inhabitant, to whose clothes a couple of stitches of grey cotton would have done no harm, was lying rather lazily on his blanket before the tent, and looking at the green masses of foliage above him. The tent was inhabited by three Germans—Renich, Haye, and Müller—so we will call the third man, as my own name is so preciously long. Reñich and Haye had gone to the store, one upon, the other by the side of, Mosquito (as we had christened the donkey belonging to the tripartite society, in honour of the gulch), and Müller might certainly have got up and made a fire, for, when his two companions came home, they would be hungry and want something to eat. In the first place, however, there was nothing edible, for the last four potatoes and two onions—the whole remains of the previous week's provisions, with the exception of some home-made bread—had just furnished out his last dinner; and besides, he "knew his Pappenheimer;" they would not come home so early, and when they did, would be suffering more from thirst than hunger. "Where there is a brewery, a baker's shop cannot exist," is a good old proverb.

Before the great tent, "Försterling," the only one who had remained behind, was collecting dry wood and leaves, to keep up the nearly extinguished fire; but even here selfishness seemed the predominant passion (if the apathetic calmness with which he did it may be called a passion), for he was hungry himself, and had kept a few cold potatoes from his very frugal dinner, which he intended to fry for his own delectation.

The sun was fast sinking behind the gigantic firs and cedars: it was a glorious sight. The hills across the stream were bathed in its magical rays; it sported in the dark summits of the pines, and gave its last lingering kiss to the tops of the most magnificent trees my eye had ever seen.

Holy silence lay upon the forest; the gentle evening breeze only whispered in the glistening foliage;

thin, airy cloud shadows floated athwart the sky, and the hollow, distant murmur of the stream below, too far removed to disturb or interrupt the sweet calmness of the whole, sounded like the solemn peals of an organ.

"Well, confound it, Müller, you'll be lying there the whole evening," Albert at length broke out; "don't you mean to get a fire ready for Haye and Renich?"

"Bah! they will not be back for a long time," Müller said, with considerable decision, but with some moral contrition, for they might return at any moment. He soon sprang up, threw his blanket into the tent, and went to work seriously to collect some wood before it became dark, and make the other necessary preparations.

Albert had in the mean while finished his supper—he and Panning divided their provisions in such a way that they always had something left for Sunday—and now waited impatiently for his companions, who usually returned at this time.

"Not a drop of brandy in the bottle," Försterling at length said; and as he came out of the tent, and held it, first to the last rays of the setting sun, and then, as if he would not believe it, to the now brightly burning fire—"haven't you got any, Müller?"

"Not a drop," was the unsatisfactory reply; brandy does not keep here, Försterling; the bottles are shaken too often."

"Oh, the shaking doesn't hurt it," said Försterling, as he took the empty bottle by the neck, and threw it as far as he could into the dry gulch, which was overstrewn with broken glass, and consequently most carefully avoided by the Indians, who frequently pay it a visit—"it's only the confounded turning bottom upwards, for brandy can't bear standing on its head. I wish, though, that Meier and the Blacksmith were come: where the deuce can they have got to so late?"

Half an hour passed, however, before the least was heard of them; in the mean while it had grown as dark as pitch, while the spot where they must cross the gulch, about half a mile higher up, with their laden beasts, was rendered far from pleasant travelling at night through the thick bushes and the holes that had been dug all around.

At length Försterling listened attentively.

"So leben wir, so leben wir, so leben wir alle Tage!"

"In der allerschönsten Saufcompagnie," sounded clearly and distinctly through the bushes.

"Ich bin liederlich, du bist liederlich, sind wir nicht liederliche Leute," a tenor voice was heard cheerily singing between whiles.

"That's that scamp the Blacksmith!" Försterling said, with a shake of his head; "he's come home in a nice state again."

"I only hope he's brought the donkey with him," Albert said; "and I don't hear Panning's voice among them."

"Bumsfallera, bumsfallera!" another voice struck up, which had not been heard till then.

"That's Haye!" said Müller; "we shall have a jolly evening."

"So leben wir, so leben wir, so leben wir alle Tage!" was now heard, with the regularly intervening chorus of "Bumsfallera," nearer and nearer; and while the bright flame sprung up through the dry wood that had been thrown on it, and was saluted by hearty cheers by the new arrivers, the long-expected, highly-delighted group made its appearance.

In front came the donkeys, Mosquito at full trot, for he knew that he would now get rid of his load, and have bread to eat; Hans, the other donkey, at a more gentle pace behind; and, last of all, the horse—a very good-tempered animal.

The beasts did not require any further guidance, but moving quickly along the narrow path, which had till then wound through a species of wild coffee bushes and then entered the cleared field, each walked to its own tent, in order to be unloaded as quickly as possible, and then enjoy its ease for the rest of the week.

"So leben wir, so leben wir, so leben wir alle Tage!" Meier shouted.

"Yes, that would be a pretty story!" Försterling expressed his opinion; "we should feel much obliged to you."

"But where's Panning?" Albert asked, with blighted hopes. That is, he asked for Panning, but meant the white mule with the provisions.

"Isn't Panning here yet?" Haye asked, with a laugh. "Donnerwetter, he rode away with us—*i. e.* he was on foot, and was close behind us."

"Has he got anything?" Albert asked, with a meaning movement of his hand.

"Anything?" Haye said, merrily. "Bumsfallera! Bumsfallera!"

For a moment utter confusion seemed to prevail in

the little camp. All ran and shouted together, and the only sensible beings appeared to be the donkeys, who stood motionless and patiently before their respective tents, waiting to be unloaded. While one party attended to this, another arranged the fire, and produced pots and pans; Meier and the Blacksmith fell on each other's necks, both declared that they were very good fellows, and the other confounded rogues were altogether not worth a dump, and then laid themselves on their blankets in the tent to rest for half an hour, after the *fatigues* they had undergone. Albert, in the mean while, asked in vain for Panning; no one knew what had become of him; and he seated himself at length to devour his supper, in solitary despair, as suddenly several voices exclaimed together:

"There's Panning!" and in truth the mule at least made his appearance in the bright light of the fire, and walked with a joyful bray towards the well-known tent.

There's the donkey, then, but where's Panning? Certainly he had disappeared; and as the only being who could furnish any explanation on the subject, the mule namely, was obstinately silent, nothing more could be done in the matter.

Mosquito had, in the mean while, employed his time famously. The provisions he had brought with him had been taken off him and lay partly in, partly before, the tent, and Mosquito received his usual reward after every Sunday's excursion—a whole ship's biscuit, which he immediately devoured, and then slowly walked round the tent to join his companions. This, at least, was his usual behaviour, but Mosquito was perfectly well aware what he had brought with him, and had no idea of leaving the nice things that were strewed about without at least making an attempt to obtain some of them. Before the tent lay a bag with dried apples and onions—(in consequence of the paucity of sacks, we were always obliged to pack several things together, and dried apples and onions agreed famously together). Mosquito was well aware of it, and when his masters turned their backs, he brought his head gently round the side of the tent and into the sack, picked the dried apples carefully from among the onions—for he was not partial to the latter—and then noiselessly disappeared in the gloomy forest, without showing himself in the firelight.

Stewing and frying were going on at all the fires. Some of the men were cooking, others singing; no one troubled himself about his neighbour till the cry of "Work, work," which they brought into the mountains from shipboard, collected several round the rough tables. The fire was then provided with dry wood, in order to furnish a decent light, and the meal commenced.

Försterling, however, had some trouble in waking his people.

"Smith—Meier—get up, supper's ready."

The smith gave a deep grunt; Meier made no reply.

"Smith, confound it, how long do you want me to shake you; supper's ready; you can sleep afterwards."

The Blacksmith at length raised himself up, and looked round in surprise. He evidently fancied it was morning. "Confound it," he said, in his soft voice, "it's quite dark yet—what's the matter with the Landrath this morning?" Försterling was universally called by this name on board ship.

While the others laughed, Försterling made a fresh attack on Meier.

"Meier, I tell you for the last time, if you don't come directly we will not wait any longer—Meier!" and he shook the sleeper with all his strength.

"Landrath," Meier muttered, for he appeared to have some faint idea from the voice who it was that disturbed him, "take care, it's perilous to rouse the lion."

"Well!" the Landrath said, as he made a new attempt to wake him, "I can't say that precisely, but it's precious difficult."

At last they were all awake, and the table-talk commenced, which had reference mainly to the events that had occurred during the day at the "store." Meier philosophized. "Yes," he said, "such are the delights of California, the same thing has no doubt happened to Panning that occurred to me this day week. A fellow goes down in the morning to the store, drinks his glass or two—that makes him thirsty, and he sets to work on champagne and porter; by the time it's evening the affair costs him his 30 dollars up to two ounces, and when he wakes in the morning he finds himself lying in the bush, and does not know where he is, much less how he got there."

"But that was a better joke of Smith's a month back," Haye said with a laugh. "I am only sorry I'm not an artist, for it would furnish a famous picture."

"You be quiet," said the smith, as he worked away

at a delicate beefsteak with fried onions; "it might have happened to any one of you."

"What was it, then?" said Wohlgemuth, a young man who had come from Calaveres to "prospect," and who was rather deaf, and held his hand to his ear.

"Ah, don't bring up an old story," the smith grumbled.

"Out with it," Meier cried, however, "that it may serve as a warning example for a careless young fellow like Wohlgemuth."

"Oh, the story is simple enough," Haye said. "Smith was coming from Charles' store and driving his donkey before him. Of course, as usual, he was the last, and half drunk in the bargain, though not so bad but that he could follow the path, or at least the donkey, which knew his road well. It was confoundedly dark in the forest, however, and about half a mile or more from Charles' store a tree lies across the path, or to speak more correctly, it fell on one side, and the roots block up the road. The donkey naturally went round the roots, struck the path again, and came home at the proper time. Smith, though, when he came to the tree, thought it was the donkey, and began pitching into it.

"'Come, Hans—come, my good beast; lazy Satan, does he mean to stop all night in the middle of the path?' and then he began hammering into the elastic roots of the tree, which, when he struck, felt very much like the rear of a patient donkey.

"In spite of Smith's well-meant advice and warnings, the usually so obedient donkey would not move from the spot, and the driver, at length more fatigued by his exertions than all the previous 'drops,' sat down near his beast, as he thought, to let it rest a little, and then make a second attempt. When Smith woke again it was broad day, and he was sitting in front of the roots."

"You would not have known anything about it if I had not told you," the Blacksmith said as the others laughed.

"And was the donkey really there the next morning?" asked Wohlgemuth, who had only heard half the story.

"Confound it, that's too bad," Meier cried, and the smith now laughed along with them.

Försterling had bread to bake the same evening, and the dough was all ready; before his tent the largest fire was therefore made, to produce the requisite heat, as we were forced to bake our bread in open pans in want of the necessary articles, and the whole little camp generally assembled there every evening.

The person who baked bread undertook at the same time the duty of providing the whole company with lights and fire, and as this was so arranged that two at the most baked on the same evening, and during each week each company baked twice, every evening there was one famous fire as a meeting-place, which flared up among the pines and quivering oak branches.

The evening, however, was not far enough advanced to collect all at one spot, and hence the most various groups were formed, for the most part so arranged that they all turned their faces to the ruddy flame.

Haye had now discovered, on going to remove the things he had brought, the trick which Mosquito had played us, and wanted to take the donkey to task; but where was Mosquito?

In his rage he could not be restrained from examining all the provisions and finding out what the donkey had really eaten, so he lighted one of the candles he had brought with him, and read the bill of fare.

It was intended to last three persons a week.

"25 lbs. flour, 4 dls. 25 cts., still there; 3 lbs. sugar, 1 dl. 50 cts., behind in the packet; 1 lb. coffee, 75 cts., here, the cheese must be with it—all right; 2½ lbs. cheese, 2 dls. 93¾ cts., by Jove! that's careful reckoning; 6½ lbs. salt pork, 2 dls. 53 cts., that's in the bag with the potatoes—here it is; 10 lbs. potatoes, at 25 cts., 2 dls. 50 cts.; 4 lbs. dried apples, 2 dls. 50 cts., are running about somewhere in the gulch—it's only a blessing that the Satan doesn't like onions; 4 lbs. beans, 2 dls. 25 cts.—here; 2 boxes lucifers, 25 cts.—well, that's sensible, we've wanted them a long while; 2 lbs. soap, 1 dl. 25 cts; ½ lb. candles, 1 dl. 25 cts., not there—oh, yes, they must be there, they're in with the flour—well, it will make them look nice, but still they'll burn; 4 lbs. ship biscuit, 1 dl.—the glutton is fonder of apples—here; 2 lbs. onions, 2 dls.—they're with the apples: no! God be praised, here; 18 lbs. fresh meat, 5 dls. 50 cts.—hang up in the bag: we had better have hung the apples up and left the meat; 3 bottles of brandy, 4 dls. 50 cts.—ah! some of that old famous 1792, what a respectable number that is, that makes altogether—"

"Come, give up your bothering accounts," Meier cried—"come here with it. This is Sunday evening, and the devil may fetch calculations and all. You, Landrath, what a miserable fire you've got for a fellow to see by!"

Meier was the chief person, and had even been previously appointed Alcalde in the German camp, to settle all disputes that occurred, which, however, not unfrequently originated with himself. He wore a straw hat with a narrow brim, but of what dimensions it would be difficult to decide, for on the crown it had been so pressed in, with more strength than artistic skill, that the crown had retired like a snail into his shell, almost down to the fabulously narrow brim, and formed a deep groove all around.

His Sunday clothes were, in miner's fashion, simple, but strong and clean; his week-day or working clothes, on the other hand, would have created a *furore* at any masquerade. The first pair of trousers he had worn at his certainly very laborious work in the gulch had gone the way, if not of all flesh, of all trousers; and not to be bothered with the toil of performing some very difficult repairs, he had put another pair over them, which were not torn in precisely the same places as the others. In the morning and evening he wore a wide paletôt, which looked like a broken down gentleman in very low company; the fashion of the coat was good, but nothing further could be said about it, for material and colour belonged to such a long past season, that both had, in a measure, disappeared.

Shoes he certainly had, and they had been formerly sewn—at least the threads and holes could be seen in the seams which the cobbler's awl had produced in them—and now they only hung together by a thread, and, perhaps, to spare the soles he walked by the side of them.

This is, besides, the surest sign of a miner—that his right shoe or boot is trodden on one side, which comes from repeated stamping on the spade. On his hat Meier wore, besides, as an ornament, an old bronze brooch with four or five artificial and partially broken pearls.

The miners, by the way, are very fond of decorating themselves in this fashion; the Landrath's hat was brilliantly adorned with an old ostrich feather, which he had procured, heaven knows how; and with an *agraffe*, formed of a tin plate, most artistically set in a row of glass pearls; and those who could not procure such decorations wore at least a brooch in their hat or cap.

The rest, perhaps with the exception of Panning, Albert, and Haye, were dressed much in the same style as I have described Meier; they formed a wild, strange band.

Meier, at any rate, appeared the nerve that gave life to the whole, and whenever he had worked himself up a little, there was no thinking of sleep. When it got to twelve or one in the morning, and the rest went off one by one to roost, he would lie for two or three hours all alone by the fire and regard the flames.

"Now, Landrath," Meier said, when supper was over, and nearly all the campers were collected round the fire, "how did you spend the day, eh?—slept, of course?"

"Ne!" said Försterling, by trade a tinker, but a

jolly companion and good soul, "I've been out shooting to-day."

"With the rifle?"

"Of course; it's a famous piece; the bullet's difficult enough to drive in, but it comes out again precious quick; it went off twice of its own accord."

"But the shot-barrel's no use," said Klaussen; "I wouldn't have the old thing as a present."

Meier and Klaussen had come together from Adelaide.

"The shot-barrel no use," Försterling exclaimed; "you've never seen such a gun in your life, Klaussen. If I fire at a tree, and have got a good charge in, there's not a leaf from top to bottom that doesn't get its share."

One of the Americans and Haye had, in the mean while, seated themselves at the fire, and were playing a game of "sixty-six." The Pole and the German from Texas had also come to the fire, and were lying right opposite to Meier.

The Pole, whose name I believe none of us knew, was only called "the Pole" (he spoke German very well, and came from one of the German-Polish provinces, but from the lowest classes), or "the poor man," because he complained incessantly, and asserted that if a fellow was once poor, he would never have a chance of getting on in the world.

"Well, Pole," the Blacksmith cried in his gentle voice, "you weren't at Charles' store to-day; was the last week a bad one again?"

"Oh, as usual," the Pole said, with a gloomy, half-resigned countenance; "a fellow like me soon gets used to it—holes six and eight feet deep, and afterwards two or three dollars in them. But who can help it? The Almighty will not help us. God d—— it."

"Have the Americans found anything this week?" another inquired.

"I do not know—they've gone down the Creek; but there's nothing except gold dust there. I don't think it's worth the trouble."

"That's all nonsense," the Landrath said; "that's the third company that's gone down, and the other two have held on bravely; if they didn't earn their day's wage, they wouldn't stop there."

"Higher up the gold's certainly coarser," Meier expressed his opinion.

"We've found it so up to the present, but that's no reason why we should say that coarse gold has not found it's way down there; the Pole, for instance, has got a good placer now, for he complains incessantly, and that's a sure sign."

"The devil fetch me, if I earn my food!" the Pole said, who had been listening attentively, and striking his hands together.

"The two Englishmen, under the fallen tree, found a famous piece of quartz yesterday," said the German from Texas; "brown quartz, with broad veins of gold across it—a goldsmith could not have made it more regularly."

"How have you two been getting on down there, Klaussen? Are things looking up?"

"Oh it's nothing; and we get tired at last of digging one hole after the other uselessly. We've not got quite down yet, though, and in one corner we found rocks, and some gold."

"What sort of rocks?" Meier asked.

"Strange stuff; it looks for all the world like coarse salt, and indeed I was forced to put my tongue to it, to see whether it was salt."

"Those are good rocks," the Blacksmith cried. "We found the best gold among them; but you must go a little deeper, and not merely scratch about the surface."

"Yes! it's a pretty game with the rocks, here about Mosquito Gulch," the Pole growled; "one time the gold lies on the top, and when we go deeper there's nothing—at another time we are forced to split the rocks, if we want to get at the gold."

"It's certainly very strange how the gold can have got here," said Klaussen. "At this gulch, for instance, we are all abroad; and the only thing that appears possible is, that a volcanic eruption strewed the melted metal so wildly around."

"It's very strange, too," said Meier, "how we are actually able to follow this eruption; and those very spots where no gold lies in the deep holes and chasms in the rock, are a proof of it, for we always find these places filled with a firm grey volcanic scoria, so that it seems as if these ashes had been thrown out first, and carried down here by the mountain stream, then pressed firmly down by the power and weight of the water, and that the gold followed afterwards; but where it came from I should like to know; for at one moment we fancy that the vein runs from the right, at another from the left, and yet there are no high volcanic mountains about."

"Yes, I should like to know that, too," the Pole growled; "afterwards, we should not want to dig so many holes to no purpose; but that's the misfortune."

"What do you call diamonds in German?" the American asked Haye, with whom he was busily engaged in playing sixty-six.

"Caro," was the answer.

"And spades?"

"Pique."

"Hm!" the American muttered, for he did not seem quite to comprehend it; "the Germans are a strange people, they call a spade a pick."

"Oh, give up your stupid game and join our circle," Meier now cried. "You, Klaussen, just sing us a song, that will cause some life among us."

"Oh, yes, I am just in the humour for singing," Klaussen said; "I've felt queer all the evening. If I'm not better to-morrow I shall take some medicine."

"You're only seedy," said the Landrath.

"It's a pity our old doctor at home is not here," Meier said; "he would have saved you taking medicine—he had a famous remedy."

"Well, he could not cure me without giving me medicine."

"Something of the sort," Meier said, with a laugh; "he was a doctor of the good old school, who would neither give up his old broad-tailed coat or his pigtail; and, in fact, the latter was as necessary as his right hand, for his universal remedy consisted in that."

"Don't tell us any more of your nonsense," the Blacksmith cried; "as if he gave his patients the pigtail to take!"

"Quiet, Smith—go to kennel," Meier said; "he certainly gave them his pigtail, for if any one was unwell, instead of ordering him an emetic, like our present physicians, who have retrograded in cultivation, he pushed the pigtail into his throat. Yes! you need not laugh at it, but this was not necessary in all cases, for his method was so well known—and he could, naturally, only employ one pigtail—that, in many instances, he only required to show his patient the pigtail in order to produce precisely the same effect as if he had adhered most strictly to his prescription."

"Was that the doctor with the flat nose?" Klaussen asked, while the others were laughing.

"Yes," Meier said, "and Klaussen will not believe that either. The little fellow had such a flat nose that my uncle often assured me he was obliged to use a pair of pincers instead of a pocket-handkerchief."

"Is the donkey here?" a loud voice asked at this moment in the midst of the laughter.

The silence of death prevailed instantly, but at the next moment the shouts broke out afresh, for behind the circle, where he had made his appearance quite unnoticed, stood Panning, looking somewhat disconcerted at the terrible noise, and regarding one after the other in astonishment.

It was a good quarter of an hour before any one could calm his fears about the mule.

"But, confound it, you're sitting here so dry," Panning cried, when the noise had slightly ceased, and Albert got up to look for some supper for the new comer, and warm his tea—"no brandy, no grog?"

"I really believe that's the first sensible idea Panning's had to-day," Meier said.

"And where have you been this evening?" Albert asked; "and which of you two was the cleverer?"

"The donkey, most assuredly, Albert, my boy," said Panning, with a laugh, for he was in much too good a humour to quarrel about a word; "the donkey, most assuredly—as he always gets home first."

"And how are they getting on at Charles'?" Meier asked; "all jolly? The truth is, we left two hours too soon to-day."

"Yes, and I should have been home long ago," Panning said, "but I had to wait for the meat; they were slaughtering an ox."

"But our meat was on the donkey?" Albert retorted.

"Indeed," said Panning, looking very cunning; "well then, Albert, there's another proof that the donkey was in the right; but still, I waited for the meat."

"Yes, Panning's a capital fellow," said the smith; "he's been knocking about in the world since he was a lad."

"You'd better be quiet, you scamp!" said Panning; "if I like to tell something—"

"If you tell that, I'll tell the other," said the Blacksmith, tauntingly.

"Hurrah! two new stories," cried the Landrath; "out with it, Panning."

But there must have been something queer about the matter, for neither cared to begin. Meier, in the meanwhile, had placed water to boil on the fire, brandy bottles were produced from various sides, and a famous bowl of grog brewed; the anecdotes, laughing, and shouting, became constantly louder. Försterling had finished his baking, and "The Pope he leads a happy Life," "Rinaldini's haughty Robbers," and "Prince Eugenius," had echoed through the silent Californian forest, when Meier at length cried:

"Stop—empty your glasses: confound it, Smith, that's my cup. And now for my song; but you must all join in the chorus." And in a loud, hearty voice he sang

THE GOLD-DIGGER'S SONG.

With the shovel, pick, and pan,
  Diggers hurrah!
And a knapsack to each man,
  Carried from afar;
Little guard for heat or cold,
  Diggers hurrah!
In the mountains, men of mould,
  Bring we from afar.

Where the gnomes their treasure bright,
  Diggers of the gold,
Hid in chasms from the light,
  Here in some dark hold,
Dig, and wash, and grope about,
  Lusty and bold,
Though it's deep, we'll have it out,
  Diggers of the gold.

Care! Who talks of care or sorrow?
  Sorrow, by my fay!
The luck may come to-morrow,
  Though it's missed to-day.
Let us never cark or pine,
  Good hearts and bold,
There is stuff shall soon be thine,
  Diggers of the gold.

Still a whisper's in my ear,
  Diggers hurrah!

Wilt thou tarry ever here,
  From thy home so far?
Canst thou careless revel keep,
  Lusty and free,
When thy love does sit and weep,
  Digger, for thee?

Heart, thy fruitless whispers cease,
  Diggers hurrah!
Can I sit at home in peace,
  When I should be far?
Men must labour, rend, and rive,
  Stout heart and bold,
And in storm and sunshine strive,
  Diggers for gold.

But there soon shall come a day,
  Diggers hurrah!
When we'll bear rich spoil away
  Coming from afar;
Homeward hieing, heavy laden,
  Stout hearts and bold,
Then for father, mother, maiden,
  Diggers for gold.

The chorus was sung with great effect, and in the last verses it became a species of Dutch melody, for they seemed to forget the tune utterly, and all sorts of possible and impossible songs were now heard. Hayo even sang "Bumsfallera" once more, and the Blacksmith his "Ich bin liederlich," while the neighbouring Americans and Englishmen had come down from the hill to hear the songs. Meier now sang the serenade "I am beneath thy window, dearest," with all the proper gesticulations, and beneath an oak-tree instead of his beloved's window. Klaussen had drunk a little too much, and had become harmonious. Wohlgemuth took Albert into a corner, and told him a frightfully long story of his school-days; how they had placed a bone under the master's chair, and with what presence of mind he had extricated himself from the affair. Renich had made fast to the Landrath, who was singing, though, between whiles, and told him a story from ancient Roman history, doubtlessly very important in itself, but a matter of perfect indifference to Försterling, which he afterwards brought into connection with later history, although his shouting victim did not pay the slightest attention to him.

In the mean while, fire and grog drew to an end; one after the other retired to his tent. Renich as well as Wohlgemuth had both lost their hearers, and Renich had also gone to bed. Meier and Wohlgemuth still held out; the former, because he never retired earlier; the latter, because he felt a necessity to have his say out.

Naturally, a quarter of an hour had not elapsed before the two were up to the ears in politics. Wohlgemuth had been formerly in the United States, and defended the forty acres grant. Meier, on the other hand, abused Germany; and whether they did not understand one another, or found sufficient points of collision, I cannot say, but they became heated, and Haye looked a couple of times out of the tent to see whether they were not fighting.

As Wohlgemuth was very hard of hearing, Meier was forced to shout; and as Meier spoke very loudly, Wohlgemuth could not support his arguments in a very gentle tone; consequently such a disturbance soon arose between the two that the sleepers were aroused, and grumbling voices were heard. At length Försterling could not stand it any longer.

"Confound it, Meier," he cried from the tent,

"you're both in the right; but now come to bed."

"Hold your row, Landrath; you don't understand it," Meier cried, in his zeal.

However, if the Landrath did not know how to damp the dispute, he was clever enough to do so with the fire. It had burnt to a little point, and as the night was very cool the debaters had drawn quite close to it, and the Landrath managed so cleverly to sacrifice the jug of water, which he had fetched for the morrow's coffee, that in a moment not a trace of burning wood could be seen.

The quarrellers would not allow themselves to be baulked by this, and continued their dispute in the dark; but the animus was wanting, and in half an hour all were silent, after murmuring, "Thank the Lord."

The cayotas, little wolves, or wild dogs, alone commenced howling, and now and then an owl croaked its monotonous night song.

With the break of day fresh life awaited the sleepers. Those who had "the week" got up and prepared breakfast, then woke the rest; and an hour later the several parties walked with their pans and water-buckets, for their tools had been left at the spot where they had struck work on the Saturday evening, to the different places at which they intended to try their luck during the week.

Immediately after, the machines began clattering in the ravine below, the axes removed trees and roots from their way, the pick was driven with powerful strokes into the hard ground, and the working life of the miners had recommenced.

CHAPTER XVII.

MADEMOISELLE RACHEL.

In February, 1821, a poor Hebrew family, consisting of Samuel or Isaac Felix, the husband, Esther Haya, the wife, and a little girl of four years of age, called Sophia (which name she eventually changed for Sarah), were forced to delay their journey at a poor village in the canton of Argau, called Munf. Our readers need not look for it on the map or in the gazetteer; it is so small as to have been utterly neglected, and yet it was the birthplace of the greatest tragic actress France ever possessed. Here it was that the Felix family were delayed on their laborious progress from one fair to another, by an interesting event; and so soon as the young Elizabeth Rachel was born, she was added to the rest of the burden, the father growling at the additional weight, and little foreseeing the wondrous treasure he was taking his turn to carry. So they went on from fair to fair, from town to town, until they at last reached Lyons, where Madame Felix gained a step in the social hierarchy by being attached to the theatre as mender-in-chief of old dresses, while the father added to his scanty fortunes by giving lessons in German and elocution. In the mean time, a son had been added to the family, and the children were compelled, by the harsh law of poverty, to seek their own livelihood. Sophia, the future Sarah, visited the cafés, singing (malice adds, very much out of tune), while Eliza, the future Rachel, went round to collect the centimes, which were grudgingly bestowed. Still Papa Felix possessed all the pertinacity of his race, and obeyed a secret impulse which told him to seek his fortune in Paris. This he decided on doing in 1830; and so scanty were the family circumstances, that they were compelled to travel on foot, meeting their expenses by singing at the public-houses along the road. At Paris, however, it was much the same as at Lyons; the mother set up an establishment for second-hand clothes, while the children went about singing as before; whether the sun scorched or the rain drenched them, they were to one thing constant ever—they must take money home with them at night.

Although not generally admirers of the Hebrews, we are bound to give them credit for the admirable manner in which they assist their poorer brethren. Such was the case with Felix père; some of his co-religionists took compassion on the poor girls, and exerted their influence to procure them admission to the school of singing and declamation kept by a M. Choron, formerly director of the Opera. The old gentleman was an enthusiast, and welcomed recruits, no matter their social position. So long as he saw in them germs of talent, he devoted his own powers to the good cause, and was indefatigable in his researches after fine voices. A curious letter is quoted by H. Jules Lecomte in *Figaro*, the first portion being written by Choron, and suggesting to the parents that the two children should remain a little longer at his school before Felix père began to make a market of them. In his verdict on the two girls, Choron says, "Eliza (Rachel) will require a little more time, for she has a worse memory and works less than her sister, who is considerably more thoughtful, and understands with greater facility." The second portion of the letter, dated 30th of November, 1832, is probably the earliest autograph existing of the great tragédienne; we quote it in its entirety, preserving the peculiar orthography:

CHERS, CHERS PARENTS,—Il m'est *imposible* de vous exprimer toute la joie que j'ai *resentée* en recevant de vos nouvelles. Je commençais à craindre qu'il *arivé* quelque chose, car voilà longtemps que vous m'avez écrit; je me réjouis à l'idée que j'aurai bientôt le *bonheure* de vous voir et *montres* les progrès que j'ai *fait*. M. Choron est assez content de moi et a pour nous mille bontés. Je ne puis prouver toute ma reconnaissance qu'en cherchant à m'*apliquer* afin de toujours contenter M. Choron autant que je désire. Adieu, mes bons parents, recevez l'assurance de tout mon *resepect*. Votre fille soumise vous embrasse sans oublier mon petit frère Raphaël et ma sœur Rebec.

"ELISA."

But M. Choron soon detected that Eliza's nature was not adapted for the trammels of song, while he foresaw a great future for her as a tragedian. Hence he mentioned her to his friend Pagnon, who kept a school of declamation with a small theatre annexed, called the Théâtre Molière, in the Rue St Martin. He soon discovered the latent talent in Rachel, and from M. J. de Lasalle we may be allowed to quote the following paragraph relating to her: "St Aulaire entered my room one morning and spoke with extreme animation about a poor Jewish girl, whom he described to me as the essence of tragedy, and the only person capable of recalling the *chefs-d'œuvre* of our tragic repertory. It was Rachel for whom the professor demanded an audience, which I granted on the spot. Mademoiselle Mars, Samson, Desmousseaux, were the only persons present. Saint-Aulaire replied to the *débutante,* who was then very small; she had selected *Hermione* in 'Andromaque,' and *Marinette* in the 'Dépit Amoureux.' She commenced with the latter, in which she displayed no remarkable talent; but she had hardly finished in 'Andromaque' the ironical passage, the 'Adieu to Orestes,' than we uttered exclamations of surprise. For a very long period we had not heard the verses declaimed with so much precision or such energy. The audience over, Mademoiselle Mars embraced the young girl, who was quite moved by the success she had just achieved, and evinced great interest in her. Upon the remark that she was very short for the part of queens and great heroines, the characters she had decided on playing, Mars reminded us that Mademoiselle Maillard, the great tragic actress, was still shorter. 'Besides,' she added, 'it is a good fault; Rachel will grow.'"

M. Thiers granted the young *débutante* a gratification of 1200 francs, while Samson, the celebrated professor, undertook her tragic education. It was with great difficulty that Rachel could be induced to give up her predilection for comedy; but at length she was pronounced fit for managerial inspection, and her parents pressing to make money out of her, M. St Aulaire invited Delestre-Poirson, director of the Gymnase, to come and hear the little Jewess. He was satisfied with her performance in "Eriphile," and engaged her at 3000 francs a year. His first care was to change her name of Eliza into Rachel, the learned Dr Véron describing the circumstance thus: "M. Poirson said to her, 'That name of Eliza will not suit the bill at all. Have you no other?' 'My name is Elizabeth-Rachel.' 'Come, that is better. Rachel! that is a name which will be remembered, and which is not borne by everybody. Call yourself, in future, Rachel. The selection of a name is of more consequence than you may imagine.'" But the *père aux écus* has forgotten that another circumstance decided Poirson on calling the young actress Rachel; Halévy's opera had brought the name into great vogue, and no manager would neglect such an opportunity of attracting popular attention. A wretched play, called "La Vendéenne," was written expressly for the young actress, and she made her first appearance in it on the 25th of April, 1837. But few of the critics recognized her marvellous power; in fact, the only favourable exception was Jules Janin, and he has not forgotten to plume himself on his discovery ever since. Here is his critique, taken from the *Journal des Débats*, May 1 :—

"In this 'Vendéenne,' the authors not only desired to make a drama, but to produce at the same time a new-born child of the drama, a little girl, scarce fifteen years of age, named Rachel. This child, thank Heaven! is not a phenomenon, and she will never cause the world to consider her a prodigy. Rachel plays with a good deal of soul, heart, talent, and very little skill: she feels naturally the sentiment of the drama entrusted her, and her intelligence suffices for her to understand it: she requires no advice or lessons.

There is no effort, no exaggeration, no cries, or gestures; a great soberness in all the movements of her body and her face; nothing that resembles coquetry but, on the contrary, something brusque, bold, even fierce in her gestures, carriage, and look. Such is Rachel. This child, who has the conscience of truth in the art, dresses herself with a scrupulous fidelity of costume: her voice is hoarse and veiled, like the voice of a child: her hands are red, like the hands of a child; her foot is like her hand, still slightly formed; she is not pretty, but she pleases. In a word, there is a great future in this young talent, and already there is a goodly crop of tears, of interest, and of emotion."

We dare say this is very fine criticism, but, in all humility, we venture to suggest it would have been more intelligible if less ornate. Still, we suppose that Janin is justly entitled to the merit of being the great Rachel discoverer. Unfortunately, the people could not be induced to look on the young actress with the same eye of enthusiasm: the piece was bad, the applause lukewarm, and Rachel was allowed gently to sink into oblivion, although we believe her salary continued to be paid. For a whole year she was not heard of in public; but during that period she was diligently studying her art under the tuition of Samson. A powerful Israelite interposed in her behalf; she was again heard at the Théâtre Français. M. Vedel cancelled her engagement with the Gymnase, and took her on to the establishment as *pensionnaire,* with a salary of 4000 francs a year. Her foot was now firmly planted on the ladder, and she never ceased her exertions till she had reached the summit. The company being aware that Mademoiselle Mars took considerable interest in the young actress, attended the rehearsals, a thing they were not in the habit of doing usually; and they had the sense to recognize her wondrous talent. Hence, before the young girl made her first public appearance, she had attained a certain degree of celebrity. On the 12th of June, 1838, the bills announced "Les Horaces," with Mademoiselle Rachel. And here we must make room for the second Christopher Columbus, Dr Véron :—

"On a lovely summer evening, seeking shade and solitude (by looking carefully, everything may be found at Paris, even shade and solitude), I entered the Théâtre Français between eight and nine o'clock. There were four spectators in the stalls, I being the fifth. My eyes were attracted to the stage by a strange face, full of expression, with a prominent brow, a dark eye full of fire; all this planted on a thin body, but possessing a certain elegance of posture, movement, and attitude. A sympathetic voice, of the most delightful diapason, and before all very intelligent, drew the attention of my distracted mind, which was more disposed for sloth than for admiration. This strange physiognomy, this eye full of fire, this thin body, this so intelligent voice—it was Mademoiselle Rachel; she was making her first appearance in *Camille* in 'Les Horaces.' The lively and profound impression made on me at the first glance by this young actress aroused in me confused reminiscences. By dint of interrogating my memory, I called to mind a singular young girl, playing the *Vendéenne* at the Gymnase. I also remembered a poor young girl, poorly clad, with clumsy shoes, who, on being asked in my presence, in the corridor of a theatre, what she was doing, replied to my great amazement, in a high tragedy voice and most serious tone, 'I am pursuing my studies.' I found again in Mademoiselle Rachel the singular physiognomy of the Gymnase and the poor girl poorly clad. The young Rachel had astonished me; her talent impassioned me; I was obliged to lay hands as speedily as possible on my friend Merle, whose tastes and literary fancies I shared, to compel him to follow the *débuts* of her whom I already called my little prodigy. 'This child,' I said to him, 'when the twelve or fifteen hundred men of talent who form public opinion in Paris have seen and heard her, will be the glory and fortune of the Comédie Française.' In 1838 I had left the Opera; the talent and success of my actress became for me a fixed idea and business. Before bidding people good day, I asked them, 'Have you seen her in 'Les Horaces,' in 'Andromaque?'' The greater number did not know of whom I was talking: I grew angry with them, and reproached their ignorance in strong language. The pleasures and joys of my summer were ensured; my emotions as *habitué* of the Théâtre Français were to take the place of the pleasures of the fields, the incidents and surprises of travels. During the whole month of June, during the whole month of July, but few people seemed to be converted to my new religion: whether Mademoiselle Rachel performed *Camille, Emilie,* or *Hermione,* the apostles of this new creed, of this new divinity, preached in the desert. From the month of August, despite the canicular heat, Rachel's performances were more closely followed. When the theatre appeared to me nearly filled, I wiped my brow, and, like the fly on the coach-wheel, I said to myself, with a satisfaction pushed almost to pride, 'Mademoiselle Rachel and I will gain our cause with the public. Here are people possessed of common sense.' At last, during the whole of October, the young actress played nine times, and the smallest receipt (*Monime*, in 'Mithridate') amounted to 3669 fr. 90 c. The receipts exceeded 6000 fr. when she played *Hermione:* it was a complete victory and deafening triumph; Racine and Corneille lived again among us, as in the great age of Louis XIV.; a feverish popularity surrounded the young *tragédienne* and the old tragedy."

So great was the success attained by the young actress, that the sociétaires spontaneously decided on raising her salary from 4000 to 20,000 francs, or 8000 francs more than Ligier, Samson, or Monrose were receiving. A short time afterwards, though still so young and inexperienced, she was summoned to take her seat in their committee of administration, so utterly had Rachel subverted all the old prejudices connected with the principal French theatre, in which, hitherto, everything had been forced to give way to precedents and tradition. One of the earliest acts of revenge Rachel took on those who had contemned her talent, was so graceful that we cannot omit it here, although it is probably well known. M. Provost, of the Théâtre Français, to whom she had applied for dramatic instruction, had somewhat brutally repulsed her by telling her to go and sell bouquets. One evening, when the theatre was crowded to see *Hermione,* and bouquets were thrown by thousands to the actress, she amused herself, so soon as the curtain fell, by filling her Greek tunic with flowers; then, going to the actor who had given her such bad advice, and kneeling with admirable grace, she said, "I have followed your counsel, M. Provost: I am selling bouquets. Will you buy some from me?" We must make room here for an anecdote not so well known, serving to display the appreciation Mademoiselle Mars felt for the young actress. We quote from M. de Varenne, who had the story at first hand from an intimate friend of the great actress:—

"It was the day of Rachel's *début*, and she was about to perform *Camille*, in 'Les Horaces.' I met at the theatre Mademoiselle Mars, who said to me, 'You are aware that there is a *début* to-day?' 'Ah!' I remarked, 'it seems there is nothing extraordinary about her.' 'On the contrary, according to competent judges, great things may be expected from her. At any rate, come with me and hear her.' I accompanied her to her box. We were alone with a young man who stood behind her, and during the whole performance criticised the young actress in the hope, of course, of gratifying the elder one. When *Camille* appeared on the stage, Mademoiselle Mars followed her attentively; then, turning to me, she said, with a half-nod and a sigh of hearty satisfaction, 'She walks well!' Those acquainted with the theatre well know what praise was contained in these simple words, especially from the lips of Mars. *Sabine* addresses a few words to *Camille* at the moment when the latter appears on the stage. Mademoiselle Rachel had not yet opened her lips, when Mars turned to me again, and, regarding me with an air of personal triumph, said, 'And she listens well!'

Listening well is the height of art which few actors possess—an art as difficult, more difficult, perhaps, than that of speaking well. Mademoiselle Mars was too profoundly, too delicately artistic, not to seize with delight the slightest *nuances*. *Camille* spoke in her turn. She had scarcely uttered half-a-dozen lines when Mars exclaimed, with a satisfaction I shall never forget, and an indescribable feeling of relief, 'Ah! she does not declaim: she speaks!' When the famous imprecation came—

> 'Rome, l'unique objet de mon ressentiment . . . .
> Rome, enfin, que je hais, parce qu'elle t'honore'—

instead of the classic elevation of voice, and those noisy outbursts of grief which carry away the audience and force applause, Mademoiselle Rachel, either through fatigue, calculation, or disdain of received traditions, uttered these words hoarsely, and with a concentrated feeling; so that the public, which expected something very different, did not applaud this consecrated passage. 'Ah!' the young gentleman remarked, 'she lacks strength.' 'But, sir,' Mademoiselle Mars exclaimed, turning sharply to him, and as if stung to the quick, 'surely you will allow her to recruit her strength. Are you fearful she will not grow older? She grows while performing, this young girl!' For my own part, though far from being ill-disposed to the young actress, I could not summon up such an amount of admiration, and was struck by Mademoiselle Mars's heat in this scene."

As Dr Véron justly tells us, great names and great fortunes are often pleased to play the part of Mecænas to rising celebrity. Hence it grew the fashion to have the wild *Hermione* in company. She soon counted among her friends the greatest personages of Spain then residing in Paris, the Duchess of Berwick and Alba being the chief among them. The Countess Duchâtel insisted on Rachel dining with her constantly, while her husband the minister presented her with a rich library, containing the *chefs-d'œuvre* of French literature. In public places her presence was an event. When she appeared at the Chamber of Deputies she attracted all the assembly of sages, and even caused a species of distraction to the illustrious orators whom she came to study. The following passage contains more truth and feeling than we are wont to expect from the Doctor:—

"What sense and good taste she must have required to support decently this abrupt transition from the most obscure misery to all the intoxications of success, to that happy character of the spoiled child of fortune, the great world, and the public. This society, which at a later date was destined to exaggerate her weaknesses and accuse her, without chariness, of unpardonable disorders, could find in her, at the dawn of her celebrity, virtues, a pure heart, a heart virgin to all evil sentiments, to all the violent passions, which she knew so well how to depict without experiencing them. The success which Mademoiselle Rachel obtained in the salons, the favour, full of tenderness, which she knew how to conquer among distinguished women, from people of talent and knowledge, can only be explained by the rare qualities—I do not say of the actress, but of a young girl who was spirituelle, amiable, and always mistress of herself."

By degrees Rachel extended her repertory. She

played thus *Phèdre,* a character she comprehended admirably, after the fashion of Euripides and not of Racine, regarding herself rather as a victim to the vengeance of the gods than as a loving and culpable woman; *Marie Stuart,* whom she succeeded in rendering touching and proud, melancholy and implacable, at once resigned and haughty, suppliant and superb, but always courageous, patient, and worthy. The pecuniary result of her extraordinary success was, however, as surprising as her great talent. It was estimated that she made an income of 400,000 francs, including her lucrative engagements at home and abroad. Her first appearance in England was in 1840, when she played her limited round of characters from Corneille and Racine. While in London she received several visits from the Duke of Wellington. Once, when complaining of her nerves, the illustrious veteran recommended her to employ some baths of *eau sale.* On Rachel naturally inquiring what degree of *saleté* would be necessary, the Duke condescended to an explanation, and Rachel then discovered that the Duke meant salt, not dirty water. Many letters are extant from the great political actor to the great tragic queen. The most interesting we quote in the original:

Londres, ce 9 *Juliet*, 1842.

Le Maréchal Duc de Wellington présente ses hommages à Mademoiselle Rachel. Il a fait prévenir au théâtre qu'il désirait y retenir sa loge, *enfin* de pourvoir y assister à la réprésentation pour le *benfice* de Mademoiselle Rachel.

Il y assistera certainement, *si il* devient possible de s'absenter ce jour-là de l'assemblée du parlement *dont il est membre.*

Il regrettera beaucoup *si il* se trouve impossible ainsi d'avoir la satisfaction de la voir et l'entendre encore une fois avant son départ de Londres.

In 1844 Rachel returned for an instant to her first love: she performed the part of *Marinette* in the "Dépit Amoureux," on the occasion of her sister's benefit. On another occasion she played the part of *Celimène*, but with equal want of success, for in Rachel's hands a fan became a dagger. The first modern character she played was the *Catherine II.* of Hippolyte Romand. She was as charming in the train of green velvet as in the antique peplum; but the dress fitting tightly to her body made her look smaller, and spite of her queen-like gestures, she had not the amplitude of stature suited for a *Catherine*. In 1845 she performed the *Virginie* of M. Latour de St Yvars, of which she made a delightful creation. In 1846 she performed in "Jeanne d'Arc," imitated from Scheller's "Maid of Orleans," but the attempt was not successful, although Rachel spoke of herself in that character as a Geneviève attired in the armour of Bradamante. A French critic accounts for her failure by stating that the unbending armour deprived her of her irresistible *serpentine* charm. In 1847 she performed *Agrippine* in "Britannicus." We believe she only assumed this character once, and in spite of her juvenile air, she performed it with considerable force. In the same year she represented *Athalie*, and was perfectly successful. In March, 1848, she played in the "Lucrèce" of Ponsard; but even her inimitable acting was not so much admired as her singing of the *Marseillaise*. The circumstance which led to her singing it is thus described by M. Lockroy:

"One evening I was in Rachel's box, when she suddenly said: 'I have dreamed of something extraordinary, which will draw all Paris. I will sing the

Marseillaise.' 'But I did not know you could sing.' 'No matter, I will make a *mélopée* of it. You shall come and hear it to-night; there will be only three or four of you present.' 'Then I am to announce that Mademoiselle Rachel will sing the *Marseillaise* at the Théâtre Français?' 'Certainly; don't you think it will bring in money at a period when the theatres are deserted?' 'That depends; I must hear it first.' In short, when the performance was over we assembled in the green-room. With her family collected around her, and the tricolor flag in her hand, she attacked the celebrated song which she had stealthily studied, verse by verse, note by note. All the world knows what she made of it! It was not singing, properly so called, but a recitation, in which the strength of accentuation and the power of expression supplied the want of melody. It made the hearers tremble and shudder. The success was as great as the conception was daring. The *Marseillaise* brought in as much money as an entire tragedy."

Soon after, Rachel performed the two characters, *Tullia* and *Lucrèce*, in Ponsard's tragedy, and her success suggested "Valeria," in which Rachel played the characters of *Valeria* and *Lysisca*, to the great scandal of those who deplored that her talents should be wasted on such unworthy subjects. But her greatest triumph in her modern repertory was *Adrienne Lecouvreur*, which she performed with evident sympathy, the circumstances were so typical of her own life. It is unncessary, however, to delay on all the characters Rachel created, as she progressed from one triumph to another. Let us hasten to the close of her career. The last European performance she gave was, curiously enough, on the boards of old Drury, on the 9th of August, 1855, on the occasion of a benefit performance on behalf of the Société Française de Secours. The next day she quitted Liverpool for New York, where she laid the foundation of that illness which led to her premature decease. She caught cold at an evening party given by M. Trévriand, editor of the *Courrier de l'Europe.* She was lightly clad; the mistress of the house lent her a pelisse, but Mademoiselle Rachel returned to her lodgings hoarse, and from that moment never ceased to cough. At Charleston she played for the last time in her life, and her last part was that of *Adrienne Lecouvreur.* She then spent some weeks in Havannah, hoping that the climate would cause some improvement in her health, and returned to Paris in February, 1856, in a very serious condition. In October, after selling her hotel in the Rue Trudon and her furniture, she proceeded to Egypt, but her health was for ever lost. In May, 1857, she returned to Marseilles, and her doctors advised her to pass the summer in a country-house near Montpellier. After a short stay in Paris, whither she went to take leave of her son, she finally returned to Le Cannet on the 15th of last September, and never rose from her bed again. No words can furnish an idea of the fearful sufferings she endured with the most unalterable serenity, to quote the words of the *Constitutionnel*: "As often happens in such cases, either by the illusion of the sufferer or the provision of Providence, as her end approached she ceased to anticipate it, and some days previous to her death she suffered pain no longer. She became resigned and docile as a child, and wrote a letter to her father full of tenderness on the occasion of the new year. She expired tranquilly, without a single murmur or a sigh, and repeating aloud the prayers of the dying. . . . . Her countenance was so beautiful at the transformation, that some one hastened to a photographist to preserve the features, so pure and calm, that they will pass to posterity without being distorted by a single pang." It has been affirmed that some few hours before death actually ensued, Rachel fell into a swoon, which was mistaken for death. The poor sufferer lived—if such a condition can be called life—nearly two hours after the telegraph had announced her decease in Paris. But we may believe that Rachel was prepared for an early death; like many other great artists, she was very superstitious, and we may quote a curious anecdote on this subject from *Le Monde Illustré*. She had the usual horror of dining thirteen at table, and a dinner given on the success of Victor Hugo's "Angelo" was liable to this objection. "What has become of the thirteen? Hugo and his wife at Jersey; Girardin and his wife—she is dead; Pradier is gone; Alfred de Musset, gone; Gérard de Nerval, suicide; Court d'Orsay, dead; my sister Rebecca, dead. I alone survive."

On Monday, the 11th of January, all that was left of Rachel was consigned to the grave in the Jewish burial-ground. All the celebrities of letters and art were present, and several speeches were, after the Gallic fashion, held. That of M. Janin was peculiarly effective; he alluded to the loss, within so short a period, of all that was renowned, glorious, and free; and he uttered his regret that the deceased was not eulogized by a man who was alone competent to do so, but who was now in exile—M. Victor Hugo. Thus passed away the greatest tragic actress France ever possessed; we say advisedly the greatest, for she was more than a mere actress; she succeeded in exciting the hearers' interest in the play itself, and when we bear in mind the general character of French tragedies, and the inflated sentiments for which they are made a medium, we cannot sufficiently admire the skill with which Rachel rendered even such verses entrancing.

Through the whole of our sketch we have purposely referred to the actress, and left the woman at peace; we have no desire to cast a stone upon her grave, and much may be forgiven in remembrance of the exceptional temptations to which she was exposed. But we are sorry to say that the French, who are ever ready to sacrifice a friend for a jest, have not been so generous, and multitudinous anecdotes have been raked up about her, which do no credit either to the actress or the narrator. Some of these, which tend to throw a light on her character, we will proceed to select, avoiding, as far as possible, all personality.

A young author, very poor, and yet enjoying a certain degree of poetical reputation, had completed a three-act comedy in verse. He presented it to the Théâtre Français, and it was rejected. The poet was in despair, when Rachel took him on one side. "I know an Englishman who has a mania for unpublished MSS.," she said to him; "will you let him have yours for 1000 fr.?" The poet gladly consented; the actress gave him the money and kept him to dinner. A week later the MS. was magnificently bound and placed in her private library.

On one occasion Rachel had to write a letter of thanks to the home minister, M. Baroche. Before sending it she showed it to Arsène Houssaye, who advised her to recopy it, and correct some orthographical errors. "Ah, bah!" she replied, "let them stand; in that way my letter will appear all the more sincere."

One day Rachel had a grand dinner party, and determined to do things in style. She called on a critic of her acquaintance to aid her in choosing her dessert. They went to Chevet's, where Rachel demanded all the finest fruit in and out of season. Just as she was going away, Chevet suggested that madame should have a pine-apple for the centre, but the price was too high; she agreed to hire it. The dinner was superb; for she did things right royally. Still, in a corner of her heart there was always a trace of that parsimony peculiar to her race. When the dessert was put on the table the pine-apple looked magnificent, and the critic maliciously suggested to the Duc de St Teodoro that he should cut it. The Duc leaned over the table and thrust a sharp knife into the forbidden fruit, which he bore off in triumph. Mademoiselle Rachel saw the deed. She was struck by it as if a tragedy dagger had been suddenly thrust into her heart. She uttered a dolorous cry, and cast a fifth-act glance on the Duc. "Mademoiselle Rachel has, then, a pine-apple for a heart," said Ponsard. Nothing could restore her good-humour that evening. It could not be avarice, for the dinner had cost 1200 fr. It was rather an attack of the nerves. It was misunderstood, however, and the story of the 70-franc pine-apple made the round of the *salons*.

During the *coup d'état*, a critic, who had not always been kind to her, was gravely compromised. She heard of it, and never rested for two whole days, until she had restored him to liberty—and to write against her still.

Rachel received 500 fr. premium for each occasion she thought proper to play more than twice a week. When the "Malade Imaginaire" was given, with the procession in which all the company defiles before the audience, she walked at the head to receive the applause of the public—and the 500 fr. The amount being at last disputed, she never appeared in the procession again; not even on the night of Molière's *fête*.

One of her companions at the Théâtre Français, a blonde with an angelic face, but terminating deplorably in enormous hands and feet, said one day before her in the green-room, "I adore Meudon—I have there a little *pied-à-terre*." "You!" Rachel exclaimed, with an indescribable air of mockery, which gained her three rounds of applause.

A good deal has been said about Rachel's avarice, and many of her admirers have been turned away from her by this charge. But there appears to be but little truth in it. She has left behind 1,500,000 fr. it is said; but, on the other hand, she gained more than four millions, and if she had spent but 50,000 fr. a year since 1838, she would have had three millions to leave behind her. Not only was she not avaricious, but she actually devoted herself to her friends with a degree of prodigality. On the day after M. Michel Lévy lost his first action against Dumas, she sent to tell him that she had 200,000 fr. at his service.

The truth appears to be that Rachel was full of contradictions and failings. As she loved gambling, she took every opportunity to organize among her family a game of cards or a loto. If she lost twenty or thirty sous she would become furious, and rage against the whole world. Then her brother would ask her for two thousand francs, of which he stood in pressing need, and she would give them without a word.

Among the letters of Mademoiselle Rachel which have been preserved, we find one admirable specimen, addressed to a well-known Hebrew banker:

Monsieur,—My friend M. asserts that I need only write *one word* to you to obtain for him fifty shares in the Austrian railways. If you will be kind enough to add fifty more for each extra word, the surplus will be for your ever devoted Rachel.

Among the curious letters which Rachel had received in the course of her theatrical career, was one she was fond of showing. She had reason to complain of the chief of the claque, and he expostulated as follows:

Mademoiselle,—I cannot remain under the obloquy of a reproach from lips such as yours. The following is an authentic statement of what occurred; at the first representation I led the attack in person not less than thirty-three times. We had three acclamations, four hilarities, two thrilling movements, four renewals of applause, and two indefinite explosions. In fact, to such an extent did we carry our applause, that the occupants of the stalls were scandalized, and cried out, "Turn them out!" My men were positively exhausted with fatigue, and even intimated to me that they could not again go through such an evening. Seeing such was the case, I applied for the MS., and after having profoundly studied the piece, I was obliged to make up my mind to certain curtailments in the service of my men. I, however, only applied them to MM. ——, and, if the *ad interim* office I hold afford me the opportunity, I will make them ample amends. In such a situation as I have just depicted, I have only to request you to believe firmly in my profound admiration and respectful zeal; and I venture to entreat you to have some consideration for the difficulties that environ me.

In the course of our reading we have naturally met with many appreciators of Rachel's acting, but none of them appear to us so truthful as that published by Mr Charles Harvey, in his "Theatres of Paris," to the following effect:—

"Nature has endowed Mademoiselle Rachel with a face and form modelled after the statues of ancient Greece; her figure, though slight, is at once graceful and commanding; her eyes are small but expressive; and there is a simple majesty in her look, walk, and manner, which art alone could never give. Her great triumphs have been in parts in which hatred, contempt, or irony forms a principal feature. Thus, nothing can be finer than her *Camille* in 'Les Horaces.' While she spoke, every eye was fixed upon her, in order that not a sound, not a gesture might be lost; her voice, though at times subdued almost to a whisper, came distinct to every ear, so deep, so unbroken was the silence; until at last, when, overcome by her own energy, and concentrating all her strength into one final effort, she, as it were, hissed out the 'Moi seule en être cause, et mourir de plaisir!' the whole house burst into one simultaneous roar of applause, and re-echoed long and loudly as well behind as before the curtain. When tenderness or grief unmixed with the sterner passions are required, Rachel is comparatively ineffective; even *Virginie,* one of her finest creations, though a consummate piece of acting, has not that influence on the spectator which is produced by her performance of *Camille* or *Hermione.* But whatever be the character sustained by her, she is always great, always admirable."

It is now clearly established that Rachel did not quit the religion of her family for that of Catholicism. Even royal influence was attempted in vain, of which a curious instance is quoted in the *Figaro.* After the death of Louis Philippe, the Prince de Joinville designed a drawing, which was sent to Paris to be lithographed. Rachel hearing of it, wrote to General Rumigny for a copy, and the Queen Amélie sent her word: "Mademoiselle Rachel will be presented with my son's drawing when she is converted to Catholicism." But Rachel always had a friendly feeling towards the family of the King of the French; for did not Louis Philippe present her with a thousand francs? and the rarity of the gift greatly enhanced its value. It appears, too, that Rachel had intended a conversion, but her desire remained unaccomplished. During the latter years of her life she devoted considerable attention and thought to the subject of religion. She read Bossuet and Fénélon with deep interest and sustained attention. It is to be presumed, therefore, that if she did not embrace Catholicism, it was because she did not find in it better claims to belief than the religion in which she had been brought up.

"One word," writes M. Jules Janin, "may serve to explain Mademoiselle Rachel entirely, and it is the remark of a dying hero. When the Maréchal de Saxe succumbed, exhausted by glory and overcome by passions, surrounded by so many pleasures, and yet wearied of so many pleasures, he said to his physician, who was weeping, 'Monsieur de Senac, do not lament: I have enjoyed a glorious dream—a dream beyond the infinite!'"

CHAPTER XVIII.

BYWAYS OF THE BLACK FOREST.

Many a free and enlightened Briton in the course of a summer tour spends a day or two at Baden-Baden, and fancies that in rambling to Lichtenthal and breakfasting at the Alt Schloss—not to mention vespertinal losses to M. Benazet—he has seen the Black Forest. It is true that Baden is situated in that portion of the world which Mrs Radcliffe and her followers thought proper to brand as the resort of banditti and midnight murderers, and which still, probably, furnishes the schoolboy with material for thrilling scenes of perilous adventure, though the only robbers now to be found consist of landlords, who bring you down with a long bill instead of a pistol-bullet; still the routine traveller in visiting Baden—we say it with all humility—knows absolutely nothing of the Black Forest. The mode of life at Baden is so entirely exceptional, so utterly cosmopolitan, that those peculiar elements which characterize the Black Forest disappear, and give place to Parisian manners and customs, very charming, it is true, *per se*, but still far from satisfying any one who interests himself in ethnology, or likes to study his fellow-men under various aspects. To find the true Schwarzwälder, he must put on his knapsack and leave the beaten track; he must wander through secluded valleys, where he will find a population, self-depending and self-satisfying, ignoring the luxuries of civilization to a great extent, and perfectly content to let the world wag on as it listeth, so that their small manufactories be not interfered with. We have had opportunities in our time for visiting the Schwarzwald thoroughly; and hence we trust we shall not be thought presumptuous if we draw our readers' attention to a district where the omniscient Murray has thought it beneath his dignity to penetrate.

On leaving Baden-Baden the traveller should proceed by railway to Achern, whence the first excursion must be made to the ruins of Allerheiligen. And we may here remark at starting, that the traveller must be blessed with good legs if he wish to enjoy the Black Forest scenery, for it is a constant succession of going up and down hill. The first object of interest seen is the Brigitten Schloss, built on such a tremendously steep rock, that it seems impossible for the owner ever to have descended to the plain without imminent risk of breaking his neck. Indeed, the story runs that the fort was originally situated at the foot of the mountain, but was lifted up to its present position bodily by the spells of the wicked fairy Brigitta. The view from the ruin, however, well repays the exertion of reaching it. It extends an extraordinary distance, comprising the valley of the Ortenau, the whole of Central Alsace, with the Rhine winding like a silver thread through the valley; while in strange and romantic contrast to this lovely scenery, the Hornissgründe rise frowningly in the rear, and the valley of the Seebach looks black as the entrance to Hades. After a rugged walk of about two hours we reach a solitary inn, and a path turns off through the heart of the forest. Suddenly the trees disappear, and we enter a sequestered valley, occupied almost entirely by the ruins of a large edifice. It seems to have been exposed for centuries to the fury of the wind and storm; but it is scarcely fifty years since the chants of the monks were heard in the halls of All Saints. In 1803 it was struck by lightning, and since that period has never been restored. The treasure-seekers then did their share in the destruction by undermining the walls in their search for the treasures which the monks were supposed to have buried there. At last the present forester's house was built to protect the few traces of the former splendour of the abbey.

But the traveller soon quits these remnants of Teutonic architecture to follow the course of the stream as it hurries to the vale below. In a few minutes the point is reached. The forest valley is suddenly broken away by a wall of naked rock, nearly perpendicular, and of immense height, through which the water has forced its way in a zigzag direction. In seven waterfalls the roaring rivulet dashes down its granite bed, and at length finds rest below in a circular basin. Various projecting rocks and cavities have been childishly christened "The Pulpit," "The Gipsy's Cave," "The Raven's Nest," "The Knight's Leap," &c., and German authors have been found to invent legends to order, justifying these titles. This is one of the greatest defects in German show places; they will not allow you to enjoy the *tout ensemble* in peace, but will insist on drawing your attention to trumpery accessories, which afford you not the slightest interest, as you cannot be expected to know the private history of every ruffian, called by courtesy knight, who has imparted a local importance to otherwise valueless points. In every direction footpaths, auxiliary steps, thoughtful banisters have been placed about the waterfall, as if the object were to lessen the really magnificent effect of the whole by a leisurely examination of the details. Still, in one respect they are useful, for by their assistance you reach in all possible comfort the valley, where the Lier now runs in a state of model civilization through gentle meadows. If you feel inclined to follow its course, it will lead you to the town of Oppenau, and thence to the railway on your homeward route.

But the traveller who has followed the road we have indicated, has, after all, only seen an interesting Schwarzwald waterfall, and has left a far more interesting picture of life in the Black Forest unnoticed. We mean the Kniebis baths, bedded in the dense forest foliage above Oppenau in the valley of the Rench, and known by the names of Freyersbach, Petersthal, Griesbach, Antogast, and Rippoldsau. Even as early as the seventeenth century, when Baden-Baden was desolated by the Thirty Years' War and that of the Palatinate, and Baden Weiler had as yet obtained no celebrity, these Kniebis baths, with their "sour" waters, were well known. Of course they never were a gathering place for the fashionable world, and it is not till the last ten years that they have been visited at all by luxury and elegance. At the present day these forest hermitages are by no means huts built of trunks of trees and covered with straw, with poor furniture and hard beds.

On the contrary, they ought rather to be compared to pleasant villas or châteaux. All that comfort, or even fashionable habits, may require, to enjoy at their ease their idyllic fancies, is found in all possible abundance. But the fact that in the majority of these baths all the visitors live in the bath-house itself, that there is no other place for their meals than the common *salon*, that every guest with his daily requirements is bound to the bath-house, gives them a resemblance with the well-known Swiss *pensions*, which, on one hand, render too great an accession of guests impossible, on the other, bring all the inmates necessarily into association. As a general rule, carefully tended gardens in the immediate vicinity of the Cur Haus form the meeting-place for the visitors. But if you wish to escape from society and indulge in misanthropic tendencies, there are plenty of smooth, gently ascending paths leading through the forest, with comfortable benches and shady resting spots, and terminating usually in some glorious view over mountains and valleys. But to the right or left of these tracts of civilization you can immediately enter the unknown portions of the Schwarzwald, you can attain a delicious solitude, where only rarely a charcoal-burner's hut, a band of woodcutters, or a grazing herd evidence the proximity of humanity, and with each declivity you can regain a road which brings you shortly to meadows, villages, and towns. And as these bathing-places are situated so near each other, their summer population generally become known, and pleasant intimacies are formed. Elegant ladies, attired in a rustic *négligé*, harmonizing well with the romantic scenery, animate the overshadowed roads, and yet the true rural life enjoyed here gradually gains the mastery over the forms of society, and many who would at first think it a crime to appear ungloved, end by being as sunburnt as the veriest peasant. The ennui of fashionable life is soon dispelled by the healthy mountain atmosphere; eau-de-Cologne is superfluous in the aromatic fragrance of the pine forest, and the cares of high life float merrily along upon the rustling waters of the mountain stream, into the Rench, into the Rhine, into the sea—of oblivion.

We do not wish to assert that in the villages where these bathing establishments have been opened Schwarzwald life has remained as clear and unpolluted as the forests which enclose them, and the streams which bound along through them. But, on the other hand, they have generally grown out of their original poverty, are adorned with pretty little cottages, and are wont to put on their holiday aspect and Sunday clothes to greet their stranger but most welcome guests. It may be that they assume from their visitors unwonted notions of luxury, and that their primitive manners and customs have been considerably modified, but we must not forget that with increased wants there is always an increase of industry. And even supposing the present generation acquires more bad than good, still the following one will grow up with wants which will render a further advance on the path of civilization absolutely necessary. While formerly feudal lords and monasteries represented the intellectual life of the people, at present the people acquires its education from intercourse with foreigners whom the charms of novelty attract to their mountain homes.

Sentimentalists may lament the disappearance of national or local costume, but on looking at the magnitude of the question such lamentations are simply absurd.

Our sketch of this Schwarzwald valley would be incomplete unless we mounted to the summit of the Kniebis, a height of 3283 feet above the level of the sea. Here we quit the luxuriance of the forest to enter a sterile and poor district. Heather, juniper-bushes, and scrubby firs clothe the sides of the pass through which the Strasburg-Stuttgardt road runs. An extensive panorama opens to the east, south, and west, too wide to possess any landscape beauty, too contracted in the contour of its horizon to allow any clear perception of objects. Still, we must not forget that many furious battles have been waged for this spot, occupied at present only by some miserable cottages called popularly "Beggar's Turnagain," and a solitary post-house. It is true the Alexander's Redoubt, built by Alexander Duke of Wurtemberg, in 1734, against the inroads of the French, is grass-grown and pulled down, and the Swedes' Redoubt scarcely exists in name. But who can decide whether the time may not return when this pass and others similar in the Black Forest may again be of the greatest possible importance? At Frankfort the organ of the Germanic Confederation has frequently brought up this subject, but it has continually been passed over.

From the Kniebis baths we should recommend our traveller to wend his way to Appenweier, and thence by railroad to Offenburg, which must be his next station. It is a pleasant little town enough, but does not possess any interesting objects to delay his onward progress. The most curious thing is a statue of Francis Drake, which the Offenburger erected to the introducer of potatoes into Europe very recently. Their reason for doing so remains a mystery, for the inhabitants possess such immense natural wealth in their vineyards and orchards that they would hardly ever be reduced to Drake's importation. Not far from Offenburg is the elegant castle of Ortenberg, recently restored in the richest mediæval style. Not only the exterior but the interior as well have been so carefully handled, that the castle well repays a visit. The next place of interest reached on ascending the valley of the Kinzig is the town of Genzenbach, which gradually collected round the stately Benedictine abbey of the same name. With its walls, towers, and gates, it still retains reminiscences of its former importance, although the majority of the buildings were destroyed by the French in their inroads. The Kinzig runs placidly through the valley, and has been employed for all sorts of useful purposes. Factories, mills, &c., stand on its banks, but the inhabitants have none of that sickly hue peculiar to manufacturing districts; on the contrary, they are healthy to a degree, and the women remarkable for beauty.

Between Hausach and Hassbach the mountain masses draw more closely together. Here, too, the real Alpine cottages commence, and we rarely meet one of the inhabitants of the valley without finding him busily engaged in plaiting straw. This is one of the most charming national labours—if we may be allowed to call it so—imaginable. The smooth clean straws glisten as they are moved between the active hands, which we could hardly expect to possess such delicacy of touch; and before we can think it possible, a broad band of straw is completed, as if in sport. What a contrast this affords to the peasants of North Germany knitting their clumsy blue woollen stockings! The practical man, of course, feels a shuddering sensation when he hears by chance what splendid tracts of corn are yearly sacrificed to this straw-plaiting mania, in the midst of its growth. And it is, in truth, a painful sight to the tourist to see many stubble-fields in the middle of June. Still, it must be borne in mind that straw-plaiting has been known in the Schwarzwald from the remotest ages, and that the women regard it as necessary to wear the straw hat under the most varying forms.

Before reaching Hausach, the Gutach falls into the Kinzig, and we turn off toward Triberg. The scenery too soon changes. The broad meadow-valley with its fruit-trees is contracted, and the granite ribs of the mountain force their way out on the wooded declivities. Suddenly, in the midst of this gorge, we come to a circular valley with an old town, above which a well-preserved castle proudly frowns. It is Hornberg, captured by the French under Villars in 1703, whence, however, they were speedily driven by the infuriated peasants. Hence its preservation. After going through many phases, aristocratic and otherwise, it has, at length, degenerated into a brewery. A beautifully smooth road leads up the valley, and the scenery grows with each minute wilder. We walk along a romantic ravine, partly under, partly through, the rocks, gradually becoming so narrow that there appears hardly space for the saucy rivulet that goes bounding along at our feet. On the summit of the jagged rocks we can only notice a few dwarf fir-trees and boulders, apparently ready to fall upon us at the slightest shock. The valley then expands again, although retaining its wildly romantic character, and suddenly there appears before us the pretty town of Triberg, only consisting at present of a single street, for in 1826 it was almost entirely burnt to the ground. The clock manufacture has here its principal station. The sign-boards on the houses reveal this fact on all sides. Nearly 2000 feet above the level of the sea, and in the very heart of the Schwarzwald, lies the home of this trade, whose results greet us in nearly every peasant home of England. And Triberg is not merely the home, but also the cradle of the Schwarzwald clock trade; for three of its discoverers were natives of the old "Triberg Lordship." These times are long, long past, for this Black Forest manufactory commenced in the early half of the eighteenth century, and it would be difficult at the present day to find a Schwarzwald clock of the construction then used. Not that this has been greatly changed, but brass wheels have been substituted for the old wooden ones, to the great benefit of the machine and saving of space. Hence, there is nothing very peculiar in the aspect of the factories. In those places where the manufactory of clocks is carried on to a large extent, they do not differ materially from what we see in Geneva, Neufchâtel, and La Chaux de Fonds, always with the exception that the Schwarzwälder prefers trusting to his own hands than to machinery. The Black Forest clockmaker is acquainted, from his earliest youth, with all the portions of the machine, and is able to earn his living in whatever part of the world he may be. A great falling off has taken place in the fabrication of the musical clocks, once so much the rage, but the legitimate trade has so greatly increased that nearly 2000 workmen are now engaged upon it through the Black Forest, without reckoning the clock-face painters.

It is a fortunate thing for the population that this trade has so extended, for the gifts of nature are but churlishly scattered over the country. After leaving Hornberg, fruit-trees become a rarity; and even the cherry, which is found to flourish 6000 feet above the sea on the middle Rhine, is lost a few hundred paces beyond Triberg. With the exception of pines and larches, the holly is the only tree of any height which appears successfully to resist the endurance of a severe winter, the changing wind currents, the late springs, and early autumn frosts. We are here on a true German alpine height, and the little town will represent faithfully enough the Swiss châlets. But the great attraction of Triberg consists in the waterfall, which is found just outside the town. From a height of more than 650 feet, the huge body of water comes rushing down over gigantic blocks of granite, broken into seven principal falls, between which a multitude of smaller cascades foam and bubble. Tall green firs on the barren rock form the dark setting of this, perhaps the loveliest, waterfall through the whole length and breadth of Germany. Light wooden bridges have been erected across it at various intervals, so slight and graceful that they render the cascade still more imposing. And at times we hear through the hoarse murmur of the water the bells of a pasturing herd, or the solemn sound reaches our ear of the Sanctus summoning the population to mass in the little church.

The road from Triberg to Furtwangen runs in a southern direction through this desolate region, at times over sterile plateaus, then through bush or forest, possessing but slight picturesque variety, though at times enlivened by a distant prospect over the Schwarzwald heights. We will, therefore, make our way to the railroad, which we reach at Denzlingen, and hurry on to Freyburg.

Freyburg in the Breisgau, as it is generally called, to distinguish it from the other town of the same name in Switzerland, is one of the most curious relics of the feudal ages still to be found in Southern Germany. As the chief seat of the Catholic university of Baden, it possesses some slight importance, and is celebrated by being the abode of that turbulent Herman von Vicari who has been trying to restore the unlimited power of papacy, and compel the grand duke to bow his knee before the supremacy of his Church. But the traveller will be inclined to forget all such disagreeable matters on his walk through the town, for his eye will be immediately attracted by the varities of dress which he will notice on the market, the Münster-square, and the Kaiser-strasse. Red and black are the predominant colours. The men wear the broad-brimmed hat, or fur cap, with green top and gold button: the women, on the other hand, the tall straw hat, made like our fashionable chimney-pots, or the flat, wide-brimmed

Bloomer straw hat, ornamented with broad, fluttering red or black ribbons, between which their long plaits of hair reach almost to the ground. As a general rule, the dress of the Black Foresters is very tasteful, but the style in which the clothes are made will not meet with approval. Imagine the waist just under the armpits, after the fashion of our George II., and then the immense coat-tails the men wear to make up for this, rendering them frightfully clumsy to look at. The women, on the other hand, wear a fearful amount of petticoats, to which our modern crinoline bears no comparison; but generally both sexes have a round-shouldered appearance, detracting greatly from their good looks. But the beauty to be found among the women is remarkable; and it would take a great deal to disfigure them. Their large black eyes and clear brown complexion would tempt a misogamist, and their broad Doric *patois* sounds charmingly from their ruddy lips and pearly teeth. As is usually the case with all German peasant women, their beauty soon fades from hard work and privation, and by the age of twenty-five they are old and wrinkled. The dress of the Black Foresters is gradually assuming an urban character, and in many valleys the men are entirely attired like townsfolk, though the women adhere strictly to old habits.

The principal object of attraction in Freyburg is the wondrous cathedral, the most perfect specimen of Gothic architecture in Germany. It occupied three centuries in building, and, as if by a miracle, has escaped all the dangers of storm and insurrection, while the other antiquities of the town have gradually disappeared. Count Conrad of Zähringen commenced it in

1122, and in 1270 it was completed by Conrad of Freyburg with the exception of the choir. The steeple, 385 feet in height, is the precise model of those which our great-grandchildren may perhaps see terminated on the Kölner Dom. The choir was not finished until 1515, by Hans von Gräz. But the principal object in our visit to Freyburg is that we may see the celebrated Höllenthal, on the road to Donaueschingen and Schaffhausen. Instead of describing it here, we will compare it to those portions of the road from Gotthard to Fluellen, immediately after passing the terrible *Schöllenen*. All that is absent is the avalanches, but the general scenery is of a very similar character. The traveller, if he like, can stay for the night at the post-house of Steig, and climb up to the summit of the Feld Berg and the Titi Lake, about 4600 feet, but we prefer returning to the railway and going on to Müllheim, whence the road runs to Baden-Weiler.

This little bathing-place is very rarely visited by English folk, and yet it well deserves a day or two. Apart from the scenery, which is magnificent in the extreme, there is another attraction in the old Roman bath, only discovered accidentally in 1784, although Baden-Weiler had been known at the commencement of the prior century as a celebrated bath. The remains are of an extraordinary size, in a very excellent state of preservation, and are probably inferior to none in Europe, with the exception, perhaps, of Titus's bath at Rome. There are no traces of other Roman buildings to be found here, unless, perhaps, the old castle may be built on the remains of a Roman fort, like Heidelberg and Baden-Baden. It is probable that this was one of a chain of posts, maintaining the strategic connection with Argentoratum. Baden-Weiler and Baden deserve a comparison from their resemblance and difference. One at the northern extremity, the other at the southern, of the Black Forest, both situate on the western slope of the mountains—both employed by the Romans—both nearly resembling in the effect their waters produce—both belonging to the family of Zähringen for centuries—both protected by castles belonging to that family—both bearing originally the same name, Baden. But Baden-Baden, the Aurelia Aquensis, was, under the Romans, an important military station, and remained the same for centuries, then became a princely residence, and even under the Merovingians was a much-frequented bath, and gradually grew in celebrity and fashion. Baden-Weiler, on the contrary, was forgotten with the Romans; its castle became the abode of a bailiff, and its waters were scarcely used till recently, and that only by patients from the adjoining villages. And yet it would be difficult to decide, as regards picturesque scenery, which of the two places deserves the prize of beauty.

Another most interesting spot, which every traveller must visit who desires thoroughly to become acquainted with the Black Forest, is the Abbey of St Blasien. After a long ramble through forest and solitude we suddenly come to a splendid church, with a dome built after the pattern of the Pantheon at Rome by the rich monastic order which resided here during the last century. The monks have all departed, and the abbey has been converted into a manufactory, much to the regret of the peasantry, who believe that all prosperity went with them. The Catholic element is stronger in this portion of the Black Forest than in any other, and, as a natural consequence, the inhabitants are the most bigoted and narrow-minded that the traveller will yet have come across. This will be found more especially the case at the little village of Hauenstein, where our trip terminates, whose inhabitants have ever been notorious for their turbulence and bigotry. The railway, however, which is soon to be made through this district to the Lake of Constance, will dissipate this, and industry and prosperity will speedily make their appearance in this part of the grand duchy, rendering it equal in every respect to the more favoured northern districts.

And here we may terminate our tour: we have traversed the Black Forest in every direction, and, we trust, have seen all that possesses any interest for the traveller. We hope, in all sincerity, then, that the few pages we have been enabled to devote to the subject will induce many of our readers to visit this curious country, for we assure them it will amply repay the trouble. They need not be afraid, either, of faring badly, for the smallest village inn has its tank, whence trout can be taken alive, and what more can a hungry traveller desire? The people will be found, as a general rule, hospitable and kind to strangers, and there are many worse ways of amusing oneself than a night spent in a Black Forest châlet. A manger is always at your service to sleep in, and, with fresh hay, it is difficult to imagine a more pleasant summer night's resting-place. The expense, too, of such a tour as we have described is trifling in the extreme, and bears no proportion to the enjoyment it will occasion. For our own part, we can only say that the Black Forest is our predilection; and though residing many years at Baden, we were glad to escape as often as we could from its tinsel and artificiality, and seek refuge from *ennui* in the secluded nooks of the Black Forest. If we can induce others to follow our example, we shall feel the gratification that the time we have devoted to this description of one of the most beautiful and unknown portions of Southern Germany will not have been bestowed in vain.

CHAPTER XIX.

A SAD STORY.

THERE is always something pleasant on a winter's night in sitting cosily by the fire, and the pleasure seems to be enhanced if the weather outside be at all boisterous; perhaps on the Lucretian *suave mari magno* principle, we feel a sort of contemptuous compassion for those poor fellows out on such a night, and poke up the fire into a brighter blaze, as we gloat over the notion we are not as they. Pleasanter than all, perhaps, is it to have two or three trusty friends with you, who make the time fly by telling you story on story, each serving as an excuse for a fresh glass of toddy. Just such a night did I spend last month in that horrid snow-storm, with my friend Dr T. and young B., and I will tell you now a story as it was told to me, and which sent me supperless to bed. It was really too bad of the doctor, for Sweeting had sent me in a magnificent barrel of oysters, which I had intended to regale on, despite the doctor's repeated hints as to their indigestibility.

We had been talking about the humanitarians, and the doctor had been venting his spleen as usual, for he was a tremendous Tory, and predicted that no good would come to the country by our mawkish sentimentalism, as he was fond of terming it. Among other strong remarks he made, he said that at the present day humanity was based on regulated murder.

"Do you mean the punishment of death?" I remarked, somewhat sarcastically.

"No; but children are born at present only to die. You know that I have been attached to a lying-in institution for the last five years, and I have seen the working of the system sufficiently. Thousands of wretched beings here await their heavy hour, in which they are to give birth to another poverty-stricken babe. Most of the mothers take service as wet-nurses in the houses of the richer class; they put out their own child to nurse with some old woman, and pay a few pence weekly. Many of the mothers are heartless, hardened creatures, who wish their children to die soon; for out of ten of such children one half die in the first month."

"Can that be true?" said B.

"I have, perhaps, understated the case. The nurses, generally old, hard-hearted women, have five, six, or more of such children to take care of. At first they pay some little attention to them, and give them delicacies, but after a short time they must take pot luck. Their young stomachs cannot bear the coarse food, the children cry, they swallow nothing, and in a short space they die of hunger."

"Terrible!"

"In one of our northern cities, where there are richly endowed institutions for the conversion of the Hottentots, and tender women knit lambswool waistcoats for the benighted heathens, a few years ago an old soldier was tried for his life, who carried on a business of this sort with his wife. When the children cried, he thought the only way to quiet them was by beating them. They were soon quiet enough. The old fellow had done no more than happens daily; he had killed the children instead of allowing them to die. And why should the little scamps live?—they might run between the legs of rich folk when they went out for a walk."

"Really, doctor, you are too bad," I remarked; "your profession has blunted all your finer perceptions."

"I only tell you what has happened, and is still happening. I could tell you a story showing the misery and revenge of a poor misguided creature. Have you the courage to hear it?"

"Tell us—tell us," said B.; "nothing can be too terrible, if it promotes the cause of truth."

"Well, then, I will."

It was just three years ago, on such a night as this, and the snow was enough to take away one's breath; I could hardly find my way through the well-lighted streets. I was summoned to the house of Mr F., the rich wine-merchant. He was very comfortably off, to use the common phrase. He had made one of those marriages of convenience which are so common, and which once caused a woman to say, "If you were not my husband I should not feel the slightest interest in you." In short, the man was happy, and now doubly so, for his wife bore a joyful hope beneath her heart. When I entered the drawing-room the tea was being served. All the front rooms in the house were brilliantly lighted and thrown into one. The young wife was ordered to take exercise, and she was now walking up and down the rooms. Not a sound was to be heard on the velvet carpets. I seated my self with the company, consisting of the wife's parents and her married sister. The mother was working at a baby cap, the sister was crocheting a dainty coverlet; in a corner stood the cradle, covered with a green silk curtain. Whenever Mrs F. was absent in the next room, they began speaking of the hour of travail, which all were awaiting with mingled feelings of apprehension and delight. I was especially requested to look out for a healthy and respectable nurse. The sister, a clever young woman, who seemed very delicate, said: "I could never make up my mind to hire a wet-nurse, and I much wished that Fanny were of the same opinion. I am always grieved to see the way in which these nurses are pampered and petted; they are treated like queens, and enjoy the best of everything, and what is to become of them afterwards? Besides, it must have a pernicious influence on the other female servants. They who have kept pure from sin are forced to wait on the fallen sister, and endure all her caprices and whims." Her husband somewhat harshly expressed his opinion about it being all stuff, while I was engaged in combating the prejudices of Mr F., who fancied that a wife retained her beauty longer if she did not suckle her children. I proved to him how utterly false and unnatural this view was. The young wife had now found us, and, for fear of exciting her, the conversation was turned to other matters. The sister sang, the father retailed some of his stock jokes to keep her in good spirits. The fair young wife, as she sat there self-forgetting, and only thinking of the future, resembled a saint. For a woman who bears a second life beneath her heart is a saint; even the roughest and wildest beings treat her with reverence.

I left the house at a late hour. As I descended the stairs I thought to myself how happy the new arrival would be—how many loving arms, how many sparkling eyes would welcome it. As I went along the street, the snow and wind almost knocked me backwards. At last I reached my residence in the Lying-in Hospital. As I walked up the steps I felt something moving at my feet. I started back, and shouted, "Who is that?"

"Oh, God!" was the reply, "have mercy upon me."

"Who are you?"

"Misery, misery! I must die—I and my child!"

I now saw by the glimmer of the lamp a girl, whose head was wrapped up in a coarse shawl: she was wiping the snow out of her eyes. I rang violently, and the poor girl embraced my knees and sobbed out:

"Oh! we must not be left to die. I have come 20 miles to-day from G——. I could hardly drag my limbs along. I could not stay there any longer: the villagers were pointing the finger of scorn at me. I went into a public-house and implored them to give me shelter, but they only laughed at me; one coarse fellow tried to insult me, and I ran away. At last I resolved to remain here till some kind gentleman came to my assistance."

Thus the girl spoke through her tears, and shuddering with the cold, until the porter at last opened the door. I ordered a nurse to be roused, and the stranger put to bed, and within an hour she was in a deep sleep, though every now and then she made a convulsive movement. For a long time I lay awake; do what I would I could not but speculate on the fate of the two children I was about to bring into the world almost at the same time. Little did I think what a fearful tragedy I was preparing.

The next morning I found the stranger refreshed, and almost quite restored. I, too, had got over that softness of heart which had so strangely unmanned me on the previous night. I went up to her bedside. I knew beforehand what lamentable story, intermingled with sobs, I was about to hear. I have been too often deceived not to be always strictly on my guard. Fortunately we are at times not so wise as we should like to be, and the uncorrupted heart will not listen to all the wise warnings of the head. Well, I found the girl in better spirits, and she thanked me heartily for my kindness. According to her statement she was the daughter of a once rich farmer, who had been brought down in the world by intoxication and bad housekeeping. She had seen better days in her father's house. Father and mother were now dead, and Jane Hardy (that was her name) had been for three years servant at the Plough, in G——. Here she fell away from virtue with the ostler. She wept bitterly as she said this, but then she wiped her tears, and her eye sparkled as she spoke of her husband, as she persisted in calling him. She represented him to be a thoroughly honest and industrious man, and was incessant in her praises.

He wanted to marry her, but they had not a shilling to begin housekeeping. She spoke of the nights she had passed in solitary sorrow, and how her mother could find no rest in the grave because her daughter had quitted the path of rectitude. She told me how her husband was going to do himself a hurt, through sorrow for his great fault. Then she added, "God will punish me for my sin, but I will endure all patiently, so long as the poor innocent creature is spared to us. I will willingly work my finger-ends off, and I and my husband will be able to save enough in the course of a few years to emigrate to Australia."

I must confess that the story affected me but slightly; but I had heard so many of them, part true, part invention. But when in the course of a few days the husband made his appearance, a good-looking young fellow, but now as hang-dog as a criminal, and with a trembling hand offered me a few shillings, then adding, through fear of insulting me, that I could lay them out in getting some dainties for Jenny, I began to form a better opinion of the couple. The young fellow pleased me remarkably: he was one of those men who are not in the habit of expressing their thanks, and who find difficulty in uttering words of humiliation, for they prefer to receive only that which they have a right to demand.

On the tenth day after her arrival Jane gave birth to a healthy boy. The joy she evinced at the sight of the infant is indescribable. At this moment she put off all her grief, all thoughts of her misfortune: she was a happy mother. And when she said that the boy was the very image of his father, her whole face shone with delight.

A week later Mrs F. also gave birth to a son. I now proposed to Jane to go there as wet-nurse, as she could earn a decent sum of money. She regarded me with widely-opened eyes, pressed her child closer to her heart, and large drops stood in her eyes. She drew breath hurriedly, and could not speak, but at last she said, "I can say nothing about it: my husband is coming to the christening to-day." The child was christened, and I was asked to be godfather, but I had no time, and to tell you the truth, no great inclination. I might have been godfather to half the world if I had accepted all the offers. Still, in gratitude to me, the boy received my name—Anthony. The husband wanted to take the child in the country with him, and have it taken care of there, and I advised the same; but Jane made it a condition that if she accepted the situation her boy must remain near her. It was handed over to one of these old nurses I was abusing just now.

The same evening I took Jane to Mr F.'s house. She shrank back involuntarily as she laid the strange child to her breast. But she got over this feeling; and Jane lived like a princess in a room where the temperature was regulated with the greatest care. She had every sort of dainty to eat and drink, the whole house was at her disposal, and Mrs F.'s child (he was christened Augustus) grew stronger hourly. Jane grew handsomer every day too; she sang and sported with the child, and could hardly invent sufficient terms of endearment. Many times did I laugh at her inventive genius. But you must not imagine that Jane was trying to stifle the cry of pain in her own heart; it is a secret impulse of nature that a nurse learns to love her foster-child. I was heartily praised for having procured the F.s such an excellent and respectable wet-nurse. I received the thanks of a slave-dealer.

The winter rapidly made way for spring, and Jane was permitted to take Augustus out for an airing in St James's Park. She carried the child warmly wrapped up, and held a parasol over his face to keep off any impertinent sunbeams. Mrs F. was seated at the window, and I met Jane just as she got into the street. She looked round timidly, and said to me she felt nervous: she was to surprise Mr F. as he came home from the City by showing him the child enjoying the air for the first time.

In the Park were several wet-nurses, mostly reckless creatures, who paid more attention to the soldiers than to the children in their arms. One of them, who had known Jane in the institution, asked her casually whether she had got rid of her trouble. She turned icy cold, for she had seen her child but once since she had deserted it. On the day when Augustus was christened, the old nurse had brought Master Tony, and had been regaled with the best of meat and drink. Jane had then felt that she was almost a stranger to her child, and now the thought of her neglect almost maddened her. She rushed down the dirty back streets of Westminster to her child. She found it crying, alone in the room; a half-peeled boiled potato lay upon the cradle. The child was wretchedly thin, and looked like death. When her eye then fell on the little Augustus (so the old nurse said) she looked as if she would have killed him with a glance. It seemed to say, " See, that is the robber who steals from you your mother, your food, your very life!" She sank down by the side of the cradle, and sobbed loudly; the two children cried with her. Then she rose again, took up her own child, kissed it and hugged it: she offered it the breast, but it would not suck: she raised it sportively above her head, and the boy merrily struck her in the face. Then she quarrelled with the old nurse; but all at once the idea occurred to her she must go home, and she hurried away with Augustus. When she reached Mr F.'s house she received a severe scolding, as far as they dared to go for fear of injuring her nursling. Everybody was suffering from the greatest alarm. The father had come home from the City, and the child was nowhere to be seen. Jane did not like to say where she had really been; so she pretended that she had lost her way. Strict orders were given that she must never go out again alone. The little Augustus cried and whined all the day. Against my will I was obliged to betray where Jane had been. Mr F. was half inclined to turn her out of the house at once; but I interposed, and promised to keep a careful watch over Jane's child. I had done so all along; but what avail is that under such circumstances?

Jane gradually became quite cheerful as she had heretofore been. On the third evening after this occurrence, Mr and Mrs F. went to spend the evening at her mother's. The house was quite quiet. Jane was singing a melancholy old English song, while the under-nurse was at work in the adjoining room. Suddenly Jane rushed to the window and threw it up. The under-nurse asked her what she was about; she was letting in a draught, and must close the window instantly. Jane asked her if she had not heard something; it seemed to her as if some one in the street kept on calling her by name. The under-nurse said she heard nothing, and it must be all fancy. But Jane could not be pacified; and she rushed about the room like a tiger in its cage. She stopped and listened at the window; all was silent, and yet she heard something again. She opened the nursery door and went out. She slipped off her shoes and gently glided down-stairs. The house door was locked, and in a second Jane was down the kitchen stairs and entered the larder, the window of which opened on the area. It was, luckily, unbolted, and she leaped out, and was up the steps in a moment. So soon as she reached the street, she hurried on along. The policeman started back involuntarily as she passed him; and she was come and gone without a sound. On she hurried, and at length reached the house where her child was. The door was on the latch, for the old nurse had gone to visit her next-door neighbour. Jane found her child quiet in bed; it no longer cried, it only groaned. The moon shone brightly in the heavens and poured down on the mother, as she bent tearless over her child. The nurse came in with a light, and Jane uttered a cry that pierced the very marrow as she saw her child; she tore her hair, but then suddenly turned calm, and laid her child to her breast. Oh! blessings on it! her boy opened his eyes, laid his wasted hands on her bosom, and drank eagerly. Cautiously she laid him down, and kissed the blanket under which he slept, or at least had closed his eyes.

I had just arrived at the house on my round of visits, and hearing an unusual disturbance, I walked in. Jane hurried to meet me, and said, joyfully, "My child is alive—my child is alive!" but I saw death, which might close its eyes at any moment. I tried to induce Jane to go home, but she was proud or lost in thought, and scarcely listened to me. She sang a nursery song, and rocked her child the while. I felt its pulse—it was quite silent—she was rocking a dead child. I now tried to force Jane home, for I hoped to hide the awful truth from her; but she seized the child once again, and I saw that the awful truth had struck her. At first, I thought she was about to faint, for she sank over the cradle; but she soon recovered, and said, "Yes, he has gone from me, my Tony, but he drank at my breast for all that, yes—yes." She turned backwards and forwards and shook her head, as if saluting a party of friends. I had several visits still to pay, and ordered that Jane should be kept there till I came to fetch her. She could not return to Mr F.'s house in her present condition. Jane allowed me to depart quietly, but so soon as I was gone, she over-persuaded the old nurse to accompany her home. She walked along the street as quiet as a lamb.

When they arrived at Mr F.'s house, the carriage was just drawing up to the door. Jane said, "Let me in now," and she stepped in without observation. She crept up to the nursery, roused the little Augustus from his sleep, kissed and cuddled him, and sang:

"Sleep, my darling, sleep,
Your father minds the sheep,
Your mother——"

At this moment the door opened, and Mrs F. walked in.

"How is my child?" she said.

"Your child?" Jane shrieked in her madness. "Away, away! Your child?—my child! Yes, your child, the murderer of *my* child." She glanced wildly around her. "Murderer! murderer!" she yelled, and hurled the child on the ground. It uttered but one groan—it was dead!

At this fearful moment I entered the room. The child was lying on the ground, the mother in a fainting condition by its side. Jane was dancing round the room, and singing merry snatches. I was petrified.

That night Jane was conveyed to Hanwell: it was said that she was attacked by a milk fever. After many weeks of fearful agony, death spared her further suffering.

Mrs F. had no more children: and she died of what is vulgarly termed a broken heart, only last year.

This was my friend Dr T.'s story.

"Horrible," said B., after a pause; and then added, "that is a fearful revenge on an individual for the crime of thousands. Something ought to be done to stop such a dreadful state of things."

"Jane Hardy," the doctor concluded, "was the last wet-nurse I recommended. I have lost half my patients by the public expression of my views. The best thing would be to bring up our girls more healthily, so that they might become mothers in the true sense of the term. Even if they were not such proficients on the pianoforte, we want before all a healthy race of men. But when it is absolutely necessary to have a wet-nurse, the parents ought to enter into an agreement to take all proper care of the nurse's child, or, better still, have it in the house along with their baby."

I took up my candle, and went off to bed without saying a word.

END OF VOL. I

CPSIA information can be obtained
at www.ICGtesting.com
Printed in the USA
LVHW111956050422
715401LV00006B/233

9 783752 58956